D1240382

ENVY
and Other Works

YURI OLESHA was born in Elisavetgrad, Russia, in 1899, the son of an impoverished landowner. He grew up in Odessa, where his fellow townsmen included several of the most gifted writers of the era. Although he published important poetry and fiction during the Revolutionary period, Olesha became celebrated only upon the appearance of *Envy* in 1927. Originally acclaimed by the official Soviet cultural arbiters who interpreted its rich complexity in rigid political terms, Olesha's masterpiece was later re-evaluated and found "formalistic." Gradually, *Envy* and the stories that had succeeded it were suppressed. Olesha took refuge in virtual silence. He died in 1960, too early to benefit from modifications in Kremlin policy toward artists.

ANDREW R. MACANDREW, has translated more than thirty books from Russian and French, including works by Dostoevsky, Tolstoy, Maupassant, Babel, and Yevtushenko.

ENVY

and Other Works
by Yuri Olesha

TRANSLATED, WITH AN INTRODUCTION, BY

ANDREW R. MacANDREW

W · W · NORTON & COMPANY

New York · London

Copyright © 1960, 1967 by Andrew R. MacAndrew

Published simultaneously in Canada by George J. McLeod Limited,
Toronto.

Printed in the United States of America

All Rights Reserved

First published as a Norton paperback 1981

Library of Congress Cataloging in Publication Data

Olesha, IUrii Karlovich, 1899–1960.
  Envy, and other works.

  Translation of: Zavist'. 1964.
  Originally published Garden City, N.Y.:
Anchor Books.
  Contents: Envy—The chain—Love—Lyompa—
[etc.]
  I. Title.
PG3476.O37A25   1981   891.78′4209   81–2583
                                        AACR2

W. W. Norton & Company, Inc. 500 Fifth Avenue,
New York, N.Y. 10110
W. W. Norton & Company Ltd. 25 New Street Square,
London EC4A 3NT

ISBN 0-393-00042-7
2 3 4 5 6 7 8 9 0

CONTENTS

INTRODUCTION

Yuri Olesha was born in Elisavetgrad in 1899. He came from the impoverished landowner class. As he explains in "I Look into the Past," his father was a card-playing excise officer, hopelessly ineffectual at both cards and career.

In early childhood Olesha began questioning the values of those around him, lumping together the Victorian tastelessness of middle-class homes and the social inequities outside them: a world of conches on the mantelpiece and beggars in the doorway.

When Olesha was still very young, his family moved from Elisavetgrad to Odessa, where he lived through the early 1920s. There he began to write poetry and, within a few years, came to rank high among a surprising concentration of gifted writers found at one particular time in what was, after all, a provincial town. Among his fellow townsmen were the satirists Ilf and Petrov, the poet Eduard Bagritsky, the novelist Valentin Kataev, and Isaac Babel.

During the Revolution and the Civil War, Odessa was the scene of many important events. Olesha, like his young intellectual contemporaries, sided with the new regime and this position was reflected in his early verse and in his novel-length fairy tale *Three Fat Men* about a revolution in a fairy-tale land that ends with a fairy-tale proletariat triumphant. It is a charming story that eventually became a play and a ballet, and it was the only work by which Olesha's name remained known throughout the grimmest years of the Stalin era.

Olesha's fateful moment came in 1927. That year he published his novel *Envy*. It was an immediate sensation.

And perhaps just as sensational, considering what the book said, was the unqualified official endorsement by the government-controlled press. The acclaim followed the full course from specialized literary journals like *Revolution and Culture* all the way to *Pravda*, the supreme repository of Soviet literary judgment.

Pravda's reviewer wrote at that time:

> . . . Olesha's style is masterful, his psychological analysis infinitely subtle, his portrayal of negative characters truly striking. . . .

And he went on to evaluate Olesha's "ideological message":

> The novel exposes the envy of small despicable people, the petty bourgeois flushed from their lairs by the Revolution; those who are trying to initiate a "conspiracy of feelings" against the majestic reorganization of our national economy and our daily life. . . .

Despite this early tribute, Olesha was soon neck-deep in trouble. Somehow, somewhere, signals had got crossed: instead of admiring and wishing to emulate the novel's "positive heroes," readers went as far as to identify with the villain, the "negative hero" who displayed the whole spectrum of loathsome, discarded, obsolete "petty-bourgeois" feelings, from bilious envy through slobbering sentimentality and deadening indifference to total degradation.

Obviously, Olesha not only had failed to deliver the proper message but had delivered a perverse one instead. So the literary critics had to revise their original verdict; this time they found Olesha guilty of "formalism," "naturalism," "objectivism," and "cosmopolitanism." These are grave charges in the vocabulary of a Soviet literary critic. They imply, respectively: (1) that Olesha was unduly preoccupied with form at the expense of content (i.e. the Party message); (2) that certain passages were no longer considered fit for consumption by the neo-Victorian Soviet family; (3) that Olesha's "negative heroes" were not nearly negative enough; and (4) that he was "kowtowing" to the West.

The same accusations were thrown at Olesha's shorter works, which appeared during the immediately following years—"Love," "The Cherry Stone," "From the Secret Notebook of Fellow-Traveler Sand," and others. As a result, Olesha's writings were soon virtually out of print.

For many years Olesha was known to the younger generation of Soviet readers as the author of *Three Fat Men* or of occasional anti-Western articles in *Literaturnaya gazeta,* the journal of the Union of Soviet Writers.

Then Stalin died and literary controls were somewhat slackened. During that period, now referred to as "the thaw," a collection of Olesha's writing, including *Envy* and other "denounced" works, saw daylight again. It was ushered in by a typical Soviet introductory piece, "explaining" to the reader that, whenever life under the Soviet regime appears unattractive in Olesha's stories, either he does not mean what he seems to be saying or he is simply overindulging in paradoxes, or—all other arguments failing—he was mistaken at the time but realized his error later and recanted. But while concluding that Olesha was, after all, on the side of Communism, the author of the introduction to the post-Stalin edition is careful not to stick his neck out as far as the critics in 1927. For who can ever be sure when assessing the whimsical imagery and symbolism of such a writer?

Apparently Olesha's complexity confounds commentators beyond the Soviet borders as well. Reviewing my English translation of *Envy, Time* (May 23, 1960) asserted that "Olesha once opposed Communism with such passion as to make *Zhivago* seem like a gentle reproof."

Is this really so? On whose side is Olesha—or, rather, where is he?

Like his beggar in "Jottings of a Writer," Olesha is "standing in a drafty passage." The beggar stands in a

passage between the drizzly street and a brightly lit store;
Olesha, between what he loosely calls the nineteenth and
the twentieth centuries. The street represents the nineteenth century, the world of his childhood, which was governed by the old, obsolete feelings without which he cannot
write. Unlike the throngs of people who rush into the store,
banging the door behind them, Olesha and his beggar cannot cut themselves off so brutally. Olesha must take his past
with him into the budding new world of industrialization
and five-year plans.

The beggar is short-legged and roly-poly like Olesha himself. Cotton wadding sticks out of his quilted jacket, which
is bursting behind the shoulders so that from certain angles
he looks like a huge, unkempt, incongruous cupid—that is,
a god of love. That beggar turns up again and again in
Olesha's writings and figures even in Olesha's speech to the
First Congress of Soviet Writers (1934).

"While I was thinking about the story of my beggar,"
Olesha declared on that occasion, "our country was building factories. It was the time of the First Five-Year Plan,
the very time when the socialist national economy was being created.

"But," he admitted sadly, "this was not a subject for
me." It was not for him, he felt, to go out on a construction
site, live in a factory among workers, so that later he could
make out of them characters for a novel. Nor could he
make up suitable stories in which "typical socialist workers" and "revolutionary heroes" would come alive. This
was not his theme.

What Olesha was pleading for was permission to "roam"
through the newly created world, to discover for himself
themes he could write about. He wanted to find out, for
instance, what Soviet boys and girls dream about, what
they really long for, whom they love. And then he would
write about it.

When he wrote *Envy*, Olesha was apparently stuck in
that passage between the two worlds. The poem-like novel

is full of nostalgia for the discarded old world and its feelings. The attitudes of the various characters toward the wholesale eradication of the unwanted but familiar and comfortable sentiments, and their replacement by new, streamlined, and rational relations, range from open rebellion to enthusiastic endorsement. And Olesha conveys these attitudes by a symbolism as subtle and concentrated as is likely ever to be found in a *profession de foi*.

Olesha's alter ego, Nikolai Kavalerov, and the older Babichev brother, Ivan, fight a losing battle against the food-industry wizard Andrei Babichev and his young protégé Volodia Makarov, athlete and engineering student, whose ambition is to become an emotionless, perfect "human machine." The stake is the future, symbolized by a charming young girl, Valia, who is loved by Kavalerov with romantic exaltation, but destined for Volodia as a matter of course.

Olesha uses these four characters like the stops of a musical instrument and plays a strange tune, woven out of notes of sadness, hope, rebellion, acceptance, and despair. The ending is a grotesquely plaintive tremolo of resignation. The men representing four distinctive attitudes toward the regime are four metaphorical milestones in time.

Ivan Babichev has both feet firmly planted in the nineteenth century and is in open rebellion against the New Order. He openly, albeit pathetically, defies the regime by building a machine-killer machine.

Kavalerov stands in the passage between the two centuries. His challenge to the regime, unlike Ivan's, is confined to daydreams. He is anxious not to be rejected by Andrei Babichev, the man he scornfully refers to as "the sausage maker."

Andrei Babichev is the new Soviet managerial type, representing the consumer-goods industry. He is nevertheless an intermediate type, still susceptible to many of the old-world feelings such as pity. It is because he is responsive to pity that he rescues Kavalerov from the gutter.

Volodia Makarov is the Soviet man of the future and his

field is heavy industry (remember the priority given to producer goods over consumer goods by Soviet planners at the time). Volodia is portrayed in a deliberately schematic way, the enigmatic future behind a "Japanese" (i.e. inscrutable) smile. He is fond of Andrei Babichev, the food-industry man, although condescendingly so. As for Ivan and Kavalerov, he looks at them almost blankly, unable to recognize human beings in these freakish vestiges of the past.

With the inexorability of a Greek tragedy or perhaps like a cog in one of his own machines, Volodia, the man of the future, will come to occupy his assigned place alongside Valia, the future itself. In the meantime, to Kavalerov's despair, the couple pursue their hygienic, comradely, and meticulously planned courtship.

There is little doubt that, like Kavalerov, Olesha was both saddened and frightened by the new world that was taking shape before his eyes. But he was not yet ready to resign himself to the fate of his hero—to wait for death in a state of drunken stupor while sharing the huge, ornamented, Victorian bed and flabby favors of Annie Prokopovich with old Ivan Babichev.

Kavalerov's end was one of the possible plights awaiting a sensitive and imaginative man in the new Soviet society, but Olesha visualized other alternatives as well. In "The Cherry Stone," the unloved narrator finds that the tree he plants has room enough to grow among the concrete giants created by the First Five-Year Plan. There is also the alternative presented by Shuvalov in "Love," where emotion triumphs in the end over the blinkered "scientific" (Marxist) reasoning that prevents people from seeing the castles in the air formed by the flight of birds and insects.

Olesha pleaded with the nascent world for the right to be admitted into it with his sentimental luggage, without which he could never be anything but a beggar and would be doomed to regret forever his possessions abandoned in the past. He describes this inner struggle between the past and the future in "Human Material," published one year after *Envy:*

"I catch myself within myself, I grab by the throat the *I* who wants to turn back, who stretches out his arms to the past, who thinks the distance between us and Europe is a purely geographical one."

Olesha returns to this "distance between us and Europe," that is, between the Soviet world and the West, in his major play, *A List of Assets*.

In it Lola Goncharova, a Shakespearean actress and another spokesman for Olesha, performs before an audience of workers the scene in which Hamlet scornfully explains to Guildenstern that a human being is not a musical instrument, that he cannot be played upon to produce the desirable sounds:

> Why look you now, how unworthy a thing you make of me! You would play upon me; you would seem to know my stops; you would pluck out the heart of my mystery; you would sound me from my lowest note to the top of my compass: and there is much music, excellent voice, in this little organ; yet cannot you make it speak. 'Sblood, do you think I am easier to be played on than a pipe? Call me what instrument you will, though you can fret me, yet you cannot play upon me.

During a question-and-answer session following this reading, a worker asks Lola why she chose *Hamlet* instead of any number of available Soviet plays. She answers that all these plays are "sketchy, false, unimaginative, heavy-handed, and obvious" and that "doing them impairs one's acting ability."

This reply could easily be transposed from Lola to Olesha himself, who feels about writing "Soviet" novels to order much the way that Lola feels about acting in "Soviet" plays. Olesha intends the musical instrument to symbolize the difficulty encountered by the authorities who assume the artist is "easier to be played on than a pipe."

But when Lola, having decided that Hamletian soul-searchings can no longer interest audiences in the new Russia, goes on tour to Paris, she finds that cultural values have been debased in the West as well, although in a different way and for different reasons.

There, Monsieur Margeret, a greedy and uncouth "capitalist" music-hall manager, reacts rather unexpectedly to Lola's offer to perform the same scene from *Hamlet* in his establishment. The idea of the recorder rather appeals to Margeret, but he feels it needs spicing up and finally thinks up a sensational gimmick: Lola, he decides, will begin her act by playing some sad little tune. Then she must swallow the recorder and play a cheerful melody from the other end of her anatomy. The public, he explains, likes to be sent home on a cheerful note.

It was perhaps the implication here that Western commercialization is at least as fatal to art as sterilizing Communist rigidity that averted an all-out attack by the Soviet critics. But the play ends on a note of despair as heartbreaking as *Envy*'s. Lola, about to leave Paris, is fatally wounded by a policeman's bullet meant for the leader of a Communist demonstration in which she takes part. She dies muttering unintelligibly something to the effect that she would like to have her body covered in the Red banner carried by the demonstrators. At that moment police troops attack; the demonstrators unfurl their banners and march on the enemy, leaving Lola's corpse lying uncovered and forgotten in the street.

This disparagement of the West was, of course, no mere bone Olesha tossed to the Soviet critics to forestall the automatic accusation that he was in the pay of the capitalists. Like George Orwell, he feared the future, not just the Soviet future.

It must be noted that later, in some quarters in the West, Olesha's *Envy* was misunderstood and mishandled almost as badly as *Hamlet* in Monsieur Margeret's music hall. But it was not commercialization in Olesha's case. In fact, Olesha was welcomed with open arms: the literary critics of the psychoanalytical school eyed hungrily the wealth of his symbols. It did not bother them in the least that these were carefully collected devices chosen to convey extremely conscious thoughts referring to very specific situations. They pounced upon them and, using their various text-books and vying with one another, explained Olesha in terms of phallic symbols, castration fears, and death wishes. Olesha may well have likened himself to the colt in Sergei Yesenin's poem—a colt who gallops pathetically across a field trying to race a train. The colt, we are told, is doomed by the new "steel cavalry" to be turned into canned horse-meat.

In the 1920s, after the First World War had obliterated the remnants of nineteenth-century optimism—and with it conventional art forms—anxiety and artistic experimentation were not confined to any one part of the world; the Soviet writers of that generation—Olesha, Mayakovsky, Zamyatin, Babel, and Pilniak—have their Western counterparts in such writers as D. H. Lawrence, F. Scott Fitzgerald, Ernest Hemingway, and Louis-Ferdinand Céline.

Of course, anxiety and a sense of doom were bound to have more personal immediacy in a regime with a mania for "co-ordinating" all national "activities." Long before most, a man of Olesha's perspicacity must have anticipated the worst aspects of Stalinism. Too lucid to hide them under euphemisms or explain them away as temporary aberrations, as many intellectuals did, Olesha resisted. As long as he could, he argued, pleaded, begged, would "not go gentle into that good night." When, at last, he found protest not only futile but potentially fatal, he simply stopped writing. To be sure, he did come up with some "beautiful little vignettes," as the Soviet writer who reintroduced Olesha to the public put it. But these vignettes were only little masks that Olesha made grin complacently or snarl with affected xenophobia, as the case demanded. And thanks to these "vignettes," Olesha was allowed to remain a member of the Soviet Writers' Union and keep his apartment in Peredelkino.

There is a curious parallel between the career of Olesha and that of his contemporary fellow townsman, Isaac Babel.

Both reached full artistic maturity in the second half of the twenties; both fell silent in the early thirties. After that, they wrote little and, as far as is known, nothing of comparable value to their early work. Within a few days of each other, Olesha and Babel addressed the First Congress of Soviet Writers (1934) in an attempt to explain their silence. But the explanations they offered were typically quite different.

Babel declared that his old style was no longer suitable. He was still searching, he said, for a "new language to fit our great era," meaning the era of nascent Stalinism.

Olesha, on the contrary, pleaded to be allowed to write in his natural style on his own themes, arguing that, if he had a personal contribution to make, he should be allowed the choice of how to make it.

Opposite though their arguments were, the result was the same—neither man wrote well again. Two delicate musical instruments could not be played on by insensitive, "goal-directed" zealots. They broke. And for safe measure, Babel was silenced altogether—"liquidated."

Olesha survived, lamely, until 1960, when he died of "natural causes." But even as he was dying, his pessimistic premonitions still seemed justified: within a year of his death, the same stupid and insensitive attitude toward the artist claimed yet another victim—Boris Pasternak.

All the works collected here, except one, were written between 1927 and 1933. "Natasha" (1936) is the only piece from Olesha's "post-literary" period that could be included without too much apology. Even so, it provides a sufficiently striking contrast to the other writings to give an inkling of what had happened to Olesha during the intervening years. In "Natasha" the former intricate lacework of symbols is no longer there. Instead, we are offered a rather insipid paradox: in the past people used to invent all sorts of stories to cover up their trysts but Natasha, a girl of the young Soviet generation, invents trysts to conceal from her father the fact that she is a parachutist. One can still recognize here Olesha's former theme: the young world does not understand the one that preceded it, and the survivors of the old world feel left out and mortified. How much more honestly, and therefore more subtly, is this theme developed in his early works. With what a bright touch, for instance, is the green-shaded lamp placed on Andrei Babichev's table, surrounding him with a circle of light from which Kavalerov is excluded; and the symbol is further strengthened when later the same lamp stands between Volodia and Andrei so that they share its light, while the drunk and furious Kavalerov is outside it again.

Olesha expresses himself almost entirely through such symbols. They are strictly functional, not at all ornamental, as some critics have suggested. Olesha uses them to create patterns of character and emotional environments.

In *Envy*, there are such major symbols as the construction site for Andrei's huge cafeteria: a magic realm through which Andrei, in his own element, can even fly from scaffolding to scaffolding—or so it seems to Kavalerov who is altogether lost there (Andrei is actually transported by crane). Or there is the glistening dump-heap of the old world, rotting and rightly cast aside; but then it also contains the buds of feelings that are trampled underfoot by the unimaginative "new men" searching for a bolt or some other "useful" item. Thus Olesha tells his tale and makes his *cris de cœur* heard without resorting to direct explanations. Even Ivan's orations are anything but a presentation of Olesha's theme in rational terms.

Ivan appears first as a reflection in a street mirror into which Kavalerov is looking. The world in the mirror is a different, transformed world, and Ivan is very much like the terrible double who haunts Dostoevsky's Golyadkin and who appears as a mirror image. Ivan is a Kavalerov pushed further: a bit shorter, a bit fatter, more hostile toward the new order, more deeply rooted in the old world. It is significant that, as they turn away from the mirror, Ivan walks ahead of Kavalerov and, when he talks to him, he *looks back* (i.e. into the past), is unable to see where he is going (the present), and keeps bumping into people.

Very significant, too, are three statements made about Ivan on three different occasions: the first, the tale of his turning wine into water at a wedding; the second, his exclamation, upon being arrested by the security police, that he is on the way to his Golgotha; and finally, the picture of him spreadeagled against a wall and pierced by the needle of his own machine. These are unmistakable allusions to Christ's miracle at the wedding in Cana (although in that case water was turned into wine), His capture by the soldiers, and His crucifixion. Ivan is a caricature of a savior, and Olesha feels perhaps that this is all the old world deserves.

The same richness of symbols and imagery is found in Olesha's shorter works. In "The Chain," the airplane, the automobile, the bicycle, the racing driver, all symbolize the future of the boy's dreams. When, finally, he is allowed to ride the bike, the dreamy, impractical child in no time loses the symbolic chain—an allegory of the imaginative artist as a modern anachronism. In "Jottings of a Writer," the old lady can see the park of the "old world," barely remembered by the narrator and, at best, a legend to the young girls. In "Aldebaran," the planetarium stars seem to satisfy the "romantic" requirements of the young generation.

Olesha's metaphors and symbols, with which he conveys his thought through artistic shortcuts, are so effective because of their freshness. He seems to raise them deep out of his childhood and then integrate them into his narrative with consummate skill, looking on with artistic detachment all the while (Olesha was a great reviser: he wrote, for instance, more than a hundred versions of the first page of *Envy*).

In his essay "On Prevention of Literature," George Orwell describes the fate of a serious writer when he is deprived of freedom:

The imaginative writer is unfree when he has to falsify his subjective feelings, which from his point of view are facts. He may distort and caricature reality in order to make his meaning clearer but he cannot misrepresent the scenery of his mind: he cannot say with conviction that he likes what he dislikes or believes what he disbelieves. If he is forced to do so, the only result is that his creative faculties dry up.

These words sum up Olesha's case.

ENVY
and Other Works

ENVY

PART ONE

1

Mornings, he sings in the lavatory. Imagine how pleased with life he is, how healthy. His singing is a reflex. These songs of his, which have neither melody nor words, just a single "ta-ra-ra" which he shouts out in different tunes, can be interpreted thus:

"How pleasant my life is . . . ta-ra, ta-ra . . . my bowels are elastic . . . ra-ta-ta-ta-ra-ree . . . my juices flow within me . . . ra-tee-ta-doo-da-ta . . . contract, guts, contract . . . tram-ba-ba-boom!"

In the morning, I pretend to be asleep as he passes me on the way from the bedroom to the door leading to the entrails of the apartment, to the lavatory. I follow him in imagination. I hear him moving in the small lavatory, which is narrow for his big body. His back bangs against the inside, shutting the door; his sides thrust against the walls; he shuffles his feet. In the lavatory door, there is an oval panel of opaque glass. He flicks the switch, the oval lights up from the inside and becomes a beautiful egg, the color of an opal. In my mind's eye, I see that egg, hanging in the dark of the corridor.

He weighs around 220 pounds. Recently, going downstairs somewhere, he noticed how his breasts quivered to the rhythm of his steps: And so he decided to add a new set to his daily calisthenics.

There's a real man for you.

Usually he does his gymnastics, not in his own bedroom,
but in the room of undefined purpose that I occupy. It is
roomier here, airier; there's more light, more radiance.
Coolness pours in through the open door of the balcony.
Moreover, this is where the washstand is. He brings a mat
from the bedroom. He is stripped except for jersey drawers,
done up by a single button in the middle of his stomach,
a mother-of-pearl one in which the pale blue and pink
world of the room spins around. When he lies on his back
on the mat, raising first one leg then the other, the button
comes undone. His groin is exposed. A splendid groin. A
tender spot. A forbidden corner. The groin of a production
manager. I saw just such a velvety groin on a buck antelope
once. Amorous currents must course through his young
secretaries and office girls at his mere glance.

He washes himself like a little boy: trumpets, dances
around, snorts, makes noises. He scoops up the water in
the hollow of his hands. Most of it splatters on the mat
before it reaches his armpits. The droplets of it that scatter
are full and clean. The lather, falling into the basin, hisses
like a pancake. Sometimes the soap blinds him; cursing, he
tears at his eyelids with his thumbs. He rinses his throat,
gargling with such zest that, under the balcony, people stop
and raise their heads.

The morning is quiet and rosy. Spring is at its height.
There are flower boxes on all the window sills. The ver-
milion of this year's blooms is already showing.

(Things don't like me. Furniture tries to trip me up.
Once the sharp corner of some polished thing literally bit
me. My relations with my blanket are always complicated.
Soup, given to me, never cools. If some bit of junk—a coin
or a collar button—falls off the table, it usually rolls under
some almost unmovable piece of furniture. And when,
crawling around on the floor after it, I raise my head, I
catch the sideboard laughing at me.)

The blue straps of his suspenders hang at his sides. He

goes into his bedroom, takes his pince-nez from the chair, puts it on in front of the mirror and comes back to my room. Here, standing in the middle of the room, he lifts the suspender straps, both at once, as if he were shouldering a load. He doesn't say a word to me. I pretend to be asleep. In the metal clips of his suspenders there are two burning clusters of sunbeams. (Things like him.)

He doesn't have to comb his hair or groom a mustache and beard. His hair is close-cropped and his mustache is small, right under his nose. He looks like a grown-up fat boy.

He takes the flask; the glass stopper squeaks. He pours eau de cologne on his palm and passes his palm over the globe of his head, from his forehead to the nape of his neck and back again.

For breakfast, he drinks two glasses of cold milk. He takes the little jug out of the sideboard, pours the milk, and drinks it, without sitting down.

My first impression of him was flabbergasting. I would never have imagined anything like it. . . . He stood there in a well-tailored gray suit, smelling of eau de cologne. His lips were fresh, slightly pouted. He turned out to be a fancy dresser.

Often, at night, I am awakened by his snoring. In a daze, I don't know what's going on. Someone seems to keep repeating threateningly, over and over: "Krakataoo . . . krra . . . ka . . . taoooooo . . ."

They have given him a wonderful apartment. It has a vase on a lacquered stand by the balcony door! A vase of the finest porcelain, rounded, tall, a tender blood-red, like a hand held against a light. It reminds you of a flamingo. The apartment is on the third floor. The balcony hangs over an ethereal space. A wide suburban street, looking like a highway. Across the street below, there is a garden: a garden thick and heavy with trees, like so many in the

Moscow suburbs, an untidy jumble grown up in an empty lot, as in an oven, hemmed in by three walls.

He is a glutton. He eats dinner out. Yesterday evening he came home hungry, decided to have a snack. There was nothing in the sideboard. He went out (there's a store on the corner) and returned loaded down with food: half a pound of ham, a can of sprats and another of mackerel, a large French loaf, a good half moon of Dutch cheese, four apples, a dozen eggs, and "Persian Pea" candy. He ordered fried eggs and tea (the kitchen in the house is communal, two cooks take turns).

"Dig in, Kavalerov." He beckoned to me and got down to it himself. He ate the eggs straight from the pan, chipping off bits of egg white as if scraping paint. His eyes became bloodshot. He kept putting on and taking off his pince-nez. He smacked his lips, snorted. His ears moved.

I spend my time observing things. Have you ever noticed that salt falls off the edge of a knife without leaving a trace—the knife shines as though nothing had been put on it; that a pince-nez sits on the bridge of a nose like a bicycle; that a human being is surrounded by tiny letters, like a scattered army of ants: on forks, spoons, plates, on a pince-nez frame, on buttons, on pencils? No one notices them, but they are engaged in a struggle for existence. They evolve from one type to another, until they become the huge lettering on posters! They rise—one species against another. The letters on street signs are at war with those on posters.

He ate himself full. He reached for an apple. But when he had lopped off its yellow cheek with his knife, he put it down.

Once a People's Commissar praised him highly in one of his speeches: "Andrei Babichev is one of our country's most outstanding citizens."

He, Andrei Petrovich Babichev, is the director of the

Food Industry Trust. He is a great salami man, a great pastry man, a great caterer.

And I, Nikolai Kavalerov, I am his jester.

2

He's in charge of everything connected with grub. He's greedy and jealous. He would like to cook all the omelets himself, all the pies, all the hamburgers, and bake every loaf of bread. He would like to be the soil that grows the wheat. He gave birth to the "Quarter."

And his offspring is growing. The "Quarter" is going to become a giant, the greatest cafeteria, the greatest kitchen. A two-course meal there will cost one quarter.

War has been declared on the kitchens.

Thousands of kitchens have submitted.

He will put an end to make-it-yourself, to food bought in fractions of a pound, to small bottles and jars. He will amalgamate all the meat grinders, all the kerosene stoves, all the frying pans, all the taps. . . . It will be, if you like, the industrialization of the kitchens.

He has set up several committees. The Soviet-made vegetable-cleaning machines have proved first-class. A German architect is building a superkitchen. Many plants are working under Babichev contracts.

I found out the following:

Babichev, a citizen of very solid, obviously statesman-like bearing, the director of a trust, briefcase under his arm, turned into a service entrance one morning, went up a flight of stairs, and knocked at random on a door. Like some Harun-al-Rashid, he visited the kitchen of a house in a working district. He saw soot and dirt and mad furies rushing around in the smoke. Children were crying. He was immediately assailed. He was in everybody's way, huge as he is, taking up so much space, light, and air. Besides, he had a briefcase, a pince-nez, and was well dressed and clean. The furies decided that, without doubt, he must be a member of some committee. Those housewives put their hands on their hips and needled him. He left. It was his fault, they shouted after him, that the kerosene stove had gone out, that a glass had cracked, that someone's soup had got oversalted. He left without saying what he had wanted to. He has no imagination. He should have said:

"Women! We shall blow the soot off you, rid your nostrils of smoke, your ears of hollering. We shall oblige a potato to peel itself, miraculously, in a split second. We shall give you back the hours that the kitchen has stolen from you—half your lives will be returned to you. You, young wife, are cooking soup for your husband. And to that miserable puddle of soup, you sacrifice half your day! We shall turn your puddles into gleaming seas, borsch shall flow like an ocean, buckwheat will be heaped in mountains and applesauce descend upon you like a glacier! Listen to me, housewives! We promise you: tiled floors with sunlight playing on them, huge burnished kettles like dark fire, plates as pure as lilies, milk so thick it will flow like mercury; and the aroma of the soup will be so sweet it will make the flowers on the table jealous."

Like a fakir, he is in ten different places at the same time.

In his official memos, he uses plenty of parentheses and underlining, afraid to be misunderstood.

Here are a couple:

To Comrade Prokudin: The wrappings for the candies (12 samples) must be made informative to the consumer (what filling, chocolate, etc.). The design to be new. No "Rosa Luxemburg" (found out this already in use for a candy bar!). Use, rather, a scientific motif (something poetical, like "geography" or "astronomy"? A serious name with an attractive sound: "Eskimo" or "telescope"?). Telephone without fail tomorrow, Wednesday, managerial offices, between one and two.

To Comrade Fominsky: See to it that every plate of the 50- and 75-kopek dinners contains a piece of meat (neatly cut, as in a private restaurant). See that this is carried out. Is it true that (1) the snack with beer is served without tray and (2) the peas are small and undersoaked?

He is petty, suspicious; fussy as an old housekeeper with a bunch of keys.

At ten in the morning, he arrived from the cardboard factory. Eight persons were waiting for him in his reception room. He received: (1) the head of the fish-smoking department; (2) the representative of the Far-Eastern Canning Trust (he seized a can of crabs, rushed out of his office to show it to someone, then came back, placed it on his desk, at his elbow, and for a long time could not calm down; he kept glancing at the blue can, laughing, rubbing his nose); (3) an engineer from the construction site of the new storage building; (4) a German, with reference to trucks (they spoke in German and he must have closed the conference with a proverb because it sounded like a rhyme and they both laughed); (5) an artist who had brought a project for a poster (he did not like it and said that the blue in it must be a chemical rather than a romantic blue); (6) some kind of restaurant manager with cuff links like little, milk-white bells; (7) a weedy man with a wave in his beard who talked about head of cattle; and (8) some delightful inhabitant of the countryside. This last conference was of a special nature. Babichev rose and moved forward, almost with his arms outstretched. The other filled the whole office, he was so charmingly clumsy, smiling shyly, suntanned, bright-eyed, a kind of Levin out of Tolstoy. He exuded a smell of wild flowers and dairy produce. They spoke of state farms. A dreamy expression lingered on the features of all those present.

At four-twenty, he left for a meeting at the Supreme Soviet for Agriculture.

3

In the evenings, he sits bathed in the palm-green light of the lampshade. His desk is covered with notebooks, typed sheets, scraps of paper with columns of figures. He turns over the pages of a desk calendar, jumps up, looks for something on a shelf, gets hold of some file. Kneeling on the chair, his belly on the table, his fat face resting on his hands, he reads. The green field of the table is covered with a sheet of glass. Well, what's so special about all that? A man is working. A man is working at home in the evening. A man, staring at a sheet of paper, is digging in his ear with a pencil. Nothing special. But everything about him says: You, Kavalerov, are a bystander. Of course, he makes no such declaration. Probably he is thinking nothing of the sort. But it is clear without words. Some third person informs me of it. Some third person drives me into a rage as I observe him.

"The Quarter!" he shouts. "The Quarter! Yes, sir!"

And then he begins to guffaw. He has seen something killingly funny in a column of figures. He calls me, beckons to me, choking with laughter. He neighs, jabbing his finger at a sheet of paper. I look and see nothing. What made him laugh? Why, I cannot even see the principles on which to base a comparison. Whereas he sees a departure from those principles so flagrant that it makes him dissolve in laughter. I listen to him, horrified. His laughter is that of a priest, a witch doctor. I listen like a blind man listening to exploding fireworks.

"You, Kavalerov, are a bystander. You don't understand a thing."

He does not say it, but it is plain without words.

Sometimes he does not return home until late at night. Then I get his instructions by phone:

"Is that you, Kavalerov? Listen, they'll be calling me from Bread Trust. Have them call 2-73-05, Extension 62.

Write it down. You have it? Consumers' Committee. Extension 62. 'Bye."

Sure enough, they call him from the Bread Trust.

"Hello, Bread Trust?" I repeat, "Comrade Babichev is at the Consumers' Committee. What? Yes, Consumers' Committee, 2-73-05, Extension 62. Got it? Sixty-two. 'Bye."

The Bread Trust calls Babichev, the director of the Food Trust. Babichev is at the Consumers' Committee meeting. What has all this got to do with me? But it is pleasant to feel that I have even an indirect part in the existence of the Bread Trust and of Babichev. I experience an administrative exultation. Certainly my part in all this is small. That of a flunky. What is it, then? Do I respect him? Fear him? No. I am just as good as he is. I am no bystander. I'll prove it.

I would like to catch him unawares, to discover his weak side, find an unguarded spot. When I witnessed his morning ablutions for the first time, I thought I had him. I felt I had broken through his inaccessibility.

Drying himself, he left his room, walked toward the balcony, and stopped not six feet from me. He continued to dry himself. Boring into his ear with a corner of the towel, he turned his back on me. I almost cried out when I saw his massive torso from behind like that. His back answered everything. His oily skin was a tender yellow. The secrets of another man's life were unfolding before my eyes. Babichev's ancestors had taken good care of their skins. The rolls of fat had been harmoniously distributed over his ancestors' bodies. And from them, the Commissar had inherited fineness of skin, nobility of coloration, purity of pigment. And I really felt I had him when I saw the birthmark on his waistline, a special, hereditary, aristocratic birthmark—a little thing filled with blood, translucent, tender, attached to the body by a frail stem, the sort of mark by which mothers recognize their kidnaped children decades later.

"You are an aristocrat, Andrei Babichev! You're just masquerading." I almost said it aloud.

But then he turned round, his chest toward me.

On that chest, under the right collarbone, there was a scar. A round one, with tiny wavelets, like the imprint of a coin on wax. One could imagine that a twig had grown out of that spot, and then had been broken off. Babichev had been deported. He tried to escape, was shot at.

"Who is Jocasta?" he asked me once, out of the blue. Completely unexpected questions pour out of him at times, especially in the evenings. During the day he is busy. His eyes slide over posters, display windows, while with corners of his ears he overhears other people's remarks. That is his raw material. I am the only one to provide him with non-business conversation. He feels the need to communicate, but he considers me incapable of serious talk. He knows that when people are relaxing they usually chat. He decides to respect certain human habits. So he asks me idle questions. I feel obliged to answer. I am his jester. He thinks I'm a fool.

"Do you like olives?" he asks.

"Yes, I know who Jocasta is and I like olives. But I do not wish to answer inane questions. I'm no stupider than you are."

That's how I should reply. But I don't have the courage. He smothers me.

4

I have been living under his roof since that night, two weeks ago, when he picked me up as I lay drunk outside the door of a bar. . . .

They had kicked me out of that bar.

The argument started unexpectedly. At first, there was nothing to indicate that a row was in the making. On the contrary, friendship could have bloomed between the two tables. Drunks are communicative. A large group, which

included a woman, asked me to join them, and I was about
to accept their invitation when the woman, who was charming, slender, and wore a silk blouse hanging loosely on her
collarbones, made a crack about me. I was offended; halfway between one table and the other, I turned on my heels,
carrying my mug of beer before me like a lantern.

This brought a hail of gibes down on me. Actually, they
may have had good reason to laugh at me. "Who's this
prickly pear?" a bass guffawed behind me. Somebody
threw a pea. I circled around my table and faced them.
Some beer spilled out of my mug onto the marble tabletop.
I could not free my thumb from the handle. Drunk as I
was, I burst into a tirade in which self-destruction and ag-
gressiveness were fused:

"You are a troupe of monsters . . . a traveling band of
freaks, holding the girl prisoner. . . ." (The people around
quieted down; the prickly pear expresses himself quite
strangely, his speech emerging from the surrounding din.)
"You, the one sitting under the palm tree—freak number
one. Stand up. Let everybody have a look at you. . . .
Take note, Comrades, respected public. . . . Quiet! Orchestra, play a waltz! Your face is a harness. Your cheeks
are pulled tight by wrinkles. And they're not wrinkles but
reins. Your chin is a nag; your nose, the cartman, a leprous
cartman. And the rest of you is the load of dung. . . . Sit
down now. Let's go on. Freak number two. The guy whose
cheeks look like knees. . . . Very pretty! Admire, citizens,
the touring freaks. . . . And you? How did you manage
to get through the door? How come your ears didn't get
caught? And you, the one leaning over the kidnaped girl,
ask her how she feels about your blackheads? Comrades . . ." (I looked around the room) "They, these ones,
imagine, *they* laughed at *me!* That one over there was
laughing! You, do you have any idea how you laugh? You
sound like an enema. . . . Maiden!

> Among flowers you have no peers.
> Oh, to conquer your eighteen years.

Maiden! Cry out for help. We shall save you. What has
happened to the world? He is pawing you and you're just
being playful and coy. Do you like being pawed?" (I
paused, then said) "I invite you to come and sit down here
with me. Why were you laughing at me? I stand facing you,
unknown maiden, and beg you: do not lose me. Simply get
up, push them away, and step over here. What do you expect from him, from any of them? Tenderness? Intelligence? Caresses? Loyalty? Come to me. It would be absurd
even to compare them to me. You will receive infinitely
more from me. . . ."

Saying this, I was horrified by what I was saying: I felt
acutely that special power which comes with the knowledge
that one is dreaming and that everything is permitted because one can wake up at will. Only in this case, no awakening was to follow. The thread of irreparability was fran-
tically winding itself taut.

They threw me out.

I was unconscious. Then, when I came to, I said:

"I call them, and they don't come. They won't come,
the bitches" (my words were addressed to all women).

I lay in the gutter above a drain, my face toward the
grating. The air I was inhaling from the drain was musty;
in the black cube of the hole something was moving, the
garbage was alive there. Falling, I had caught sight of the
drain and the memory of it governed my dream. The hole
was the condensation of anxiety and fear, of what I had
felt in the bar, of humiliation and fear of punishment; in
my dream it dressed itself up into a plot about being pursued—I was running away, trying to escape. I made a final,
desperate effort to escape, and broke the dream.

I opened my eyes, trembling with the joy of liberation.
But my waking was so vague that I took it for the transition from one dream to another, and in this new vision it
was the Deliverer who played the main part. The one who
had saved me from pursuit, the one whose hands and
sleeves I was covering with kisses, thinking that I was kiss-

ing them in my dream, the one round whose neck I threw my arms, sobbing aloud.

"Why am I so unhappy? Why is it so difficult to live?" I mumbled.

"Raise his head higher," the Deliverer said.

I was being driven somewhere in a car. Coming to my senses I saw a pale sky, growing lighter, rushing like water from the soles of my feet to somewhere behind my head. This sight and the rocking made me dizzy and ended each time in a fit of nausea. When I woke up in the morning, in my fear I stretched my hands out toward my feet. Before I even knew where I was or what was happening to me, I recalled the jerks and the swinging. The thought stabbed through me that while I was drunk they had cut off my legs. I was expecting my hand to touch the thick, barrel-like roundness of bandages. But it turned out that I was simply lying on a sofa in a large, clean, light room with two windows and French doors leading to a balcony. It was early morning. The stone of the balcony was turning pink and gradually warming up.

When we made each other's acquaintance in the morning, I told him about myself.

"You looked so miserable," he said, "I felt terribly sorry for you. Perhaps you're offended and think, why does he meddle in other people's affairs? In that case, please forgive me. But if you would like to live a normal life for a while, I'd be very pleased. Plenty of room. Light and air. And there's a job for you here, some editing to do, selection of materials. What do you say?"

What caused the great man to condescend so much to an unknown, unprepossessing-looking guy like me?

5

One evening, I found out about two secrets.

"Comrade Babichev," I asked him, "who's that in the picture in the frame?"

There is a photograph of a swarthy young man on his desk.

"What's that?" He always asks one to repeat. His thoughts stay stuck to the paper and he cannot tear them off immediately. "What?" He is still far away somewhere.

"Who is that young fellow?"

"What, that, his name's Volodia Makarov. A remarkable young man." (He never speaks to me in a normal tone, as if I couldn't ask him anything seriously. I always expect to get a proverb, a limerick, or just plain mooing for a reply. And indeed, instead of simply saying "remarkable young man," for my benefit he makes it "ree-markah-ah-ble!"

"What's so remarkable about him?" I ask, avenging myself with the irritation in my tone. But he does not notice my irritation.

"Well, no. . . . Simply a youngster, a student. You sleep on his sofa. The thing is . . . he is like a son to me. He lived with me for ten years. Now he is in Murom, staying with his father."

"So that's who he is. . . ."

He rose from his table and walked across the room.

"He's eighteen; a first-class soccer player."

(Ah, a soccer player, I thought.)

"True," I said, "that's really wonderful. It is a remarkable quality in someone to be a first-class soccer player." (What am I saying?)

He didn't hear me. He was deep in his pleasant thoughts. From the doorway of the balcony, he looked out at the sky, thinking of Volodia.

"There's nobody quite like that youngster," he said suddenly, facing me (I feel that my very presence is offensive to him when he is speaking of Volodia Makarov). "In the first place, I owe my life to him. Ten years ago, he saved me. They held me down, the back of my neck on an anvil, and were about to hit me in the face with a hammer. He saved me." (He obviously relishes talking about the fellow's heroic deed, he must often think of it.) "But that is not the important thing. What's most important is that he's a completely new human being. Well, that's that." (He returned to his desk.)

"Why did you pick me up and bring me here?"

"What, what's that?" he mooed. I knew it would take him a second to hear my question. "Why did I bring you here? You looked so miserable and it was hard not to be moved. You were sobbing. I felt terribly sorry for you."

"And the sofa?"

"What about the sofa?"

"When your young friend comes back . . . ?"

Without giving it a thought, he answered simply and cheerfully:

"Then you'll have to move off the sofa."

I ought to get up and take a swing at him. You see, he took pity on me. He, the exalted public figure, has taken pity on a wayward young man. But only temporarily, until the main character comes back. He is simply bored in the evenings. Later he will kick me out. He is quite cynical about it.

"Comrade Babichev," I say to him, "do you realize what you just said? You are a pig."

"What's that you say, what, what?" He is unsticking his thoughts from the paper. Now the sounds will reach his nerve ends, and I wish the sounds would make a mistake. Could he have heard? Well, let him. Let's get it over with, once and for all.

But an external circumstance interferes. It is not my fate to be kicked out yet. In the street, under the balcony, someone is shouting "Andrei!"

He turns his head.

"Andrei!"

He stands up jerkily, pushing himself from his desk with the palms of his hands.

"Andryusha, old man!"

He steps out onto the balcony. I go to a window. We both look down into the street. Outside it's dark. The only light comes from the windows, and it shines wanly onto the middle of the street. In the center of it stands a short, squat man.

"Good evening, Andryusha, how're you getting along? How's the Quarter?"

(Through my window, I make out the balcony with the huge Andryusha on it and I can hear his heavy breathing.)

The man in the street keeps exclaiming, but somewhat less loudly.

"Why don't you answer? I have news for you. I've invented a machine. It's called Ophelia."

Babichev turned his body abruptly and came back into the room. His shadow rushed diagonally across the street and almost caused a storm in the foliage in the garden opposite. He sat down behind his desk, drumming on it with his fingers.

"I warn you, Andrei, don't let it go to your head!" the other shouts from outside. "I'll get you yet, Andrei."

Then Babichev jumps up again. His fists clenched, he rushes out onto the balcony once more. Now there is definitely a storm in the trees. His shadow, like a Buddha, falls on the city.

"What are you fighting, you scum?" he thunders. The metal railing of the balcony rings out. He has hit it with his fist. "What are you against, you scum? Get away from here. I'll have you locked up!"

"See you soon," comes the answer from down below. The fat little man takes off his headgear (a bowler hat, can it be a bowler?). His politeness is affected. Andrei is no longer on the balcony. With small drumming steps, the short man is walking down the middle of the street.

"Here," Babichev shouts at me, "how do you like him? My little brother Ivan. The son of a bitch!"

Seething, he walks up and down the room. He shouts at me again.

"Who is he? Ivan? A lazy bum, a harmful, contagious man. He ought to be shot."

(The swarthy youth in the picture is smiling. He has a plebeian face. He shows his gleaming teeth in a specially

masculine way. A whole cageful of teeth, which he exhibits
like a Japanese.)

6

Evening. He's working. I'm sitting on the sofa. The lamp
is between us. From where I am, the lampshade blots out
the top part of his face—it just isn't there. Below the lampshade hangs the lower hemisphere of his head. On the
whole, it resembles a painted terracotta piggy bank.

"My youth coincides with the youth of the century," I
say.

He does not listen. His indifference is insulting.

"I often think of the century. Our century is a great one.
And it's wonderful, isn't it, if they coincide, the youth of
the century and the youth of a man?"

"Century—man," he repeats. And if I told him that he
had heard and repeated two words, he wouldn't believe it.

"In Europe, there is great scope for a talented man. They
love other people to become famous over there. Please,
just do something remarkable, and they will pick you up
and lead you on the path to fame. . . . Here, we have no
path for individual success, have we?"

Talking to myself would have had the same effect. I am
making sounds, mouthing words. . . . Well, go on making
sounds. They don't bother him.

"In this country, the gates on the roads to fame are
down. A talent must either fade or dare to face the scandal
and lift the barrier. I, for one, feel like arguing. I want to
show the strength of my personality. I want my own glory.
We are afraid to pay attention to a man. I want a great
deal of attention. I would like to have been born in a small
French town, to grow up with my head full of dreams, to
find a lofty goal for my life; then, one day, to leave the
small town and walk on foot to the capital, and there, by
frantic effort, reach my goal. But I was not born in the
West. And now they tell me: it's not just you, even the
most remarkable personality is nothing. I am beginning

gradually to get accustomed to this truth, which is a debatable one. Here's how I figure it: it is possible to become famous by being a musician, a writer, a military leader, by crossing Niagara on a tightrope. . . . These are legitimate ways of gaining fame; in them, the personality tried to express itself. . . . And what about here, where they talk so much about efficiency, usefulness, where they demand a sober, realistic approach to things and events, what about suddenly doing something absurd, pulling off some trick of genius and then just saying: that's your way and this is mine. To go out into a public square, do something like that, and then take a bow: I have lived my way and done as I pleased."

He doesn't hear a word.

"Even, say, kill myself. A suicide for no reason. Just a flippant suicide. To show that everyone is free to do what he pleases with himself. Even now. I could hang myself in the entrance to your house."

"If I were you, I would rather hang myself at the entrance to the Commissariat of the National Economy, on Nogin Place, you know, the former Barbara Place. There's a huge arch there, have you noticed? It would look quite impressive."

In the room where I used to live, before I moved here, there was a terrifying bed. I feared it in the way that one fears ghosts. It was curved, like a barrel. Bones rattled in it. It was covered with a blue blanket which I bought at the market in Kharkov during the year of the famine. A peasant woman was selling pies. She kept them warm under a blanket. Losing heat, the pies clung to the warmth of life, almost squeaking and wriggling like puppies. Life was tough then, for me as for the rest, and there was so much well-being, homeliness and warmth in the scene that I firmly decided to get myself just such a blanket. Eventually, I did so. One wonderful evening I crept under the blue blanket. I baked under it, turning from side to side, the warmth setting me in motion as though I were made of jelly. I slipped blissfully into sleep. Gradually, the designs on the blanket swelled and turned into pretzels.

Now I sleep on an excellent sofa.

By deliberate movements, I cause a ringing in the taut, new, virginal springs. The result is droplets of ringing, rising up from the depth below. I imagine bubbles of air rushing to the water's surface. I go to sleep like a baby. On this sofa, I fly back into my childhood. It's blissful. Like a child, I have at my disposal the tiny time interval between the first heaviness felt in the eyelids, the first melting away of things, and the beginning of real sleep. Once again, I know how to prolong this interval, enjoy it, fill it with the thought I want; before sinking into sleep, still in control of my conscious mind, I observe how my thoughts acquire a body of dream substance, how the ringing bubbles from the submerged depths become rolling grapes, how a heavy bunch of grapes is formed, a whole vineyard thick with bunches, and then there is a sunny road beside the vineyard, and the warmth. . . .

I am twenty-seven.

Once, changing my shirt, I saw myself in the mirror and suddenly caught a striking resemblance to my father. In reality there is no such resemblance. I remembered: my parents' bedroom, and I, a boy, am watching my father as he changes his shirt. I feel sorry for him. It's already too late for him to be handsome, famous. He is already cooked, finished, already not famous for anything. He can't be anything except what he is. That's what I was thinking, pitying him and feeling quietly proud of my own superiority. And now I recognize my father in myself. Not a formal resemblance—no, something else, I would say—a sexual resemblance, as if I suddenly perceived in me, in my very substance, my father's seed. It was like being told: you're cooked, finished, there's nothing more for you. Produce a son.

Now I'll never be either handsome or famous. I will not set out for the capital from my little town. I will be neither a general nor a People's Commissar, nor a scientist, nor a sprinter, nor an adventurer. All my life I have dreamed of a rare love. Soon I will go back to my old place, to the room with the terrifying bed. It's an odious neighborhood. The widow Prokopovich lives there. She's maybe forty-five, perhaps. Still, in the house, they call her Little Annie. She cooks for the hairdressers' co-operative. She has installed a kitchen in the corridor. The oven is in a dark recess. She feeds cats. The thin, silent cats follow the flight of her hands as if mesmerized. She throws them some sort of offal. As a result, the floor seems to be decorated with mother-of-pearl gobs of spit. Once I slipped, having stepped on something's heart—small and neatly outlined, rather like a chestnut. She walks around tangled up in the intestines and veins of animals. A knife gleams in her hand. She elbows her way through the guts, like a princess through cobwebs.

The widow Prokopovich is old, fat, and flabby. You can squeeze her out like a tube of liver paste. In the morning I would stumble upon her as she stood at the sink in the corridor. As a rule, she wasn't dressed and she smiled at me with a womanly smile. By her door, on a stool, stood a basin, with some loose hairs floating on the water.

The widow Prokopovich is a symbol of my humbled masculinity. Her whole attitude seems to say: by all means, I am ready, mistake the door at night, I purposely don't lock mine, you'll be welcome. We will live and enjoy ourselves. Give up your dreams of a rare love. All that is past. And you, neighbor, have had it yourself. Your pants look shrunk on you—you've already got middle-aged spread. Well, what more do you want? One with fine, smooth hands? The one in your imagination? With a delicate oval face? Forget her. By now, you could be a father yourself. Come on; I have a wonderful bed. The late lamented won it in a lottery. There's a quilt. I'll look after you. Sympathize with you.

At times the way she looked at me was downright shameless. At times, when we met, there popped from her throat a tiny sound, a round vocal droplet ejected by a spasm of delight. I'm no consort to you, you lousy cook! I'm no mate for a slimy reptile!

I fall asleep on Babichev's sofa.

I dream that a wonderful girl with a powdery laugh slips under the sheets to join me. My wish has come true. But how can I reward her? I become frightened. Nobody has ever loved me for nothing. Prostitutes have always tried to squeeze all they could out of me. What will she demand? As happens in dreams, she guesses my thoughts and says:

"Don't worry . . . just a quarter."

I remember myself as a schoolboy being taken to a wax-works museum. Inside a cube of glass, a handsome man in white tie and tails, a smoking wound in his chest, was dying in somebody's arms.

"That's the French President, Carnot; he was wounded by an anarchist," my father told me.

The President was dying, he was breathing heavily, his eyes rolled back. I stared at him spellbound. A magnificent man was lying inside a cube of greenish glass with his goatee thrust forward. A magnificent sight. That was when, for the first time, I heard the roar that time makes. Time was flying past above my head. I gulped back enthusiastic sobs. I decided to become famous so that one day my wax twin, filled with the roar of centuries only a few are privileged to hear, might also adorn the inside of a greenish cube.

Now I am writing a music-hall revue. Monologues and couplets. It's all about financial inspectors, our Soviet young womanhood, our new profiteers, alimony, and the like.

> Since the day they gave the drum,
> To machinist Liz Kaplan,
> The shop is filled with trum-bum-bum,
> And they fail to fill the plan.

And maybe, sometime or other, there will stand in a museum the figure of a strange-looking man: thick-nosed, with a pale, kindly face and tousled hair; boyishly plump, in a jacket with one button left on the paunch. On the cube there will be a sign:

NIKOLAI KAVALEROV.

Nothing else. That's all. And everyone who sees it will say: "Ah!" And will remember certain stories, legends perhaps. "Ah! That's the one who lived in a famous time, hated everyone and envied everyone, bragged, let himself get carried away, harbored great plans, wanted to do many things and did nothing—and ended by committing an odious, loathsome crime. . . ."

7

From Tverskaya Street, I turned into a side street. I had to get to Nikitskaya Street. It was early in the morning. The side street is jointed. Like painful rheumatism, I move from joint to joint. Things don't like me. I make the street ache.

A little man in a bowler hat was walking ahead of me.

At first I thought: he's hurrying somewhere. But soon I realized that his jerky gait, propelling his whole body forward, was a peculiarity of his.

He was carrying a large pillow in a yellow cover by its ear. It kept banging against his knee, and this caused dents to appear and disappear in it.

In the center of a town, in certain side streets, one sometimes finds a romantic, flowering hedge. We were walking alongside such a hedge.

A bird on a bough sparkled, jerked forward, and clicked, reminding me of a hair clipper. The man walking ahead looked back at the bird. Walking behind, I managed to catch just a glimpse of the first phase, the crescent moon, of his face. He smiled.

"Doesn't the bird sound like one?" I almost exclaimed, certain that the same resemblance must have occurred to him.

He has a bowler hat.

He has taken it off and is carrying it under his arm. In his other hand is the pillow.

The windows are open. On the second floor I see a little vase with a blue flower in it. The little man is attracted by the vase. He steps off the sidewalk, crosses to the middle of the street, stops in front of the window, and lifts his face toward it. His bowler hat, which he has put back on, slips down onto the nape of his neck. He is holding on tight to the pillow. There is some down flowering on his knee.

I observe all this from a recess.

He is calling to the little vase: "Valia!"

Immediately, the vase tips over and a girl wearing something pink appears in the window.

"Valia," he said, "I have come for you."

Silence. The water from the vase runs down the wall.

"Look what I have brought with me . . . can you see?" He took the pillow in both hands and lifted it above his belly. "Do you recognize it? You used to sleep on it." He laughed. "Come back to me, Valia, come back. Don't you want to? I'll show you my Ophelia. Won't you come?"

Silence again. The girl was leaning, motionless, on the window sill. Her head and her loose, tangled hair hung down. Near her the vase rocked. I remembered now that, a second after she appeared, the girl, seeing the man in the middle of the street, had let herself fall onto her elbows on the window sill and her elbows had collapsed.

Clouds are moving across the sky and the windowpanes, and in the windows their paths were becoming entangled.

"Please, Valia, come back, please. Just slip downstairs." He waited.

Some passers-by stopped.

"You won't, then? Well, good-by."

He turned, adjusted his bowler hat on his head, and started off in my direction.

"Wait! Wait, Daddy! Daddy! Daddy!"

His steps grew faster. He started running. I saw he was not young. His breath came short; he turned pale from the effort. A funny, fat little man was running, hugging a pillow against his chest. But there was nothing insane in that.

The window was empty now.

She rushed after him. She reached the corner. The privacy of the small street ended there. She did not find him. I was standing near the hedge. I took a step toward her. She thought I could help her, that I knew something, and stopped. A tear was tracing a curved path down her cheek like a droplet of water on a vase. She was all pent up, ready to ask me something. But I beat her to it and said:

"You passed me with the rustle of a bough full of flowers and leaves."

In the evening I was proofreading.

. . . thus, the blood collected during the slaughter of cattle can either be processed for salami or used for the production of glue, buttons, dyes, fertilizers, feed for cattle, fowl or fish. The fat-containing organic waste products can be processed into edible fats like margarine and oil or, for technical use, made into glycerines, stearine, and machine oil. The heads and legs of sheep, by means of electrical spiral drills, automatic cleaning machines, gas lathes, cutting machines, and boiling drums, can be turned into food products, technical grease, cleaned hair, and bone for various uses. . . .

He is on the telephone. They call him ten times an evening. Usually I pay no attention. He talks to all sorts of people. But then I suddenly begin to register what he is saying:

"There is nothing cruel about it."

I begin to listen.

"There's nothing cruel in that. Well, you asked me and I'm telling you. That's not cruelty. No, no! You have nothing to worry about, do you hear? He's abasing himself? What? Stands under your windows? Don't you believe it! He's just being difficult. He's been under my windows too, you know. He likes it. I know him. What? You did? You cried? All night, did you say? Well, you were wrong to cry all night. He'll go mad? Do. We'll send him to the proper place. Ophelia? Which? Ah, that . . . the hell with it, pay no attention. He's raving. Just please yourself. But I assure you, you did the proper thing. Yes, sure. What? The pillow? Really?" (He laughs into the receiver.) "I can imagine. What? The one you slept on? So what, why is it better than the one you sleep on now? But every pillow has a history. Well, to make it short, don't hesitate. What? Sure, sure. . . ." Here he stopped and listened for some time. I could hardly keep my seat. He laughed thunderously. "A bough? Come again, what bough? Laden with flowers? Flowers and leaves? What? Probably some alcoholic, one of his buddies."

8

Imagine an ordinary piece of cooked salami. A thick, smooth, round cylinder, lopped off one end of the huge, multi-pound original. The blind end of it, with its wrinkled skin, is tied with a string that hangs down like a little tail. A piece of salami like any other piece of salami. It must weigh somewhat more than two pounds. Its surface is sweating. Under it, you can see the yellow bubbles of subcutaneous fat. On its cut face, the lard forms white polka dots.

Babichev was holding this piece of salami in the palm of his hand. He was speaking. The doors opened and closed. People kept coming in. It was crowded. In his pinkish statesman's palm, the salami looked like a live thing.

"What do you say, great, isn't it?" he asked all of them. "No, just look at it! A shame Shapiro isn't here. We must call Shapiro. Ha-ha. Great! You've called Shapiro? Busy? Try again."

Then the salami was on the table. Lovingly, Babichev made a bed for it. Without taking his eyes off it, he backed away, found an armchair with his backside, eased himself into it, put his fists on his thighs, and burst into happy laughter. He raised a fist, saw some grease on it, licked it off.

"Kavalerov," he said, when he was through laughing, "are you doing anything? Would you please go and find Shapiro? He must be at the storage house. Go straight there and take it to him." He pointed to the salami with his eyes. "Let him have a look at it and call me."

I went out to take the salami to Shapiro, while Babichev was phoning all over the place.

"Yes, yes," he was roaring, "yes! Absolutely out of this world! Let's send it to the show. To the Milan exhibition. Italy, yes. Yes, seventy-five per cent veal. Great victory, certainly. No, not a quarter, ha-ha . . . are you trying to be funny? . . . Thirty-five. Lovely, isn't it? A beauty!"

He drove off.

Through the window of his limousine swayed the pinkish disc of his laughing face. At various buildings, hardly stopping, he would thrust his Tyrolean hat into the doorman's hands with his eyes popping out of his head, rush upstairs, heavy, noisy, temperamental as a wild boar. "Salami!" resounded in many offices. "The very one I mentioned to you. . . ." And, while I drifted through the sunlit streets, he kept calling Shapiro.

"It's on its way to you! You'll see for yourself, Sol, you'll burst. . . ."

"Haven't you got it yet? Ha-ha, Sol."

He was wiping his sweaty neck, thrusting a handkerchief deep inside his collar, almost tearing it open, frowning, suffering.

I reached Shapiro's. They saw I was carrying the salami and stepped out of my way. My path was magically cleared. They all knew that the messenger with Babichev's salami had arrived. Shapiro, a melancholic old Jew whose nose in profile looked like a figure six, stood under a wooden awning in the courtyard of the storage house. The door to the huge shed gave onto shimmering summer darkness like the doors of all packing houses, a tender, chaotic darkness as when you close your eyes and press your fingers against the lids. By the doorjamb there was a telephone. Next to it, a nail stuck out of the wall with yellowed sheets of paper speared on it.

Shapiro took the salami I had brought, weighed it in his hand, balanced it in his palm, and, shaking his head, brought it up to his nose and sniffed at it. Then he emerged from under the wooden awning and placed the salami on a crate. With a pocketknife, he carefully cut a small, soft slice off it. In solemn silence the slice was chewed, pressed against the palate, slowly sucked, and swallowed. The hand holding the pocketknife came down, trembling slightly, while its owner analyzed his sensations.

"Ach!" he sighed, when he had swallowed the piece of salami. "Atta boy, Babichev. That's a salami. It's the truth: he's done it! Thirty-five kopeks for such a salami. I'm telling you, it's incredible."

The telephone rang. Shapiro got up slowly and went to answer it.

"Yes, Comrade Babichev. Congratulations. I could kiss you."

From somewhere Babichev was hollering so loudly that even from where I stood, quite a distance from the phone, I could hear his voice and the crackling and exploding sounds. The receiver, shaken by powerful vibrations, was almost torn out of Shapiro's weak hands. He even shook a finger of his other hand at it, as if at a naughty child preventing him from listening.

"What shall I do?" I asked. "Does the salami stay here?"

"He asked me to have it brought to his place. He invited me to come over and eat it with him."

I could not restrain myself.

"Do I really have to drag it back home? Why not buy another one?"

"It's impossible to buy a salami like this," Shapiro said. "They're not on sale yet. This is a factory sample."

"It will go bad."

Shapiro closed his knife by sliding it in his hand down the side of his pants, feeling for his pocket. When he spoke, it was slowly, with a tiny smile, his lids lowered. He lectured me:

"I have just finished congratulating Comrade Babichev for creating a salami that does not go smelly in one day. Otherwise I would not have congratulated Comrade Babichev. We shall eat it today. Put it down. Never mind the sun. Don't be afraid, it will have the aroma of a rose."

He disappeared into the darkness of the shed, came back with a piece of wax paper, and a few seconds later I was holding in my hands a professionally made package.

From the first days of my acquaintance with Babichev, I had heard about the famous salami. Somewhere they were experimenting with the production of a special kind, nourishing, clean, and cheap. Babichev kept making inquiries in various places about the results, his voice trembling with concern. He gave advice and asked questions, returning from the telephone sometimes discouraged, sometimes happily excited. Finally the species was evolved. From out of the mysterious incubators, swaying with the movement of its heavy trunk, came crawling a fat, tightly stuffed hose.

When Babichev held a piece of this hose in his hands, he turned crimson. He even looked coy at first, a bit like a bridegroom at a wedding who suddenly realizes the beauty of his bride and her spellbinding effect upon the guests. In happy confusion he looked around at everyone. He put the salami down and raised his upturned palms, as if to say: "No, no. Better not. I'd rather give it up now than eat my heart out later. Such luck does not come in an ordinary lifetime. It's a snare set by fate. Take it away. I am not worthy."

Carrying two pounds of this amazing salami, I drifted along aimlessly.

I stood on a bridge.

The Palace of Labor was on my left; behind me, the Kremlin. In the river there were boats, swimmers. From my bird's-eye view, a tugboat slid by swiftly. From this height, I saw, not a tugboat, but something like a huge almond cut in half lengthwise. The almond vanished under the bridge. Only then did I remember seeing the tugboat's funnel and, near the funnel, two characters eating borsch from a pot. A white puff of smoke, transparent and disintegrating, flew in my direction. Failing to reach me, it kept taking on different shapes, and reached me only with its hindmost tail, coiling in a hardly visible astral hoop.

I was about to throw the salami in the river.

Andrei Babichev is a remarkable man. He is a member of the society of former political exiles, a statesman who considers today his personal holiday. Just because they showed him a salami of a new type. . . . Can it really be a holiday? Can this be glory?

Today he was shining. Yes, the seal of glory was visible on him. Why then don't I feel passion, exaltation, awe, in the presence of this glory? I am filled with hatred. He is a statesman, a Communist. He is building a new world. And the glory in this new world flares up when a new salami is delivered by a salami man. I do not understand this glory. What is the meaning of it? It is not the sort of glory I have learned from shrines, from history. . . . Does this mean that the nature of glory has changed? Has this happened everywhere or only in this country, where a new world is being built? I know that this new world is the most important thing, the triumphant future. . . . I am not blind, I have a head on my shoulders. You don't have to teach me, to go into long explanations. I am quite literate. It is in this world that I long for glory! I want to shine here

like Babichev shone today. But a new kind of salami won't
make me shine.

I drift along the streets with the package. A lousy piece
of salami governs my movements, my will. I refuse!

Several times I was on the verge of tossing the parcel
over the railing. But no sooner did I imagine the damned
salami escaping from its wrapping as it flew downward
with the efficiency of a torpedo than another picture super-
seded this vision and made me shiver. I saw Babichev's
shadow moving on me, a terrifying, unconquerable idol
with popeyes. I am afraid of him. He oppresses me. He
looks at me and sees through me. In fact, he does not look
at me. I can see his eyes only from the side, because when
his face is turned toward me he has no eyes, only his
sparkling pince-nez—two round, blind, brilliant things. He
is not interested in looking at me, he has no time for it,
no desire, but I know he sees through me.

In the evening, Solomon Shapiro came over with two
other men and Babichev made quite a party of it. Old
Shapiro brought a bottle and they drank, taking bites of
salami between small glassfuls of vodka. I declined an invitation to take part in their feast. Instead I watched them
from the balcony.

Paintings have immortalized many feasts. Military lead-
ers, Venetian doges, and just ordinary lovers of good food
hold feasts. Whole periods are recorded in these paintings.
Plumes flow in the air, garments slip off shoulders, cheeks
gleam and glisten. . . .

We need a new Tiepolo! Here is a new set of feasters
for you! They are sitting around a table under a hundred-
watt bulb and are engaged in lively conversation. New
Tiepolo, I want you to paint "The Feast in the House of
a Food-Industry Manager."

I imagine the painting in a museum. People stand before it, trying to guess what the fat giant in blue suspenders,
painted with such inspiration, can be talking about. The
giant is holding on his fork a round slice of salami. This
slice should have disappeared long ago into the giant's

mouth but he is much too absorbed in what he is saying. And what *is* he saying?

"In this country, they do not know how to prepare sausages!"

That's what the giant in blue suspenders is saying. "I don't call those sausages. Shut up, Sol. You're a Jew and understand nothing about pork sausages. You like dried-out, kosher meats. . . . And so we have no sausages. . . . Ours are nothing but sclerotic fingers. Genuine sausage must squirt juice when pricked. I'll obtain results, you'll see. I'll produce such sausages!"

9

We gathered at the airfield.

I say "we," but I myself was an appendage, brought along by sheer chance. Nobody spoke to me, my impressions interested no one. I could have stayed at home.

The latest-model Soviet plane was about to take off. Babichev had been invited to attend. The select guests entered the enclosure, Babichev dominating the gathering. As soon as he engaged someone in conversation, a circle formed around them. Everyone listened to him, respectfully intent. He was magnificent in his gray suit, imposing, the arch of his shoulders looming above all the other shoulders. Black binoculars on a black leather strap hung on his belly. Listening, he put his hands in his pockets and slowly rocked on his widespread feet, from toes to heels, from heels to toes. He kept scratching his nose, then bringing the fingers of one hand, tips together, up to his eyes and looking at them. Those who were listening did so like schoolboys, automatically imitating his movements and facial expressions. They scratched their noses, to their own surprise.

I walked off in a rage. I found an open-air restaurant, sat at a table, and, caressed by a breeze from the fields, ordered a beer. I drank it watching the wind mold delicate shapes out of the corners of the tablecloth.

Many miracles were happening simultaneously at the airfield. Daisies grew there very close to the enclosure: ordinary daisies emitting yellow pollen-dust. Low over the airfield, parallel with the line of the horizon, round rolling clouds made me think of cannon smoke. At the crossing of red-lead paths there were wooden arrows indicating all directions. Nearby, in the air, the silky trunk of a wind indicator was shrinking, stretching, and swinging, showing the direction of the wind. Over the grass of ancient battles, of reindeer, of romanticism, crawled the flying machines. I was delightedly savoring these enchanting contrasts and combinations. The rhythm of the shrinkings of the silky hose was conducive to thought.

Transparent, vibrating, like the upper wing of an insect, the name Lilienthal has had an enchanted ring to it for me since childhood. Airy, flying kite-like, stretched on a light, bamboo frame, this name was bound up in my memory with the beginnings of aviation. The flying man, Otto Lilienthal, got killed. Flying machines no longer resemble birds. The light, translucent, yellow wings have been replaced by struts. They seem to beat against the ground at take-off, when a cloud of dust rises. Now the flying machine looks like a heavy fish. How quickly aviation has become an industry!

A march broke out like a thunderclap. The People's Commissar for War had arrived. Passing the others, he walked quickly down the path. The power and speed of his step caused a draft: leaves whirled behind him. The orchestra played smartly. The Commissar stepped out smartly, his whole being in rhythm with the orchestra.

I rushed to the gate leading to the field, but they held me back. A soldier said "You can't" and placed his hand on the top rib of the gate.

"What do you mean?" I asked.

He turned away. His gaze was drawn to where interesting things were happening. The pilot-designer, in a rosy leather jacket, stood facing front before the Commissar. A tight leather belt emphasized the massiveness of the

Commissar's back. They both held a salute. Everyone was robbed of movement. Only the orchestra was in full motion. Babichev stood with his stomach sticking out.

"Let me by, Comrade," I repeated, touching the soldier's sleeve, and heard in answer:

"I'll have to expel you from the airport."

"But I was in there! I left for only a minute. I'm with Babichev!"

I had to show an invitation card. I didn't have one. Babichev had simply brought me along with him. Ordinarily, it wouldn't have bothered me at all, not to get onto the field. Besides, behind the barrier there was an ideal vantage point. But I kept insisting. Something more important than the simple desire to see everything at first hand made me try to scale the fence. It suddenly dawned on me: the extent to which I didn't belong with those who are invited to big, important occasions, the terrible superfluity of my presence among them, my lack of connection with every great achievement of these people, here or elsewhere.

"Comrade, I am no ordinary citizen," I began excitedly, unable to find anything better to say. "What do you think I am? Just a bystander? Kindly let me through. I belong over there." I waved toward the group of people around the Commissar of War.

"You do not belong over there," the soldier smiled.

"Ask Comrade Babichev."

I cupped my hands, rose on tiptoe, and hollered:

"Andrei Petrovich!"

Just then the orchestra stopped. The last drumbeat escaped in an echoing roll.

"Comrade Babichev!"

He heard me. The People's Commissar for War also turned his head. The pilot brought his palm to his flying helmet, picturesquely sheltering his eyes from the sun.

I became frightened. I was shuffling around, somewhere behind the fence, a fat-bellied little guy in my too narrow, too short pants. How did I dare to distract these people? And when silence reigned, while they still wondered who had cried out, were frozen in expectant poses, I could not find the strength to call again.

But he knew, he saw, he heard me calling him. One second, and it was all over. They reverted to their earlier poses, I was ready to cry.

Then, once more, I raised myself on my toes, and through the megaphone of my hands, deafening the soldier, sent a resounding yell toward the forbidden area:

"Salami man!"

And once more:

"Hey, salami!"

And many more times:

"Salami! Salami! Salami!"

I saw only him, Babichev, towering above the others, his Tyrolean hat sticking out over the crowd. I remember longing to shut my eyes and squat down behind the fence. I do not remember whether I did so or not but, in any case, I saw the main thing: Babichev's face was turned toward me. For one-tenth of a second, it remained turned toward me. There were no eyes in it. There were two obtuse circles, gleaming like mercury. The terror of impending retribution plunged me into a nightmare state. I was dreaming. It seemed to me that I was asleep. And the most terrible thing in my dream was the way Babichev's head turned toward me. It turned toward me on an immobile body, swinging around on its own axis, as if on a bolt. His back remained unturned.

10

I left the airport.

But the festive noise called to me. I stood on a green bank, leaning against a tree, with the wind blowing dust all over me. Like a plaster saint, I was surrounded by shrubbery. I tore the tender, acid buds off a shrub, sucked at them, and spat them out. I stood there with my pale, kindly face raised, and looked at the sky.

A plane took off. With a deafening mewing, it passed

over me, a slanting yellow shape as on a poster, almost cutting through the foliage of my tree. I followed it with my eyes, shuffling my feet on the bank, as it went higher and higher, now sparkling in the sun, now turning into a black dash. As the distance increased, the plane kept changing into various objects. Now it was a gunlock, then a pocketknife, then a trodden lilac blossom. . . .

The new-model aircraft had become airborne in my absence. I was at war. I had insulted Babichev.

Now they would come bursting through the gates, the whole bunch of them. Their drivers were coming for them. There was Babichev's blue limousine. Driver Alpers saw me and made signs. I turned my back on him. My feet got caught in the green noodles of the grass.

I ought to talk to him. He will understand. I must explain to him that it's all his fault, not mine. Yes, his. But he will not come out alone. I must talk to him, man to man. From here he will drive to the administration building. I must get there ahead of him.

There they told me: he is at the construction site.

"At the Quarter?" So I rushed to the Quarter.

I rushed there, my heart weighing me down. It was as though some word that must be said to him had already broken through my lips and was flying toward him. I was hurrying after it, afraid to miss it, to lose it and forget it.

The construction site appeared before me like a yellowish mirage hanging in the air. There it was, the Quarter! Over there, behind the houses, far away. The separate parts of the scaffolding were fused into one mass which loomed like an ethereal bee's nest from that distance. . . .

I came closer. Din and dust. I grew deaf and cataracts covered my eyes. I walked along the planking. A sparrow took off from a tree stump. The boards bent slightly under me, making me laugh, recalling a sensation of seesaw and childhood. I walked over the falling sawdust, smiling at the way it whitened my shoulders, like an old man's head. . . .

Where should I look for him?

A truck blocks the way, unable to enter. It fusses, raises itself, and falls back, like a beetle in a box trying to climb from the horizontal floor onto the perpendicular side.

The paths I must follow become involuted like the inside of an ear.

"Comrade Babichev?"

They show me; over there. Somewhere. There is hammering in the background.

"Where?"

"Over there."

I cross a girder over a chasm. I balance myself. Something like a hold of a ship yawns below.

Limitless, black, and cool. Altogether, it reminds me of a dry dock. I get in everyone's way.

"Where?"

"Over there."

He is unreachable.

I caught a glimpse of him: his torso flashed by above some sort of wooden edge. Disappeared. And there again he appeared, up above, far off—between us there was a huge emptiness, which soon would be one of the courtyards of the building.

He is held back. There are several others with him: caps, overalls. Just the same, I'll call him aside, to tell him I'm sorry.

They showed me the shortest way to the other side.

One ladder remained. I could already hear voices. There were just a few rungs to overcome. . . .

In order not to be swept off, I bent down, grabbing a wooden rung with my hands. He flew by above me. Yes, he literally rushed past through the air. In an absurd foreshortening, I saw his motionless flying figure; his face, only his nostrils: I saw two holes, as if I were looking at a monument from underneath.

What was it?

I rolled down the ladder.

He was gone. Flown away. On an iron wafer, he had flown off. A crisscross shadow accompanied his flight. He stood on an iron thing, describing a semicircle with a clanking and whining. A technical device, a crane. A platform of girders, crossed girders. It was through the spaces between the girders that I had seen his nostrils.

I sat on the rung.

"Where is he?" I asked.

The workers around me were laughing, and I was grinning at everyone like a clown after he has ended his performance with hilarious tumbling.

"It's not my fault," I said, "it's his fault."

11

I decided not to go back to him.

Someone else was occupying my former lodging. A padlock hung on the door. The new tenant must have been out. I remembered: the widow Prokopovich's face looked like a padlock. Was she really about to re-enter my life?

A night spent in a park. A beautiful morning spread itself out above me. Nearby, bums were still asleep on the benches. They lay doubled up, hands thrust into sleeves and pressed against stomach, like bound and beheaded Chinamen. The dawn touched them with cool fingers. They oh-ed and ah-ed, groaned, shook themselves, and sat up without opening their eyes or removing their hands from their sleeves.

The birds woke up. Small sounds arose: small voices talking among themselves—voices of birds, voices of the grass. In a brick niche, pigeons began to fuss.

I got up shivering, yawning helplessly like a dog.

(Gates were opening. A glass was filled with milk. Judges passed sentence. A man, having worked through the night, walked to the window and was surprised to find he didn't recognize the street in the unusual light. A sick man asked for a drink. A little boy ran into the kitchen to see whether a mouse had been caught in the trap. The morning had begun.)

That day I wrote a letter to Andrei Babichev.

I ate at the Palace of Labor—fish and pickled cabbage, Nelson steaks—drank beer, and wrote:

Andrei Petrovich:
You took me in out of the cold. You took me in under your wing. I slept on your delightful sofa. You know how lousily I had lived before that. Came the blessed night. You took pity on me, gathered up a drunk.

You put me between linen sheets. The material was so smooth and cool; it was calculated to soothe my anger and ease my anxiety. It did.

Even mother-of-pearl pillowcase buttons came back into my life—with iridescent rainbow rings swimming in them. I recognized them at once. They emerged from a long-forgotten corner of childhood.

I had a bed.

The word itself had a poetic remoteness for me, like the word "hoop."

You gave me a bed.

From the height of your well-being, you lowered a cloud-bed, a halo that surrounded me with magic warmth, wrapped me in memories, nostalgia without bitterness, and hopes. It seemed I could still have much of what had been intended for me in my youth.

You are my benefactor, Andrei Petrovich!

Just think: a famous man made me his close companion! A remarkable public figure settled me in his home. I want to convey my feelings to you.

Strictly speaking, it's all one feeling: hatred.

I hate you, Comrade Babichev.

I'm writing this letter to bring you down a peg.

From my first day with you, I felt afraid. You stifled me. You crushed me under your weight.

You stand in your underpants giving off the beery smell of sweat. I look at you and your face becomes strangely enlarged, your torso becomes bloated—the lines of a clay idol curve out, swell. I want to shout out:

Who gave him the right to crush me?

How am I worse than he?
Is he more intelligent?
Is he richer spiritually?
Is he on a higher level of organization?
Stronger? More important?
Superior not only in position, but in essence?
Why must I acknowledge his superiority?

These were the questions I asked myself. Every day, observation gave me a fraction of the answer. A month went by. I know the answer. And now I'm not afraid of you. You're just an obtuse dignitary. And nothing more. It was not the importance of your personality that crushed me. Oh no! Now I see through you, look you over; I've got you in the palm of my hand. My fear of you has passed, like something childish. I have thrown you off my back. You're not much really.

At one time I was tortured by doubts. Can it be that I am a nonentity compared to him? I wondered. Can it be that for an ambitious man like me he is plainly an example of greatness?

But it turned out that you are nothing but an empty shell, ignorant and stupid like all figureheads, those who have gone before and those who will come after. And, as it does with all figureheads, your position has gone to your head. Only conceited stupidity could account for the hurricane you raised over a bit of ordinary salami or, for that matter, the fact that you took in off the street an unknown young man. And perhaps it also accounts for your closeness to Volodia Makarov, about whom I know only one thing, that he is a soccer player. Yes, you are a big bourgeois. You must have jesters and hangers-on. I don't doubt Volodia Makarov left you because he could not stand the indignities heaped upon him. You must have deliberately tried to turn him into a fool, as you did with me.

You stated that he lived with you like a son, that he saved your life; you even got quite worked up over these reminiscences. But it's all lies. You are simply trying to

camouflage your bourgeois instincts. I have seen the birthmark on your waistline, you know.

At first when you told me that the sofa belonged to him,
that when he came back I would have to get the hell out
of there, I was offended. But the next minute I understood
that you are cold and indifferent to both of us. You are a
baron and we are your hangers-on.

But I dare assure you that neither of us will come back
to you again. You don't respect people. He will return only
if he is more stupid than I am.

It so happens that I do not have to my credit either deportation under the old regime or a revolutionary record.
So they won't entrust me with responsible work, like the
manufacture of soda pop or the running of a bee farm.

But does that make me an unworthy son of our century,
and you a good one? Does that make me nothing and you
a big something?

Sure, you found me on the street. . . . But how stupidly
you behaved!

On the street you decided, well okay, the guy's not much,
still let's see if I can fit him in somewhere. A copyreader
perhaps, a proofreader, a copyholder. You didn't try to
descend from the heights, to approach the young man in
the gutter, to understand. You were too full of yourself.
You're a bureaucrat, Comrade Babichev.

Who did you think I was? A drowning remnant of the
lumpenproletariat? You decided to hold me up? Thanks.
I am strong enough, do you hear me, strong enough to
drown and to come up again, and to drown once more.

I wonder how you'll react when you read this. Perhaps
you will try to have me deported, or put me into an institution. You can do anything: you're a big man, a member of our administration. You even said that your own
brother should be shot. You said yourself: we'll clap him
into a madhouse.

Your brother is an unusual man. He intrigues me. I
don't understand him. There's a mystery here of which I
know nothing. There's something strangely appealing about

the name "Ophelia." And it seems to me that it frightens you.

Just the same, I can make a conjecture or two. I feel something's about to happen. But I'll prevent you from carrying out your schemes. You want to take away your brother's daughter. I saw her only once. Yes, that was me. I compared her to a branch laden with leaves and flowers. You have no imagination. You ridiculed me. I overheard that telephone conversation. You slandered me in the girl's eyes, as you slandered her father. You can't admit that the girl whom you are planning to carry off for your amusement—as we were for your amusement—that this girl should be so vulnerable inside, full of tenderness and torment. You want to utilize her, as you utilize (I use your word intentionally) "the lambs' heads and feet, ingeniously with the aid of electric spiral drills" (I quote from your brochure).

But no, I won't let you. Sure you've found yourself a dainty morsel! You belly-worshiping glutton. Is there anything you wouldn't immolate for your own physiological needs? What's to stop you from seducing the girl? The fact that she's your niece? But you sneer at the very idea of family. You want to have her eating out of your hand.

And that's why you talk about your brother with such hatred, while anyone who stops and looks at him can see what a remarkable man he is. Although I still don't know him, I'm sure he is a genius. In what way, I don't know. You are persecuting him. I heard your fist against the railing of the balcony, heard how later you persuaded the daughter to leave her father.

But you won't hunt *me* down.

I am going to protect your brother and his daughter. Listen to me, you obtuse lump who laughed at the branch laden with flowers and leaves, because that exclamation was the only way I could express my ecstasy when I saw her. And you, what words do you use for her? You called me an alcoholic because I addressed a girl in metaphoric language which you couldn't understand. What cannot be understood inspires either laughter or fear. Today you laugh, soon I'll make you tremble. I can express myself in ordinary words too, not only in images. All right, I will tell you about Valia in everyday language. I will describe a few things in language within your grasp, to tantalize you with a picture of something you won't be able to get your hands on, my exalted sausage maker!

As she stood in front of me—let me say it first in my own way—she was lighter than a shadow. The lightest of shadows, that of falling snow, would have envied her lightness. Yes, I'll say it first in my own words: she listened to me, not with her ear but with her temple, with her head bent forward slightly; her face was reminiscent of an almond— its color and its shape, high-cheekboned and tapering off toward the chin. You can understand that, can't you? No? Then here's some more for you. From running, her dress had come undone and I saw that she was not yet tanned all over. I saw a small, pale-blue, Y-shaped vein on her chest. . . .

Now, in your lingo, here's the description of the choice morsel you intend to lay your hands on. Before me stood a girl of sixteen or so. Almost a child. Her shoulders were rather broad, her eyes gray, her short-cut hair tousled. A delightful adolescent, straight as a chess piece (but that's rather my way of putting it), not too tall.

And you won't get her.

She'll be my wife. All my life she has filled my dreams.

We shall fight it out! You are thirteen years older than I am, years that are behind you and ahead of me. An achievement or two more in the salami business, another couple of cheap cafeterias—those are the limits of your active life.

But I, I have different dreams.

Valia will be mine, not yours. We shall thunder through Europe, through the lands where people love glory. And Valia will be mine, a compensation for everything: for the humiliations, for the youth which I did not have time to savor, for my dog's life.

Remember the cook I told you about, how she washes in the corridor. Now, here's another picture: I visualize a room, brightly lit by the sun. By the window, a bluish sink filled with limpid water and the reflection of the window dancing in the sink as Valia splashes with her hands, playing on the liquid keyboard. . . .

I'll do anything to make this picture come true. You'll not make use of Valia for your own ends. Good-by, Comrade Babichev.

How could I have stood a whole month in this humiliating position? I am not going to take any more of it. Just keep waiting, perhaps fool number one will come back to you. Convey my sympathies to him. I am so happy not to be coming back!

Each time my self-respect is wounded by something, I know that, through an association of ideas, I will be carried back to one of the evenings I spent near your desk. You are radiating conceit: "I am at work," your radiation crackles. "Hey, Kavalerov! Can you hear? Don't disturb me. I am working, understand? You're just a bystander."

And in the mornings you were praised by a number of mouths.

"A great man! He's amazing, really. Extraordinary personality, our Andrei Petrovich Babichev!"

But at the very same time as these lickspittles were paying their tribute, when conceit was bloating you, a man lived by your side. Nobody showed him any consideration, nobody asked for his opinion. The man lived alongside you and observed your every movement. He studied you, watched you; not like a slave, from below, but like a human being, calmly. And this man concluded that you are nothing but an exalted clerk, only a very ordinary person brought to an enviable height by purely external circumstances.

No need to beat about the bush. That's all I had to tell you.

You tried to make me your fool and I became your enemy. "With whom are you at war, you scum?" you

shouted at your brother. I don't know what you had in
mind: yourself, your Party, your factories, your stores,
your sausages, I cannot tell. But I know whom I am against:
a very ordinary middle-class gentleman, an egotist, a vo-
luptuary, a fool; a man who is convinced that he can get
away with anything. I am fighting for your brother, for the
girl to whom you lied. I am fighting for tenderness, for
pathos, for individuality; for names that touch me, like
"Ophelia," for everything that you are determined to op-
press and erase. Give my regards to Solomon Shapiro.

Yours cordially,   N. KAVALEROV

12

I was let in by Babichev's cleaning woman. Babichev
himself was out. He had downed his traditional glass of
milk. The opaque glass stood on the table. Next to it there
was a plate with crackers shaped like Hebraic characters.

Human life is not much. The movements of the heavenly bodies are awesome. When I came to live here, a
patch of reflected sunshine, like a round rabbit, sat on the
doorstep at two p.m. Thirty-six days have gone by and the
sunny rabbit has jumped into another room. The earth has
relentlessly covered this last stretch and the rabbit, a child's
plaything, reminds us of the infinite.

I stepped out on the balcony.

On the corner, a small group of people were listening to
the church bells. The church there is famous for its bell
ringer. Idlers often watch him at work.

Once I myself spent a good hour standing on that corner.
Under its arches I could see the insides of the bell tower.
There in the smoky darkness of the loft among planks
wrapped in cobwebs, the bell ringer gave his all. Twenty
bells tore him apart. Like a coachman, he leaned back,
bent his head, perhaps shouted commands as to horses.
His body curled up at the central point of the grim web.
Then he dived into a corner, distorting the pattern of the

web—the mysterious musician, indistinct, black, perhaps ugly, like Quasimodo.

(Possibly, of course, it was the distance that made him awesome. He could also be described as a laborer throwing around different-sized pieces of hardware. And the sound of the famous carillon could be presented as a mixture of the noises in a restaurant and a railway station.)

From the balcony, I was listening: "Tom-vee-ree-lee! Tom-vee-ree-lee! Tom-vee-ree-lee!"

There was some Tom Vereley floating around in the air,

> Tom Vereley with a rucksack
> Handsome Tom Vereley . . .

The disheveled bell ringer had put many of my mornings to music. "Tom" is a stroke of the big bell, "vee-ree-lee" are the little bells.

Tom Vereley came to me on one of the wonderful mornings I experienced in this house, and the musical phrase translated itself into words. I have a vivid picture of him.

A young man taking in the city with a roving glance. A young man, completely unknown, is on his way here. He comes still closer, can already see the sleeping city unaware of his existence. The morning mist is just beginning to disperse. The town looms up in its valley like a greenish sparkling cloud. Tom Vereley is smiling. His hand on his heart, he searches the city for landmarks familiar to him from the picture books of his childhood.

The young man has a rucksack on his back.

He can do everything. He personifies the haughtiness of youth, the secret pride of daydreams.

Days will go by (the sunny rabbit will have jumped only a few times from the doorstep into the next room). Soon boys who dream of arriving themselves with a bag on their backs, in the outskirts of the city, on a May morning, will sing about the man who did as he pleased:

> Tom Vereley with a rucksack,
> Handsome Tom Vereley . . .

This is how the ringing of the bells of a small Moscow church was transformed inside me into a daydream of an indubitably Western nature.

I will leave my letter on the table, collect my few things (in a rucksack?), and go. The letter was folded into a square and placed on the glass top of the desk, next to the portrait of the one whom I considered my companion in misfortune. Then there was a knock on the door. Him?

I opened. He stood on the threshold, holding a bag, smiling gaily (a Japanese smile) as though he had seen through the closed door a dear, much-missed friend. Shy, in some way reminiscent of Valia, Tom Vereley stood facing me.

This, then, was the swarthy young Volodia Makarov. He looked at me, surprised. His eyes traveled round the room. Several times his look returned to the sofa: my shoes could be seen under it.

"Hi!" I said.

He walked over to the sofa, sat down, remained seated for a while, then went into the bedroom, remained there a moment, came out, and paused next to the flamingo vase.

"Where's Andrei? Is he in the office?"

"I'm not sure. He'll be back this evening. Possibly he'll bring a new fool along with him. You're fool number one, I am number two, the next one will be number three. Unless there were some fools before you? It's also possible he'll bring along a girl."

"Who?" Tom Vereley asked. "What?"

He screwed up his face in his effort to understand. His temples tensed. He sat down again on the sofa. My shoes under it obviously bothered him. I'm sure he would have liked to touch them with the back of his heel.

"Why did you come back?" I asked. "Why the hell did you come back? Your role here, like mine, is finished. He's busy with someone else now. He is leading astray a young girl, his niece, Valia. Do you understand? Listen, go away. . . ."

I rushed toward him. He was sitting immobile.

"Listen to me, do what I have done! Tell him the whole truth. . . . Here," I grabbed the letter from the table, "here's a letter I have left him. . . ."

He waved me aside. His bag sank down in its habitual spot, next to the sofa. He walked over to the phone and called Babichev's office.

And so my things remained there uncollected. I fled.

13

The letter remained with me. I decided to destroy it. This soccer player lived with him like a son. The way his bag found its place in the corner, the way he looked around the room, the way he picked up the receiver and called Babichev's extension—it was obvious that he was in familiar surroundings, that this house was his. Lack of sleep the previous night had affected me. I hadn't written what I wanted to write. Babichev would have misunderstood my indignation. He would have thought it was based on envy. That I envied Volodia.

It's lucky that I kept the letter. Otherwise it would have been like firing a blank.

I was misguided when I thought that Volodia lived with him as his fool, to amuse him. Hence I shouldn't have tried to be protective of him in my letter. On the contrary, now that I have met him, I have seen how haughty he is. Babichev is rearing and cherishing someone like himself. Another bloated, blind creature will emerge.

Volodia looked at me as if to say: "I am sorry, you've made a mistake. I am not a parasite like you. I am a full-fledged young lord."

I sat down on a bench in a square and discovered something horrible. The folded paper I had taken with me was not the right one. Mine was larger. This was not my letter. In my hurry I had grabbed the wrong one, which read:

Dear, dear Andrei Petrovich, hello! Are you sure you are all right? Hasn't your new lodger strangled you yet? Hasn't Ivan Petrovich set his Ophelia on you? Watch out lest the two of them, Kavalerov and Ivan Petrovich, combine efforts and succeed in exterminating you. You better look out for yourself. Remember you are a helpless little thing, so damned vulnerable. . . .

Since when have you become so trusting that you bring every bit of jetsam into your house. Kick him out now! The very next morning you ought to have said: well, young man, you've had your sleep, good-by now. What's all the sentimental fuss about? When I read your letter in which you say you took pity on that drunk because you thought of me, that you picked him up because you imagined me lying in a ditch, when I read all that stuff, I thought it amusing, but odd. Doesn't sound like you at all; more like Ivan Petrovich.

It was just as I knew it would be. You brought the sly bum home and didn't know what to do with him. It's somehow awkward to ask him to clear out. You're in a hell of a fix, aren't you? See, I am lecturing. Your type of work makes people that way. It leads to sentimentality: fruit, herbs, bees, calves, that sort of thing. I am a heavy-industry man. You can laugh, Andrei Petrovich, you are always laughing at me. I am of the new generation.

When I come back, what will happen to your queer bird? What if he begins to cry, refuses to evacuate the sofa? You'll take pity on him once more. Yes, I am jealous. I'll get him out of there, beat him up if it comes to that. . . . You're too soft. You just shout, bang your fist against things, inflate yourself; but when the chips are down, you're full of pity. If it had not been for me, Valia would still be suffering with Ivan Petrovich. What are you doing to prevent her from going back to her father? You know very well how cunning your brother is, that he knows how to trick people. He even calls himself a cheap charlatan. So, no mercy.

Start preparing a place in an institution for him: he'll

vanish. Perhaps you could offer Kavalerov a cot there too. He'll resent that.

Don't get sore; remember your words: you'll teach me and I'll teach you. Well, we're learning.

My father sends you his best. I'll be back soon. One of these days. I'll say good-by to this town. At night when I am out walking, I realize that, strictly speaking, Murom isn't much of a town at all: just workshops, an accumulation of workshops. Everything is for them. The night is thick and black over the town. It looks fit for ghosts. But nearby, across the fields, the lights of the workshops gleam. Very festive.

And in the town, I saw a calf chasing a district inspector, for the briefcase he was holding under his arm. The calf, moving its mouth, wanting to chew at something. . . . The scene: a hedge, a puddle; the inspector, red, hot, wearing a hat, steps out energetically. Behind him, the calf aims at his briefcase. All these contrasts, contradictions, you see?

I do loathe calves like that one. You won't recognize me: I have become a human machine. And if I am not really one yet, it is what I want to be. The machines in the workshops here are pedigreed! They are terrific, so proud, so dispassionate, nothing like the ones in your sausage factories. Yours are just artisans. All you do is slaughter calves. I want your advice. I want to be proud of my work, to be indifferent to everything outside it. So I have become envious of the machine; why am I not just as good? We invented, designed and constructed it. It turns out to be much harder than we are. Switch it on and it starts working. It won't make a single unnecessary wriggle. That's the way I would like to be: not a single unnecessary wriggle. I am longing to talk to you.

I imitate you a lot. I even smack my lips when I eat, in imitative zeal.

Often I think how lucky I have been. Few Young Communists live as I do. And I live with you, Andrei Petrovich, with a very wise, remarkable man. Who wouldn't

give a lot for a life like mine. I know that many people
envy me. Thank you very much. Don't laugh. It's a declaration of love, you may think, a declaration of affection from
a machine. But I mean it: I will become a machine.

How's business? How is the Quarter coming along?
How's the construction site? Did anything collapse?

And how are things at home? So an unknown citizen is
relaxing on my sofa? Remember how they carried me in
from that soccer game? I can still feel it at times. Remember how you got frightened when they brought me in?
You are so slobbery, old man! I was lying on the sofa.
My leg was heavy as a steel rail. I was looking at you
sitting and writing at your desk under the green shade.
And suddenly you looked at me. I closed my eyes. Just
like my mother.

Speaking of soccer. I have been picked to play with the
Moscow representative team against the Germans. And,
unless they take Shukhov at the last moment, I will also be
on the U.S.S.R. squad. Ain't that something?

And how's Valia? Sure I'll marry her. In about four
years. You say we won't hold out? But I am telling you:
four years. Yes, I'll be the Edison of this century. We shall
kiss, Valia and I, for the first time, on the inauguration day
of your Quarter. You don't believe it? She and I, we have
an agreement. The day the Quarter is inaugurated, we shall
kiss on the platform as the orchestra plays.

Don't forget me, Andrei Petrovich. Don't let me come
back and find that your Kavalerov is your best friend, that
you have forgotten me, that he has taken my place. Perhaps that he does calisthenics with you, that he accom-
panies you to the construction site. Maybe he has turned
out to be a remarkable fellow, much better company than
I am. Maybe you have become really close to him, and I,
the Edison of the century, must gather my things together
and get the hell out of there. Perhaps you are sitting with
him now, with Ivan Petrovich and with Valia, all of you
laughing at me. And perhaps it's your Kavalerov who'll
marry Valia? Tell me the truth, Andrei Petrovich. If I

am right, I will kill you, I give you my word. Kill you for betraying all our talks, all our plans. Understand?

Well, this is much too long. I don't really want to take the important man away from his work. I was talking about eliminating every unnecessary wriggle and look at this. I suppose it's because I miss you. Good-by, my dear, venerable friend, good-by. See you soon.   VOLODIA

14

A huge cloud, shaped like South America, stood over the city. The cloud gleamed in the sun but its shadow looked threatening. The shadow, with astronomical slowness, was creeping over Babichev's street.

All those who had already entered the mouth of the street and were moving against the current saw the approach of the shadow and felt things darkening before their eyes. The shadow was sweeping the soil from under their feet. They were walking as if on top of a revolving sphere.

I was struggling along with them.

The balcony hung over the street. A jacket was hanging on the guardrail. There was no longer any ringing from the bell tower. I stood at the place where the groups of idlers had watched the bell ringer. A young man appeared on the balcony. He was surprised by the glowing gloom. He raised his face, looked up, and leaned over.

The staircase. The door. I knock. My left lapel is jerked up and down by my heartbeats. I have come to fight.

They let me in. The person who has opened up withdraws, holding the inward-swinging door. And the first thing I see is Andrei Babichev. Andrei Babichev is standing in the middle of the room, his feet spread wide enough apart to let an army of Lilliputians pass between them. His hands are thrust into his pants pockets. The jacket is unbuttoned and rippling behind the dikes of his hands. His posture says: "Well?"

I can see only him although I hear Volodia Makarov's voice.

I step toward Babichev. It has started to rain.

In one second I will fall on my knees in front of him.

"Do not chase me away, Andrei Petrovich, don't! Now I understand everything. Believe me, as you believe Volodia. I am young too and I will also be an Edison of this century. I will worship you as Volodia does. How could I be so blind, how could I have failed to do everything in my power to make you love me! Forgive me. Let me in. Give me time. Four years."

But I do not fall on my knees. Instead, with a sarcastic little smile, I ask:

"How come you're not in your office?"

"Get the hell out of here!" he answers.

His answer was immediate, as though we were repeating the lines of a play, but it took a while to penetrate to my conscious mind.

Then something unusual happened.

It was raining. Possibly it was a thunderstorm, lightning. I do not want to speak in images. I want to express myself simply. Once I read Camille Flammarion's *Atmosphere* (Flammarion, what an astral name! Flammarion is a heavenly body himself). He was describing spherical lightning, its extraordinary effect: a full, smooth ball rolls into a space and fills it with blinding light. . . . Oh, far be it from me to use stale comparisons. The cloud looked suspect. The shadow was advancing as in a dream. But it was raining. A window was open in the bedroom. One should never leave the windows open during a thunderstorm. Because of the draft!

With the rain, with the raindrops, bitter as tears, with the bursts of wind under which the flamingo vase was like a flame setting the curtains afire, rushing toward the ceiling—with all this, Valia appeared from the bedroom.

But I was the only one to be struck by her presence. Actually, everything was very simple: a friend had come back and his friends had hurried over to see him. Possibly Babichev had picked up Valia on his way here, since she must have been waiting so eagerly for this day. Everything is simple. As for me, I must be sent to a special institution to be treated by hypnosis, to cure me of thinking in images, of ascribing to a girl the effects of spherical lightning.

Well then, I'll just mess it up for you!

My mind re-registers the words: "Get the hell out of here!"

"It's not quite that simple. . . ." I begin.

There is a draft. The door has remained open. I have grown a wing, because of the wind. It is flapping crazily behind me. My eyelids are forced shut by all the blowing. The draft anesthetizes half my face.

"It's not quite that simple," I say, holding on to the doorjamb so as not to break the horrible wind. "While you, Volodia, were away, Comrade Babichev was having an affair with Valia. And while you are waiting your four years, Babichev will have his fill of her. . . ."

I was behind the door. One half of my face was anesthetized. So maybe I hadn't felt the blow.

The door catch clicked above me like a broken branch and I fell from the wonderful tree, an overripe fruit, lazy and soft.

"It's all over," I said calmly as I got up. "Now I will kill you, Comrade Babichev."

15

It is raining.

The rain is walking along Flower Street. It strides by Circus Square, turns onto the boulevards, and when it reaches Petrovsky Heights it suddenly becomes blind and loses its assurance.

I am crossing a street thinking of the fabulous swordsman who walked under the rain splitting the raindrops with his sword. His sword glistened, the ends of his cape blew in the wind; the swordsman's body was twisting, moving back and forth like a harmonica. He remained dry. He had to keep dry to qualify for the inheritance left him by his father.

But I was wet through to my ribs. Moreover, it seemed I had been slapped.

I find that a landscape viewed through the wrong end of binoculars gains in brightness and relief. Colors and contours seem more precise. Familiar objects suddenly become new in their unfamiliar smallness. The observer sees them the way he saw them in his childhood. It's like dreaming. The odds are that a man looking through the wrong end of binoculars will at some point dissolve into a blissful smile.

After rain the city acquires brilliance and stereoscopic relief. Anyone can see it: the streetcar is carmine; the paving stones are far from being all the same color: some of them are even green; a housepainter who was sheltering from the rain like a pigeon has come out of his niche and is now moving against the background of his brick canvas; in a window, a little boy is catching the sun in a splinter of mirror. . . .

I bought myself an egg and a loaf of French bread. I cracked the egg by banging it against the side of a streetcar coming from Peter's Gate. The passengers stared at me.

In a park I climbed a slightly humped path. The benches on either side were about at the level of my knees. Magnificent mothers were sitting on them. On their suntanned faces their eyes glistened like fish scales. The suntan extended to their necks and shoulders. But the lower slopes of their large young breasts, which could be seen under their blouses, were white. Lonely and hunted as I was, I soaked up this whiteness nostalgically. This whiteness, for me, was milk, motherhood, marriage, self-respect, and cleanliness.

A nanny was holding a baby who looked like the pope. The shell of a sunflower seed was stuck to the lower lip of a girl with a red band around her hair. She stepped into a puddle without noticing it. She was listening to the brass band. The mouths of the trumpets resembled the ears of African elephants.

To all of them, to the mothers, the nannies, the girls,

the musicians entwined in their brass, I was a comical sight. The trumpet players squinted at me and their cheeks became even more inflated. The girl with the red band guffawed and the sunflower seed dropped from her lip. At the same time she discovered that she was standing in the puddle. As if holding me responsible, she turned away in disgust.

I shall prove to them there is nothing comical about me. Nobody understands me. And what is not understood becomes either ridiculous or frightening. They will all be frightened.

I stopped before a mirror in the street. I love full-length mirrors in the street. They appear suddenly. Your path is usual and quiet, an ordinary urban route promising no miracles or visions. You walk along unsuspecting. Then you raise your eyes and suddenly it dawns upon you: incredible changes have taken place in the world, in the universal laws.

The rules of optics, of geometry, have been broken. The natural motive force behind you is broken—the one that made you go precisely where you did go. You begin to think that you are seeing through the nape of your own neck, you even begin to smile at the passers-by, embarrassed by your special gift. You sigh very quietly: "Ah-ah-ah . . ."

The streetcar that just now disappeared from your sight is again rambling past you, cutting off the edge of the avenue like a knife lopping off a slice of cake. A straw hat hanging on a blue ribbon over somebody's wrist is back, you had seen it earlier. It attracted your attention but you did not have time to turn toward it.

There is an open space in front of you, almost certainly a house, a wall. Thanks to your gift you know it is not a house. You have destroyed a mystery. It is not a wall; there is a mysterious world here where everything you have just seen is repeated with the stereoscopic clarity and neatness of outline one gets from looking through the wrong end of binoculars.

You have walked yourself into drunkenness; so unexpected is the collapse of law, so welcome this dizziness,
you love it. . . . Then you guess, and hurry toward the
bluish square. Your face hangs immobile in the middle of
the mirror—the only thing that has kept its familiar shape;
the only particle remaining of the regular world in which
all else has collapsed, been transformed, acquired a new
regularity to which you will never become accustomed
even if you stand for an hour before the mirror where
your face is set in an exotic tropical garden. The grass is
too green, the sky too blue.

It is impossible to tell which way a pedestrian is going
as long as you do not turn your face away from the mirror. . . . I was looking into it chewing the last of my
French loaf.

Then I turned my head.

A pedestrian was walking toward the mirror, having
emerged from somewhere to one side. I obstructed his
reflection and received the smile he had prepared for himself. He was considerably shorter and raised his face.

He had been in a hurry to reach the mirror in order to
locate and brush off a caterpillar that had crawled over his
shoulder. He flicked it off with a snap of his middle finger,
having previously twisted his shoulder round like a violinist.

I was still thinking about optical illusions, about the mirror tricks. So I asked the newcomer, who I still had not
recognized:

"Which side did you come from? Where did you
emerge?"

"Where from?" he said. "Where from?" He looked at
me with clear eyes. "I have invented me myself."

He took off his bowler hat, displayed his bald patch, and
greeted me with exaggerated solemnity; the way beggars
once greeted almsgivers. He had big bags under his eyes
the color of thin black silk stockings. He was sucking a
hard candy.

I realized immediately: here was my friend, my teacher, my consolation.

I seized him by the hand and restraining myself from embracing him, I said:

"Tell me . . . answer me. . . ."

He raised both eyebrows.

"What is it?" I said. "Ophelia?"

He was about to speak. But a trickle of sweet juice dribbled from his lips. Enraptured, I waited longingly for his reply.

PART TWO

1

The approach of old age did not frighten Ivan Babichev.

Still, from time to time he would complain that this life was flowing by too fast in wasted years, that he suspected he had stomach cancer. . . . But these complaints were made too cheerfully, probably not quite sincerely; rhetorical complaints.

Sometimes, he put his left hand (palm down) on the left side of his chest and said, with a smile:

"I wonder what it sounds like when a large vessel bursts here."

Once he raised his hand to show some friends the back of it where the veins formed a tree.

"This," he said, "is a tree of life. This tree tells me more about life and death than the blooming and shedding trees in our parks. I cannot remember exactly when I discovered that there was a tree growing on the back of my hand; but it must have been during that wonderful time when the blooming and shedding trees made me think not of life and death but of the end and the beginning of the school year. Then this tree was sky blue, it was blue and supple, and the blood, which at that time I believed was a light rather

than a fluid, spread like a pink dawn above it, giving the
landscape the quality of a Japanese watercolor. . . .

"Years passed. I changed. The tree changed. I can recall a wonderful time when it was in full bloom. I proudly
watched it grow powerful: purplish and stocky, symboliz-
ing strength. But today, friends, see how old it is, how
rickety!

"I imagine sometimes the branches are breaking off,
that, here and there, hollows appear. . . . That is sclerosis,
my friends! The skin stiffens and grows brittle over the
watery tissues. It is the evening fog setting in over the tree
of my life, a fog that will soon envelop my whole being.

"There were three of us, three brothers Babichev. I was
the second. The eldest, Roman, was a member of a fighting
revolutionary organization and was executed for a terrorist
act.

"The youngest, Andrei, had emigrated abroad. I wrote
to his Paris address: 'Guess what, Andrei, we now have a
martyr in the family! Just imagine how pleased our
grandma would have been.' Andrei answered tersely with
characteristic uncouthness: 'You are nothing but a son of a
bitch.' Thus the difference of opinion between the two
surviving brothers began."

Ivan Babichev went on with his story. He told how, in
childhood, he had surprised his relatives and friends. At
twelve, he had demonstrated to his family a strange apparatus resembling a lampshade with pendants and cow-
bells, and tried to assure everyone that the machine could
induce any dream one might wish.

"Fine," said his father, who was a school principal and
a classicist, "I believe you. I want a dream about the history
of Rome."

"What specifically?" the boy asked, business-like.

"Anything—the Battle of Pharsalus. But if it doesn't
work, you will be spanked."

Late that evening, a wonderful ringing filled the Babichev apartment. The father lay on the leather couch in his
study, symmetrical and straight with rage, as if in a coffin.

The mother waited nervously outside the slammed door of the study. Little Ivan walked up and down by the leather couch, smiling benignly and holding his lampshade above his head as a tightrope walker holds his Chinese parasol. . . .

The next morning, the father jumped up from his couch. Without bothering to dress, he reached the nursery in a hop, a skip, and a jump. He extracted Ivan from his bed—kind, fat, lazy, sleepy little Ivan. The day was still puny, but the father pushed the curtains back, staging a false welcome to the morning. The mother tried to sabotage the spanking. She kept putting her hands over her child's posterior and repeating:

"Let him be, Peter, let him be. . . . He made a mistake. . . . I give you my word. . . . What of it if you didn't have the dream. . . . His ringing missed the mark. . . . You know how damp this apartment is. So it was I who dreamed of the Battle of Pharsalus! I did, Peter, believe me. . . ."

"Don't lie to me," the father said, "or tell me the difference in the armament of the Balearic slingshot men and the Numidian infantry. Well, go on. . . ."

Mrs. Babichev was given a few seconds to answer. She could only burst into tears, and little Ivan got his spanking. The young truth-seeker took it like a Galileo.

Later that same day, the maid told Mrs. Babichev she had decided not to marry the man who had proposed to her.

"He's no good," she said, "a liar. He can't be trusted, ma'am. All night I kept seeing horses. Galloping. Horrible horses, wearing masks. Horses in a dream mean lies. . . ."

Mrs. Babichev lost all control over her lower jaw and marched like a sleepwalker to her husband's study. The cook by the stove stared in amazement and began to lose control of *her* lower jaw.

Mrs. Babichev touched her husband's shoulder. He was sitting at his desk trying to replace the metal monogram on his cigarette case. The mother said:

"Peter dear, I believe Frosia dreamed of the Battle of Pharsalus. . . ."

We do not know how the school principal reacted to the maid's dream. But a month or two after the dream-induction incident, Ivan was telling everyone about his new invention.

It was a special soapy solution and a special little tube with which to blow an amazing soap bubble. In its flight, this bubble would grow from the size of a Christmas tree decoration to that of a basketball, then of a sphere with the circumference of a flower bed. Finally, attaining the proportions of a balloon, the bubble would explode and fall in a golden rain on the city.

The father was in the kitchen. He belonged to that gloomy species who are proud of a few culinary secrets; who consider it their exclusive privilege to determine the amount of bay leaf needed for some family heirloom of a soup, or the time needed for boiled eggs to reach the ideal *mi-mollet* stage between hard and soft.

Little Ivan was outside the open kitchen window, near the courtyard fence. Through his yellowish ear, the father registered what his son was saying. He looked out. Ivan, surrounded by several other boys, was lying to them about his soap bubble. It was going to grow and grow and become as large as a flying balloon. . . .

The father's bile rose. Roman, his eldest son, had left home a year earlier. The father was taking it out on his younger sons.

God had not been too kind to him in the matter of sons. He turned his back to the window. He was so angry he was smiling.

At dinner he waited for Ivan to start chattering. But the boy said nothing. "I believe he looks down on me, takes me for a fool," the father seethed inwardly. Later that day, near dusk, Babichev was drinking tea on the porch when suddenly he saw something, high above the buildings. Something was melting, sparkling yellow in the rays of the setting sun. Then, across the father's field of vision, there appeared a large orange sphere. It floated slowly, cutting the plane in a slanting curve.

The father rushed inside the house and the first thing he saw was Ivan sitting on a window ledge, loudly clapping his hands.

"That day was completely satisfying," Ivan Babichev reminisced. "Father was scared. For a long time afterward, when I tried to look into his eyes, he hid them from me. I took pity on him. He turned sort of grayish; I thought he was going to die. So I generously discarded my cloak of glory. My dad was a dry, petty person who failed to notice many things. He had not known that Ernesto Vitollo was scheduled to fly over the city in a balloon that day. Magnificent posters had informed me. I confessed my unintentional deception. Because, I must tell you, my experiences with soap bubbles did not bring the results I had anticipated."

(It is a fact that, at the time Ivan was a twelve-year-old schoolboy, manned flight was not very common and it was rather unlikely that a flight be staged over a provincial city. Whether this story was true or not does not matter. Fantasy is the beloved of reason.)

In any case, Ivan Babichev's friends were delighted by his tales.

"I believe," he went on, "that the night after that humiliating day, my papa *did* dream of the Battle of Pharsalus. In the morning he didn't leave for school. Mother took a glass of mineral water to his study. Possibly he was shocked by some of the details of the battle. Perhaps the dream made a farce of his idea of history and he couldn't get over it. Possibly the battle was decided, in his dream, by Balearic slingshot men who landed from balloons. . . ."

On another occasion, Ivan shared with his friends the following incident from his youth:

"A student whose last name was Chemiot was sweet on a girl. . . . I can't think of her name . . . well, let's call her Lilia Kapitanakis. Her heels clicked like the hooves of a dainty she-goat. We boys knew of everything that happened in the neighborhood. Chemiot would hang around in front of Lilia's porch, determined and panicky at the same time, hesitating to summon, from the gilded entrails beyond, this sixteen-year-old girl who to us kids seemed like an old woman.

"Chemiot's college cap was blue and his cheeks were crimson when he arrived on his bike. And I remember his indescribable sadness on May Sunday. It was one of those Sundays of which there are no more than ten in the annals of meteorology, a Sunday when the breeze is so light and tender that one longs to tie a blue ribbon around it. The student, who had ridden up to the porch at full speed, saw Lilia's aunt sitting there. There were so many colors and flowers concentrated in the aunt that she looked like an armchair cover in a small-town living room; she was all in curls, crescents, and pleats; her hairdo made one think of a snail. . . .

"It was obvious that the aunt was delighted with Chemiot's arrival. From her height, so to speak, she opened her arms to him. In a mashed potato voice wet with saliva and so full of tongue it seemed she was chewing something hot, she announced: 'Lilia is leaving for Kherson today, for a long time, for the whole summer. She asked me to give you her best.'

"With lover's intuition, the student understood. He knew that in the goldish depths of the room behind the porch Lilia was in tears, longing to come outside; that she could see him as a bright splash. (He wore a white jacket and, according to the laws of physics, white reflects the greatest amount of light and glistens like blinding Alpine snow.) But the aunt was all-powerful and bent on keeping them apart. . . .

"I said to Chemiot: 'Make me a present of your bike and I'll avenge you. I know for a fact that Lilia does not want to go anywhere. There's been a lot of shouting going on since they've started trying to send her off. Make me a present of your bike.'

"Chemiot looked frightened of me. 'How will you avenge me?' A few days later I took Lilia's aunt a special remedy for warts, telling her my mother had sent me. The aunt had a large wart in the hollow under her lower lip. This aging lady hugged me and kissed me. Her kisses felt exactly like stones fired at close range from a slingshot with a brand-new rubber band. . . . My friends, the student was avenged. A flower grew out of the aunt's wart, a fragile wild violet. It quivered delicately in the breeze of the aunt's breath. She was disgraced forever. When she saw the violet, the aunt raised her hands to heaven and rushed headlong through the streets. . . .

"Mine was a double joy. In the first place, I had solved the problem of growing flowers out of warts. In the second place, the student had given me his bicycle. And at that time, you know, bicycles were not too common. They used to draw cartoons of bicycle riders. . . ."

"What became of the aunt?" a listener asked.

"Well, my friend, she lived with the flower until the fall. She waited impatiently for the autumn winds, and when they came, she left the city by the back streets, avoiding the busy thoroughfares, and went into the green sub-urbs. . . . Moral suffering was tearing her apart. She tried to hide her face in a scarf. The flower tickled her lips lovingly, like the whispering of sadly spent young years, like the ghost of a kiss, almost the only one, extracted from someone by stamping the feet. . . . She stopped on a hill and removed her scarf. 'Come, wind,' she said, 'blow these horrible petals off me, scatter them in all directions, come, wind.' But, as if to spite her, the wind dropped. In-stead, a crazy bee arrived from somebody's empty sum-merhouse and, taking aim at the flower, began to trace zooming figure eights around the wretched woman. The aunt took flight and struggled home, ordering her maid not to admit to anyone. She sat in front of her mirror staring at her mythically flower-adorned face, which was swelling visibly from a bee sting and becoming a sort of tropical plant with edible roots. What a horror! To simply cut the flower was too risky: one never knows with warts. There is the possibility of septicemia."

Young Ivan was a Jack-of-all-trades. He was good at composing verses and little musical plays, and at drawing. He could do many things. He even invented a dance which was specially designed to suit his physical characteristics—fatness and laziness. (Like many remarkable people, he was a fat lump in his young years.) He called the dance the Little Jug. He sold paper snakes, whistles, Chinese lanterns. The neighborhood boys admired him and nicknamed him The Engineer.

Later, Ivan Babichev graduated from the Petersburg Polytechnical Institute, in the very same year in which his brother Roman was executed. He worked as an engineer at the Naval Plant in Nikolaev, near Odessa, until 1914, when the war broke out in Europe.

Then . . .

2

But was he ever really an engineer?

The year they were building the Quarter, Ivan's way of earning his living was rather undignified. In fact, it was a disgrace for an engineer.

Just imagine, he drew portraits of people in bars, composed little verses ad lib, read palms, demonstrated his powers of memory by repeating up to fifty words read to him without interruption.

Sometimes he would produce a pack of cards from his inside pocket, at once acquiring a resemblance to a professional cardsharp, and would do card tricks.

Some people would offer him drinks; he would sit at their table until the feature entertainment began—Ivan Babichev's preaching.

What did he talk about?

"In us, the human race has reached its apex," he announced, banging his glass like a hoof on the marble table. "Hear me, you strong personalities, you people who have

decided to live as you wish—to you I appeal, to you, the
most richly endowed with intelligence, to you, my van-
guard! Hear me, you who stand in the front ranks. An
epoch is coming to an end. The wave has broken against
the rocks, it is seething, frothing, glistening. What do you
want then? What? Do you want to disappear gradually like
the tiny drops of frothing brine? No, my friends, you do
not have to perish! No. Come to me and I will teach you."

His audience treated him with a certain consideration
but paid little attention to what he was saying, although
from time to time they interrupted him with applause or
with such exclamations as "hear, hear," "right," and "you
said it!"

Then he would suddenly disappear, after reciting the
same four-line farewell verse

> I am not a foreign faker,
> Neither am I John the Baptist;
> I'm a modern miracle maker,
> I'm a modest Soviet artist.

At one time or another he would also say:

"The gates are closing. Can you hear their hinges creaking? Don't rush. Don't try to get through. Stop. To stop is
to show you have pride. Be proud. I am your leader, I am
the king of the trite. To him who can sing and weep and
dip his nose in the puddles of beer on his table, and draw
with it after the beer glasses are all empty and they are no
longer serving, to him I say: your place is here, next to
me. To him who kills out of jealousy, to him who is tying
a noose for himself, I call: you children of the sinking
century, come here; thinkers in stereotypes, come to me;
dreamers, fathers of families doting on your daughters,
honest petty bourgeois, people faithful to tradition, slaves
of honor, duty, love, those who fear blood and disorder,
come, my dear soldiers and generals, let us march. Where?
I'll lead you."

He liked to eat crabs. A crab carnage would appear under his hands. He was slovenly. His shirt, which looked

like a saloon napkin, was always open on his bare chest.
To make it worse, he would sometimes appear in starched
cuffs. Dirty ones. If slovenliness can be combined with
pretensions to old-fashioned elegance, then he was the man
who could do it. Witness, the bowler; witness, the flower in
his buttonhole (which remained there almost until it had
gone to seed); witness, his frayed pants and nothing but
little tails where some of his jacket buttons used to be.

"I am a devourer of crabs. Look: I don't eat them, I
destroy them, like a priest. Do you see? Wonderful crabs.
They are entangled in seaweed. Oh, it's not seaweed? Ordinary greens, you say? Isn't it all the same? Let's agree on
seaweed. Then we can compare the crab with a ship,
raised from the bottom of the sea. Wonderful crabs. From
the Kama."

He licked his fist all around and, peering up the cuff of
his shirt, extracted a fragment of crab from it.

Could he really have been an engineer, ever? Hadn't he
made it all up? It was impossible to associate him with the
idea of an engineer's mentality, a closeness to machines,
to metal, to blueprints. He looked more like an actor or an
unfrocked priest. He realized his listeners didn't believe
him. He spoke with a certain malice in the corner of his
eye.

Now in one bar, now in another, the fat little preacher
would appear. Once he went so far as to climb on a table.
. . . Awkward and rather out of training for the performance of such a trick, he clambered over heads, hanging on
by the palm leaves—bottles were broken, the palm tree
tipped over—he established a foothold on the table. Brandishing two empty beer mugs like dumbbells, he began to
shout:

"Here I stand on the heights, overlooking a teeming host
rallying to my side. Come to me! Come to me! Great is my
army! Little actors dreaming of fame! Unhappy lovers!
Aging spinsters! Accountants! Ambitious ones! Fools!
Knights! Cowards! Come to me! Your king, Ivan Babichev,

is come! The time is not yet, but soon we will march. . . .
Rally around me, my army!"

He flung away his mug and snatched a harmonica out
of someone's hands, wiping it against his paunch. The groan
he drew from it produced a storm: paper napkins flew to
the ceiling. . . .

From behind the bar, aproned figures hurried forth.

"Beer! beer! Give us more beer! Roll out a barrel of
beer! We must drink to the great event!"

But they wouldn't give him more beer; they kicked the
whole company out, and Ivan after them—the shortest of
the lot, but heavy, stubbornly resisting ejection. In his stub-
bornness and anger, he acquired the weight and dead in-
ertia of an oil drum.

To humiliate him, they pushed his bowler down over his
eyes. In the street he staggered from one side to the other
—as if he were being passed from hand to hand—all the
time making a sad noise which might have been either a
song or a groan, and which discomfited passers-by.

"Ophelia," he kept repeating, "Ophelia." Just that one
word. It floated along above him, above the streets, tracing
a series of shining figure eights.

That night he went to see his famous brother. Andrei
Babichev and Volodia sat at the table facing each other,
separated by the lamp with the green shade. Volodia was
asleep, his head resting on a book. Ivan, drunk, hurried
toward the sofa. For a long time he struggled, trying to
pull the sofa under him, the way you pull up a chair.

"You're drunk, Ivan," his brother said.

"I hate you," Ivan said. "You're an idol."

"You ought to be ashamed of yourself, Ivan. Lie down,
sleep it off. I'll give you a pillow. Take off that bowler of
yours."

"You don't believe a word I say. You're a blockhead,
Andrei. Don't interrupt me or I'll break the lampshade
over Volodia's head. Shut up. Why don't you believe in
the existence of Ophelia? Why don't you believe that I have
invented a wonderful machine?"

"You've never invented anything, Ivan. That's just an *idée fixe* of yours, a bad joke. Now, aren't you ashamed? Do you really take me for such a fool? What kind of machine is it? How could there be such a machine? And why do you call it Ophelia? Why do you wear a bowler? What are you, a rag-and-bone man or an ambassador?"

Ivan remained silent for a while. Then, as if suddenly sobered, he got up, clenching his fists.

"So you don't believe me?"

Threateningly, he advanced on his brother:

"Get up. The leader of an army of millions is addressing you. You have the effrontery to disbelieve me? So there is no such machine? Now listen to my solemn pledge: by that machine you shall perish."

"Take it easy," Andrei said, "you'll wake Volodia."

"You know what you can do with your Volodia. I'm on to you and your schemes. You want to give him my daughter. You want to produce a new species. But my daughter is no incubator. You won't get her. I won't give her to Volodia. I'll strangle her with my own hands first."

He paused. Then, eyes sparkling, hands thrust into pockets as if to support his rotund belly, which was beginning to sway, he sneered:

"You are wrong, brother dear. You think you are fussing over Volodia because he is a new kind of man? Nonsense, Andrei, nonsense. . . . It's not that, Andrei, not that at all."

"What is it then?" Andrei asked threateningly.

"You are getting old, Andrei. You need a son. You are simply indulging your fatherly feelings. The family is an eternal concept, Andrei. You're trying to present a very unremarkable (except in soccer) young man as a symbol of the New World. That's sheer bunk. . . ."

Volodia raised his head.

"Greetings to the Edison of the new age!" cried Ivan. "Hoorah!" He bowed solemnly.

Volodia looked at him in silence. Ivan roared with laughter.

"What's the matter, Edison? Are you skeptical about Ophelia too?"

"You, Ivan Petrovich, should be institutionalized," Volodia said, yawning.

Andrei whinnied.

The preacher flung his bowler hat on the floor.

"Pigs!" he shouted. Then, after a pause: "Andrei! Why do you allow this foundling to insult your own brother?"

Ivan couldn't see his brother's eyes, only the glitter of his glasses.

"Ivan," said Andrei, "I must ask you not to come here any more. You're not a madman. You are a son of a bitch."

3

Many tales spread about the new preacher.

The rumors, originating in the bars, traveled up back staircases, slipped into the communal kitchens where some of the inhabitants of the divided apartments were lighting their primus stoves or dancing under the taps during their morning ablutions. Everyone repeated the gossip.

The rumors percolated into offices, nursing homes, and markets.

A story went around that an unknown citizen had come to the wedding of a tax collector's daughter. The uninvited guest wore a bowler, looked suspicious and shabby, and from certain other signs could only be Ivan Babichev. At the climax of the festivities, the intruder demanded everyone's attention and delivered an address to the newlyweds:

"Why love one another? Why join your lives together? Bridegroom, forsake your bride. What will be the fruit of your love? You will bring your own enemy into the world, and he will devour you."

The bridegroom wanted to hit him. The bride fainted. The intruder left in high dudgeon. At that moment, it is said, the port in all the bottles and glasses on the festive table turned to water.

There was yet another strange story going around.

A solid, respectable citizen, heavy and ruddy-cheeked, was riding down a central street in his chauffeur-driven, open convertible. Suddenly, the scandalous Ivan ran out from among the crowd on the sidewalk and opened his arms wide, blocking his brother's car. He stood there like a scarecrow of someone trying to stop a bolting horse. The chauffeur slowed down, letting the car roll slightly forward and tooting the horn. But the scarecrow refused to yield.

"Stop!" Ivan shouted at the top of his voice. "Stop, Commissar! Stop, child-abductor!"

And the chauffeur was forced to apply his brakes. The stream of traffic stopped. Many cars almost got up on their hind legs to avoid collision. A bus roared, screamed, and came to a halt, trembling on its elephantine tires, ready to flee. . . . The outstretched arms of the man standing in the middle of the street demanded quiet.

And everything fell silent.

"Brother," the man said, "you are being driven around in a car while I have to walk. Open the door, move over, let me get in. It isn't proper that I should walk. Sure, you are a leader of men. But so am I."

At these words people ran up to him from all sides. Some jumped out of the bus, others emerged from the neighboring bars, still others rushed from the park. The brother in the car stood up, huge (even bigger standing in the car), and saw before him a living barricade.

He looked so terrifying that it seemed he would just step forward, over the car, over the chauffeur's back, and trample the barricade of their bodies, crushing them like a steamroller down the whole length of the street.

Ivan was raised above the crowd on the shoulders of his partisans. He swayed, sank, drew himself up again; his bowler slipped onto the nape of his neck, uncovering the high, shining forehead of a tired man.

Andrei grabbed him by the pants and pulled him down from his height. He almost flung him at a policeman.

"Take him to the G.P.U.," he said.

The magic word had hardly been uttered when everything came out of its trance: spokes glittered, hubs began
to spin, doors slammed; all operations were resumed.

Ivan was arrested and held for ten days.

When he was released, his drinking companions asked
him if it was true he had been arrested on the street by
his brother under such extraordinary circumstances. He
laughed.

"That's a lie. A legend. They simply picked me up in a
bar. I suppose I had already been under observation for a
long time. But anyway, it's good they're already making up
legends about me. The end of an epoch, the period of
transition, must have its myths and tales, however tall. So
I am glad to be made the hero of one of them. And there'll
be another, about a machine called Ophelia. . . . Our
epoch will die with my name on its lips. To that end, I
will direct my efforts."

They let him out, threatening him with deportation.

What could they accuse him of in the G.P.U.?

"Did you describe yourself as a king?" the interrogator
asked him.

"Yes . . . king of banality."

"What does that mean?"

"You see, I am helping a whole category of people to
see . . ."

"To see what?"

"To see their own doom."

"You said a whole category of people. Whom do you
include in that category?"

"All those whom you call decadent. The bearers of decadent dispositions. If you will allow me, I will explain in
detail."

"I wish you would."

"I believe that many human feelings are scheduled for
liquidation."

"Such as?"

"Pity, tenderness, pride, jealousy, love—in a word, almost
all the feelings of which the human soul was made up in

the vanishing era. Socialism will create a new set of states
for the human soul, instead of these feelings."

"Is that so?"

"I see you understand me. The Communist who is stung
by the serpent of jealousy is oppressed. And so is the pitying Communist. The buttercup of pity, the lizard of vanity,
the serpent of jealousy—this flora and fauna should be
purged from the heart of the new man. Please excuse me,
I am talking a bit metaphorically. Do you find it flowery?
Is it hard to follow? Thank you. Water? No, I don't want
any water. . . . I like to express myself elegantly. . . .
We know that the grave of a Young Communist who has
committed suicide is adorned with alternate layers of
wreaths and the curses of his comrades. The man of the
new world says suicide is a decadent act. The man of the
old world used to say he had to end his life to save his
honor. Thus we see that the new man is schooling himself
to scorn the old feelings glorified by the poets, by the muse
of history herself. Well, there we are. I want to organize a
final parade of those feelings."

"And is that what you call the conspiracy of feelings?"

"Yes. That is the conspiracy of feelings, and I stand at
its head."

"Go on, please."

"Yes. I wanted to rally around me a group of people.
You see? You must admit that it is conceivable that the
old feelings were beautiful. Instances of great love, for
women, for one's country. Or anything you like. You must
agree that some of those great loves move one still. It's
true, you know. And so I'd like . . .

"You know, sometimes it happens that an electric bulb
goes out unexpectedly. It burned out, you say. And if you
shake that bulb, it will flare up and burn again for a little
while. Inside the bulb, a catastrophe is occurring. Tungsten
filaments are snapping; with the contact of the fragments,
life returns to the lamp. A short, unnatural, clearly doomed
life—a fever, a too-bright incandescence, a gleam. Then
darkness falls, life will not return, and in the darkness only

the dead filaments will rattle when you shake it. Do you understand me? But that short-lived gleam is beautiful! I want to shake. . . . I want to shake the heart of a burnt-out era. The heart-lamp; oh, to make the fragments touch and evoke the momentary, beautiful gleam. . . .

"I want to find the representatives of what you call the old world. I mean feelings like jealousy, love for a woman, vanity. I want to find a blockhead so that I can show you: here, comrades, is an example of that human condition known as stupidity.

"Many characters played out the comedy of the old world. The curtain is coming down. The characters must gather on the proscenium and sing the final couplets. I want to be the intermediary between them and the audience. I will direct the chorus and the last exit from the stage.

"To me has fallen the honor of conducting the last parade of the ancient, human passions. . . .

"Through the slits of her mask, history will follow us with a twinkling eye. I want to point them out to her: here is a lover, here an ambitious man, here a traitor; this one is recklessly brave, this a true friend, this a prodigal son. Here they are, the bearers of great feelings now found insignificant and vulgar. For one last time, before they vanish, before they are exposed to mockery, let them be seen at a climactic moment.

"I listen to a conversation. They are talking about a razor. About a madman who has cut his throat. A woman's name flutters through their talk. The madman isn't dead; they have stitched up his throat, and he has slashed himself again in the same place. Who on earth can he be? Show him to me, I need him. I have been looking for him; for her too, the demon woman, and him, the tragic lover. But where shall I look? In which hospital? And her? Who is she? A clerk? A tradeswoman? It's very hard for me to find heroes. There are no heroes. I peep into strangers' windows, climb strangers' stairs. At times I run after a stranger's smile, skipping along like an entomologist chasing a butterfly! I feel like calling out: Stop! From what

flowering bush has your rash, fleeting butterfly smile flown?
What feeling does the bush symbolize? The pink wild rose
of sorrow or the black currant bush of petty vanity? Stop!
I need you. . . .

"I want to rally a mass of people around me, to have a
choice and to choose the best, the brightest of them, to
make a sort of shock troop . . . a shock troop of feelings.
Yes, this is a conspiracy, a peaceful revolution, a peaceful
demonstration of feeling.

"Let's say that somewhere I find a full-blooded, one
hundred per cent vainglorious person. I will tell him: Show
yourself! Show those who won't give you a chance, show
them what it means to love glory. Perform a deed which
they will say: Oh, vile vanity! Oh, the strength of vanity!
If I am lucky enough to find a perfectly thoughtless man,
I shall say: Show yourself, show the strength of thought-
lessness, so the spectators will throw up their hands in
despair.

"The genii of feelings will take possession of souls. The
genie of pride will rule one soul, the genie of compassion,
another. I want to extract them, these imps, to unloose
them in the arena."

Interrogator: "Well then, have you managed to find
someone?"

Ivan: "I have been searching for a long time. It's very
hard. Maybe they don't understand me. But I have found
one."

Interrogator: "Who is he?"

Ivan: "Are you interested in the feeling of which he
appears to be the bearer, or in his name?"

Interrogator: "Both."

Ivan: "Nikolai Kavalerov, the Envious."

4

They walked away from the mirror.

Now the two ridiculous figures were walking together,
the slightly shorter and fatter one half a step ahead of the

other. This was a peculiar habit of Ivan Babichev's. He was forced to look back constantly in order to talk to his companion. If he had to utter a long sentence (and his sentences were hardly ever short), he would repeatedly bump into passers-by. Whereupon he would tear his bowler from his head and burst into flowery apologies. He was a very polite man; an amiable smile never left his face.

The day was closing shop. A gypsy in a blue waistcoat was carrying a clean brass bowl on his shoulder. The day was moving off, riding on the gypsy's shoulder. The disc of the bowl was bright and blinding. The gypsy walked slowly, the bowl swayed gently, and the day wheeled inside the disc. The two wayfarers stared. As the sun set, the disc disappeared around a corner. The day was gone. They turned into a bar.

Kavalerov told Ivan how an important person had kicked him out of his house. He did not mention any names. Ivan told a similar story: an important person had thrown him out too.

"I bet you know him. Everybody does. He's my brother, Andrei Babichev. Ever heard of him?"

Kavalerov turned crimson. He lowered his eyes and said nothing.

"That makes our lives similar; we must become friends," Ivan suggested radiantly. "Besides, I like your name. Kavalerov—it sounds highfalutin' and vulgar."

Kavalerov thought: That's exactly what I am: highfalutin' and vulgar.

"Wonderful beer," Ivan said. "The Poles sometimes say of a woman: her eyes are the color of beer. Isn't that good? But most important, this big man, my brother, has stolen my daughter. I will make my brother pay for that.

"He stole my daughter. Well, I don't mean that he literally stole her, of course. Don't make such big eyes, Kavalerov. And it would be a good thing if you could reduce your nose a bit too. With a thick nose like yours, you ought to be famous. You cannot be happy as an ordinary onlooker. You see, he exerted moral pressure on her. You know, he could be made legally responsible. I could go to the public prosecutor. She left me. But I don't even consider Andrei to be as guilty as the bastard who lives with him."

He was speaking of Volodia.

Kavalerov's big toes squirmed in embarrassment.

"That boy has ruined my life. Oh, I wish he'd get his kidneys kicked loose playing soccer. Andrei takes his advice on everything. That nasty youngster, if you please, is the New Man! That snot-nose declared that Valia was unhappy because I, her father, am mad (the bastard!), and have been systematically driving her mad, too. Bastards! Between them they talked her into it, and Valia ran away. Some girl friend or other has taken her in. I cursed that friend. I wished that her gullet and her rectum would change places. Can you see it? They're a bunch of blockheads. . . . Woman was the best, the most beautiful, the purest flower of our civilization. I searched for a being of the female sex, for a being in whom all womanly qualities would be combined, for the quintessence of womanly qualities. Femininity was the glory of the old era. I wanted to make that femininity shine. We are dying, Kavalerov. I wanted to carry Woman above my head like a torch. I thought Woman would be extinguished with our era. Thousands of years are piled in a dump-hole in which are scattered machines, lumps of iron, old cans, old bolts, rusty springs. . . . It's a dark, bleak pit. And the only light comes from rot, from phosphorescent fungi, from mold. Those are our feelings! That's all that's left of our feelings, of the flowering of our souls. Then the new man comes to the pit, gropes around, climbs down into it, picks out what he needs—maybe a machine part, maybe a wrench—and tramples upon the shining rot, extinguishes it. I dreamed of finding a woman who would blossom in that pit with unprecedented feeling, the miraculous flowering of a fern. So the new man coming to steal our iron would be frightened, would withdraw his hand, close his eyes, blinded by the light of what he had thought was rot.

"I found such a being right beside me: Valia. I thought Valia would glow over the dying century, light its way to the great funeral. But I was wrong. She has fluttered away. She has deserted the bedside of the old era. I thought Woman belonged to us, that tenderness and love belonged to us alone, but there it is—I was wrong. I wander by the edge of the pit, the world's last dreamer, a wounded bat."

Kavalerov thought: I will snatch Valia from them. He wanted to tell Ivan he had been a witness to the incident in the street with the flowering hedge, but for some reason he abstained.

"Our fates are similar," Ivan continued. "Give me your hand. Good. Welcome. Very pleased to see you, young man. Cheers. So they kicked you out, Kavalerov? Tell me, tell me about it. Oh, but you've told me already. A very important person turned you away? You don't want to name names? Well. Okay. You hate the man very much, don't you?"

Kavalerov nods.

"Oh, my dear fellow, I see! You, as I understand it, have sent a powerful man to hell. Don't interrupt. You have conceived a hatred for a man who has gained universal recognition. It seems to you, certainly, that it is he who has insulted you. Don't interrupt me. Drink up. You are sure it is he who is preventing you from proving yourself, that he has stolen your rightful place, that where you think you should excel, *he* does. And you are seething. . . ."

The orchestra hovers in the smoke. The violinist's pale face lies on his fiddle.

"The violin looks like the violinist," says Ivan. "It's a little violinist in a wooden tailcoat. Do you hear? The wood is singing. Can you hear the voice of the wood? The wood in the orchestra sings in different voices. But how horribly they play, God, how horribly!"

He turned toward the musicians.

"You think that's a drum you have? No, that's the god of music rapping you with his fist. My friend, envy is eating

us away. We envy the future. It is the envy of senility, if
you wish. Mankind has grown old. It is the envy of a generation of mankind grown old. Let's talk about envy. Give
us some more beer. . . ."

They sat near a wide window.

It had rained once more. It was evening. The city sparkled as if hewn out of Cardiff coal. People glanced in the
window from the street, and some pressed their noses to
the pane.

"Yes, envy. Here a drama should be played out, one of
those grandiose dramas in the theater of history that evoke
tears, ecstasy, pity, and anger. Without even realizing it,
you are the bearer of a historical mission. You, we may
say, are a clot of envy. A clot in the bloodstream of the
dying era, which envies the New that will take its place."

"But what can I do?" Kavalerov asked.

"My dear fellow, either take things as they come or kick
up a row, go out with a bang. Slam the door, as they say.
The bang is what matters. Scratch history's mug for her.
Show them, damn you! They won't let you into history
anyway. Don't give up without a fight. I want to tell you
about something that happened in my childhood.

"There was a party. The children put on a play, did a
ballet on a specially constructed stage in the big living
room. And a girl, see what I mean, a typical little girl,
twelve years old, thin legs, short dress, all pink and satin,
dressed up—all in all, with her ruffles and ribbons, looking
like a snapdragon—a little beauty, haughty, spoiled, tossing
her curls. She was the queen of the ball. She had it all her
way. Everyone admired her, everything radiated from her
and was drawn in around her. She outdanced everyone
else, outsang them, leaped higher, thought up better games
to play. She received the best presents, the best candies,
flowers, oranges, compliments. . . . I was thirteen, a high-
school student. I didn't have a chance, despite the fact that
I was also used to admiration, to an enthusiastic following.
In class, I too was top man, a pace-setter. I couldn't stand
it. I caught the girl in the corridor and gave her a going

over: tore her ribbons, mussed her curls, scratched her
charming features. I grabbed her by the nape of the neck
and banged her forehead several times against a column.
At that moment I loved that girl more than life itself,
worshipped her, and hated her with all my strength. Muss-
ing up her pretty curls, I thought I would dishonor her,
dispel her pinkness, her glow; I thought I would show
everyone they were wrong. But nothing came of it. I was
the one disgraced. They kicked me out. However, old man,
they remembered me all evening; I spoiled their party for
them; they talked about me everywhere the beauty went.
. . . That is how I came to know envy. The terrible heart-
burn of envy. It is burdensome to envy! Envy catches you
by the throat, squeezes your eyes from their sockets.
When I was tormenting her there in the corridor, my victim, my captive, tears poured from my eyes, I was choking
but, all the same, I ripped her delightful clothes, shivering
at the feel of the satin. It almost set my teeth on edge and
made my lips tremble. You know what satin is like: just
as a touch on the spine pierces the whole nervous system,
so the feel of satin makes your face twitch. All the powers
that be rose up against me in defense of that nasty girl.
A poison that had been concealed poured out from what
had seemed so charmingly innocent in the living room:
from her dress, from the pink satin dress which was such a
joy to look at. I don't remember saying anything when I
was beating her up, but I must have whispered: This is
my revenge! Don't try to outdo me! Don't try to take
what's mine by right.

"I hope you have followed me because I want to draw
an analogy. I am thinking of the struggle between two eras.
At first the comparison may seem flimsy. But you understand me, don't you? I am speaking of envy."

The orchestra stopped playing.

"Well, thank God for a little silence," Ivan said. "Look
over there at the cello. It didn't shine like that before it
was used. They've been tormenting it for a long time and
now it shines as if it were wet—absolutely a freshened-up

cello. You ought to take down my comments, Kavalerov.
I don't talk, I carve my words on marble. Don't you think
so?

"My dear fellow, we were pace-setters, we too have
been spoiled by admiration, we also have been accustomed
to lead back there in the dimming era. Now a wonderful
new world is rising. A brilliant carnival they won't let us
attend. Everything radiates from it, from the new era,
everything is drawn in around it. It gets the best gifts and
all the admiration. I love this world bearing down upon
me, more than life itself. I worship it; at the same time, I
hate it with all my strength! I am choking, tears pour from
my eyes in a shower. But I want to sink my fingers into its
clothes and rend them. Don't push me out! Don't take
away what belongs to me.

"We must avenge ourselves. You and I—there are many
thousands of us—must avenge ourselves. Kavalerov, enemies don't always turn out to be windmills. Sometimes
what we long to take for a windmill is the enemy, the conqueror, bringing death and ruin. Your enemy, Kavalerov,
is a real enemy. Avenge yourself. Trust me. Let's go out
with a bang. We will take the young world down a peg.
We are tough. We too have been the pets of history. Make
them talk about you, Kavalerov. It's clear: everything is
going down to destruction, it's all planned, there's no way
out. You have to perish, you with your thick nose! Each
minute will increase the humiliation, with every day the
enemy will blossom forth like a cherished youth. To perish: that's clear. So dress up your destruction, adorn it
with fireworks, tear the clothes off the one who is trying to
knock you down, take your leave in such a way that your
good-by will roll down through the centuries."

Kavalerov thought: He is reading my thoughts.

"Did they insult you? Did they kick you out?"

"They insulted me terribly," Kavalerov said hotly. "For
a long time they humiliated me."

"Who insulted you? One of the elect of the century?"

Kavalerov wanted to cry out: "Your brother, the one
who insulted you!" But he remained silent.

"You are lucky. You know the face of the conqueror. You have a tangible enemy. And so have I."

"What shall I do?"

"You are lucky. While avenging yourself, you can avenge the era which gave you birth."

"What shall I do then?"

"Kill him. Leave an honorable memory of yourself, as the hired assassin of the era. Squash your enemy in the door, on the threshold between the two eras. He is swaggering; he thinks he is already across the threshold. He is already a cupid, hovering with his scroll by the gates of the new world. Already his nose is in the air and he doesn't see you. Give him a farewell crack on the nose. I bless you. And I," Ivan raised his beer mug, "and I too will annihilate my enemy. Let's drink to Ophelia, Kavalerov. She's my weapon of revenge."

Kavalerov opened his mouth to tell him the important thing: we have a common enemy, you have given me your blessing and told me to kill your brother. But he didn't say a word because a man came up to their table and asked Ivan to follow him immediately, without questioning. And Ivan was arrested.

"Good-by, my dear fellow," said Ivan. "They are taking me to Golgotha. Go and see my daughter." (He named the little street which had been a bright spot in Kavalerov's memory for some time already.) "Go and have a look at her. You will understand that if such a creature has forsaken us, then there is only one thing left: revenge."

He drank up his beer and went out, a step ahead of the mysterious man.

As he left he winked at the other customers, lavished smiles, glanced into the mouth of the clarinet. When he reached the door, he turned. Holding his bowler in his outstretched hand, he declaimed:

> "I am not a foreign faker,
> Neither am I John the Baptist,
> I'm a modern miracle maker,
> I'm a modest Soviet artist."

5

"What are you laughing about? You think I'm sleepy?" asked Volodia.

"I wasn't laughing, I was coughing."

And Volodia fell asleep again, hardly reaching the chair first.

It was the younger man who tired first. Andrei Babichev was a titan. He worked all day and half the night. Andrei banged his fist on the table. The lampshade jumped like the lid of a kettle, but the other slept on. The lampshade jumped and Andrei remembered: James Watt watches the kettle lid bobbing above the steam. A famous story, a famous picture. James Watt invents the steam engine.

"And what will you invent, my James Watt? What machine will you invent, Volodia? What new secret of nature will you uncover, new man?"

For a while Andrei Babichev left his work, stared at the sleeping young man, and thought:

What if Ivan is right after all? What if I'm nothing but an average man with family feelings? Am I fond of him because he has lived with me since he was a child? Has he grown on me, have I grown to love him like a son? Is that the only reason why? Is it that simple? And what if he was stupid? Everything I live for has become centered around him. I have been lucky. The life of the new man is still remote. I believe in it. And I have been lucky. He has fallen asleep so close to me, my wonderful new world. The new world lives in my house. I'm terribly attached to him. A son? A mainstay? Someone to close my eyes for me when I die? No, it's not true. That's not what I need! I don't want to die on a high, gilt bed surrounded by pillows. I know: the masses and not my family will take my last breath. Nonsense! As we cherish the new world, so I cherish him. And he is dear to me as the personification of a hope. I will kick him out if I am deceiving myself about him, if he is not something new, something com-

pletely different from me, because I am still up to my big
belly in the old world and for me it is too late to get out.
I would kick him out then; I don't need a son, I'm not a
father and he is not a son, we are not a family. I believed
in him and he justified that belief.

We are not a family, we are mankind.

What does it mean then? Does it mean that the human
feeling of fatherly love must be annihilated? Why then does
he love me, the new man? It means that there, in the new
world, love between father and son will also bloom. That
gives me the right to exult: I can rightfully love him both
as a son and as a new man. Ivan, Ivan, your conspiracy is
meaningless. Not all feeling is doomed. Your rage is sense-
less, Ivan! Something will be left.

Long, long ago, on a dark night, falling into water-filled
ditches, up to their knees in reflected stars, shaking more
stars from the bushes, two people were fleeing: a Commissar and a boy. The boy had saved the Commissar. The
Commissar was huge; the boy, tiny. Anyone seeing them
would have thought that there was just one running, a giant,
throwing himself to the ground, getting up again. The boy
could have been taken for the palm of the giant's hand.

They were united forever.

The boy lived with the giant, grew, grew up, joined the
Young Communist League, became a student. He had been
born in a railroad workers' village, the son of a track re-
pairman.

Other children liked him, grownups liked him. Sometimes it worried him that everyone liked him. At times it
seemed undeserved, mistaken. His strongest feeling was his
feeling of comradeship. Sometimes, feeling the need for a
mysterious justice, trying to correct the irregularity of nature in distributing her gifts, the boy used various strata-
gems in an attempt to play down people's opinion of him,
to dim his glow.

He wanted to compensate less successful comrades by
showing his attachment to them, by being ready for self-

sacrifice, by fervent displays of friendship, by discovering
the remarkable features and talents in each of them.

His presence incited his friends to emulation.

"Why are people angry with each other, why do they
get offended," Volodia would say. "Such people don't understand our times. They are not acquainted with technology. Time is also a technical concept. If everyone was a
technician, wickedness, vanity, and other petty feelings
would disappear. You smile, but one must understand time
in order to get rid of petty feelings. A feeling of offense,
let's say, lasts an hour or a year. Men have enough imagination to make it last that long. But a thousand years is
beyond their scope. They see only three or four divisions
on the dial; they crawl, butt into each other. . . . They
are not up to it! They cannot conceive of the whole dial.
In fact, just try telling them there's a dial at all. They won't
believe you."

"Why only petty feelings? After all, lofty feelings are
also short-lived. What about magnanimity, for instance?"

"In magnanimity there is a sort of pattern . . . a technical pattern. Don't smile. Yes, yes. No, as a matter of
fact, I think I've got it all mixed up. You're confusing me.
No, wait! The Revolution was . . . well, how shall I put
it? Certainly, it was very cruel. But for the sake of what did
it cause so much hardship? It was magnanimous. It was
kind in terms of the whole dial! Wasn't it? Offense must
not be taken for what happens within two divisions, but
only for the dial as a whole. . . . Then there is no difference between cruelty and magnanimity. Then there is just
one thing: time. The iron logic, as they say, of history.
History and time are twins. Stop laughing, Andrei. I tell
you, a man's main feeling should be an understanding of
time."

He also would say:

"I'll show the bourgeois world what's what. They mock
at us, the old fogies; they keep buzzing: and your new
engineers, surgeons, professors, inventors—where are they?
I'll form a group of my comrades, a hundred strong. Its

purpose will be to teach the bourgeois world a lesson. You think I'm bragging? You don't understand a thing. I'm not getting carried away. We'll work like mad. Then you'll see. They'll be traveling here to congratulate us. And Valia will be one of us."

He woke up.

"I had a dream," he said, laughing. "I was sitting on a roof with Valia, looking at the moon through a telescope."

"What? Uh? A telescope?"

"And I said to her: 'Look over there, that's the Sea of Crises,' and she asked: 'The Sea of Lice?' "

In the spring of that year, Volodia had left to pay a short visit to his father in the town of Murom. His father worked in the Murom locomotive-building plant. Two lonely days went by. On the night of the third day, as Andrei was being driven home, the chauffeur slowed down at a corner. It was dawn, and Andrei saw a man lying by a wall.

The man lying on the grating somehow reminded him of the absent youth. This impelled him to lean forward to the chauffeur. "But there's nothing in common between the two of them," Andrei almost cried out. And indeed, there was absolutely no resemblance between the man lying there and the absent youth. He simply had a vision of Volodia and thought: What if Volodia somehow found himself in such a pitiful position. Stupidly, he gave way to sentimentality. The car stopped.

Nikolai Kavalerov was picked up, his delirious words were heard, and he was taken to the house of Andrei Babichev, who dragged him up to the third floor, laid him down on Volodia's sofa, made him a bed there, and covered him up to the neck with a blanket. There Kavalerov lay on his back, crisscross marks from the grating on his cheek, while Andrei went placidly off to bed: the sofa was no longer empty.

And that night he dreamed the young man had hanged himself on a telescope.

6

The wonderful bed that stood in Annie Prokopovich's room was made of expensive wood and varnished with dark-cherry lacquer. It had inset mirror-arcs on the insides of its ends.

Once, in a year of profound peace, at a public feast, Annie's husband, strewn with confetti, climbed onto a wooden platform to the sound of a fanfare, presented a lottery ticket, and got from the master of ceremonies a receipt of ownership for the wonderful bed. They used a cart to haul it away. Boys in the street whistled after it. The blue sky appeared and disappeared, reflected in the swaying mirror-arcs, as if the lids of a pair of beautiful eyes were opening and slowly drooping again.

The couple lived a married life and then it was over, but the bed rode out all the storms.

Kavalerov now lived in the corner behind the bed.

He had come to Annie and said:

"I can pay you thirty rubles a month for a corner of your room."

And Annie had agreed, smiling broadly. He had nowhere else to go. A new lodger was firmly installed in his former room. Kavalerov had sold his own horrible bed for four rubles and it had groaned as it left him.

Annie's bed was like an organ. It filled half the room. Its upper reaches dissolved in the twilight of the ceiling.

Kavalerov thought:

If I were a child, Annie's little son, how many poetic, magic stories my childish mind would have made up, inspired by this extraordinary object. But I am an adult now and can take in only the general outline plus a few odd details. Then, I could. . . . Then, neither distance nor scale nor time nor weight nor gravity had to be taken into consideration, and I could have crawled inside the narrow passages between the frame of the bedspring and the edge of the bed; I could have hidden behind the columns which

today seem to me no thicker than a broomstick; I could
have set up imaginary catapults on its barricades and
opened fire on the enemy who would have beat a hasty
retreat over the soft, boggy ground of the quilt, leaving
behind the dead and the wounded; I could have held re-
ceptions for foreign envoys under the mirror-arcs, exactly
like the king in the novel I had just read; I could have gone
off on fantastic journeys along the fretwork—higher and
higher, up the legs and buttocks of the cupids, climbing
over them like climbing a gigantic statue of Buddha, seeing
only one bit of the huge details at a time. Then, from the
last arch, from a dizzying height, I would have slithered
down the terrifying precipice, onto the icy whiteness of the
pillows.

Ivan Babichev leads Kavalerov along a green bank. The
down of dandelion clocks flies up from under their feet; it
floats in the air and its floating is a dynamic reflection of
the heat. Babichev grows pale; his round face shines as if
the heat were modeling a mask out of it.

"Over here!" he commands.

The suburb is in bloom. They cross an empty lot, walk
along by the fences. German shepherds rage behind the
fences, rattling their chains. Kavalerov whistles, teasing the
dogs—but everything is possible: what if one of them manages to break its chain and leap over the fence? And so a
tiny capsule of terror keeps dissolving somewhere deep in
the pit of the teaser's stomach.

Ivan and Kavalerov go down the green slopes, landing
almost on the roofs of the little red houses in their gardens. Kavalerov does not know this part of town; even
when he sees Krestovsky Towers ahead, he still isn't certain where he is. They can hear the whistles of locomotives
and the clanking of trains.

"I will show you my machine," Ivan says, turning his
head back toward Kavalerov. "Here, pinch yourself, like
that. . . . That's right . . . again . . . once more. . . .
See, it's not a dream. No. Remember: you weren't asleep.

Remember: everything was quite commonplace; we crossed an empty lot; a puddle, the kind that never seems to dry up, was glistening in the sun; there were pots drying atop the palings. Now, you are sure to remember this, my friend: we came across some wonderful things in the gutter by the fences. Here, for instance, is a page from a book. Pick it up, look at it, before the wind carries it away. See, it's an illustration from *Taras Bulba*. Do you recognize it? They must have used it to wrap food and then thrown it out of that little window over there. And over here, what's that? Ah! There's the eternal, traditional rubbish-dump shoe. It's not worth our attention, being too academic a symbol of desolation! There's a bottle. It's still whole, but tomorrow the wheel of a cart will smash it and if some dreamer follows our path, he will have the pleasure of contemplating the famous bottle glass, celebrated by writers for its ability to reflect the light, to flash amidst garbage and bleakness, create mirages for lonely travelers. Observe, my friend, observe. There are buttons, hoops, a shred of bandage; there are the Babylonian turrets of fossilized human defecation. In a word, my friend, the usual aspect of an empty lot. Remember it. Everything was just commonplace. And I brought you here to show you my machine. Pinch yourself again. That's right. So then, it's not a dream? Well, all right. Still, later—you know how it is—later, you'd say that you didn't feel too well, that it was too hot, possibly that a lot of perfectly ordinary things seemed strange to you in this heat or because you were tired, and so on. No, my friend, I demand that you make a statement that you are in full possession of your faculties. What you are about to see may give you too great a shock."

Kavalerov made the statement:

"I am in possession of all my mental faculties."

And then they came to a fence. A small, low, plank fence.

"It's in there," Ivan said. "Wait. Let's sit down. Here, above this little gully. I've already told you that my dream has been a machine's machine, a universal machine. I thought up a perfect instrument. I hoped for one small apparatus combining hundreds of different functions. Yes, my friend, I was faced with this beautiful, noble problem. It was worth becoming a fanatic over. I wanted to tame the mastodon of technology, to make him a domestic, hand-fed pet. To give man this little lever, simple, familiar, unfrightening; something he could get used to, like the knob on his door."

"I don't understand anything about mechanics," Kavalerov said. "I'm afraid of machines."

"And I succeeded. Listen, Kavalerov, I have invented such a machine."

The fence beckoned Kavalerov; yet he felt the odds were that no secret lay behind those commonplace gray boards.

"It can blow up mountains. It can fly. It lifts weights. It will crush ore. It will replace the kitchen stove, the baby carriage, the long-range gun. It is *the* mechanical genius. . . ."

"What are you smiling about, Ivan Petrovich?"

Ivan was playing with the corner of his eye.

"I am blooming. I can't talk about it without my heart jumping around like an egg in boiling water. Listen. I have imparted hundreds of skills to it. I have invented a machine that can do everything. Do you understand? You'll see it right away, but . . ."

He stood up, placed his hand on Kavalerov's shoulder, and said solemnly:

"But I have forbidden it to do all those things. One fine day I understood that I had been given a supernatural power with which to avenge my era. . . . I have perverted the machine. On purpose. Out of spite."

He laughed happily.

"Try to understand, Kavalerov, what a great satisfaction it was. I gave the most vulgar human sentiments to the greatest technical creation. I dishonored the machine. I avenged my era, the brain that was given me, that lies in my cranium; my brain, that conceived the extraordinary mechanism. To whom could I leave it? To the new world?

They are devouring us, like food. They are devouring the nineteenth century, as a boa constrictor devours a rabbit. They swallow us whole and digest us. What they can use, they feed on and assimilate; what is bad for them, they eject. They expectorate our feelings, and feed on our technology. I must avenge our feelings. They won't get my machine, they won't make use of me, they won't feed on my brain. My machine could bring happiness to the new era, all at once, from the very first day of its existence, could bring technology to its Golden Age. But there it is, they won't get it. My machine is a dazzling flash, a sneering tongue stuck out by the dying era at the newborn one. Their mouths will water when they see it. The machine, think of it, their idol, the machine . . . and suddenly. . . . And suddenly the best machine will turn out to be a liar, a sentimental wretch, full of petty-bourgeois traits. It can do everything. But what will it actually do? It will sing our love songs, the silly love songs of the dying century, and gather the flowers of the past era. It will fall in love, become jealous, cry, dream. I did this. I have insulted the machine—the god of these people, of the future. I have even given it the name of a girl who went out of her mind with love and despair. I've called it Ophelia, the most human, the most touching name."

Ivan dragged Kavalerov after him.

He bent down and put his eye to a chink, presenting to Kavalerov his heavy, shiny buttocks that looked very much like dumbbells. Perhaps the heat was really having its effect, or perhaps it was the unfamiliar, suburban quiet, the novelty of a landscape rather surprising in Moscow. Perhaps Kavalerov, abandoned by the usual city noises, had fallen victim to some sort of mirage, some sort of acoustic hallucination. It seemed to him that he heard Ivan's voice carrying on a conversation with someone on the other side of the chink. Then Ivan recoiled. And so did Kavalerov, although he was standing a good distance from Ivan. It was as though fear, hiding in the trees opposite, was dangling them both on a single string.

"Who is that whistling?" cried Kavalerov, fear ringing in his voice, as a shrill whistle flew over the suburb. He turned away a fraction, hiding his face in his hands, as if protecting himself from a cold draft. Ivan ran back from the fence mincingly, bumping into Kavalerov. The whistle flew after him, as if Ivan was not running at all, but was being carried along, impaled on the dazzling beam of the whistle.

"I'm afraid of it, I'm afraid of it!" Kavalerov heard Ivan's choking whisper.

Holding on to each other, they rushed downhill, accompanied by the curses of a hobo over whom they had stumbled, having mistaken him for an old, discarded horse collar.

The hobo, yanked out of his sleep by the scruff of his neck, sat on a knoll groping in the grass for a stone. They disappeared into a little street.

"I'm afraid of it," Ivan kept repeating rapidly. "She hates me . . . she's betrayed me . . . she'll kill me. . . ."

Kavalerov regained his senses and became ashamed of his cowardice. He remembered that at the very moment he had seen Ivan begin his headlong flight, something else had come within his range of vision that, in the fright, he hadn't registered.

"Listen," he said, "it's all bunk. It was a boy whistling with two fingers in his mouth. I saw him. A boy appeared on top of the fence and whistled. . . . A boy, that's all."

"Didn't I tell you," said Ivan, "you'd start looking for all sorts of explanations? Remember, I asked you to pinch yourself as hard as possible."

They quarreled. Ivan turned in to a bar they finally found. He did not invite Kavalerov, who stumbled ahead not knowing his way, his ears exploring space for the ringing of a streetcar bell. At a corner he stamped his foot and retraced his steps toward the bar. Ivan met him with a smile and with the open palm of his hand gestured toward a chair.

"Tell me," Kavalerov whined, "why are you doing all

this to me? Are you trying to fool me and yourself? Of course there isn't any such machine. It's all delirium. Why are you lying to us both?"

Exhausted, Kavalerov let himself drop onto the chair.

"Here, Kavalerov, order yourself some beer and I will tell you a fairy tale. Listen."

THE TALE OF THE MEETING OF TWO BROTHERS

. . . Scaffolding surrounded the tender, growing body of the Quarter.

A scaffolding like any other; girders, planks in tiers, passages, crosswalks, all that. A crowd had gathered in front of it. The people reacted in all sorts of ways. Some with a predilection for simplicity said that the construction made a nice crosshatching. A man remarked:

"Wooden structures are not meant to grow too tall. Planks too high in the air offend the eye. Scaffolding detracts from the majesty of a building. The tallest mast is easily broken. Such a huge edifice of wood is vulnerable, whatever you say. The thought of fire comes to mind automatically."

Another exclaimed: "Just look over there, on the other side! The beams are stretched out like strings! It looks like a guitar. A guitar, I tell you, a guitar."

"Well, wasn't I just saying how fragile wood is? It should be content to serve music."

"And what about brass?" someone interjected sarcastically. "I only like brass instruments."

A schoolboy found an arithmetic in the arrangement of the planks that nobody else had noticed. However, he could not determine what the planks were multiplying, or what the parallel girders were equalizing. He never did find out: the resemblance was a flimsy one and soon dissolved.

The poet thought: The siege of Troy. The besieged towers . . .

The comparison was strengthened when musicians appeared. Under their trumpets, they crawled into a sort of wooden trench at the foot of the structure.

The evening was black. The lanterns were white and spherical. The bunting was strikingly crimson. The depths under the wooden steps were deathly black. The lanterns swayed back and forth on their humming wires. It was as though the darkness were raising and lowering its eyebrows. And around the lanterns, insects fluttered and died. The lanterns, swaying upward, caused windows in their arc to blink. As they descended again, they tore away the outline of some far-off house and hurled it at the construction site. Then, until the wind-swayed lanterns stopped, the scaffolding came violently alive: everything was set in motion, and the structure set sail for the crowd like a high-decked galleon.

Andrei Babichev was making his way along a wooden walk toward a wooden platform. The platform had sprung into existence spontaneously, with all its accessories. The orator was provided with steps, a ramp, a handrail; with a dazzlingly black background, and light shining on him from behind and in front. There was so much light provided that even a very distant observer could see the water level in the decanter on the chairman's table.

Babichev was moving along above the crowd. He was a splash of bright colors, like a mechanical tin mannequin. He was scheduled to make a speech. Down below, in the natural shelter, actors were preparing to give their performance. An unseen oboe, which the crowd did not understand, was wailing sweetly. Just as incomprehensible to them was the drum opposite, grown silvery in the intense light. The actors were adorning themselves in their wooden recess. Those walking above forced the planks apart at each step, and caused a fog of wood dust.

Babichev's appearance on the platform was greeted with laughter. They took him for an MC. Everything about him was much too neat, too purposeful, too theatrical.

"Fatso!" somebody in the crowd exclaimed admiringly.

"Bravo!" they hollered from scattered spots.

But when one of the men at the chairman's table announced Comrade Babichev, the hilarity vanished. Many stood on tiptoe. Their attention was intensified. Everyone felt good seeing Babichev. He was a famous man, and he was fat. Fatness made the famous man familiar, understandable. They gave him an ovation, in homage to his bulk. He delivered his speech.

He spoke about the future activities of the Quarter—the number of meals, its catering capacity, its nutritional coefficient. He was extolling the advantages of communal feeding.

He spoke about the nourishment of childen—the Quarter would have a special children's section—he spoke of the scientific method of preparing oatmeal with milk; he spoke of growth and anemia.

Like every orator, his eyes were focused on a far-off point beyond the audience, and that is why, until his speech was finished, he remained unaware of what was happening under the dais. In the meantime, a small man in a bowler had long since distracted the audience in the front rows who were now giving their full attention to him. The man's behavior was perfectly peaceful. True, he had taken a chance by slipping under the rope that separated crowd from platform. He was standing all by himself in that place, implying special privilege whether rightful or usurped.

His back was turned to the crowd; he stood leaning back or, rather, half-sitting on the rope. His behind hung over it, and he seemed unconcerned about the havoc that would ensue if the rope broke. Rocking with Olympian serenity, he apparently enjoyed the situation.

Perhaps he was listening to the speaker and perhaps he was observing the actors. A flashing ballerina's tutu and all sorts of strange faces could be seen through the gaps between the planks.

The funniest thing about this little man was that he had brought along a large pillow in a yellowish pillow slip, well dented by many heads. When he had made himself comfortable on the rope and put the pillow down beside him, it sat like a pig.

When the speaker had concluded, and was wiping his lips with a handkerchief with one hand and pouring water from the decanter into a glass with the other, as the applause subsided and the audience was shifting its attention to the actors—the little man, raising his behind from the rope, drew himself up, taking advantage of every inch of his small stature. He extended the hand holding the pillow, and shouted:

"Comrades, I demand the floor!"

That was when the orator first saw his brother Ivan. His fists clenched involuntarily. Ivan was mounting the steps onto the platform. He was coming up slowly. Somebody from the chairman's table rushed toward the railing. He meant to stop the stranger with gestures and words. But his arm hung in the air and, as though counting the stranger's ascending footsteps, moved downward in short, spasmodic jerks.

"Fee-fi-fo-fum . . ."

"That's hypnotism!" Squeaks of delight came from the crowd.

The stranger advanced, carrying the pillow by the scruff of its neck. Then he was on the platform. Another wonderful mechanical toy had appeared against the black background, which was like the blackboard in school, so black that fancied chalk lines flashed in many eyes. The rolypoly mechanical toy stopped.

"The pillow!" The whispered word rolled all through the crowd.

And the stranger spoke: "Comrades! They are trying to take your most treasured possession away from you: your homes. The steeds of the Revolution, thundering up the back stairs, are trampling over your children and your cats, breaking into your kitchens, smashing your beloved stoves and sinks. Women, your pride and your glory—your homes—are in danger. Mothers and wives, the elephants of the Revolution are stampeding, and they will raze your kitchens!

"What was he saying, this man. He was sneering at your

pans, at your little pots, at your quiet, at your right to
stick a pacifier between your own children's lips. . . . He
was trying to teach you to forget. To forget what? What
was he trying to push out of your hearts? Your own
homes, your own dear homes! He wants to turn you into
homeless tramps roaming the wilderness of history. Wives,
he is spitting into your soup. Mothers, he dreams of wiping
family resemblances from your babies' little faces, the beautiful, sacred family resemblance. He violates your little secret corners, scurries like a rat along your shelves, pokes
under your beds, crawls under your shirts, sniffs at the hair
of your armpits. You must send him to hell! . . .

"See this pillow? I am the king of pillows. Tell him:
We wish to sleep, each of us on her own pillow. Don't you
dare touch our pillows! Our heads have rested on them,
our kisses have fallen on them during our nights of love,
we have died on them and those whom we have killed have
died on them too. Keep your hands off our pillows! Stop
calling to us! Stop beckoning to us, trying to lure us! What
can you offer us to replace our capacity to love, to hate, to
hope; to cry, to pity, to forgive? See this pillow? It is our
coat of arms. Our symbol. Bullets get buried in a pillow.
With a pillow we shall smother you."

His speech was snapped. Even so, he had said too much.
It was as though they had caught him by his last sentence
and twisted it behind his back like an arm. He broke off,
suddenly frightened: the man he was belaboring simply
stood there and listened in silence. The scene could easily
have been part of a show; many assumed it was. Actors
are often made to come on stage from the audience, after
all. The impression was strengthened when the real actors
appeared from their wooden shelter. Yes, the ballerina
fluttered out from under the planks just like a butterfly.
The clown, in a monkey suit, was climbing onto the platform; with one hand he gripped the horizontal rail; in the
other he clutched a strange-looking musical instrument—a
long trumpet branching into three; in some magic way, he
seemed to be shinnying up his own trumpet. Somebody in

a tailcoat scurried about below the platform, trying to
round up the actors who wanted to get a glimpse of the
extraordinary orator. The actors also assumed the little
man was just another performer who was to come on stage
with his pillow and heckle the main speaker and was about
to do his number. But no. The clown slid down in terror on
his preposterous trumpet. There was a general furor. It was
not the subversive words, flung at the crowd, that caused
it. On the contrary, the fat little man's speech had been received exactly like a piece of showmanship. It was the en-
suing silence that made the skin of their skulls tighten under their caps.

"Why are you staring at me like that?" the little man
asked. He dropped his pillow.

The voice of the giant (no one knew it was brother talking to brother), a brief bark, was heard by everyone in
the crowd below, in all the windows and doorways of the
surrounding house. In their beds, old men raised themselves on their elbows.

"Whom are you fighting, you scum?" the giant asked.

His face became congested. A dark liquid seemed about
to flow from his face, out of all its openings, and cause
everyone to wince in horror. . . . These words were not
spoken by the giant, but by the girders around him; by the
concrete; by the imaginary graphs and formulas traced on
the black background that suddenly seemed to be really
there. It was their anger that was congested in him.

Ivan did not retreat, although the crowd expected he
would back up, back and back until, stumbling against his
pillow, he would find himself sitting on it. Instead, he suddenly regained his determination, straightened up, and approached the handrail. Screening his eyes with his hand,
Ivan called out:

"Where are you, Ophelia? I'm waiting for you!"

The wind had been blowing in bursts all the while. The
lanterns had kept swaying. . . . The audience was already
accustomed to the combining and dissolving of the shadow
designs (trouser-like squares constructed by Pythagoras on

the sides of a right-angled triangle, Hippocrates' little moons). The many-decked galleon of the structure, dragging her anchor, had kept sailing into the crowd. So the new blast, from which many shoulders and heads were turned, would have been just another nuisance and immediately forgotten, had it not been for . . .

And later they said it came from behind and flew over the heads of the crowd.

The huge sailing vessel was sailing straight at the crowd, its wooden sides creaking, the wind howling in its sails, when a black bird-like body hit a girder high in the air, broke a lantern, and tore away to one side. . . .

"Are you scared, brother?" Ivan asked. "Here's what I'm going to do. I'm going to send Ophelia to attack the scaffolding. She will raze your building to the ground. The screws will unscrew themselves, the nuts will fall off, the reinforced concrete will disintegrate like decaying matter. What would you say to that? She will teach each girder how to disobey you. Well? All this is going to collapse. She will turn every one of your neat little numbers into a useless flower. That, brother Andrei, is what I can do to you."

"Ivan, you are very ill," said the man from whom everyone expected thunder and lightning. "You're delirious, Ivan," he said, warmly and softly. "What are you talking about? Whom do you mean by 'she'? I can't see a thing. Who's going to turn numbers into flowers? It was nothing but the wind that blew a lantern against a girder and broke it. Oh, Ivan, Ivan . . ."

And Andrei Babichev stepped toward Ivan Babichev, his arms outstretched. Ivan brushed him aside.

"Look, over there!" he shouted, raising his hand. "No. You're looking the wrong way. . . . See, over there, more to the left. What do you think that is sitting there on the girder? See? Take a drink of water. Hey, give Comrade Babichev a glass of water. . . . What's that sitting on the girder over there, do you think? You do see it! You're scared, scared!"

"It's a shadow," Andrei said. "It is nothing but a shadow,

brother. Let's leave here. I'll take you home. Let the concert begin. The actors are beginning to fret. The public is getting impatient. Let's go, Vania, let's go. . . ."

"So you think it's a shadow, Andryusha. Well, it isn't. It is the machine you used to jeer at. That's me sitting up there on the girder, Andryusha; me, the old world, my century, is sitting up there. The brain of my century, Andryusha, a brain that could compose songs as well as scientific formulas, a brain full of the dreams that you are out to destroy."

Ivan raised his hand and shouted:

"Come on, Ophelia, off you go!"

The object on the girder flashed a beam of reflected light as it turned around. It began to rattle, shuffled like a bird before taking off, dived into the darkness, and disappeared out of sight.

Panic ensued. People pushed one another, fled, hollered. Now the thing could be heard rattling along the planks. Then, suddenly, it came back into sight, giving off an orange light. It whistled; its vague shape hung spider-like and weightless in the air. . . . Then it settled down on some other rib, half turned toward the crowd.

"To work, Ophelia, get going!" Ivan shouted, darting back and forth on the platform. "You heard what he had to say about the home. I order you to destroy this construction. . . ."

People were fleeing, and their flight was accompanied by the flight of the clouds.

The Quarter collapsed.

Ivan interrupted his tale and fell silent for a moment.

. . . A drum was lying among the ruins, and Ivan Babichev climbed on top of it. Ophelia was dragging the badly mauled, dying Andrei toward him.

"Let me put my head on your pillow, brother," Andrei whispered. "I want to die on the pillow. You win, Ivan, I give up."

And Ivan concluded:

I put my pillow on my knees and he placed his head on it. Then I said: "We've won, Ophelia."

7

On Sunday morning, Ivan Babichev came to visit Kavalerov.

"Today," he said solemnly, "I want to show you Valia."

They set out. Their walk could well be described as enchanting. It took them across a deserted city. They walked around Theater Square. There was almost no traffic. The upslope of Tverskaya Avenue loomed blue. A Sunday morning offers one of the prettiest views of the Moscow summer. The lighting, unbroken by the traffic, remained all in one piece, as though the sun had just risen. They crossed geometrical patterns of shadow and light, or rather a three-dimensional field, since light and shadow intersected each other in the air as well. Before they reached the Moscow City Soviet, they found themselves completely immersed in shadow. However, in the gap between two buildings there was a large block of light, very thick and dense. It was no longer possible to doubt that light was made of matter: the dust tearing around inside it could easily pass for waves in the ether.

In the small lane joining Tverskaya Avenue with Nikitskaya Street, they stopped to admire a blooming hedge.

They passed through a gate and climbed a wooden staircase to a glass-covered porch, shabby but enlivened by its colored glass and the sky showing through the grid of the panes.

The sky was broken up into sections of varying blueness and varying remoteness from the observer. About one pane in four was missing. The little green tails of a plant that had crawled along the outer edge of the porch slipped in through the lower row of tiny windows. Everything seemed

designed for happy childhood. It was the sort of porch
where one finds white rabbits.

Ivan was in a hurry. There were three doors in the
porch. He rushed toward the farthest one.

As they passed, Kavalerov tried to tear off one of the
green tails. As he pulled at it, the whole unseen network
outside was dragged along behind the tail. Somewhere a
plaintive sound was emitted by a wire which had somehow
invaded the life of the vine, or at least that's how Kavalerov
visualized it. (One would think they weren't in Moscow at
all but in Italy or somewhere like that.) Kavalerov pressed
his temple to a window and saw a yard surrounded by a
stone wall. The porch was at an intermediary height—
between the second and third stories. From there, the view
opened out beyond the wall (it was still like Italy . . .),
and he saw a piercingly green patch of grass.

Even before they had entered, he had heard voices and
laughter coming from that very spot of green. Before he
had time to make anything out, Ivan distracted him. Ivan
was banging at the door: once, twice, again. . . .

"Nobody in," he grunted. "She's already over there."

Kavalerov's attention returned to the lawn seen through
a broken pane. Why? So far he had seen nothing extraordinary. He had taken in, before his attention had been
diverted by Ivan's hammering, just one flash of multicolored
movement, just one beat with a gymnastic rhythm. It was
simply that the greenness of the lawn was surprisingly sweet
and cool to the eye after the usual courtyard. Most probably, he persuaded himself later on, it was the enchantment
of the lawn that had immediately gripped him.

"She's left already," Ivan repeated. "Just one minute,
may I?"

And he glanced through one of the windows. Kavalerov
immediately followed suit.

What had struck him as a luxurious lawn turned out to
be a small courtyard overgrown with weedy grass. The
main source of greenness was the tall, thickly crowned trees
that stood around the yard. All this vegetation glistened

green under the huge, blind wall of the house. From his vantage point above, it seemed to Kavalerov that the little courtyard was groping for breathing space. The surrounding stone hulks were pressing in on the little yard, which lay like a doormat in an overfurnished room. Strange roofs revealed their secrets to Kavalerov. He saw weather vanes full size and skylights whose existence nobody down below suspected; he caught a glimpse of a child's ball irretrievably lost when it had rolled into the gutter. Among the antenna-spiked buildings beyond the yard, the cupola of a church, freshly painted with red lead, filled an empty spot in the sky. It seemed to have been wafted along on the breeze until Kavalerov's eye had caught it. He saw a trolley in the terribly remote street, looking like Siamese-twin question marks facing each other. Another observer was leaning out of a faraway window, either eating something or sniffing at it. In his obedience to perspective, he was almost leaning on the trolley.

But the main thing was the lawn in the little yard.

They descended. There was an opening in the stone wall that separated the large, empty, boring yard from the mysterious little green one. Some stones were missing from the wall, loaves of bread removed from the oven. Through this embrasure they could see everything.

The sun burned the back of Kavalerov's head. He watched a high-jump practice. A rope was stretched between two posts. The young man took off, body sideways, stretched parallel, almost gliding over the rope. He seemed to be rolling instead of jumping. Once he had rolled over, he threw his legs up and kicked, the way a swimmer propels himself. In the next split second, his upside-down, distorted face flashed by on its way down, and immediately afterward, Kavalerov saw him standing up on the ground, which he had met with a sound like "haff"—either the expulsion of breath cut short or the bang of his heel against the grass.

Ivan pinched Kavalerov's elbow.

"There she is. . . . Look . . ." he whispered.

Everybody shouted and clapped. The high-jumper, almost naked, was walking off to the side slightly favoring
one foot, probably out of athletic jauntiness.

It was Volodia Makarov.

Kavalerov felt lost. Shame and fear overwhelmed him:
Volodia had displayed a whole gleaming grate of teeth
as he smiled.

Up on the porch, someone was knocking at the door
once more. Kavalerov turned his head. It would be very
stupid to be caught like a Peeping Tom behind the wall.
Somebody was walking along the porch; the windows were
dismembering him as he went. Different parts of his body
moved independently. It was an optical illusion. The head
was too far in front of the rest of the body. Kavalerov
recognized the head. Andrei Babichev was sailing down
the porch.

"Andrei!" Valia calls out to him from the lawn. "Andrei,
here we are, here!"

The terrible visitor disappears. He has left the porch,
searching for a way to the lawn. All sorts of barriers hide
him from Kavalerov's eyes. It's time to flee.

Valia's voice keeps ringing out: "Here, here. . . ."

Kavalerov sees Valia standing on the lawn, her legs wide
apart. She wears very short, black shorts. Her legs are
terribly bare and their shape is clearly distinguishable. She
wears white sneakers which make her stance even more
firm and solid—not at all the stance of a woman but of a
man or perhaps a child. Her legs are dirty, suntanned, and
shining with sweat. They are the legs of a little girl, exposed
to air and sun, to falls on grass and thorns, to bumps; legs
dotted with the pale scars from prematurely picked-off
scabs; knees rough like the skin of oranges. Valia's youth
and her unconscious feeling of physical wealth give her the
right to treat these legs so carelessly, not to spare them, not
to pamper them. But higher up, under the black shorts, the
purity and cleanliness of the body give an idea of how
charming the owner of the legs will be as she matures into
a woman and her attention becomes centered on her body,

when she will want to make herself beautiful, when the scratches are healed, the scabs have fallen off, the coloring has become even all over.

He pushed himself away and began to run along the blind wall away from the embrasure. A chalky whiteness rubbed off onto the shoulder of his jacket.

"Where're you off to?" Ivan called after him. "Wait! Wait!"

Kavalerov was horrified: He's shouting so goddam loud, they'll hear, they'll see me.

And indeed, behind the wall, it had suddenly grown very quiet. They were listening. Ivan caught up with Kavalerov.

"Hey, listen, did you see him? That's my brother! Did you see him? And they were all there, Volodia, Valia, the lot of them. Wait. I'll climb up on top of the wall and insult them. . . . You're covered with dust, Kavalerov, from the wall, like a baker. . . ."

Kavalerov said in a very low voice:

"I am very well acquainted with your brother, thank you. It was he who kicked me out. He is the important public figure I mentioned to you. . . . Our destinies, yours and mine that is, are similar. You said that I must kill your brother. . . . Well, what am I to do?"

Valia was sitting on top of the wall.

"Dad!" she exclaimed with a moan.

Ivan caught her legs as they hung down from the wall.

"Valia, pluck out my eyes; I want to be blind." He was out of breath. "I don't want to see any of this; no lawns, no branches, no flowers, no knights in shining armor, no cowards. I must go blind. I was wrong, Valia. . . . I thought that all feeling had perished—love, devotion, tenderness. . . . But it has all remained, Valia. . . . Only, Valia, not for us. All we have left, Valia, is envy. Just envy and envy. Pluck my eyes out, Valia, I want to go blind. . . ."

His hands, his face and chest slipped down the girl's sweaty legs, and he fell heavily at the foot of the wall.

"Let's drink, Kavalerov," Ivan said. "Let's drink to youth

that is past, to the conspiracy of feelings that has failed, to the machine that does not exist and never will. . . ."

"You are a son of a bitch, Ivan Babichev!"

Kavalerov caught Ivan by his collar.

"No," he said, "youth is not past! You hear me, it's not! You're lying. I'll prove it to you . . . tomorrow, do you hear? I'll kill your brother during the soccer match."

8

Nikolai Kavalerov had a seat in the grandstand. To his right, in the wooden enclosure, surrounded by the enormous letters of various posters, Valia sat amidst a group of young people.

The day was very bright and gusty; the wind blew and whistled through the stands. The huge field of smooth grass shone a brilliant green.

Kavalerov stared at the enclosure. He strained his eyes when they grew tired, he allowed his imagination to take over, trying to make up for what he could not see or hear. Many others besides him with seats near the enclosure, despite their excitement over the forthcoming spectacle, were staring at the delightfully pretty girl in pink, almost a child. She seemed still completely unself-conscious in movement and attitude, although she had something about her that made people try to attract her attention, as though she were a celebrity or the daughter of a famous man.

Sixty thousand spectators filled the stadium. They had come to see the long-awaited soccer match between Moscow's own squad and a selected German team.

In the stands people were arguing, hollering, quarreling about trifles. The stadium seemed distorted by this excited mass of people. While looking for his seat, Kavalerov got entangled in other people's knees. Working his way past these obstacles, he saw a respectable old man in a cream-colored vest lying with his arms stretched out crosswise on the track encircling the field. The people pouring past him paid no attention to him. Above, pennants and flags fluttered like flashes of lightning.

Kavalerov's body and soul strove toward the enclosure. Valia was above him and somewhat to his right sixty feet or so away. Optical illusions mocked him. Now and then, he thought their eyes had met, and would leap to his feet. It seemed to him that the little medallion round her neck had caught fire. The wind could do whatever it pleased to her: she kept clutching at her little hat of shining straw. The wind would blow the sleeve of her blouse up onto her shoulder, uncovering the top of her arm, slender and shapely as a flute. A leaflet escaped from her hand and, after a few wingbeats, fell into the denseness of the crowd.

For a whole month, people had been speculating on whether the Germans would bring their famous centerforward Getzke, the star of their attacking line. Getzke was in the line-up. The German team appeared from the underground passage, accompanied by the sounds of a military march. Before the players had time to take their positions on the field, the public (as it always does) at once recognized the celebrity among the other players.

"Getzke! Getzke!" Shouts came from the crowd thrilled at seeing a famous player and applauding him with zest.

Getzke turned out to be a medium-sized, swarthy, roundshouldered man. He stepped slightly to one side, stopped, clasped his hands over his head, and shook them. This unfamiliar foreign way of responding to applause excited the spectators even more.

The vivid German jerseys shone through the pure air like colors of an oil painting against the green background: orange, almost golden shirts with purplish-green eagles on the right breasts. Their wide, black shorts flapped in the wind.

Volodia Makarov, still shivering slightly from the coolness of his new sweater, was peering out of the window of the home team's locker room. The Germans had reached the middle of the field.

"Shouldn't we start?" he asked.

"Let's go," the team captain said.

The Soviet team trotted out in their red shirts and white shorts. The spectators leaned over the guardrails, stamping their feet against the boards. Their roar drowned out the orchestra.

The Soviet captain won the toss and elected to play the first half against the wind.

The Russians played their best while keeping a sharp eye on the Germans' style of play. Since the game lasts ninety minutes with only a brief rest at half-time when the teams change sides, it is an advantage to play against the wind during the first half when the players are still fresh.

The ball was constantly blown toward the Soviet goal-posts, and the game practically never left the Russian half of the field. After the high, parabolic kicks of the Russian fullbacks, the ball would slide down the wall of wind, its new yellow leather flashing, and reverse direction. The Germans attacked with abandon. Their famous Getzke was worthy of his reputation; he presented a constant threat to the Soviet goal. The crowd was soon giving its undivided attention to him.

As soon as he got the ball, Valia, from her height, would scream as though about to witness some horrible crime. Getzke would break through the Russian defenses leaving the Soviet backs sprawled in his wake, unable to cope with his bursts of speed and his feints. Then he would shoot. Valia would sway to one side, grabbing her neighbor's arm with both hands, leaning her cheek on it, desperately trying not to see the horrible, inevitable outcome. But she watched the fearful movements of Getzke through squinting eyes. He looked almost black from all his running around in the sun.

Then the Soviet goalie, Volodia Makarov, would intercept the ball. Getzke, gracefully changing his follow-through after shooting into an about turn, jogged back, head bent forward, orange shirt darkened by sweat. Valia, immediately recovered, laughed because she was happy the ball had been kept out of the Soviet goal and because she had just squeaked so stupidly and grabbed her neighbor's arm.

"Makarov! Makarov! Good boy!" she shouted with the rest.

Every minute or so the ball was hurled at the Russian goal. Again and again, it hit the sideposts or the crossbar. The goal moaned, raining whitewash. . . . Or else Volodia would get hold of the ball when it seemed physically impossible to do so. The entire audience, the whole live slope of the stands would become steeper as every spectator, again and again, rose to his feet, propelled by the terrible, impatient expectation of seeing the most dramatic thing that could happen: the scoring of a goal. The referee would shove the whistle into his mouth on the run, ready to recognize the first goal. . . . But Volodia would grab the ball, tearing it out of its line of flight, transgressing the laws of physics, for which the indignant elements tried to retaliate. Projected into the air with the ball, he would spin around on his own axis, exactly as if screwing himself into it. Then, having finally pulled it down, he would control it with his belly, his knees, his chin. Volodia would hurl his body on Getzke's low, bolt-like shots as one throws a wet rag on a flame to douse it. The speed of the intercepted ball sometimes tossed Volodia six feet or more to one side; he fell like a colored paper bomb. When the opposing forwards rushed him, the ball finished every time, at his fingertips, high above the melee.

During lulls when the game had left his immediate vicinity, Volodia could not stand still. He paced back and forth in a straight line from one goalpost to the other, unable to contain the overflowing energy released by his struggle with the ball. Inside him, everything was humming. He swung his arms, wriggled his shoulders, kicked at bits of turf on the sparse patch before his goal. So neat at the beginning of the game, he was now a bundle of rags, with bits of sunburnt body showing and big leather gloves on his hands. But these lulls never lasted long. The German attack would again roll toward the Soviet goal. Volodia terribly wanted to win and was wrapped up in every move his teammates made. He couldn't help feeling he alone knew how to play against Getzke, how to cope with his attacks, how to exploit his weaknesses. He was anxious to learn Getzke's opinion of Soviet technique. When a Soviet fullback succeeded in stopping a German attacker, Volodia longed to shout to Getzke: "Well, what do you think? Are we doing well?"

As a player, Volodia was just about as different from Getzke as could be. Volodia was a sportsman; Getzke a professional. Volodia was interested above all in the whole game, in victory for his side. Getzke was there to display his individual art. He was an old, experienced player, very little concerned with the honor of his team. His personal success was what mattered. He was not a permanent member of any organization, because he had kept changing clubs, lured by under-the-table deals; he had even lost his amateur status. He had been barred from the German national championships and was used only in exhibition games and on trips abroad.

A team on which Getzke played could always be dangerous, although he despised his teammates as much as his opponents. Knowing that he could score against any team, he cared about nothing else. Because of this he could not be a truly great athlete.

Even before half-time, the spectators realized the German team had nothing on the Russians; their attacking strategy was faulty. Getzke spoiled their combinations. He played only for himself, taking needless risks, hogging the ball, failing to launch an unguarded partner. When he had the ball he monopolized the game, tangling it up, making it lopsided, moving from one wing to the other according to his own private scheme, relying only on his speed and feinting ability.

As a result, the spectators felt the Germans would be completely routed in the second half, when Getzke had exhausted himself and the Russians had the wind in their backs. If only the Russians could hold out till then, without letting the ball into their net.

But Getzke, the virtuoso, did score. Ten minutes before
the intermission, he broke out to the right side of the field,
carried the ball as though it were glued to his foot, then
stopped abruptly so that the pursuit thundered past him.
Then, before they had time to stop, he darted toward the
center of the field and, having feinted a Soviet fullback in
his way, streaked toward the Soviet goal, looking now at
his feet and now at the posts, calculating the strength and
direction of his forthcoming shot.

An uninterrupted "oooooo" rolled down from the
stands.

Volodia, his feet and arms flung wide as though holding
an invisible barrel, was ready to dive at the ball. The other
kept coming without shooting. Volodia dived at Getzke's
feet. The ball was caught between the two of them like a
bird; whistling and stamping engulfed them. One of the
two must have pushed the ball into the air and Getzke,
suddenly soaring high after it, thrust it into the Russian net
with a single movement of his head, resembling a gracious
bow.

The Soviet team was one goal behind.

The stadium roared. Field glasses were trained on the
Soviet goalposts. Getzke, looking down at his flashing boots,
was gracefully trotting toward center field.

Volodia was being picked up by his teammates.

9

All heads turned in one direction, Valia's too, and
Kavalerov caught sight of her face. He was sure she had
seen him too. He shivered. His agitation increased when
he began to suspect people around him of noticing his
state and laughing at him. He began to stare at his neighbors, one by one. Suddenly, to his surprise, he recognized
Andrei Babichev in his row, not too far away. Once again,
Kavalerov became indignant at the large white hands holding the field glasses, the large torso stuffed into the gray
suit, the clipped mustache. . . . The straps of Babichev's

field glasses hung down from his cheeks, like fuses on a bomb.

Down in the field, the Germans were attacking again.

Suddenly the ball, propelled high into the air by a powerful and miscalculated kick, flew sideways in Kavalerov's direction, beyond the limits of the field, whistled past the ducked heads in the first rows of spectators, stopped for a split second in air, and then, all its leather sections spinning, collapsed at Kavalerov's feet. The game was interrupted. The players froze in their tracks, caught by the unexpected. The picture of the field, green with multicolored spots, a picture that had been moving all the time, now became immobile the way a film stops when the projector breaks down and the star remains motionless in a pose that only makes sense in rapid motion. Kavalerov's irritation increased. People were laughing. Somehow, people always laugh when the ball falls among the spectators. It is like a moment of truth, a temporary awakening. People suddenly realize the absurdity of adults chasing a ball for an hour and a half and forcing complete outsiders to react seriously and passionately to their completely unserious pursuit.

During those seconds, all the thousands present in the stadium did their best to bestow their unwanted attention upon Kavalerov, and their attention was of the laughing kind.

Possibly Valia too was laughing at him, at the man who happened to be where the ball fell. Possibly she doubly enjoyed laughing at an enemy who found himself in a ridiculous position. He grinned, moving his feet away from the ball. Having lost its support, it rolled under Kavalerov's heel with cat-like attachment.

"Well!" Babichev exclaimed with impatient surprise. Kavalerov remained completely passive. Somebody picked the ball up and handed it to Babichev. Babichev got up, straight and tall, pushed his belly out, holding the ball in both hands above his head, and swung back to throw it as far as possible. He could not be really serious about this business, but, thinking he ought to be, he overdid the gravity of his expression, frowned, and blew out his red, smooth lips. Then, with a strong forward swing, he threw the ball, and the field was magically freed from its fetters.

"He does not recognize me." Kavalerov's spite kept accumulating.

The first half ended with the Germans leading 1–0. The players, dark sweat running down their faces, green threads of grass sticking to their clothes, were walking toward the underground passage, raising their bare knees high, as though moving through water. The Germans, their faces outlandishly red from the temples down, had been shuffled with the Muscovites in a multicolored herd. As they walked, the players could see the spectators above the wall of the passage without being able to make out individual faces. They smiled vaguely toward the crowd. Their blank eyes seemed transparent in their darkened, sweaty faces. Those who, just a few moments back, had seen them as little, darting, falling, multicolored dolls now met them at close quarters. The still-warm noise of the game moved along with them. Getzke, looking like a gypsy, was sucking at a small, fresh scratch just above his elbow.

This close view revealed many new, unexpected details about the size of a player, his build, his scratches, his heavy breathing, and the disorder of his clothes. From afar he was a more ethereal, graceful sight. Kavalerov worked his way out, pushing at other people's ribs. He breathed with relief when his foot felt grass under it. He found himself in the shade behind the semicircle of the stands, amidst a throng of people, hurrying toward the refreshment kiosk on a lawn under the trees, which was rapidly becoming crowded. The old man in the battered cream-colored suit was eating ice cream, still throwing resentful, suspicious glances at those around him. A little further on, a crowd was besieging the locker rooms.

"Makarov! Makarov! Bravo!" they were shouting in exaltation. Fans were climbing over the fence, kicking the barbed wire away with their feet, like someone flicking off a bee. They were climbing to the tops of trees that swayed in the wind outside the enclosure, displaying the agility of forest sprites.

Then a body appeared above the crowd, exposed, naked patches flashing: Volodia Makarov was being carried on hundreds of shoulders.

Kavalerov did not have the courage to force his way into the triumphal ring around Makarov. He was content to peep through the cracks between bodies.

Volodia now stood on the ground. One of his woolen socks had slipped down and formed a doughnut around a pear-like calf lightly covered with hair. His torn shirt hardly clung to his body. His arms were modestly crossed on his chest.

Valia stands next to him. With her is Andrei Babichev. And around them idlers are clapping.

Babichev looks at Volodia, profound affection in his gaze.

Then the wind intruded. A striped awning collapsed. All the treetops swung far to the right. The ring of idlers dissolved. Pictures disintegrated. People ran to find shelter from the dust. Valia took the full force of the blast. The light dress, pink as a shell, flew up and Kavalerov saw how transparent it was. The wind blew the dress over Valia's face and Kavalerov saw it outlined in the pink, fanned-out material. . . . He saw it all through a cloud of dust. He saw Valia get caught and spun around and nearly fall to one side. She tried to catch the hem of her dress between her knees, to hold it down, but failed and decided to be content with half measures: she stopped and covered her unveiled thighs with her arms, like a bather surprised in the nude.

Far away, the referee's whistle sounded. A military band played a few bars of a march. The gay interlude was over. The second half was about to start. Volodia ran away.

"At least two goals for our side, right?" a schoolboy shouted, rushing past Kavalerov.

Valia was still struggling with the wind. In pursuit of the
hem of her dress, she had to change position at least ten
times. She finally found herself within whispering distance
of Kavalerov.

She stood with her legs spread apart. In one hand she
held her hat, caught in its flight after the wind blew it off.
Not yet recovered from her struggle, she looked straight at
Kavalerov without seeing him; her head, with its short
chestnut-colored bangs, bent slightly to one side.

Sunlight slipped down her shoulder; for five seconds,
her collarbones flashed like two daggers. Kavalerov grew
cold as he realized what an incurable nostalgia would remain in him forever. He knew he was watching a creature
from a different world, alien and puzzling; yet he felt how
hopelessly charming she looked, how oppressively unattain-
able she was because she was a little girl; because she
loved Volodia. He couldn't control himself though.

Babichev was waiting for her, his hand outstretched.

"Valia," Kavalerov said, "I have waited for you all my
life. Take pity on me. . . ."

But she did not hear. She ran, leaning against the wind.

10

Kavalerov came home drunk. On his way along the corridor, he stopped at the basin for a drink. He turned on
the tap full blast and got soaking wet. He left the tap on.
The jet of water produced a sound like a trumpet. As he
entered Annie's room, he stopped. The light was on. The
widow, surrounded by the cottony yellow light, sat on the
huge bed, her bare legs hanging down. She was ready for
the night.

Kavalerov took a step forward. She remained silent, as
if spellbound. Kavalerov fancied she was smiling, beckoning
to him.

He approached.

She did not think of resisting. In fact, she opened her
arms.

"You," she whispered, "you little piggy . . ."

Later, he kept waking up. He was tormented by thirst, by a drunken, maniacal longing for water. He kept waking up to find himself deep in silence. Just before he awoke, he remembered the jet of water splashing into the basin, and the memory would jolt him out of his dream. But there was no water, so down he went again. While he slept, the widow had been busy: she had shut the tap, undressed the sleeper, and mended his suspenders. The morning arrived. At first Kavalerov could make no sense of it. He lay there like a drunken beggar in a comedy, found by a millionaire and taken to his palace. The beggar lies there, dazzled by the luxury surrounding him. He saw an uncommon sight in a mirror: the soles of his feet close-up. Behind them he lay majestically, one arm folded under his head. The sun lighted him from one side. He appeared to be hung floating in the wide, smoky strips of light. Above him hung heavy clusters of grapes; cupids pranced, apples rolled out from horns of plenty. He could almost hear the hum of a solemn organ. He was lying in Annie's bed.

"You do remind me of him," Annie whispered ardently, leaning over him.

The glass-covered photograph hung over the bed. In it there was a man, somebody's youngish grandpa, in formal attire, one of the latest cutaways of a bygone era. One could feel he had a solid, many-barreled nape to his neck. A man of perhaps fifty-seven.

Kavalerov remembered his father changing shirts. . . .

"You do remind me a lot of my husband," Annie repeated, putting her arms round Kavalerov. His head began to sink into her armpit. The widow had opened the tents of her armpits. Joy and shame raged within her.

"He conquered me the same way . . . by cunning . . . he was always, always so quiet . . . he wouldn't say much . . . and then, suddenly! . . . Oh, you, my little piggy . . ."

Kavalerov hit her.

She was stunned. Kavalerov jumped off the bed, tearing

aside layers of sheets and eiderdowns. A sheet clung to him, followed him. She rushed toward the door, her hands and arms crying out for help. She was fleeing, pursued by lava like a Pompeian woman. A washbasket collapsed, a chair tilted over.

He hit her several times in the back, on her waistline encircled by its tire of fat.

The chair was standing on one foot.

"He used to beat me too," she said, smiling through her tears.

Kavalerov returned to the bed and fell on it, feeling ill. For a whole day, he lay unconscious. In the evening, the widow came and lay next to him. She snored. Kavalerov imagined the roof of her mouth as an arch leading into darkness. He hid in the recesses under the arch. Everything shook, knocked; the ground rocked. Kavalerov slipped and fell under the stream of air pouring in from the abyss. In her sleep she would moan, then stop suddenly after loudly smacking her lips. The architecture of her palate became twisted. Her snoring became powdery, then carbonated.

Kavalerov tossed in the bed and wept. She got up and put a cold towel on his forehead. His whole being groped toward the moist coolness: he raised himself, found the towel, squeezed it, put it under his cheek, kissed it.

"They have stolen her . . ." he whispered. "It's hard for me to live in this world. . . . It's terribly hard for me. . . ."

The widow was no sooner back in bed than she was asleep. Sleep smeared her all over with sweetness. She slept with her mouth open, little gurgling noises trickling out of it.

Bedbugs lived their lives. There was a rustling about, as though someone were stripping the wallpaper. The bedbugs revealed their secret recesses, never suspected by daylight. The wooden parts of Annie's bed grew and swelled.

The window sill began to turn pink.

The darkness was concentrated around the bed like heavy, black smoke. The mysteries of night came down from corners of the ceiling, crawling down the walls, slipping over the sleepers, finding final refuge under the bed.

Suddenly Kavalerov sat up, his eyes wide open. Ivan was standing over the bed.

11

Kavalerov began to get ready. Annie was asleep, lying on her side in a sitting position, her arms around her belly. Careful not to wake her up, he removed the blanket from the bed, put it around himself like a cloak, and stood facing Ivan.

"Very good," Ivan said, "your body is gleaming like a lizard's. This is how you will appear before the people. Come on, let's go, we must hurry."

"I am terribly sick," Kavalerov sighed. He was smiling meekly in apology for his reluctance to look for his pants, jacket, and shoes. "Does it matter very much if I go barefoot?"

Ivan was already in the corridor. Kavalerov hurried after him.

I have been suffering all this time for no reason, Kavalerov thought. At last, the day of redemption has come.

He was caught up in a human stream. Around the next corner, a sparkling road opened up.

"Here it is!" Ivan said, squeezing Kavalerov's hand. "This is the Quarter."

Kavalerov saw gardens, spherical cupolas of foliage, an arch of transparent stone, glass-covered porches, the flight of a ball above the green. . . .

"Here!" Ivan ordered.

They sprinted along the top of a creeper-covered wall. Then they had to jump. The blue blanket helped Kavalerov in his leap: he floated above the crowd and landed at the foot of a strikingly wide staircase. Immediately he became frightened and began to crawl away with his blanket over him, an insect crawling away with its wings folded. They did not notice him. He sat behind a column.

At the top of the stairs, surrounded by several people, stood Andrei Babichev. He had his arm around Volodia's shoulders.

"They'll bring her in right away," Andrei said, smiling to his friends.

Kavalerov saw a band marching along the asphalt driveway leading to the stairs. Valia was floating above it, held in the air by the music emerging from the instruments. The sounds were carrying her. She rose and dipped above the trumpets according to pitch and volume. Her hair flew above her head; her dress flapped like a sail.

The last musical phrase tossed her to the top of the stairs where she fell into Volodia's arms. Everyone stepped aside. The two of them remained there, alone at the center.

Kavalerov did not see what came next. He was seized by sudden panic. A strange shadow suddenly slipped down close to him. Overcoming his paralysis, he turned toward it. On the grass, a step away, sat Ophelia.

"Ah-ah-ah-ah-ah-ah!" He howled and dashed off. Ophelia emitted a tinkling sound and grabbed him by the blanket, which slipped from his body. In this shameful state, stumbling, falling, banging his chin against the stone steps, Kavalerov climbed the stairs. The group at the top looked down at him. Valia stood there radiant, bending forward.

"Back, Ophelia, back!" he heard Ivan's voice. "Oh, she won't listen to me. . . . Ophelia, stop it, stop it. . . ."

"Hold her!"

"She'll kill him!"

"Oh!"

"Look! Look! Look!"

Halfway up the stairs, Kavalerov looked back. Ivan was trying to climb the wall. The creeper was falling away in his hands. The crowd drew back. Ivan was hanging on the wall, gripping it with spreadeagled hands. The awesome metal object was slowly moving toward him over the grass. A shiny needle slowly emerged from the part that may be described as its head. Ivan was whimpering. His hold was weakening; he let go. His bowler fell off his head and rolled among the dandelion clocks. He sat down, back to the wall, covering his face with his hands. The machine slowly approached, uprooting dandelions on its way.

Kavalerov rose and shouted in a voice full of despair:

"Save him! Is it possible you'll stand by and watch a machine kill a man?"

No answer.

"My place is next to him," Kavalerov said. "Teacher, I'll die at your side."

But it was too late. Ivan's rabbit-like squeal knocked Kavalerov off his feet. Falling, he saw Ivan pinned to the wall like a butterfly.

Ivan was slightly bent forward, turning on the gruesome axis of the pin.

Kavalerov buried his head in his arms to avoid seeing or hearing anything. Nevertheless he could still hear a slight tinkling behind him. The machine was coming up the stairs.

"No! No!" he hollered as loud as he could. "She'll kill me! Forgive me! Have pity on me. It was not I who tried to discredit machines. No, not I. I am innocent. Valia, Valia, save me!"

12

Kavalerov was ill for three days and nights. When he felt better, he ran away.

He got out of bed, keeping his eyes fixed on one single point: the corner under the bed. He was dressing automatically when he discovered a new leather strap with a button-hole, instead of the safety pin, on his suspenders. Annie had sewn it on for him. Where had she got it? Had she torn it off her husband's old suspenders? Kavalerov felt disgusted with what he had become. He dashed off down the corridor without his jacket. On his way, he took off his red suspenders and threw them away.

He paused before stepping outside. There were none of the usual voices floating in from the courtyard. When he passed the dividing line and went out, all his thoughts became confused. He felt the sweetest sensations—languor and joy. The morning was a delight. The breeze was as light as though caused by turning pages in a book; the sky was azure. Kavalerov stood by a filthy spot. A cat he had scared rushed out of a garbage can dragging some horrible things in its wake. What poetry could there be in this alley buried under several layers of curses and filth? Nevertheless, he stood there, head thrown back, arms outstretched.

At that second he felt the time had come, a line had been drawn between the two ways of life; it was a cataclysm. To break, to break with all that used to be, to do it now, immediately, in a couple of heartbeats; to cross the line and leave the repulsive, ugly life behind, not his, the other one. . . .

He stood with his eyes wide open and, perhaps because he was out of breath from the running and the excitement and because he was still weak, his entire field of vision turned reddish and pulsated.

He realized the extent of his degradation. It had been inevitable. His life had been too irresponsible, too self-centered; he had overestimated his own importance, his lazy, unclean, whimsical self. . . .

Kavalerov understood everything, looking down on the alley. . . .

He retraced his steps, picked up his suspenders, finished dressing himself. A spoon clinked against a plate: the widow beckoned to him. But without looking back he left the house. He spent the night in the square and again came back, having, however, firmly resolved:

I'll put the widow in her place. I won't even allow her to hint at what happened between us. All kinds of things happen to people when they are drunk. But I can't go on living in the street.

The widow was lighting the stove. She glanced at him from beneath her temple and smiled conceitedly. He stepped into the room. Ivan's bowler was hanging on a corner of the chest of drawers.

Ivan was sitting on the bed, looking like a reduced version of his brother. A blanket enveloped him like a cloud. A bottle stood on the table. Ivan was sipping red wine from a glass. Apparently he had only recently awakened: his face had not yet had time to settle back into its mold, and he was still scratching some part of himself under the blanket.

Kavalerov asked the classic question:

"What does this mean?"

Ivan smiled brightly.

"This means, my friend, we must have a drink. Annie, give us another glass!"

Annie came in and opened the cupboard.

"Don't be jealous, Nicky," she said, giving Kavalerov a big hug. "He is so lonely. Just like you. I am sorry for both of you."

"What does this mean?" Kavalerov asked quietly.

"Well, what do you keep repeating that for?" Ivan said impatiently. "It means nothing, that's what."

He climbed down from the huge bed. Holding the bottom of the bottle in his palm, he poured some wine into Kavalerov's glass.

"Let's drink, Kavalerov. We used to talk so much about feelings. But we forgot the main one: indifference. I believe indifference is man's best state. What do you say? Let's be indifferent, then, Kavalerov. Look around you: it is peace we have found here, my friend. Drink it down then. To indifference. To Annie! Fine. And now, Kavalerov, here's a piece of good news for you. Tonight, it is your turn to sleep with Annie. Cheers!"

(1927)

THE CHAIN

A college student called Seva Orlov was an admirer of my sister Vera.

He came to our summer house on his bicycle. The bicycle stood by a flower bed, leaning against the veranda. It was a horned bicycle.

Orlov removed his flashing trouser clips that were something like spurs without a jingle from his ankles and tossed them onto the wooden garden table. Then he removed his college cap with its sky-blue visor and wiped his brow with a handkerchief. His face was brown, his forehead white, his head crew-cut, rainbow-colored, and with a lump on it. He didn't see me. I saw everything. He didn't say a word to me.

The wooden table was warped. A vase of flowers stood on it. Orlov blew at the flowers and the flowers turned away. Orlov looked into the distance where he could see the blue rim of the sea.

"Bleriot has flown across the Channel," I said.

I was still at an age when a person has to swallow some saliva before saying something.

"That's right, he has," the college student said.

Then there was silence again.

I have no right to participate in world events. I even feel a bit guilty about expressing myself so cleverly: "Bleriot, the Channel . . ."

Orlov pulls a flower out of the vase. It has two open blossoms and one bud on it. Orlov bites the bud off. The bud is tight, shiny, and cylindrical. It resembles a bullet. Orlov sucks in his cheeks and shoots the bud out. It hits the bicycle—the spoke of a wheel. The wheel makes a sound like a harp.

"Do airplanes have bicycle wheels?" I ask.

I know very well that planes have bicycle wheels. But still, I have the impression that this college student is stupid. I feel quite sure that I am better informed about aviation than he is. But I am embarrassed to admit it and so give the college student a chance to appear better informed.

"Right," he says, "they have bicycle wheels."

There's a triangle situation here: the bicycle, the student, and me.

I blush. I'd like to talk about the bicycle all the time. But I feel it would be a shameful thing to do and my face gets redder and redder. Orlov is stupid as a log. I know it. I can see right through him.

"Your friend Seva is a goose," Daddy said to Vera.

And it's true—Seva Orlov is a goose. But I can do nothing about it—he owns the bicycle. So I show off, I flatter him. When he's around I feel as if I'm running a temperature.

What I'd like to say to him is this:

"Mr. Orlov, please allow me to take a little ride on your bicycle. I won't go far. I'll just ride down the garden path. At the end of it, at the gate, I'll turn around. It's very smooth there. I'll be very careful. Or I don't even have to go all the way to the gate. It'd be nice just to ride down the path here."

That's what I long to say to him. Even my eyebrows rise in my shame. Leaning with my elbow on the table, I use my fingers to pull down my eyebrow.

Yesterday, he let me take a ride. I can't ask him too often. I'd better wait till tomorrow. Or even better the day after.

I look at the bike. Any moment Orlov may catch me looking at it. If he does, I'll raise my eyes a tiny bit and then they'll be looking at the vine on the wall just above it. There's a cat hanging in it. A small white Siberian cat, fluffy (oh, almost feathery!), a wayward descendant of a famous line, is hanging there amidst complete silence.

The college student catches sight of the cat.

"Ah, you louse!" Orlov said. "What does she think she's doing eating grapes!"

Cats never eat grapes. And anyway, they're wild grapes. But he gets up and I'm not about to speak up for the cat. On the contrary, I start leaping up and down. Orlov grabs the cat, pulls her out of the vine, and tosses her away.

Orlov strolls off into the garden. Any moment now Vera will be back from the beach. Here she is. I can see her behind the wire fence, speeding up when she sees her goose. She's running. Ah, they've come together. She's folding her pink parasol.

Orlov had said:
"All right, go ahead."

I open the saddlebag, pull a wrench out of it, loosen a nut, and lower the saddle. Ah, the lovely coolness of the fiber grips on the handlebars! I roll the bike down the steps into the garden. It skips and jingles. It nods with its light. Once down below, I turn it around and as I do so I see the green lettering of the make flash on the front of the frame. Another movement and the lettering vanishes like a lizard.

I am riding.

The gravel scrunches. From above I watch the tire of the front wheel turning and turning. The garden gate! It tries to slip under my armpit like a crutch as I pass through it. . . . Some bolt on the ground looks hairy with rust. . . . This is how the journey begins!

My course seems to follow the bisector between the rapidly narrowing arms of an angle.

Some bug gets into my eye. Oh, why did that have to happen to me? The space over which I'm moving is immense and my speed is so great that it would seem quite impossible. . . . Yes, what chances are there for two completely unrelated courses—mine and the insect's—to collide precisely in my eye!

My field of vision becomes bitter. I close my eye, screw-ing it up so hard that my eyebrow brushes against my cheek. I cannot let go the handlebars. I'm trying to raise my eyelid which is trembling. . . . I apply the brakes, get off. The machine lies on its side. The wheel is still turning. I open my eye with my fingers. My pupil is turned down and I see the red plush of the lower lid.

How come an insect dies immediately when it gets in my eye? Can it be that I secrete some poisonous stuff?

I'm rolling again.

A bird takes off from right under my wheel. At the very last split second. It isn't afraid. It's a little bird. As to the pigeon, it doesn't even bother to get out of my way. It doesn't even look at me, the bicycle rider.

The motion of the bike is accompanied by the sound of frying. Every now and then it lets out a crack a bit like a firecracker. But it doesn't matter. It's a detail for which I could think of hundreds of reasons. It's no stranger than that some cows seem to have a sort of framework inside them which stretches their sides and makes them look like tents. Or that other cows should wear white suede masks. What does matter is that I have lost my bicycle chain. Without it, it is impossible to ride a bicycle. The chain slipped off as I was going full speed and I noticed too late that I didn't have it.

It is lying somewhere on the road. I must go back and pick it up. It's not so terrible, really. I walk back leading the bike, holding it by its fiber grip. The pedal pokes me behind my knee. I see three boys, three boys I've never seen before running along the edge of the gully. They're receding, gilded by the sun. A blissful weakness spreads somewhere under my stomach. I grasp the situation: the boys have found the chain. They're waifs and now they're already merging into the background of the landscape.

This is how the catastrophe occurred.

And I imagine the following scene:

I return to our summer house as if nothing had hap-pened. I roll the incapacitated bicycle up to the edge of the

veranda and lean it against the wall there. They're having
tea: Father, Mother, Vera, and Orlov. They've been served
a plum tart with their tea—a flat, purple circle. I sit down
at the table. I'm facing Orlov. The situation can be described thus: Orlov had a bicycle and I damaged it. I
could make it stronger: Orlov had a wife and I poked out
one of her eyes. Evening arrives. This is the way I imagine
it: evening comes down, a lamp is brought out onto the
veranda; a moonlit path appears on Mother's bosom, on the
artificial jet.

Orlov stands up and announces:

"I suppose I ought to be on my way."

He walks toward his bicycle.

The silence of the grave follows.

No, not really a silence. . . . Actually, Vera is saying
something and Mother's saying something too. The silence
is in me. Orlov leans over the bicycle and I feel that his
head is about to turn in my direction—and already the silence is stretching between him and me.

"Where's the chain?" he asks.

"What chain?" I ask.

"What do you mean 'what chain'?"

"Which one?"

"Have you lost it?"

"There was no chain," I say. "I rode without any chain.
Why, do you mean there was a chain?"

"He's gone mad," Father declares. "Look, he's sitting
there with his tongue hanging out."

Silence. I sit there with my tongue hanging out.

This is how I imagine the scene. I cannot possibly get
out of trouble by legitimate means. There's only one way
left—to break the law. Then I decide to act as I act in my
dreams. And from somewhere deep inside me comes the
recollection of an occasionally recurring dream in which
I kill Mother. I get up. Vera covers her face with her
hands. Mother seems to sag, becomes fatter, loses her neck.

This is how I imagine what would happen if I went back
home.

I cannot go back home. They'd discover it right away.

I go to the Gurfinkels' summer place. Grisha Gurfinkel is a boy from my class and he'll help me. I'll go there and cry, and Dr. Gurfinkel, who is a famous surgeon, will be very sorry for me. I'm an anemic boy and I'll cry and sob before the famous doctor. After all, how much can a bicycle chain cost? They'll give me however much it may be and we'll buy a new chain.

So I went there, rolling along next to me someone else's wife with a gouged-out eye. We kept looking back to see whether we were being pursued.

But the Gurfinkels were not in their summer house. They had left for Chabot to take the grape cure. So I go further. A crowd has gathered by a soda fountain. And I hear the name Utochkin flying from mouth to mouth.

An automobile is standing there, a terrifying automobile. I saw it once before as it dashed down Langeron Street, spitting smoke and sounding like a cannonade, not rolling along like other cars but advancing in a succession of leaps.

The car stands there, and its engine has no hood on it. It is dirty, glistening with oil, dripping, with something hissing inside it.

Utochkin is drinking a soda at the counter. The people gathered around the soda fountain keep talking about the great racing driver Utochkin. Some refer to him affectionately as "Red." I hear someone say that he stammers.

The crowd splits up as the great racing driver steps out. He is hatless and his hair is red. He is accompanied by some people, also red-haired. He walks ahead. On the race-track he has come in front of Peterson and Bader.

Utochkin is supposed to be an eccentric and people somehow tend to laugh when they are around him. I don't quite understand why. He was one of the first to take up the bicycle, the motorcycle, and the automobile, and was one of the first to fly. People laughed. He crashed during the Petersburg–Moscow flight, smashed his aircraft, and got hurt. They laughed. He was a champion, but in Odessa people looked upon him as the city's madman.

I looked at Utochkin.

He is wearing something baggy, stained, shiny, cut open at the top. He has finished a creamy cake. His hands are in leather gauntlets. The cake crumbles over his gloves like lilac. There are also scattered lilac flowers on his lips and on one of his cheeks. They start the engine which begins to fire like a cannon. The whole countryside shakes; a whirl starts. I fall over along with the bicycle. I clutch at the spokes. The car reminds me of some letter lying on its back, maybe an *E*, maybe an *F*.

Utochkin comes over and picks me up.

Amidst all that havoc, a touching scene takes place. I grab his hand in its stiff leather glove and I tell him what has happened to me—about the college student, about the bicycle, about the castastrophe. . . .

The bicycle is placed behind and across the automobile. The infernal machine is thus given a transparent decoration. Five people, including myself, install themselves in the belly of the letter *B*. Oh, what an engineering fairy tale! I don't know, I don't remember anything now! Still I do remember one thing, but only that: all the dogs stood up on their hind legs as we roared past them.

Of course I won't die. I'll live on and on, even after this day, and tomorrow, and for a long, long time to come. Nothing will change. I'll still be a small boy and there'll be Seva Orlov, and the tragedy with the bicycle chain can't end easily and painlessly. But right now . . . Now, I'm arrogant, I'm scornful and cruel. Where am I flying to? I'm flying to punish Mother, Father, Vera, and Orlov. . . . If I saw them dying, right now, in front of my very eyes, I'd nudge Utochkin and say, laughing:

"Look there, Utochkin . . . ha-ha-ha! They're dying. . . . And we're all black, sitting in this automobile. . . . What was it that said 'Love, obedience, mercy'? We don't know, we don't care—we have black silk hats, gasoline, headlights—we are men. And here comes the great man Utochkin, coming to punish my father!"

We drive up to our garden gate and stop. I used to be

so meek, so obedient: I used to ask and sometimes I was given permission. That was an hour ago. And now suddenly I reappear wrapped in thunder and lightning and in the company of a magician. I am bold and untamable!

"You m-mustn't b-be s-s-so n-nasty t-to th-the k-kid," Utochkin said to Orlov, frowning and stammering. "G-give 'im back his ch-chain."

But it all ended with the automobile leaping away from our gate and with Orlov shouting after the departing storm:

"The pig! The bully! The madman!"

This is a story about a day long past.

My great dream was to have a bicycle. And now I'm a grownup and this grownup says to me, the schoolboy:

"Well then, go ahead and demand things now! Now I can stand up for you. Just speak up—say what your secret wishes are."

But no one answers me.

Then I say again:

"Look at me: I haven't gone that far away from you. And yet, look, I'm already all soggy and stuffed. You were born with the century. Remember? When Bleriot crossed the Channel. Now, I've fallen behind. Look how far I've fallen behind. I'm puffing along—a fat little man on short legs. . . . See how difficult it is for me to keep up, but I go on trotting. I'm out of breath, my feet sink in the mud, but I still run after the roaring storm of the century!"

(1929)

LOVE

Shuvalov was waiting for Lola in the park. It was noon and it was hot. A lizard appeared on a rock. Shuvalov thought: on that stone the lizard can be spotted easily. Mimicry, he thought. Mimicry brought chameleon to mind.

"Here we go," Shuvalov said. "That's all I needed, a chameleon."

The lizard scuttled away.

Angry, Shuvalov got up from the seat and walked rapidly down the path. He was offended, felt like rebelling against something. He stopped and said quite loudly:

"To hell with it! Why should I be thinking about mimicry and chameleons? Thoughts like that are completely useless to me."

He emerged from under the trees into a clearing and sat down on a tree stump. Insects were flying about. Stalks quivered. The architecture of the flight of birds, flies, ladybugs was transparent, but it was possible to discern some dotted outline: arches, bridges, towers, terraces, constantly expanding and contracting, forming the skyline of a city distorting itself; elastic castles-in-the-air.

I am being subjected to outside influences, Shuvalov thought. The field of my attention is being polluted. I am beginning to see things that don't exist.

Lola was late. His wait in the park was a long one. He walked up and down, compelled to become convinced of the existence of many species of insect. A bug was crawling up a stalk. He picked it up and put it in the palm of his hand. Its belly glittered. He became angry. "To hell with it, half an hour more and I'll be a naturalist."

Stalks, leaves, tree trunks—quite a variety. Some blades of grass were jointed like bamboo; he was struck by the variety of colors in what is called turf; the different colors in the soil itself came as a complete surprise.

"I don't want to be a naturalist," he begged. "I have no use for these haphazard observations."

Still there was no Lola in sight. He had already drawn statistical conclusions, had classified his data. He could affirm that, in the park, trees with wide trunks prevailed, their leaves shaped like playing-card clubs. He could recognize different insects by their buzzes. Against his will, his mind was filled with things of no interest to him.

And still no Lola. He was sad and angry. Instead of Lola, an unknown citizen appeared, wearing a black felt hat. He sat down on the green bench next to Shuvalov, drooping slightly forward, one white hand on each knee. He was young and quiet. Later it turned out that he suffered from color blindness. They got into a conversation.

"I envy you," the young man said. "They tell me that leaves are green. I've never seen green leaves. I am forced to eat blue pears."

"Blue is inedible," Shuvalov said. "A blue pear would make me vomit."

"I eat blue pears," the color-blind man said sadly.

Shuvalov started.

"Tell me," he said, "have you ever noticed that when there are birds flying around you, they create a city of imaginary lines?"

"Never noticed."

"So would you say your senses convey a correct picture of the world to you?"

"The whole world except for certain color details."

The color-blind man turned his pale face toward Shuvalov.

"You in love?" he asked.

"I'm in love," Shuvalov answered honestly.

"You see, in my case, there is only a certain confusion of colors. For the rest, everything is fine."

The young man made a condescending gesture.

"Still, blue pears are no joke," Shuvalov snorted.

Lola appeared, still far away. Shuvalov jumped up. The color-blind man got up, raised his black hat, and started to walk away.

"Aren't you a violinist?" Shuvalov shouted after him.

"You're seeing things that don't exist."

Shuvalov shouted aggressively: "But you look like a violinist!"

The color-blind man continued walking. He said something that sounded to Shuvalov like:

"You're on a dangerous path."

Lola was approaching rapidly. Shuvalov got up and took a few steps. The branches swayed with their club-shaped leaves. Shuvalov stood in the middle of a walk. The trees rustled. Lola was approaching, welcomed by this ovation from the foliage. The color-blind man, following a path that curved to the right, thought:

Why, it's windy!

He looked up at the foliage, behaving as would any foliage disturbed by the wind. The color-blind man saw swaying blue treetops. Shuvalov saw green treetops. But then he came to an unnatural conclusion: "The trees are greeting Lola with an ovation." The color-blind man was wrong; Shuvalov was even more wrong.

"I am seeing things that don't exist," Shuvalov repeated.

Lola came up to him. In one hand she had a bag of apricots. She held out the other to him. The world suddenly changed.

"Why are you screwing up your face?" she asked.

"It's as if I were wearing glasses."

Lola took an apricot out of the bag, pulled apart its tiny buttocks, extracted the stone, and threw it away. The stone fell into the grass. Frightened, Shuvalov looked back, and saw a tree had appeared at the spot where the stone had fallen; a slender, bright little tree, an enchanted umbrella. Then Shuvalov told Lola:

"There's some kind of nonsense going on. I'm beginning

to think in images. I'm no longer bound by laws. In five years, an apricot tree may grow in that spot. Very possible. That won't go against science. But now, against all natural laws, I have just seen the tree, five years early. Nonsense. I am becoming an idealist."

"It comes from love," said Lola, bleeding apricot juice profusely.

She was leaning against the pillows waiting for him. The bed was wedged into a corner of the room. The coronets on the wallpaper were gold and shiny. He came up to her and she put her arms around him. She was so young, so light that, scantily clad in a skimpy nightdress, she seemed unbelievably naked. Their first embrace was a stormy one. The little medallion she had had since girlhood flew from her breast and got caught in her hair like a canary. Shuvalov lowered his face to hers, which sank into the pillow like the face of someone dying. The light was on.

"I'll turn it off," Lola said.

Shuvalov lay under the wall. The corner had advanced. He moved his finger over the pattern on the wallpaper. It had a double existence: the usual one, the daytime one, ordinary coronets with nothing remarkable about them; and a nighttime one that only revealed itself to him five minutes before he plunged into sleep. Suddenly, a part of the pattern came close enough to touch his eyeballs, was magnified to show previously unseen details, altered its appearance. On the threshold of sleep, close to childhood's sensations, he did not resist the transformation of familiar and lawful forms. The transformation was touching: instead of rings and spirals he discerned a she-goat and a chef in his white cap. . . .

"And that is a violin key," Lola said, understanding him.

"And the chameleon . . ." he said, already asleep.

He awoke early in the morning. Very early. He woke up, looked around him, and let out a shout. A blissful exclamation. That night the transformation of the world,

begun the day they met, had been completed. He awoke
on a new earth. The brilliance of the morning filled the
room. He saw the window and, on the sill, pots of multicolored flowers. Lola was sleeping with her back to him.
She was rolled up in a ball, back rounded, spine showing
under the skin like a slender reed. A fishing rod, Shuvalov
thought, a reed. On this new earth everything was touching
and funny. Voices flew in through the open window. Some
people outside were discussing the flowers on the window
sill.

He got up and dressed, making an effort to remain on
the earth. The earth had lost its gravity. He had not yet
mastered the laws of this new universe and therefore had
to be careful; he was afraid to cause an explosive effect
through some little carelessness. It was even risky to think,
to recognize the things around him. What if, during the
night, he had been given the power to materialize his
thought? He had reason to suspect it: buttons buttoned
themselves; when he had to wet his brush to freshen his
hair, he heard the sound of falling droplets. He turned his
head. On the wall, under the sun's rays, hung Lola's dresses,
iridescent as soap bubbles.

"Here I am," the tap's voice informed him.

Under the multicolored dresses, he found the sink and
the tap and a piece of pink soap. Now Shuvalov was afraid
to think of something fearful. A tiger entered the room, he
was about to think, but managed to distract himself. Nevertheless, full of terror, he glanced at the door. The materiali-
zation had taken place, but the thought had not been fully
formulated. Its effect was reduced, only approximate: a
wasp flew in at the window. It was striped and bloodthirsty.

"Lola! A tiger!" Shuvalov hollered.

Lola woke up. The wasp suspended itself over a plate,
humming like a gyroscope. Lola jumped off the bed. The
wasp flew toward her. Lola waved her arms. The wasp
and her medallion circled around her. Shuvalov stopped
the medallion with his hand. They ambushed the wasp.
Lola covered the wasp with her crackling straw hat.

They took leave of each other standing in the draft, which in this world seemed to be very active and many-voiced. The draft opened the doors downstairs. It sang like a cleaning woman. It made an eddy in Lola's hair, picked up Lola's hat, released the wasp, and blew it into the salad. It was whistling. It picked up Lola's nightdress and stood it up.

They parted; his happiness prevented him from feeling the steps. Shuvalov got downstairs and went outside. He did not feel the sidewalk, and discovered it was no illusion: he was actually floating in the air, flying.

"Flying on the wings of love," somebody said inside a window as he passed. He soared. His shirt turned into a crinoline. His upper lip throbbed. He was flying along snapping his fingers.

At two in the afternoon he went to the park. Exhausted by love and happiness he fell asleep on a green bench. He slept, his collarbones prominent under his open shirt.

A man wearing heavy blue glasses, a black hat, and a coat reminiscent of a cassock, was walking up the path slowly, ponderously. His hands were joined under his posterior; he kept raising and lowering his head.

He came and sat on the bench next to Shuvalov.

"I am Isaac Newton," he introduced himself, lifting his black hat slightly. Through his glasses he scrutinized his blue, photographic world.

"Hello," Shuvalov said.

The great physicist sat stiffly, on the alert, ready to leap up in one motion. He listened, ears jerking; the index finger of his left hand pointed upward, as though demanding the attention of an invisible choir which was ready to burst into a hymn on signal. All around, plant and beast were still. Shuvalov slipped behind the bench and hid there. Newton was listening to the silence of the elements. Far away, above the cupolas of leaves, a star became discernible; it grew cooler.

"Listen, listen," Newton suddenly said. "Can you hear?"

Without turning his head, Newton caught Shuvalov by
his shirttail and forced him out of his refuge.

They walked across the grass. The physicist's ample shoes
trod softly, leaving white footprints behind them. A lizard
slithered ahead of them, often glancing back. They went
through a thicket; the metal frame of the great man's
glasses was adorned with fluff and ladybugs. In the clearing,
Shuvalov recognized the sapling that had appeared yesterday.

"Apricots?" he asked.

"Of course not," Newton answered with irritation. "It's
an apple tree."

The frame of the apple tree, square, light, and fragile,
like the frame of a dirigible, showed through its scanty
cover of leaves. Everything was still and quiet.

"Here," Newton said. He bent down and his voice came
out like a bark. "Here!" He held out an apple. "What does
this mean?"

It was easy to see he was not in the habit of bending.
When he had straightened up again, he pushed his shoulders back several times, to relax the old bamboo rod of his
spine. The apple was resting on a support formed by three
of his fingers.

"What does this mean?" he repeated. His snorts muffled
his voice. "Wouldn't you care to explain why this apple
has fallen?"

Shuvalov stared at the apple the way William Tell must
have done.

"The law of gravity . . ." he muttered.

Then, after a pause, the physicist said:

"If I am not mistaken, you have been flying today, young
man?"

He asked the question like an examining magistrate. His
eyebrows shot high above his eyes.

A ladybug crawled from Newton's finger onto the apple.
He followed it, eyes squinting. The ladybug looked blind-
ingly blue to him. He screwed up his nose. Then she took
off from the very highest point of the apple, using a pair

of wings which she took out from somewhere behind her back, as one might take a handkerchief out from underneath the tails of a frock coat.

"You have been flying today, haven't you?"

Shuvalov said nothing.

"Pig," Isaac Newton said.

"Pig." Lola was standing over him. "Pig, you fall asleep waiting for me."

She picked the ladybug off his forehead, smiling when she realized the insect had a metal belly.

"Hell," Shuvalov said, "I hate you. Once I used to know that was a ladybug and nothing more. Perhaps I could make a few conjectures about the origin of its name, conceivably religious. But now, since I have met you, something has happened to my eyes. I see blue pears; I note the resemblance between a toadstool and a ladybug."

She wanted to put her arms around his neck.

"Leave me alone!" he shouted. "I've had enough of it! I am ashamed of myself."

Shouting these words, he galloped away like a deer. Snorting, bounding along wildly, he ran, pushing himself off from his own shadow, his eyes squinting. He stopped, out of breath. Lola had vanished. He decided to forget everything. The lost universe had to be recovered.

"Good-by," he said, "we won't see one another again."

He sat on the slope of a hill from which he had a view of a wide space sown with summerhouses. He was sitting on the crest of a prism, feet resting on a sloping plane. Below him the umbrella of an ice-cream cart was turning. The outfit of the ice-cream vendor reminded him of an African native village.

"I am living in paradise," the young Marxist said in a broken voice.

"Are you a Marxist?" Shuvalov heard a voice next to him.

It was the color-blind young man in the black hat. He was sitting next to Shuvalov.

"Yes," Shuvalov said.

"Then you cannot live in paradise."

The color-blind man was playing with a twig. Shuvalov sighed.

"I cannot help it. The earth has become a paradise."

The young man was whistling softly. He scratched his ear with the twig.

"Do you know how far I went today?" Shuvalov continued in a complaining, whining tone. "I flew today."

A skate was stuck on the sky. Not quite straight, like a postage stamp.

"Shall I demonstrate to you? Shall I fly up there?" Shuvalov pointed to the skate.

"No thanks, I don't wish to witness your degradation."

Shuvalov said, "Yes, it is terrible." He remained silent for a moment and repeated: "I know, it's terrible." Then he added suddenly: "I envy you."

"Do you really?"

"I give you my word. It is so wonderful to understand the world correctly and be confused only about a few details of color. You do not have to live in paradise. The world has not disappeared for you. Everything is in place. And me . . . Just think, I am completely healthy, I am a materialist . . . then, suddenly, before my eyes, occurs a criminal, antiscientific perversion of elements, of matter. . . ."

"Yes, it is terrible," the color-blind man said, "and it all comes from love."

"Listen to me!" With sudden heat, Shuvalov grabbed his neighbor by the arm. "I agree. Give me your cornea and take my love in exchange."

The young man began sliding down the slope.

"Forgive me, I'm in a hurry. Have a good time in your paradise."

It was difficult for him to move down the slope. He pressed his body close to the soil, losing his resemblance to a man, beginning to look like a man's reflection in water. Finally he reached the flat surface, straightened himself up, and walked off chirpily. Then he threw his twig up in the air, blew Shuvalov a kiss, and shouted:

"Give my best to Eve!"

Lola was still asleep. One hour after his meeting with the color-blind young man, he found her in the heart of the park. Since he was no naturalist, he could not determine what surrounded her, whether it was hazel, hawthorn, elder bushes, or wild roses. From every side, branches and bushes pressed in on him. He walked like a merchant with baskets on the upturned palms of his hands, baskets loaded with the light tangle of vegetation. He kept discarding these imaginary baskets; berries, petals, thorns, birds, and eggs were scattered around him.

Lola lay on her back, her pink dress open at the breast; he heard the crackling of membranes inside her nose swollen by sleep. He sat down next to her.

Then he put his head on her breast. His fingers felt the thin cotton, his head lay on her sweaty breast, he could see a pink nipple, with wrinkles as delicate as those of the skin on boiled milk. He heard a crackling, the sigh and breaking of dry branches.

The color-blind man stood behind the leaves of a bush. The bush was in his way.

"Look here," he said.

Shuvalov raised his head. One of his cheeks felt warm.

"Will you stop following me about like a dog?" he said.

"Listen, I am willing now. . . . Help yourself to my cornea and give me your love. . . ."

"Go and eat your blue pears," Shuvalov said.

(1928)

LYOMPA

Young Alexander was planing wood in the kitchen. The cuts on his fingers were covered with golden, appetizing scabs.

The kitchen gave onto the courtyard. It was spring and the doors were always open. There was grass growing near the entrance. Water poured from a pail glistened on the stone slabs. A rat appeared in the garbage can. Finely sliced potatoes were frying in the kitchen. The primus stoves were burning; their life began in a burst of splendor when the orange flame shot ceiling-high. It ended in a quiet blue flame. Eggs jumped around in boiling water. One of the tenants was cooking crabs. With two fingers, he picked up a live crab by the waist. The crabs were greenish, the color of the waterpipes. Two or three drops suddenly shot out of the tap. The tap was discreetly blowing its nose. Then, upstairs somewhere, pipes began talking in a variety of voices. The dusk was becoming perceptible. One glass continued to glisten on the window sill, as it received the last rays of the setting sun. The taps chattered. All sorts of moving and knocking started up around the stove.

The dusk was magnificent. People were eating peanuts. There was singing. The yellow light from the rooms fell on the dark sidewalk. The grocery store was brightly lit.

In the room next to the kitchen lay Ponomarev, critically ill. He lay in his room alone. There was a candle burning; a medicine bottle with a prescription attached to it stood on a table at his head.

When people came to see Ponomarev, he said to them: "You can congratulate me: I'm dying."

In the evening he became delirious. The bottle was staring at him. The prescription was like the train of a wedding dress, the bottle a princess on her wedding day. The bottle had a long name. He wanted to write a treatise. He was talking to his blanket.

"You ought to be ashamed of yourself. . . ."

The blanket sat next to him, lay next to him, told him the latest news.

There were only a few things around the sick man: the medicine, the spoon, the light, the wallpaper. The other things had left. When he found he was critically ill and about to die, he realized how huge and varied was the world of things and how few were the things that remained to him. Every day fewer of these things were left. A familiar object like a railroad ticket was already irretrievably remote. First, the number of things on the periphery, far away from him, decreased; then this depletion drew closer to the center, reaching deeper and deeper, toward the courtyard, the house, the corridor, the room, his heart.

At first, the disappearance of things did not particularly sadden the sick man.

The countries had gone: America; then the possibilities: being handsome, rich, having a family (he was single). . . . Actually, his sickness was unrelated to their disappearance. They had slipped away as he had grown older. But he was really hurt to realize that even the things moving parallel with his course were growing more remote. In a single day he was abandoned by the street, his job, the mail, horses. Then the disappearances began to occur at a mad rate, right there, alongside him: already the corridor had slipped out of reach and, in his very room, his coat, the door key, his shoes had lost all significance. Death was destroying things on its way to him. Death had left him only a few things, from an infinite number; things he would never have permitted in his house by choice. He had things forced on him. He had the frightening visits and looks of people he knew. He saw he had no chance of defending himself from the intrusion of these unsolicited and, to him, useless things. But now they were compulsory, the only ones. He had lost the right to choose.

Young Alexander was making a model plane.

The boy was much more serious and complex than people imagined. He kept cutting his fingers, bleeding, littering the floor with his shavings, leaving dirty marks with his glue, scrounging bits of silk, crying, being pushed around. The grownups considered themselves absolutely right, although the boy acted in a perfectly adult way, as only a very small number of adults are capable of acting. He acted scientifically. He was following a blueprint in constructing his model, making calculations, respecting the laws of nature. To adult attacks he could have opposed an explanation of the laws, a demonstration of his experiments. He remained silent, however, feeling it was not right for him to look more serious than adults.

The boy was surrounded by rubber bands, coils of wire, sheets of plywood, silk, and the smell of glue. Above him the sky glistened. Under his feet, insects crawled over the stones, and a stone had a little petrified shell embedded in it.

From time to time, while the boy was deep in his work, another boy, quite tiny, would approach him. He was naked except for a tiny pair of blue trunks. He touched things and got in the way. Alexander would chase him away. The naked boy, who looked as if he were made of rubber, wandered all over the house. In the corridor was a bicycle leaning with its pedal against the wall. The pedal had scratched the paint, and the bike gripped the wall by the scratch.

The little boy dropped in on Ponomarev. The child's head bounced around like a ball near the edge of the bed. The sick man's temples were pale, like those of a blind man. The boy came close to Ponomarev's head and examined it. He thought it had always been this way in the world: a bearded man lying in a bed in a room. The little boy had just learned to recognize things; he did not yet know how to distinguish time in their existence.

He turned away and walked around the room. He saw

the floorboards, the dust between them, the cracks in the plaster. Around him lines joined and moved and bodies formed. Sometimes a wonderful pattern of light appeared. The child started rushing toward it, but before he had even taken a full step, the change of distance killed the illusion. The child looked up, back, behind the fireplace, searching for it and moving his hands in bewilderment. Each second gave him a new thing. There was an amazing spider over there. The spider vanished at the boy's mere desire to touch it with his hand.

The vanishing things left the dying man nothing but their names.

There was an apple in the world. It glistened amidst the leaves; it seized little bits of the day and gently twirled them round: the green of the garden, the outline of the window. The law of gravity awaited it under the tree, on the black earth, on the knoll. Beady ants scampered among the knolls. Newton sat in the garden. There were many causes hidden inside the apple, causes that could determine a multitude of effects. But none of these causes had anything to do with Ponomarev. The apple had become an abstraction. The fact that the flesh of a thing had disappeared while the abstraction remained was painful to him.

"I thought there was no outside world," he mused. "I thought my eye and my ear ruled things. I thought the world would cease to exist when I ceased to exist. But I still exist! So why don't the things? I thought they got their shape, their weight, their color from my brain. But they have left me, leaving behind only useless names, names that pester my brain."

Ponomarev looked at the child nostalgically. The child walked around. Things rushed to meet him. He smiled at them, not knowing any of them by name. He left the room and the magnificent procession of things trailed after him.

"Listen," the sick man called out to the child, "do you know that when I die, nothing will remain? They will all be gone—the courtyard, the tree, Daddy, Mummy. I'll take everything along with me."

A rat got into the kitchen.

Ponomarev listened: the rat was making itself at home, rattling the plates, opening the tap, making scraping sounds in the bucket.

"Why, someone must be washing dishes in there," Ponomarev decided.

Immediately he became worried: perhaps the rat had a proper name people did not know. He wondered what this name could be. He was delirious. As he thought, fear seized him more and more powerfully. He knew that at any cost he must stop thinking about the rat's name. But he kept searching for it, knowing that as soon as he found that meaningless, horrifying name, he would die.

"Lyompa!" he suddenly shouted in a terrifying voice.

The house was asleep. It was very early in the morning, just after five. Young Alexander was awake. The kitchen door giving onto the courtyard was open. The sun was still down somewhere.

The dying man was wandering about in the kitchen. He was bent forward, arms extended, wrists hanging limp. He was collecting things to take away with him.

Alexander dashed across the courtyard. The model plane flew ahead of him. It was the last thing Ponomarev saw.

He did not collect it. It flew away.

Later that day, a blue coffin with yellow ornaments made its appearance in the kitchen. The little rubber boy stared at it from the corridor, his little hands holding one another behind his back. The coffin had to be turned every which way to get it through the door. It banged against a shelf. Pans fell to the floor. There was a brief shower of plaster. Alexander climbed on the stove and helped to pull the box through. When the coffin finally got into the corridor, it immediately became black and the rubber boy ran along the passage, his feet slapping the floor:

"Grandpa! Grandpa! They've brought you a coffin."

(1928)

THE CHERRY STONE

On Sunday I went to visit Natasha at her summer place. There were three other guests besides me: two girls and Boris Mikhailovich. The girls went off boating on the river with Natasha's brother. We—that is, Natasha, Boris Mikhailovich, and I—went for a walk in the woods. In the woods we came to a sunlit clearing and lay down on the grass. Natasha raised her face and suddenly it looked like a shiny china saucer to me.

Natasha treats me as an equal but she behaves toward Boris Mikhailovich as a child toward a grownup—she fawns upon him. She knows that I don't like it, that I'm envious of Boris Mikhailovich. So she often touches my hand and, whenever she says something, turns to me and asks:

"Isn't that right, Fedya?"

It's as if she were begging my forgiveness, not directly though, but in a roundabout way.

The odd voice of a bird came from the bushes and we started talking about birds. I said, for instance, that I had never in my life seen a thrush; what's a thrush like anyway? I asked.

The bird flew out of a thicket. It flew across the clearing and sat down on a protruding branch not far from our heads. Actually, it didn't sit but stood on the swaying branch. It blinked. And I thought to myself what unattractive eyes birds have, with no eyebrows but strongly pronounced lids.

"What's that?" I asked in a whisper, "a thrush? Is that a thrush?"

No one answers me. I have my back turned to them.
My hungry glance isn't turned on them and they are enjoying their privacy. I look at the bird. Glancing round, I
see Boris Mikhailovich stroking Natasha's cheek. His hand
is thinking: Let him look at the bird, the aggrieved young
man! I can't see the bird any more. I'm listening: I hear
the unsticking sound of a kiss. I don't look around, but they
know they're caught: they see me shudder.

"Is that a thrush?" I ask.

The bird has gone already. It has taken off, up through
the crown of the tree. The flight through the leaves is
difficult—they scrape against the bird as it passes.

Natasha offered us cherries. Out of childhood habit, I
kept one of the stones in my mouth. It rolled about in my
mouth and I sucked it clean. I took it out; it looked wooden.

I left Natasha's place with the cherry stone in my mouth.

I travel through an invisible land.

There I go, returning to the town from the country
place. The sun is setting; I'm going east. I'm making a
double trip. One of my trips is quite obvious: an observer
coming in the opposite direction would see a man walking
across the green and deserted countryside. But what is going
on in the mind of this quiet walker? He sees his shadow
before him. The shadow slides along the ground, stretching
itself out very far; it has long, pale legs. I cross an empty
plot and the shadow climbs up a brick wall and suddenly
loses its head. The observer coming from the opposite direction doesn't notice it; I alone see it. I step into the passage
between two buildings. The buildings are immensely tall
and the passageway is full of shadow. Here the ground is
a bit moldy, yielding, like the earth of a vegetable patch.
A stray dog comes hobbling toward me, keeping close to
the wall to get out of my way in advance. We pass each
other. I look back. The entrance to the passage, through
which I came in, is bright and shining. There at the entrance, for one brief second the dog is blotted out by some
projection in the wall. Then it runs out onto the empty

plot and only now can I make out what color it is: rust colored.

This all takes place in the invisible land, because in the land that is accessible to normal perception, something altogether different is happening: simply, a traveler meets a dog, the sun is setting over a dark green, empty lot. . . .

The invisible land is the land of sensitivity and imagination. The traveler isn't alone. Two sisters walk at either side and lead the traveler by the hand. One sister is Sensitivity, the other Imagination.

Well, then, what does this mean? Does it mean that, disregarding order and society, I create a world which is not subject to any laws except the shadowy laws of my private fancies? What, in the end, is the meaning of this? There are two worlds: the old and the new, so what kind of a world is this? A third world? There are two ways a man can follow. So what's this third one?

Natasha makes a date with me and then doesn't show up.

I arrive half an hour before time.

There is a clock hanging over the streetcar lines by the intersection. It makes you think of a barrel, doesn't it? Each bottom a face. "Oh, empty barrel of time!" I might exclaim.

Natasha is supposed to come at three-thirty.

I wait. Ah, of course she's not coming. It's ten past three.

I stand at the streetcar stop. Everything is moving around me. I alone stand out among the crowd. Those who lose their way can see me from far off. And here it starts. . . . An unknown woman comes up to me.

"Would you be so kind as to tell me," the unknown woman says, "whether I should take a 27 to get to Kudrinskaya Street?"

No one must know that I am waiting for a date. Let them rather think something like this: This broadly smiling young man has come to this intersection to look after the welfare of other people. He'll tell us everything, he'll tell

us how to get where we want to go, he'll comfort us. . . .
Let's go to him! Let's go!

"Yes, indeed," I reply, almost dizzy with civility, "Number 27 will take you right to Kudrinskaya Street. . . ."

But right away I realize my mistake and rush after the woman:

"No, no! You want a 16."

Let's forget about the date. I'm not in love. I'm the benevolent spirit of the street. Come this way! Over here! To me!

Three-fifteen. The hands joined on the horizontal line. I looked at them and thought:

It's a fly rubbing its legs together, the restless fly of time.

How stupid! What's this stuff about a fly of time!

She's not here, and she won't come at all.

A Red Army man comes over to me.

"Tell me," he says, "where's the Darwin Museum?"

"I don't know. . . . I think it's over that way. . . . No, wait . . . just a minute. . . . No, I don't know, Comrade, I'm sorry, I don't know. . . ."

Next. Who's next? Don't be bashful, people!

A taxi, making a swerve, slows down and draws up to me. Just look how the driver despises me! Oh, not wholeheartedly, no! He wouldn't condescend to despise me with his whole heart. . . . He despises me with his glove! Comrade driver, believe me—I'm just a dilettante after all, I don't really know which way you should turn your machine. . . .

I'm not really standing here to show people the way. . . . I have my own affairs to think of. . . . My standing here is forced upon me, it's miserable. My smile doesn't come from my heart, it's a forced smile . . . look closer!

"Which way to Varsonofievsky Avenue?" the driver asks over his shoulder.

And I busily explain to him: "This way, that way, and then that way. . . ."

Well then, since it's gone this far, why shouldn't I stand

in the middle of the street and get down seriously to the business which they're pressing upon me?

A blind man comes.

Oh, this one simply shouts at me! He pokes me with his cane. . . .

"Is that a number 10 coming?" he asks. "Uh? Number 10?"

"No," I answer, almost stroking him. "No, Comrade, that's not a 10. That's a 2. Ah, but here comes a 10 now."

It's already ten minutes past the appointed time. Why should I wait any longer? But perhaps she's somewhere hurrying, flying?

"Oh, I'm late! Oh, I'm late!!"

The unknown woman has already rolled away on the number 16, the Red Army man is already walking through the cool halls of the museum, the driver is already tooting on Varsonofievsky Avenue, the blind man, touchy and self-pitying, is climbing onto the front platform, holding his cane out in front of him.

They're all content! They're all happy!

And I stand there, smiling inanely.

And more people come up to me and ask questions: an old woman, a drunk, a group of children with a flag. And I'm already beginning to wave my hands about, but now I don't simply nod like an ordinary man in the street who's asked a question by chance—no! Now I stretch out my arm, my hand stiff and perpendicular. . . . Another minute and a nightstick will grow out of my fist. . . .

"Get back there!" I'll shout. "Halt! This way to Varsonofievsky Avenue. Turn at that corner! Old woman—to the right! Stop!"

Oh, look! A whistle is dangling between my lips. . . . I whistle. . . . I have the right to whistle. . . . Children, you can envy me! Get back! Oho . . . just look: now I can stand between two streetcars coming in opposite direction —look, I stand there, with one leg thrust out, and my hands clasped behind my back, my shoulder blade propped up by my crimson nightstick.

Congratulate me, Natasha. I've turned into a traffic cop. . . .

Then I see Abel standing at a distance and watching me. (Abel is my neighbor.)

Natasha won't come—that's obvious. I call Abel over.

Me: Did you see, Abel?

Abel: I saw all right. You're crazy.

Me: Did you see, Abel? I've turned into a traffic cop.

(Pause. Yet another glance toward the clock. Hopeless now. Ten to four.)

Me: Actually, it's beyond you. My metamorphosis into a traffic cop took place in the invisible land.

Abel: Your invisible land is an idealistic delirium.

Me: And d'you know, Abel, what's the most surprising thing about it all? It's that in that magic land I should somehow fit in as a traffic cop. . . . I would've thought I'd stalk about there, calmly and majestically, like a proprietor with the flowering staff of a sage glowing in my hand. . . . And now look: I'm holding a traffic cop's nightstick instead. What a strange hybrid of the everyday and the imaginary.

(Abel is silent.)

Me: And it's even stranger that the reason for my change was my unrequited love.

Abel: I can't understand what you're talking about. Sounds like some sort of Bergsonism to me.

I decided to bury the cherry stone in the earth.

I picked a spot and buried it.

Here, I thought, a cherry tree will grow which was planted by me in memory of my love for Natasha. Perhaps some day, in the spring, five years or so from now, Natasha and I will meet by the young tree. We'll stand one at either side of it—cherry trees aren't very tall; if you stand on tiptoe you can shake the very topmost blossom. It will be a clear day, the sun will shine, the spring will still be a bit bare—it'll be one of those spring days when the gutters

along the sidewalks lure the children—and when this paper
tree has already started to bloom.

I'll say:

"Natasha, it's a bright, clear day and the wind is blowing,
fanning the day to an even brighter blaze. The wind is rocking my tree and its lacquered limbs are creaking. Its every
blossom stands up and then lies down again and this causes
it to turn first pink, then white, then pink again. It is the
kaleidoscope of spring, Natasha. Five years ago you offered
me some cherries, remember? Unrequited love makes recollections clear and miserable. I still remember: the palm
of your hand was stained violet by the juice of the cherries
and you clenched it into a funnel to pour the fruit into my
hand. I carried away a stone in my mouth. I planted this
tree to commemorate the fact that you didn't love me. It
is blossoming now. You see, you laughed at me then. Boris
Mikhailovich was a manly figure and he conquered you.
I was dreamy, infantile. I was searching through the world
for a thrush while you were kissing. I was a romantic. But
look now: this firm, manly tree has grown from the romantic's stone. You know—the Japanese believe the cherry
blossom is the soul of a man. Look: here stands a strong,
squat Japanese tree. Believe me, Natasha, romanticism is a
manly thing and it shouldn't be laughed at. . . . After all,
it all depends on the way you look at it. If Boris Mikhailovich had seen me squatting in the empty lot, planting that
infantile cherry stone, he would have savored his victory
over me even more—the victory of a man over a dreamer.
And yet, then I was hiding a charge in the ground. It
burst and sent forth a blinding flash. It was a seed I hid
in the ground. This tree is my child by you, Natasha. Bring
along the son which Boris Mikhailovich made you. I want
to see if he is as healthy, clean and without blemish as this
tree born of a man afflicted by infantilism."

No sooner had I come home from the country place
than Abel popped up from the other side of the wall. He's
a union official. He's short, wears a cotton, Tolstoy blouse,

sandals, navy-blue socks. He's shaven but his cheeks are always blue. It always looks as if he could do with another shave. You might even think that instead of two, he has only one blue cheek. So Abel has a hawk nose and one blue cheek.

Abel: What's the matter with you? I took the commuter train today and I saw you squatting in one of the empty lots, raking over the earth with your fingers. What's the idea?

Me: (Silence)

Abel (wanders around the room): A man squatting and digging in the earth. What's he doing? Mystery! Is he carrying out an experiment? Or is he having a fit? Mystery. Do you actually have fits?

Me (after a pause): Know what I was thinking about, Abel? I was thinking that dreamers oughtn't to produce children. What does the new world need with dreamers' children? Let the dreamers produce trees for the new world.

Abel: That's not provided for in the National Economic Plan.

The land of impressionableness begins at the bedside, on the chair which you moved closer to your bed when you were undressing before going off to sleep. You wake up early in the morning, everyone in the house is still asleep, but the room is full of sunshine. Quiet. Don't stir or you might disturb the stillness of the light. Your socks lie on the chair. They're brown. But in the still, bright light you suddenly notice that in the brown woolen fabric there are some individual, curly, multicolored threads—crimson, pale blue, orange.

Sunday morning. Again I'm on the familiar road to Natasha's. I should write a book called *Journey Through the Invisible Land.* If you're interested, here's a chapter from the *Journey* which should be entitled: "A Man Who Was in a Hurry to Cast a Stone."

There were bushes growing by the brick wall. I followed a little path by the bushes. I saw a niche in the wall and wanted to throw a little pebble into it. I bent down—the stone was lying at my feet. . . . Just then I saw an anthill.

The last time I saw an anthill was twenty years ago. Oh, of course, in the course of those twenty years I'd stepped on anthills many, many times. And no doubt I even caught sight of them occasionally, but even then I didn't actually think: I'm walking on anthills—just the word "anthill" flashed through my mind, and that was all. The real, live thing was at once blotted out by its handy designation.

Oh, I remembered: anthills suddenly discover themselves to the sight. One. . . . Oh! There's another! Then —look! look!—yet another! . . . And that's exactly what happened now. Three anthills came into sight, one after the other.

From my height, I couldn't see the ants: I could only make out a certain disturbance of forms which could just as easily have been taken for motionless. And my sight readily allowed itself to be tricked: I looked and was quite ready to believe that it was not the ants swarming around the anthill, but the anthills themselves crumbling like dunes.

The stone in my hand, I stood four paces or so from the wall. The stone was to land in the niche. My arm swung back. The stone flew off and hit a brick. A puff of dust arose. I'd missed. The stone bounced off into the bushes at the foot of the wall. It was only then that the stone's outcry reached me, although it had been uttered while the stone was still in my fist, before my hand had unclasped.

"Wait!" the stone had yelled, "look at me!"

And true enough, I'd been much too hasty. I should have examined the stone first. I'm sure it was a remarkable stone. And now it was in the bushes, in the undergrowth— vanished! And I, who held the thing in my hand, don't even know what color it was. Perhaps it was purplish; perhaps it wasn't a monolith, but was made up of several substances: perhaps some fossil or other was embedded in it—the remains of a beetle or a cherry pit; perhaps the stone was porous; or, perhaps it wasn't a stone I picked up from the ground at all, but a petrified bone!

On my way I met a group of tourists.

Twenty people were walking across the empty lot in which the pit was resting. Abel was leading them. I stepped out of their way. Abel didn't see me, or rather, he saw me but didn't register; like all fanatics, he gulped me down without caring whether I minded or not.

Abel detached himself from his flock, turned his face toward them—his back to me—and shouted, forcefully waving his hand:

"Right here! Right here! Right here!"

Pause. Silence.

"Comrades from Kursk!" Abel shouted. "I hope that you have imagination. So, imagine away—don't be afraid!"

I see! Abel is trying to break into the land of imagination. Perhaps he even wants to show the tourists the cherry tree blossoming in memory of unrequited love?

Abel is searching for a path leading into the invisible land. . . .

He takes a few strides. He stops, one foot dangling in the air. He kicks. He kicks again. He is trying to free himself from some finely curling plant which wound itself around his foot as he was walking.

He stamped his foot, the plant cracked, and little yellow balls rolled out of it. (There are so many plants in this story, so many trees and bushes!)

"Right here, on this spot, shall rise the giant I told you about!"

. . . Dear Natasha, I have overlooked the most important thing: the Plan. There's the Five-Year Plan. I acted without checking first whether it fitted in with the Plan. Five years from now, in that place where now there is nothing but ditches and useless walls, there will rise a concrete giant. My sister, Imagination, is really an impulsive person. Come spring they'll start laying the foundations. And then what will become of my silly pit?

Yet some day, in the invisible land, the tree I dedicated to you will bloom. . . .

Tourists will come to the concrete giant.

They won't see your tree. Is it really impossible to make the invisible land visible? . . .

This letter is an imaginary one. I didn't write it. I could've written it if Abel hadn't said what he did.

"This building will be laid out in a semicircle," Abel said. "The entire part inside the semicircle will be a garden. Do you have imagination?"

"I have," I said. "I see it, Abel. I see it clearly. The garden will be here. And in the place where you are standing, a cherry tree will grow."

(1929)

ALDEBARAN

They sat on a bench, the girl, the young man, and a certain learned old man. It was a summer morning. Above them rose a mighty tree with a hollow in it that exuded a slightly musty smell. This made the old man think of childhood expeditions to the cellar.

The young man said:

"I am free today, all day."

"So am I," said the old scholar.

The young man drove a Buffalo steamroller. He rolled asphalt roads. He was a Latvian and his name was Zwibol, Sasha Zwibol.

A gypsy girl the height of a feather duster came along. She was selling lilies.

"Go away," the old scholar said.

Zwibol became indignant.

"So it touches you," the scholar said. "Isn't it rather strange to hear a Young Communist defending tramps?"

"She's just a child," said the girl who was with them.

"A child, eh? So according to you socialism is a sort of Christian paradise for children and beggars?"

The old man spoke in a loud tenor voice. He was handsome and extremely healthy, one of those old men who smoke, drink, follow no diet, sleep on their left sides, and who think "I'm quite a fellow." His name was Bohemsky, and he was staff consultant on the board of the *Great Soviet Encyclopedia.*

He fell in love with the girl. She was sitting next to him. She put her hand on the young man's knee. The old man asked:

"Perhaps you feel I am in your way?"

The young man sighed. He took off his cap. He had close-cropped hair. He was blond and his head shone like golden chicken broth. He scratched the crown of his head.

The old man got up and threw his cigarette end into the hollow of the tree.

"Sasha and I will go to the river," the girl said.

Implicitly, the old man was not invited to go to the river.

"Would you walk with us to the bus stop?" the girl said.

They went. She walked a step ahead. Bohemsky looked at her back and thought:

No, this cannot be love. This is a whim. A disgusting, senile whim. I want to eat her. Do you hear me, I want to eat you? I would like to start at the back, just under your shoulder blades. . . .

"Isn't she pretty?" Zwibol said.

He pronounced these admiring words with his foreign accent. It sounded virile. Enthusiasm restrained by virility resulted in a sort of shy ardor. The old man envied him.

"Katia, your boy friend makes me think of a Roman," he called out to the girl.

"I am from Riga," Zwibol said.

"Well, it's the same style, the Order of the Templars. . . ."

"Templev District has been renamed Lenin District," Katia said over her shoulder.

They came to the bus stop.

"What if it rains?" Bohemsky asked.

"It won't rain," Zwibol said.

All three looked up. The sky was clear. It was blue.

"Rain is the enemy of lovers," the old man said. "It chases them from the parks. It is a fierce defender of morals."

The bus arrived. They had no time to say good-by to the scholar. He watched Katia inside, making her way down the aisle. Through the glass of the wide window her movements seemed fluid, like those of a pink goldfish.

Bohemsky walked in an indeterminate direction. He was tall and spare, with the springy walk of a young man. His unbuttoned jacket flapped. His black hat was tilted back, uncovering white, wavy hair. Dogs fear this type of pedestrian. As he walks along, a dog running in his direction stops dead, stares at him for a second, then crosses to the other side of the street. There he hugs the wall, stops when the pedestrian is already far away, and looks at him.

Bohemsky walked along, thinking of the girl. A first-rate girl. She has no idea of her own class. Under different objective circumstances she could have played a part in history. He thought of the century of enlightened absolutism. La Duchesse du Barry. The *salons*. *Le Directoire*. Barras. The rise of Bonaparte. Madame Récamier. The women conversing in Latin. The *calembours*. Political strings held in a delicate hand. George Sand. Chopin. Ida Rubinstein. . . .

. . . Sasha Zwibol. A soldier, Bohemsky thought, a Don José. What a sad story: A Young Communist in love with Carmen. Sasha Zwibol, a simple soul of a shepherd, has been hooked. Very interesting. She's wrought havoc in him and he doesn't even suspect where her strength lies. He is like a boor at a fair, grabbing those handles charged with electricity, getting a shock, grimacing, not understanding *why* he's grimacing. Young Communists both, very funny. I have lived in this world for very many years. I remember the French can-can danced in Paris. I know what there is to know; I have thought a lot. I am a very old man, Katia. I am the Dreyfus affair, I am Queen Victoria, I am the opening of the Suez Canal. Zwibol, whom you love, speaks to you of many wonderful things, of economic development, of socialism, of science, of discoveries that will remake man. And, Katia dear, your sweetheart speaks to you of the class struggle. . . . This strikes me as very funny. It must be so easy for him to hold forth about anything when you smile like that. While I, who am twice as old as the Moscow Art Theater, and who do not rate your smile, I wish to paraphrase the words of the poet, to tell you that

of love, all classes are the subjects. . . .

At this moment, he imagined, they must be undressing in a wooden structure on piles. Under the piles, the water is still, basalt-colored. It is noisy in the wooden room where they undress: voices, the stamping of bare feet on the wooden planks. The river can be seen through the windows: the guardrails, flags, boats. Oars plash in the river. They emerge from the wooden rooms and walk along hot, sunny planks. Somewhere a band is playing. The air vibrates and passes the vibration to the planks. Here and there, splinters fall from the planks into the water. Perhaps a flag flapping in the blueness of the summer sky combined with a military band *could* be the most moving sight in a human life.

The old man arrived home and lay down. He let his imagination wander. Women like her get killed. Ah, Paris, Paris! He imagined a horrible scene: the end of an unwritten tragedy. The denouement he believed was the inevitable consequence of Katia's beauty: a murder.

She is rushing about in a room. Chairs tip over. The glass doors of a closet fly open with a wild flash. Her pursuer is none other than himself, the old man, whose reasoning is opaque with passion. He fires through the mirror. Six rounds. Fragments of mirror. Silence. He stands in the middle of the room, his hand on his forehead. Pink wallpaper. The dust particles revolve in a beam of sunlight. Neighbors arrive to see a gray-bearded old man with a noble forehead, looking a bit like Turgenev.

What year was it, what century, where? What's the difference? Love, death, sex, it's always the same.

The closet opens, a corpse falls out sideways; its forehead bangs against the parquet floor.

"Let me!" the old man shouts, and rushes to the body. He emits a deep, hopeless howl of unquenched passion. He places his gray head between the girl's widespread

breasts. He raises his eyes to the people crowding around
him and says:

"This bit of her is so pure and feels so cool on such a
torrid day."

Late that evening he spoke to her on the phone.

"Katia, I love you very much. Funny, isn't it? Do you
hear me? Does an old man's love make you laugh? I don't
ask much. If you were a thunderstorm, I would be content
with a raindrop. . . . It is rather difficult to use imagery
over the telephone. Are you listening? You spend every day
with Zwibol. On clear evenings you sit with him under the
stars. Yes, yes, I have seen it. I understand a love for stars.
Does Zwibol know their beautiful names? Vega, Arcturus,
Antares, Aldebaran. Why are you laughing? At Aldebaran?
Listen, I have been wanting to take you out to the movies
for a whole month, but the weather hasn't helped me. On
summer nights you prefer the stars. What? But the weather
can change. Our technology cannot control the weather
yet. Let Zwibol have the azure, the river, the stars—and
leave me the rain. All right? Katia, I am using a pay phone.
I am being rushed. They're banging on the glass, making
obscene faces. Here is my request: if the weather breaks
tomorrow, if it rains, would you be willing to go to the
movies with me? If there are no stars, that is?"

"Okay, if there are no stars."

The morning came. It was clear, cloudless.

Bohemsky stood on a road. Three Buffalo steamrollers
were working on it. Zwibol was driving one of them, wearing a once-blue T shirt now black with sweat.

"Hot," Bohemsky shouted to him.

"Hot," Zwibol said.

Without letting go the wheel, he used his shoulder to
wipe the sweat off his temple. It was terribly hot, very
much like hell: the heat steaming from the fresh tar, the
glittering brass machine parts, the blaring radios. Some
idlers gaped by the side of the road.

During a break, Bohemsky walked over to Zwibol.

"What did you do last night?"

"I went for a walk."

"Katia go with you?"

"Yes."

"Where did you go?"

"Nowhere in particular."

"Was it a nice, starry night?"

"Yes."

"What about tonight?"

"We'll go again."

At this point the radio interfered: "Abundant rain fell in the Central Black Earth belt. . . ."

"You hear?" Bohemsky asked.

"He said abundant," Zwibol noted. "Good."

The radio was now predicting "precipitation in the Moscow region very soon."

"I hope it comes very soon," Zwibol said.

After a pause the old man remarked:

"It may even rain tonight."

"Possibly."

"And there'll be no stars. . . ."

"And you will take Katia to the movies," Zwibol said.

"You say that as though you thought nothing of giving up the evening with your girl, as long as it rains, since rain is in the national interest."

"Yes, the collective farmers need rain. . . ."

"Here, Zwibol, let me shake your hand. You're really amazing. I am beginning to understand now what the Communist attitude toward life really means."

And a cloud really came up. First to arrive was its forehead. A very wide forehead. It was a tadpole-like cloud and it came climbing up from somewhere below. Now a lump from nowhere, it stretched out huge paws, temporized for a while, rose above the town, and began to fall over on its back. . . .

The downpour lasted two hours. Then there was an abortive clearing up, followed by moderate rain.

The evening came. There were no stars. The rain kept

starting and stopping. Bohemsky bought two tickets for the last performance and went to meet Katia by the statue of Gogol, as they had agreed.

She did not turn up. He waited for her a whole hour and then another quarter of an hour. The puddles glistened. It smelled of vegetables. Inside an open window, someone was playing a guitar. Heat lightning was flashing.

He walked to a small street and stopped by the sacred house surrounded by its garden, where Katia lived. He pushed open the gate with his foot. He walked in the mud, leaving behind him footprints as deep as his rubbers. He walked around to the side door of the house and looked up at a window. It was dark. She was not at home.

He walked out of the garden gate into the street and started pacing up and down. He stopped and stood there wrapped in his dark raincoat, a dark pyramid lit by the light from a window, as in an illustration.

They came into sight from around the corner. Katia and Zwibol walked with their arms around each other's shoulders, like Napoleon's grenadiers.

He sprang up as if out of the ground in front of them, and they let go of each other.

"You broke your promise, Katia."

"No."

"But it rained, and there were no stars."

"The stars were there."

"You're lying, there was not a single star to be seen."

"But we saw them."

"Which ones? Name them."

"All of them," Zwibol answered, "Arcturus, Antares . . ."

"Aldebaran," Katia said, and laughed.

"Aldebaran nothing; we saw the Southern Cross," Zwibol said.

"And the Magellanic Cloud," Katia backed him.

"Rain didn't prevent us," Zwibol said.

"I see," Bohemsky mumbled.

"We were in the Planetarium," Zwibol said.

"Progress. . . ." Katia sighed.

"It rained—our agriculture needed it," said Zwibol.

"We needed it too," said Katia.

"And the stars we needed shone at the same time," Zwibol said.

"Our Socialist Republic needed them too," Katia said.

(1931)

FROM THE SECRET NOTEBOOK OF
FELLOW-TRAVELER SAND

I have a passionate craving for power.

I look at myself in the mirror very often. When I'm working, I leap up every minute and rush up to the looking glass. I rivet my eyes on it and look at myself. What am I trying to find in the mirror? It is some sort of a habit and I don't know how I got into it. Well, why not. . . . Perhaps it would make me feel better if I reminded myself that all writers have had their own peculiar habits which manifested themselves during their creative hours, such as Schiller's rotten apples or the cold footbaths of someone or other. And so I console myself: Schiller with his apples, Fellow-Traveler Sand with his mirror. Makes me sick.

There are men who never feel the need to look at themselves in a mirror. They find themselves looking into one by chance. But I, I even try to peek into a mirrored wardrobe as it is being loaded onto a furniture van. I go up on tiptoe and look. The mirror is flying off—a house soars into the air, the lamppost shoots away. . . . I just manage to catch sight of my face tearing off into the blue.

There are no purer mirrors than those the moving man carries out into the street.

When I think that I am a writer living in an era of the ascent of a new social class, when I begin to examine myself, to look back and try to appraise what I have achieved —it becomes obvious to me that my work, which at certain moments seems so all-important to me, fades into utter insignificance compared with the great events that make the history of these days and years.

In the window of a bookstore there is an etching. It makes me shudder.

It represents a throng of people pushing one another. They are pushing, elbowing one another at the entrance to a theater. There are arms in the air, hats pushed sideways and back. . . . There are boys darting to and fro in the foreground. And above the crowd. . . .

Above the crowd there's a man in a lace collar. He is thin and wrapped in a cloak. The crowd is striving toward him from every side. Here and there carriage lanterns flash, the coachmen tower on their boxes with their whips standing next to them, and there are flunkeys on the footboards in the back.

Do you know what it is?

Well, it is the rising class greeting its poet.

It is Schiller acclaimed after the first performance of *Intrigue and Love*. A mother holds her baby high above her head, showing it the Poet. This is glory. He wrote *Intrigue and Love*, he created the bourgeois drama. He is the poet of the ascending class. . . .

Now I am a writer too.

So how can I not long to write my own *Intrigue and Love*, a new type of play, a play that would stir the imagination of the proletariat just as much as Schiller's drama stirred those burghers' imaginations? And how could I not crave for power? How could I not crave for writing power, howling and weeping when I feel frustrated, because I need it now that a new class is rising to power.

Benvenuto Cellini writes:

Although I was moved by honorable envy* and I wanted to produce a work of art that would equal and even surpass the work of such a craftsman as Lucag-

* Olesha's source renders the Italian *"onesta invidia"* as "honorable envy," although the possible alternative "honorable rivalry" used in the English translation by J. A. Symonds seems to yield a more logical meaning. (A. MacA.)

nolo, I did not because of this neglect my own fine art of jewelry; and so both brought me much profit and even greater honor; and in both I kept creating things unlike any made by others.

At that time a highly talented man from Perugia lived in Rome. His name was Lautizio. He worked in only one form of art where he was unrivaled throughout the world. You must know that in Rome every Cardinal has his own seal with his title engraved on it. These seals are made the size of the hand of a child of twelve and, as I mentioned before, the title of the Cardinal is engraved on them together with a great many ornamental figures. They pay a hundred and more crowns for a good seal of this description.

I felt noble envy toward this great craftsman also although his art is far removed from other branches of goldsmithery and Lautizio having specialized in that form of art could not do anything else. So I began to study that art too although I found it very difficult; never shirking the efforts it cost me I ceaselessly tried to improve and to learn.

There was also in Rome another excellent craftsman who was from Milan and was called Messer Caradosso. He worked exclusively in engraving medals on tablets and such things; he made a few paxes in half-relief, and a few Christs the length of one's palm, wrought of the thinnest gold plates and so exquisitely executed that I considered him the greatest master in that domain I'd ever come across, and I envied him more than all the others.

Thus writes Benvenuto Cellini in his *Autobiography*.

And then there was an American by the name of Jack London who was a hobo, who sailed on schooners, hunted, and often had to repel those who attacked him. And, at one point, as he went hoboing around, trying to earn his living and to meet as many people as possible, he drifted to some tropical islands where all sorts of adventures happened to him.

This Jack London wrote stories that no one wanted to publish. But later they did publish his stories and he wrote more and more and in these stories he told of the things he had seen and other things he made up, and because he was brave and had gone through many dangers and many humiliations from which he had always emerged triumphant, other people, reading him, wanted to become bold and energetic themselves. He wrote many excellent stories and novels and, in fact, they are so well done that I consider him the greatest master in this kind of writing I have ever come across and I am full of a noble envy for him.

And I feel all the stronger because I happen to live in a country where people go out to wild places to build new towns and power stations, where they lay railroads and reverse the course of rivers, where these people display amazing daring and enterprise, just as happened once in America. And when I think of that, my envy increases because I could have been writing things just as excellent since life itself is a help to me, having created such favorable conditions.

There was yet another master—Balzac. He wrote day and night and as he wrote, he tore his shirt on his chest and howled and wrote on until he collapsed from exhaustion. Balzac looked like a butcher and he was fat and sweaty and dirty and had a bull neck. He is supposed to have said that, since Napoleon had been able to achieve the supreme heights in statesmanship and the conduct of war, he, Balzac, would become the Napoleon of literature.

Balzac divided Paris into circles, in each of which were people of various occupations: goldsmiths, moneylenders, bankers, barbers, generals, shopkeepers, priests, whores, actors, adventurers, artists. . . . He made them intermingle because the lot of them made up one bourgeois society and pursued one common goal—each wanted to acquire as much money as he possibly could. Balzac then proceeded to write an incredible number of novels about them, thus

creating his *Comédie humaine*. He portrayed all those characters so well that we can piece together a complete picture
of life at that time from his books, revealed by a magician
who could see and sense how all those around him lived,
what everyone was after and what he was thinking about.
Well, I envy Balzac too.

Then there was that man Pushkin. He wrote epic poems
and jocose verse and epigrams. He was also a tragic poet
and on top of it all wrote prose fiction, critical essays and
songs and was also an editor. He is really to be envied more
than any other man because by the time he was twenty-
four he had written the tragedy *Boris Godunov*.

Pushkin liked playing cards and having a gay time but
then, at the very early age of twenty-four, he turned out
that tragedy which is perfection of a kind that has never
been equaled. This man, so remarkable in all forms of
poetry, said that a poet must be abreast of the knowledge
of his age. He seems to have lived up to that motto, for
when he died, still young, he left behind a library of five
thousand volumes all of which he had read with the greatest attention, for on every page of each of those five thousand books there were annotations in his handwriting. This
makes it even more remarkable that he should, like all
members of the class to which he belonged, have had a
gay time, played cards and burned out his life.

There was yet another writer, a count, one Leo Tolstoy.
That man was so great and felt his superiority over others
so acutely that he couldn't accept the idea that there were
other great men and ideas in the world that he couldn't
take on and overcome in the end. So he chose the most
powerful opponents, so powerful that all mankind pros-
trated itself before them. These were Napoleon, Death,
Christianity, Art and Life itself, which is the reason why
he wrote *The Kreutzer Sonata* in which he appealed to
people to give up reproducing themselves, in other words,
to renounce Life itself. That man, at the age of seventy-
five, learned to ride a bicycle.

It is impossible to envy such a man because he was a

natural phenomenon, like a star or a waterfall, and it is impossible to try and become a waterfall or a star or a rainbow, or to try to acquire the properties of a magnetized needle and to always point toward the North.

I am envious of everyone though. I admit it. But that is because there is no such thing as a modest artist. If he pretends to be modest, he's faking and lying, and hard though he may try to hide his envy, it will still burst out with a hiss through his clenched teeth.

I am firmly convinced of this but not in the least depressed. On the contrary, it leads me calmly to the conclusion that envy and vanity are forces propitious to creativity, that there is no need to be ashamed of them, and that they are not black shadows left outside the door but the genius's two full-blooded sisters who are next to him when he sits down to work.

When great deeds are being accomplished, when everything around has the seal of greatness, when the word *giant* has become of current use, there is nothing shameful in my wanting to emulate artistic giants, particularly since I happen to be an artist, because the task facing me, the task of portraying the birth of a new mankind—is a task for a giant.

I saw a strong man. He went out into the garden. His undone suspenders hung down his back. He was a rotund little man. He kept looking back at the dangling suspenders, catching them, but then forgetting and letting them go again. He had on a good-quality white shirt with faint blue stripes. He had stocked up last spring when he had attended a congress of chemists in Dresden. He was Kolotilov, a chemist.

I was watching him from the terrace. Why had he gone out into the garden improperly dressed? What could he be doing in the garden anyway? He hadn't finished his coffee. Ah, the funny fatso! He's really a bit of a nut, this fat little guy! Looks as if he had no special reason for rushing out into the garden—he's simply enjoying himself.

Suddenly he begins to hop and skip. Then he stops and digs in the gravel with his toe.

A bush shuddered. There's a bird there. He crawled under the bush. No bird. What the hell's going on! He looks at the bush. The blue suspenders hang down. His pants creep freely down onto his shoes.

The bush shudders again. He squats. Maybe it's a lizard? Ah, the little fatso! There's no lizard there. The suspenders lay on the ground. As he moved forward, the bush rustled and that scared him. He looked back quickly, thinking: A lizard! He leaped to his feet. Very interesting: birds, lizards!

Now he is facing the terrace, walking toward me. He doesn't see me. His face is untidy: ginger mustache, freckles; boldness and hairiness; a good-quality shirt with the top stud buttoned but no collar; the stud is golden. A little round belly, fat little hands with reddish hair.

Suddenly, at last, at the very last minute, he found it! No, it wasn't a bird, nor was it a lizard. But it is just as interesting. It's not a lizard but something of that kind. He bends down. Look! Isn't it cute!

A caterpillar.

He tore off a leaf and turned it into a spade. The caterpillar crawls along the ground. He put his spade in front of it. The caterpillar climbed onto it and he picked up his spade. Then he started running.

The table is covered with a dazzling white tablecloth. A bridge of sunlight connects the table with the window. The coffeepot and the little guardrails on the silver glass-holders glow.

Kolotilov puts the leaf on the tablecloth.

One side of the leaf is rough, the other is smooth and lacquered. And on the green lacquered surface lies a fat, red and yellow, finger-shaped caterpillar. It is tremendously heavy and tremendously clutching. Kolotilov pokes its side with his finger. Then he pushes a match under it, picks it up from the leaf and shouts:

"Look at those feet! Ah, what feet! Watch them, just watch them! Let's watch them, let's . . ."

The strong have strength for everything. Strength is love of life.

Kolotilov is a scientist with a world-wide reputation. And here he has found a caterpillar in the garden, something that has nothing to do with his field of science. And upon this caterpillar he bestowed the full power of his superb attention. And he displayed such heights of delight as are only reached by children taken to the circus for the first time.

Kolotilov loves life.

I, for instance, hold that the main thing in life is art. Art encompasses my life as the sky does the earth. But Kolotilov tells me that life is a huge affair and that art is only one aspect of it. Just as his science is.

I spent the night in his house. The house was filled with a silence that had nothing sinister in it, a silence leaning on the alarm clock that heard everything, didn't sleep and held in its swollen cheeks the jet of ticking sound, like a boy holds water he is about to spurt out; filled with the non-sinister stillness of quiet sleep when a man sleeps through the night in the same position in which he dozed off—the stillness leaning on the three-paned window with its clean, uncluttered window ledge, a window through which streetlights and the modern world of metal, lighted throughout the night, can be seen.

Later the sun rose, birds sang and prepared to take off, standing on the outer edge of the window sill, their two feet together, as if someone had carefully placed them there one by one.

Water pouring from a hose makes a crackling sound.

I looked out of the window. It was the car having its bath.

I went out of my room and walked around the house. I found Kolotilov in a room of glass. I stopped in the doorway. This was his home lab.

In that minute, I understood everything. This head turned

up toward the sun, this head with the pinkish bald patch, these eyes, one narrowed like a marksman's, the other wide open, admitting a sunbeam that has passed through a test tube before reaching the eye of the observer, this test tube that the observer holds between himself and the sun, between the registering instrument of attention—the scientist's eye—and the sun which is life itself, this pink stuff inside the test tube which is no longer a fluid but not yet a gas—all this combined in my mind to produce a sparkling conclusion:

"The strong man is he whose attention is concentrated upon the outside world!"

For him, for the investigator, the chemist, the outside world is the test tube, and also the reagent, the experiment, and all matter. For me, the writer, the outside world is an epic.

Yes, yes—an epic!

Writing is to portray events, characters, passions—outside.

Passions?

How could I describe another man's passion without inoculating myself with the germ of that passion?

If I want to describe avarice or, say, playfulness or compassion—I must stir something inside myself and make the seed of that passion spurt up in me. I must raise the sapling of that passion inside me if it isn't already blooming there! And when I pull on that sapling, I set into motion all the entangled roots in my soul and there goes my attention, back into the gaping inner world. So that's what it is: my trade itself is such that my attention cannot be exclusively on the outside world.

"Kolotilov, could you get me some job working under you, because I don't want to go on being a writer. I could wash your test tubes, for instance. After work we could go out into the garden looking for caterpillars, drink coffee, sleep peacefully at night. It is a great misfortune to be connected with art, to be a writer. Neither success, nor money, nor what is called moral satisfaction can make up for the permanent torment, for the severance from the simple joys of life, from gardens, caterpillars, birds, cars having a bath; they can never compensate for the horror of being constantly absorbed in oneself, an absorption which always leads in the end to the thought of death and the fear of death, to a wish to get rid of that fear, that is to blow your brains out."

(And, by the way, I understand that Jack London, whom I mentioned earlier, shot himself in the end too.)

"Are you afraid of dying?" Kolotilov asked me. "You're funny. Why, death is also part of life, isn't it? It is always someone living who dies."

My mother gave me a necktie. She went to a department store and spent a long time picking one out; she bought me a beautiful tie.

Mother and I turn this way and that in front of a mirror. She is helping me to tie it properly.

"Look, Mother," I say to her, "don't I look a lot like you? Fellow-Traveler Sand looks very much like his mummy, Ekaterina Sand, the wife of a musician."

The mirror! The mirror!

Why, is it possible that a strong man should look like his mummy?

The piano is shining.

Mother sits down and plays some Chopin.

This is some sort of an answer to my complaint.

Never to look into a mirror! Never! Get rid of that pitiful, infantile habit—scrutinizing oneself. It is a peculiarity of the weak. A baby in his bath examines its tiny hands, feet, its little body. . . .

I would like to blot out of my consciousness everything that indicates weakness. I want to reform. I solemnly swear that I shall reform thoroughly.

She is offering me Chopin's oversensitivity. What is it, waltz, plush or pelisse?

She put together his portrait for me.

This forehead is begging for the palm of a hand to lean on and already some hand or other is moving close to it. But at the last second he reels back, afraid. Who is that striving toward him? He tries to see the hand nearing him and that is why his eyes are slightly raised and crossed. . . .

There are colds—it is, "Why, you're coughing again," it is, "You mustn't go out in this damp weather." He was irritated with his tailors and wrote to a friend—a Polish insurgent—and he called this man, who bore the Roman name of Titus, all sorts of tender names as if he were a young girl writing to another young girl. This was not the emotional warmth of two men hugging each other on meeting unexpectedly. No, Chopin was immature and vulnerable and the strange tenderness of his words originated in his infantile self-love and in fear of what might happen to him.

"I would like to be a fool, Mother," I said. "I consider imbecility to be a lucky break, a state conducive to happiness! Come over here, Mother. Now, see this tie? It is a beautiful tie and it is very beautifully tied. And wouldn't it be a good idea if I grew myself sideburns? Not too long, velvety sideburns. And to be sunburned. And also I'd like to be tall and have bigger shoulders. And then it would be nice to do something unscrupulous, like forging a document or something. And not to have any feelings about the world. . . ."

Now about Bazilevich. Bazilevich is a Bolshevik. He is an editor and is forty-five. His looks are ordinary. He wears an overcoat with a sheepskin collar—an ordinary black overcoat—a scarf, a fur cap with ear flaps, and rubber galoshes. He has a wife who is friendly, kind, and in no way remarkable.

I went to see him in the evening. He was out and didn't come home until after eight.

"It's freezing cold outside," he said.

Coming in from the cold, the man seemed huge. Then,

perhaps a minute after he had pulled the door to behind him, he became reduced to his normal size.

"It's unheard of," his wife said. "Just imagine, he leaves in the morning and doesn't have anything to eat during the whole day. Look at yourself—your face is completely gray. The whole day without eating! This can't go on. From now on, I'll prepare sandwiches for you and you must take them. It couldn't possibly hurt you to take a couple of sandwiches in wax paper every morning. Do you want to get a stomach ulcer or something? . . ."

Bazilevich walks over to the sink. From a few steps away, his wife throws a towel over his shoulder. He washes his hands and, as if to symbolize the end of the operation, he shakes his palms over the bowl. Then he dries them without removing the towel from his shoulder. The water drains noisily from the sink. He turns his head back to see if he hasn't forgotten to turn off the tap.

While he is doing all this, I tell him how difficult it is to be a writer. I tell him about lofty aspirations and painful bewilderment.

And he, looking at me short-sightedly, groping against the wall with the towel in search of the nail, says:

"You really should share the life of the masses."

A stereotype. Of course, it is nothing but a cliché. You can find it in every newspaper, in every magazine.

To merge with the masses.

He is an intelligent man, though, a man who leads a normal life. He goes about the business of publishing—reading, selecting and editing manuscripts, dealing with the printers, living with his wife whom he loves, going out into the cold, wearing his rubbers. . . . And here he utters this cliché with the same lively conviction he showed when he said that it was freezing cold today.

Perhaps, then, the fact that it is a cliché does not prevent a phrase from expressing an aspect of life.

I tell him in an exclamatory tone that I intend to write my own *Intrigue and Love*. This is a high-faluting phrase too but I pronounce it with lively conviction because the phrase is part of my life, one of the facets of which my whole life consists, and so this loud phrase is also an expression of life.

Now these two phrases meet and this meeting is witnessed by Bazilevich's wife, a simple woman who does not seem particularly moved. This would suggest that we're talking about quite usual things.

He does not stop to think for one second but says immediately:

"You ought to share the life of the masses."

He is still groping for that nail on the wall. Finally he finds it.

At that second he feels that something inevitable and good has taken place. A subconscious substitution takes place in his mind—the finding of the nail is replaced by something else but just as inevitable and good for which he has a ready-made verbal symbol.

"You must," he says, "merge with the masses."

(1931)

NATASHA

The little old man sat down at the table set for breakfast. It was set for one. There was a coffeepot and a milk jug. The spoon standing in a large coffee cup burned in a morning sunbeam like a blinding match. Two boiled eggs lay on a saucer next to the eggcup.

As soon as he had sat down, the little old man began to think the things he always thought in the morning when he sat down to his breakfast. He thought that his daughter Natasha did not like him. Why, if for no other reason, he could tell by the fact that she made him eat breakfast alone. She was supposed to respect him so much that she felt he needed all this privacy.

"You're a famous scholar and you must have every possible comfort."

Imbecile, the professor thought, what an imbecile. So I must eat my breakfast all alone. And while I eat it, read my paper. That's the way she wants it. Where did she get such ideas—from the movies? The idiot.

The professor took an egg, put it in the silver eggcup and banged its unshiny summit with the silver spoon. He was irritated with everything. He remembered that Columbus had done something to an egg and that irritated him too.

"Natasha!" he called.

Of course, Natasha wasn't home. He decided to have a talk with her. He loved his daughter. He knew of no prettier sight than the young girl dressed in a white linen dress with shining mother-of-pearl buttons. Yesterday she

had ironed that dress. The ironed dress had smelled of
lavender.

Having finished his breakfast, the old man put on his
panama hat, threw a raincoat over his arm, took his walking
stick and left the house.

The car was waiting for him.

"Where do we go, Professor?" the chauffeur asked him.
"The same place?"

"Yes," he said.

"I was told to give you this," the chauffeur said and
handed the old man an envelope. They started. Bouncing
up and down on the seat cushions, the professor read the
note:

"Don't, don't, don't be angry. I had to rush off to a date.
Don't you get angry, you hear me? Stein is an awfully nice
guy. I'm sure you'll like him. I'll bring him to meet you.
You aren't angry, are you? Did you have your breakfast?
I send you my love. I'll be back in the evening. Tonight
you're off, remember, and dining at the Shatunovs, so I'm
free."

"What's the matter, Kolia?" the professor suddenly
asked the chauffeur.

The chauffeur turned around and looked at him.

"I thought you were laughing."

He had thought the chauffeur was laughing but his face
was serious. Still, this did not remove the suspicion that he
was laughing inwardly. The professor believed that the
chauffeur had been covering up for Natasha. He did not
approve of his taste in dress. Always those extraordinary
sweaters. He must think of me as "the old man." Now he's
thinking—the old man is in a bad mood.

They were driving down a suburban road. Trees in
bloom, hedges and passers-by dashed to meet them.

She'll bring Stein to meet me, the professor was musing.
She says he's a nice guy. We shall see. Today I'll tell her:
bring Stein.

Then the old man was walking through knee-high grass,
swinging his walking stick.

"The coat, the coat . . . where's the coat?" He suddenly realized he did not have it. "I must have left it in the car."

Walking uphill he got a little out of breath, took off his panama hat, wiped the sweat from his forehead with his hand, looked at his wet palm, went on hitting at the grass with his stick. The grass shone and lay on its side.

He could already see the parachutes in the sky. He thought: This must be the spot where I stood the last time. Yes.

He stopped and began to watch the parachutes appearing in the sky. One, two, three, four. . . . Aha . . . one more over there . . . and there, another one. . . . What's that—a scallop shell filled with sun! How high up! But they say the fear of heights disappears. . . . Ah yes, there it is, the striped one! Funny, a striped parachute. . . .

The professor turned his head to look back. The little blue, capsule-like car was standing at the bottom of the hill. There were flowers blooming there and trees gently swaying. Everything was very strange and dream-like: the sky, the spring, the floating parachutes. The old man felt sadness and tenderness and the sun reached through to him through the little cracks in the brim of his panama.

He stood like that for a long time. Then he drove back home. Natasha wasn't there. He sat down on the sofa. In the uncomfortable position of a man who is just about to get up, he sat there for a whole hour. Then he got up, knocking over the ashtray, and walked over to the telephone. At that very second the phone rang. The professor knew exactly what they were going to tell him; it was merely a question of the address. They told him the address and he answered:

"I'm not worried. Who told you I was worried?"

Ten minutes later, after a mad drive through the streets, the little old man was putting on a white smock and walking along a long parquet corridor.

He opened a glass door and saw Natasha's laughing face in the middle of a pillow. Then he heard someone saying, "Nothing grave." A young man standing beside the pillow had said it. "She didn't land right."

She had twisted her ankle. It was all quite strange. Then, instead of talking about the accident, they all somehow began to discuss the fact that the professor looked like Gorky with the difference that he was short while Gorky was a tall man. All three of them and another woman in a white smock were laughing.

"So you knew?" Natasha asked.

"Of course I knew. I went there every time and stood in the grass watching, like an idiot."

At this point the old man began to cry. Natasha cried too.

"Why do you worry me?" she said. "It's bad for me." And she cried more and more and put her father's hand against her cheek.

"I thought you would try to stop me from jumping."

"So you tried to fool me," he said, "pretended that you were dating a young man. Very stupid. I had to stand in the grass like an idiot and wait for that striped thing to open. . . ."

"My parachute wasn't the striped one. Stein has the striped one. . . ."

"Stein?" the old man asked, growing angry again. "What Stein?"

"I am Stein," the young man said.

(1936)

I LOOK INTO THE PAST

I was a small schoolboy the day Bleriot flew the Channel.

That summer, we didn't go out to a summer place because of financial difficulties.

Dad played cards, came back home at dawn and slept during the day. He was an excise official. His job consisted of ensuring that no government sales regulations were broken in the liquor stores. He did not attend to his duties too well and I don't know how he managed to keep his job. But still, he was getting his salary. The main thing in his life was his club and cards. He lost mostly and it was a well-known fact that Dad wasn't lucky. He spent days on end at the club.

And so, as I said, Bleriot flew the Channel. It was summer and we had a summer dinner. I remember it was a hot, sticky day and someone was cutting a melon.

About melons it was known that Uncle Tolia ate them with salt. No melon was ever satisfactory. It was only we, the children, who liked every one we ate. Mummy said: "Tastes just like a cucumber." Dad remarked, "Why don't you buy melons from Lamazka?" And Auntie often warned: "One should be careful because of dysentery."

We were a petty-bourgeois family.

A big, horny conch rested on the mantelpiece. You were supposed to hold it to your ear and listen.

"Can you hear the sea?" the grownups asked then.

The conch in which the sea could be heard was, in a sense, part of a setting, like Uncle Tolia eating melon with salt. In all the homes around, there were similar conches thrown up by God knows what seas.

Dad wanted me to become an engineer. To him the word engineering represented work as an official in a government department. He imagined a badge, and the phrase "like Mr. Kovalevski" came automatically to his lips.

In our house there was not a single thing which had its particular significance; there was nothing by which one could tell, for instance, whether the master of the house was, say, an idiot, a liar or a skinflint. It was quite impossible to tell.

The master of the house was a gambler. Dad was supposed to be a man out of luck. "It was all the fault of the cards."

Dad's life at the club remained unknown to us. Perhaps he broke out in a sweat when he was losing. Perhaps he told funny jokes to put those he was about to touch for three rubles into a good mood. Maybe, talking to him, the other club members exchanged discreet glances.

His life at home was roughly like this: when he woke up, he took his tea and bread and butter in bed, after which he went back to sleep with his fists clenched on his chest. He appeared for dinner fully dressed, wearing starched cuffs with gold cuff links. He was kind, soft-spoken; the hair on his temples was still wet from being combed.

"Bleriot has flown the Channel," I said.

My announcement could only have touched a prepared audience. My aunt didn't know where the Channel was, who Bleriot was, why he was supposed to fly over anything, or why it should interest anyone anyway.

Moreover, the grownups suspected that in everything said, thought or desired by a child there lurked something suspect.

My parents were constantly apprehensive about the possibility of some disorder in my mental make-up, some disorder having a sexual connotation.

"He probably plays with his hands under the blanket."

They exchanged glances and I intercepted alarm in those glances of theirs.

So, Dad, you want me to be an engineer? Well, here's some engineering for you! I'd like to tell you something about the most magic engineering there is, but you won't listen to me. I am thinking of the engineer whose invention has made the flying man possible, while you want me to become an engineer with a badge in his lapel and a seashell with sound in it on the mantelpiece of the house in which he lives.

You reproach me for not reading enough.

So let's talk about the bookcase. It is filled with Turgenev, Dostoevsky, Goncharov, Danilevsky and Grigorovich.

Tolstoy is missing because the magazine *Niva* just didn't give Tolstoy as a literary supplement.

And there's no Chekhov because you discontinued the subscription to *Niva* before it started carrying him.

I open the door of the bookcase. The smell coming out of it isn't repellent at all. Here one might expect a description of a smell of mustiness and mice wafting over the book as it is taken from the shelf.

No smell of mice emanates from your bookcase. The bookcase is a recent acquisition. It is new and the shelves are fresh. It is kept with great care. It is upright, not too big, and not a single decorative wiggle has yet been bitten off by time; in one spot there's even a drop of the original glue still showing from under a piece of ornament. It has stopped in its run, hardened into amber, and hasn't yet been poked out by children. And the fragrance coming from the fresh shelves reminds me sometimes of a vague aroma of chocolate.

All the books are in black cloth bindings with leather spines and your initials. I pick up a book and pass the palm of my hand over its cover. Pimples appear on the calico. And it is at this point that mustiness begins.

I think this way: Once my dad decided to have all his books bound. One day, Dad said: "These books ought to be bound." A bookbinder was summoned, the price was agreed upon and everything was put in order.

I didn't suffer from the Bad Habit: I had no intention of playing with my hands under the blanket. It was they who forced this desire down my throat. They always suspected me. They scrutinized me and deciphered nonexistent sexual preoccupations.

Besides Bleriot, there were such names as Latham, Farman, Wilbur and Orville Wright, Lilienthal and the Voisin brothers. There was also a place near Paris called Issy-les-Moulineaux.

No one in my house, in my family, in the homes of our acquaintances—none of those people who knew so well how to live and what to become—had heard about how Otto Lilienthal got killed when flying in his glider, none of them suspected that, before taking off, an airplane must make a run along the ground, or that the Wright brothers' machine looked more like a bird than any other aircraft.

I was the only one aware of these things.

The small boy of the family was a European, a journalist and an aircraft engineer. I was offering my family a chance to catch up with the times. I could have stood up in the middle of dinner and, raising my fingers as though I were holding a tuning fork, sung out the word:

"Issy-les-Moulineaux!"

I would have taught them how, at the sound of these syllables, they could become receptive to the vibrations of the magic tuning fork.

Issy-les-Moulineaux. . . . I would've made them see the green field, the grass of the early runways lighted by the sun of the young century, that beautiful clear green space surrounded by a throng of bustling men in bowler hats, hurrying amidst the daisies toward the great shadow that is sliding under their feet.

Look! One of them is running holding a watch in his hand. . . . Can you see them tearing off their bowler hats, raising their walking sticks? Now look, look, see that object—that yellowish, shiny thing, knuckly, drumming silkily, scattering patches of reflected sunlight from its wheel-spokes, settling down on the turf. . . . This thing has just flown, d'you hear? This machine was airborne! Do you know this man? Well, he is the flying man, understand!

That happened long ago, before I started reading books. But even then I had somehow become fated to read the classics in pimply covers.

Ah, it really doesn't matter what sort of covers there are on the classics. I didn't care in the least whether they were in morocco or in cardboard. That's not what I'm talking about.

What I am talking about is that the bookbinder who answered my dad's call could have turned into a parquet polisher as he walked into our kitchen through the back door, without anyone's noticing the difference. And he could have turned just as successfully into a paperhanger or into anyone else, except, perhaps, a messenger.

Yes, if he had turned into a man from the messenger service, the transformation would not have gone unnoticed because messengers wear red caps. The red cap of a messenger is one of the first things I learned about the world.

What I'm trying to say here is that the bookbinder belonged to the category described as service people. One person would polish floors, another paper walls, a third bind books. This bookbinder was sent to us by some lady of our acquaintance. Another such lady could recommend us a floor polisher. About the floor polisher it could have been said that he used good floor wax, while of the bookbinder it could be said that he provided good calico.

And this is why I mentioned mustiness.

The thing is that these books were intended to be read by me. I was growing up and they were waiting for me. The day was to come, that solemn moment, when a boy begins to read.

That day came. I began to read the great classics. An event that couldn't fail to have far-reaching consequences took place.

For the first time in my life I got to know Don Quixote.
I got to know a man created by another man and with him
I received the concept of immortality in the form in which
it can exist on this earth. And I became a particle of that
immortality—I began to think. This is a unique and ir-
replaceable experience—like one's first woman.

Blessed is the man who, possessing his first woman, is
protected by love. Blessed is the youth who, beginning to
think, has a guide to lead him.

And so who was my guide? Who was there to prepare
me for my encounter with ideas? Was it the lady of my
parents' acquaintance or the floor polisher who incidentally
turned out to be a bookbinder, or was it my father who
knew that classics were only such books as came with the
Niva as literary supplements?

I had no guide.

I opened the bookcase and my knowledge about the
lady who recommended the bookbinder, about Uncle Tolia,
about the distrust of me, about the fact that I must become an engineer—all that turned inside me sickeningly,
gave me a sensation of hunger together with the taste of
enamel that is left in the mouth after a man has drunk too
much water, and with all that, I was pervaded by despondency, boredom and laziness.

That is the kind of mustiness that filled my dad's bookcase.

But then I found myself sitting and reading. A bright
lamp is hanging over the round dining table. The famous
circle of light is moving on the oilcloth in the center of the
table, as though leaving without leaving, turning around
without turning. This is the very same circle of light that
is so easily taken as a symbol of peace, family and quiet.

In front of me is an open book. And what do I know
when I read it? What have my guides told me about
reading?

All they have said amounts to warnings of one sort or
another: they were worried about my fingers, my saliva
and the lower corners of the pages. . . . They were wor-

ried about the way I was to turn the pages. That in the
first place.

And in the second place, they were worried about my
poor posture, so harmful to my health, about the anti-
hygienic aspects of it. . . . They held over me threateningly the story of Vitia Bulatovich, a boy just like me,
who somehow went the wrong way about turning the pages
of some book, caught scarlet fever and died.

This is the mustiness I had in mind.

So, Dad, you think I don't read enough. You're pleased
when you find me with a book.

"Dosia is reading!"

You stop by the table and put your hand on my head.

My hair is short cropped, my head isn't round. It isn't
a typical child's head: the back of it is somewhat flattened,
lopped off. In general, many things in me hint at sickliness.
Perhaps a phrenologist would detect a predilection for soli-
tude, shyness and easily provoked embarrassment. When
all these features are found in a child, he is, for some
reason, said to be in delicate health.

So you put your hand on my head:

"So you're reading, eh?"

And saying that, you smile as if you'd like to wink at
someone to make him understand: "See, Dosia is reading!"

And you are not in the least interested in what is going
on in my mind while I am reading.

It is infinitely less important to you to know where I am
going than to watch my gait. The sight causes you to be
pleased with yourself, brings to your mind some of your
own imaginary accomplishments and arouses your pride
and, for some reason, a desire to laugh which seems to
me moronic. I don't like reading where you can see me.
I scamper off.

Summer. The sky is blue. I sit on a step of the iron staircase in the courtyard. I am reading. The book is on my
knees. All our neighbors are away at their summer houses.
It is a Sunday.

Yesterday I cut my forefinger on some glass. The cut
was quite deep and I was taken to the pharmacy. There,
they poured collodium on it.

In the pharmacy it was dark and cool but at the same
time it was there that I had the strongest realization that
it was summer, just as I feel the summer most in the bedroom, in the early morning, when the curtains are just being drawn.

I was installed on a wooden bench. Mummy held my
hand. My blood spread all over my palm, emphasizing
the lines by which palmists predict the future. The collodium dried right away. They pulled the skin together and
bound my forefinger in a half-bent position, the bandage
crossing my palm. Then, the bandage was cut lengthwise
and the two ends were tied on the back of my hand in a
neat little butterfly.

The bandage on my hand looked dazzlingly white and
it made my hand heavy, independent and beautiful. Then
I started pulling individual threads out of the gauze bandage. They didn't break but parted daintily, revealing the
lattice-like texture of the bandage. When these threads got
onto my clothes it was impossible to get them off. My
wounded hand prevented me from bending down to pick
them up, as it had to be held up all the time in the direction
of the sore finger. By the end of the day, the finger had
become swollen and, in its loosened bandage, had taken
on the appearance of the neck of a bottle.

I'm reading as I sit on a step of the iron stairs in the
backyard. Everyone around has left for the seaside and the
country. I have a wound on my finger and I like having
that wound. I am alone and there is no one to offend me.
But by thinking about the pain in my finger and about
all the others being away in their summer houses, I somehow manage to become resentful.

The resentment is accompanied by a retinue of feelings,
all cheerful. I begin to laugh, wondering how resentment
and self-pity could turn out to be so pleasant and so
cheering.

I possess the secret of turning sadness into gaiety. I can use this secret process any time I choose. But what I most enjoy is being sad. I close my eyes and pleasant shivers pass through me. I open my eyes and in the middle of the blue sky I see a rainbow, because the light is refracted by the tears hanging on my eyelashes.

I like to act a whole part to myself while I am reading. I cry, realizing very well that I really feel very happy. I substitute myself for the hero and I want to be just like him.

Sometimes he seems quite out of my reach. Sometimes I say to myself that no life like the one destined for me could exist either in reality or in fiction, because I am superior to them all and my destiny will be really remarkable.

The hero lives in France.

I lift my eyes. In front of me I see bricks and leaves. The leaves are swaying in front of the bricks. This combination of red brick and green is my France. The hero and I walk at the foot of a brick wall under the swaying, leafy branches, in some country called France that is the land of my future. . . .

And this, Daddy, is what I'm reading!

I feel that the life of a man, the shaping of a boy's character, is determined, to a considerable degree, by his attachment to his father or the lack of it.

Perhaps the masculine character should be divided into two categories: those men who were molded by the effect of filial love, and those who were guided by the overriding need to escape paternal domination, the secret, unacknowledged longing that in a dream takes the surprising form of shameful exposure, as when a man is stripped and publicly examined.

Thus we develop notions about running away, becoming a tramp, the delight of being humiliated, compensating pity, war, the soldier, amputation of an arm.

Thus there are nights when a boy thinks he is a foundling. Thus begins the search for a father, for a homeland, for a profession, for a lucky charm that may be fame or power.

Thus we create loneliness, which dooms a man forever to be alone, to remain alone everywhere and in everything. They call him a dreamer; they laugh at him. He allows it and ends by laughing at himself along with the others. They conclude from this that he has no character, that he is servile. He continues all alone, his head sunk between his shoulders; buzzing with vanity, conceit, self-abasement and scorn for men; alternating between ecstasy and thoughts of death; forming an endless storm.

The storm never breaks beyond the confines of his sore skull; the man tries to control it by withdrawing his head between his shoulders. Only now and then he turns his head to stare after those who are laughing at him, and they may notice then that on this face that has always made them laugh canine fangs are bared in a snarl.

(1928)

HUMAN MATERIAL

I am a schoolboy.

When I grow up, I'll be just like Mr. Kovalevski.

That's the way my family wants it.

I'll be an engineer and an owner of real estate.

The balcony door is wide open. I can hear the noises coming from the port. On the balcony, there's an oleander growing in a green tub. Mr. Kovalevski has come to have dinner with us. He stands against the backdrop of the balcony doorway, black as a shadow, on thin, widespread legs.

My dad is an excise official, an impoverished gentleman, a gambler. We are poor but belong to respectable society. Dad is still every bit a gentleman and no one has turned away from him.

I come into the drawing room to greet Mr. Kovalevski. I arrive—small, stooping, ears sticking out. Indeed, I step forward between my own ears. Dad is walking behind me. He is showing me off. I am a child prodigy. The guest stretches his hand, which seems spotted like a hen, toward me.

Dad knows exactly how I should live in order to be happy, that is, rich, independent and occupying a respectable position in society. Like Mr. Kovalevski. Dad considers his own life unhappy. Like every man who has squandered his money, he considers himself wronged and humbled. Everything is lost, it's too late for regrets, life is over. Well, all right, what's done is done. But he has something to show for it all: the map of his journey through

life. On that map are marked all the disasters, gulfs, barriers.

Besides the map of his own life, my father also has an
approximate map of the life of Mr. Kovalevski. It is quite
easy to compare these two maps, to superimpose them.
Similarities, differences and contrasts are marked. As a result, Father obtains a map of the ideally happy life he
could have had if he had been fated to be happy.

But since one cannot live a life twice over, what use can
this third map be put to? Obviously—hand it over to the
son. And so I am to use as my guide a map drawn by my
father as a result of envy and frustration and based on the
longings, dreams and talents that are peculiar to him alone.
This plan is thrust upon me as the very best guidance possible and I have no right even to discuss it.

Dad realizes very well the gap between himself and Mr.
Kovalevski. It is immense: he himself will never be able
to bridge it. But here am I, and as I come into the room,
Dad announces:

"Dosia is first in his class."

This is to say that I have overcome one of the obstacles
that is marked off as catastrophes on Father's life map.

I am the first student in my class. I am younger than my
classmates, and brighter. This is very important. Mr.
Kovalevski should be greatly impressed by it. I am a quiet,
uncommunicative boy. Even the fact that I am a bit anemic
raises Dad's chances in his competition with Mr. Kovalevski. Let the man realize that I have every prerequisite for
success. An uncommunicative character, studiousness,
anemia—all these are very promising qualifications. It seems
I have an unexpected and brilliant asset for the plan for an
ideally successful life—anemia!

We are facing one another—I, a sixth-grade schoolboy,
and Mr. Kovalevski, an engineer, an owner of real estate
and the chairman of something or other.

I raise my eyes and I see a beard. The beard is long,
blond and wavy. In its shadow, like a Dryad in the forest,
nests a star of the Order of Merit.

Come to think of it, I don't see any beards nowadays. There are no more bearded people around.

We were small schoolboys and we had fathers, grand-fathers, uncles and big brothers. They formed a gallery of examples. We were led down that portrait gallery and turned from one side to the other while the names of uncles, cousins, famous relatives and acquaintances were whispered in our ears.

Human models presided over our childhood: engineers, bank directors, lawyers, chairmen of the board, property owners, doctors.

The Japanese War, the heroic exploit of Army Private Riabov, the first movies, the two-hundredth anniversary of the Battle of Poltava, the Jewish pogroms, General Kaulbars, the assassination of Queen Draga: these are the symbols of my childhood. And, in addition, the human models, the bearded ideals of my dreams, beards, beards and beards. . . .

Some beards were parted in the middle. Their owners had, as a rule, bright, smiling, salmon-colored lips, the lips of debauches, the lips of seducers of schoolgirls.

Some beards were gray, long, tapering downward like swords. Those who wore them had knitted brows and they were the conscience of the generation.

Some beards were short and wide. These mighty beards were firmly gripped in the fists of generals and railroad presidents.

I will become someone like Mr. Kovalevski. I'll have a beard.

Today we both wear uniforms—the schoolboy and the government official; he in his black coat, I in my gray school jacket.

Oh, gray school uniform! You didn't follow the con-tours of my body; you stood around my torso, being taller, and your shoulders had nothing in common with my shoulders. You surrounded me, round, wide, immobile, like the back of a chair.

I am a small schoolboy wearing clothes that are too big

so that I won't outgrow them too quickly. We are both wearing uniforms, Mr. Kovalevski and I. We are two links in the same chain; brass things, emblems, badges, glisten on our chests. We are two well-regulated persons: the young student of a Government school, the important engineer in the Government service.

"How do you do, sir?"

"Ah, hello!" Mr. Kovalevski exclaims. "How are you getting along, young man of pleasant appearance and graceful build."

After a brief pause, Dad speaks up.

"Dosia," he says, "wants to be an engineer."

Here, I could have objected that future engineers usually specialize in modern studies and science while I am taking classics and humanities. Why did you send me to a classical school if I'm supposed to become an engineer?

I must be an engineer and must also study Latin. But why does an engineer need Latin? But you are a good student and should know everything, get ahead of the other boys of your age. Then you'll be able to catch all the rabbits you want. You must do that, because, before your birth, your daddy lost an entire fortune at cards and he wants to get even.

And so, on my birthday I was given a set of geometrical instruments. Let Dosia draw blueprints.

I started to draw geometrical figures, suffering useless and boring pangs of creation that could not possibly reward me with success. For, in that part of the brain where a future engineer has a disposition for tracing, I had nothing but a blind spot. I felt the scientific impossibility of setting into motion something that simply wasn't there, and this realization was made manifest as a pain in the forehead, a weight pressing on the frontal bone.

In the velvet bed of its case lies a cold, glittering pair of dividers with the legs pressed tightly together.

It has a heavy head. I pick it up. It suddenly opens up and pricks my hand. I am holding one of its legs in my fist. Its mobility is amazing: each time its motions take me by surprise and are quicker than my reflexes of self-defense. I bring my hand to my mouth to lick off the blood and before the phrase "watch out" can form in my mind, the dividers has turned in my fist, its frightful point already glaring into my eye. I don't understand what's going on. What is it, this glitter, this dot that I cannot physically comprehend and which is now threatening my life?

I unclench my fist. The dividers is standing on the table. It looks around, takes a step, stops and falls on its head, its legs wide open, its feet deadly and sharp. Probably I am fated to fall on them, both pupils at once.

Today, I look around and find that everyone about me is an engineer.

But none of them is a property owner—just an engineer.

Among them, I am a lonely writer.

And no one demands that I should become an engineer.

I used to hear much spoken about justice. I heard it said that mended clothes are in their way beautiful and that one must be fair. One must be kind and not despise the poor. When the Revolution took place I witnessed the greatest human justice: the triumph of the oppressed class. Then I realized that not every patched jacket, not every misery, is a virtue. I learned that the only things that are just are those that are conducive to the emancipation of the oppressed class. I was never told of that justice by those who tried to teach me how to live. I must grasp it myself now with my own head. And what did they drum into that head of mine? A desire to become rich, a desire to force others to bend before my will.

I catch myself within myself, I grab by the throat the *I* who wants to turn back, who stretches out his arms to the past, who thinks the distance between us and Europe is a purely geographical one.

The *I* who views everything that happens only in relation to the way it will affect his life, that unique, inimitable and all-encompassing life beyond which there is nothing.

I want to smother my second *I* and my third *I*, who keep crawling out of the past.

I want to destroy the petty sentiments.

If I cannot be an engineer dealing with elemental forces, perhaps I can be one dealing with human material.

That sounds pretentious and loud, but I don't care. I shout: "Long live the effort to reconstruct the human edifice and the all-encompassing engineering of the new world!"

(1928)

JOTTINGS OF A WRITER

I was born in Elisavetgrad in the former Kherson Province.

Some memories of my babyhood linger in me.

A field covered with wild, coarse weeds; or rather an empty lot behind the blind wall of the house. . . . Twilight, and in the twilight, behind a fence, boys lighting matches that burn in flames of different colors.

For some time after that I thought that Swedish matches were the kind that burn in different-colored flames. I longed to have some matches like that. I'd say to people: "Remember, when I was little there were those Swedish matches. . . . You know, they made strawberry-colored or green flames. . . ."

The boys with the matches were called Sasha and Serozha. I also remember a family name—Voronin. I don't remember him but it seems he was the shoemaker. I wasn't allowed to go there. Also, I remember us walking through the coarse grass of the empty lot.

Later I learned that we had our own carriage and horses. There was a black trotter with a white spot on his forehead. That, I do not remember, but I willingly accept as recollection the picture of that horse readily formed by my imagination.

Father was an excise officer at a vodka distillery.

At the age of eighteen I went to Elisavetgrad on a trip. Before I left, Mother said: "Take a look at such-and-such a number on Petrovskaya Street; that's where you were born."

I went to have a look. No impression whatever. A two-story brick house. Some greenery by the entrance. I stood there and looked at it, expecting my heart to sink, expecting to shiver all over. But nothing came of it.

When I was three, my family moved to Odessa which, incorrectly, I consider my birthplace. In any case, all the lyricism connected with the concept of a native town is associated in my mind with Odessa.

I am very old.

I was able to read by myself the huge headlines of a newspaper announcing peace. That was the peace following the Russo-Japanese War. Hence, I've been reading now for twenty-five years.

A few days ago I was sitting in a streetcar next to a policeman. He had a big blond mustache, a sort of Viking mustache. He was a police officer, uniformed and armed, a big, powerful, grown-up man. And suddenly it dawned upon me: this police officer is younger than I am. This grown-up family man with a strongly developed chest and shoulders, wearing big, sweaty boots, is younger than I am!

For, although I'm thirty-one and already detect in myself signs of physical aging, I've never once yet felt myself to be a grownup.

I cannot plan anything in advance. Everything I have written, I wrote without a plan. Even a play. Even my adventure novel *Three Fat Men*.

For a whole year now I've been thinking of a novel.

I know its title: *The Beggar*.

The image of the beggar has been tormenting me since my boyhood. Perhaps I was struck by a cheap popular print. I don't remember clearly . . . a dry, sunny, deserted landscape. . . . A figure in the landscape, one Dmitri Donskoi, stretches his hand toward a kneeling beggar. I recall being fascinated by the words publican and sackcloth. Someone took pity on the publican. Salvation.

Once, this winter, I was walking down Nevsky Avenue. A beggar was kneeling at the top of a stairway leading down to a brightly lit basement store.

I didn't see the beggar right away. My hand was dangling
level with his lips as though I expected he'd seize and kiss
it. He was kneeling, his torso straight, black and immobile,
like an idol. As I walked past, my peripheral vision somehow registered him as the statue of a lion. "And where is
the second lion?" I looked back: a beggar.

He knelt with his face uplifted and its features, pulled
together by the darkness, composed something reminiscent
of the dark board of an icon. I shuddered.

He didn't budge. He remained kneeling and he had been
kneeling for many hours—perhaps since morning. He was
a bearded peasant.

I'm walking on a hot day on the edge of the city by an
old, ruined brick wall in silence and isolation. I'm sweaty
and barefoot; my shirt is completely unbuttoned.

Then I hear the distant voices of men working on the
railroad line and the musical clang of a falling rail. The
sound of the falling rail seems to reach me through water
rather than through air.

I am striding along unseen and forgotten by all, in search
of my original impressions.

Far, far ahead, I can see huge letters on the back of a
factory.

A ravine crosses my path. It is that dump heap over
which, in my boyhood, the genie of travels floated. Yes, it
was out of that dump that the dreamiest genie of my childhood emanated. Maybe it was because the dump glittered
like a moat on the boundary of the town.

Perhaps it was because children knew they'd be punished
if they were caught coming here, to this forbidden place.
And so, they recklessly rushed toward danger: a mutt that
could be rabid darting out from behind a hillock; two
hobos playing at toss-penny; a ragged boy showing off an
army knife with a brass handle; and, above all, the water
tower—for only in this deserted zone was it possible to get
really close to the water tower.

There's nothing on earth like that tower!

What does it have in common with the houses of the
city, the roofs, the balconies, the courtyards, the doorways? Not a thing!

The water tower is no longer part of the city. It looms
up far out in the Journey, it is already in the Future. An
iron staircase twists around it. Outlandish vegetation grows
at its foot and outlandish little black windows dot its immensely tall body.

The pharmacy was located in one of the central streets
of the city.

It was in a building that took up a good half of the
block. One side of that building gave onto a side street
that it squashed under its gray bulk, only the upper
reaches of which were lit up, catching the red glow only
at sunset on its row of windows right under the roof. The
huge house had been built toward the end of the last century and belonged to a merchant.

An old-fashioned carved oak door led to the pharmacy.
The door had glass panels. The handle was glass too. It
was faceted, and on sunny days produced a rainbow.

The door was very heavy. To open it, one had to pull
hard on the handle, holding it like a beer mug.

Inside there were some steps leading toward another
door that was always kept open.

The space between the two doors formed a sort of cave
that, depending on the season, was filled with either dust
or dampness, was either pierced with drafts or stuffed with
sunlight that, coming through the grimy glass in the door,
turned yellow like the sun on the wooden benches of railroad carriages. On those sunny days, the black shadow of
the cross stuck on the glass panel of the door lay in a
broken line on the steps.

Once on a drizzly, muddy autumn evening, a man
opened the pharmacy door, but did not slam it hurriedly
behind him and rush up the steps as others did. Instead,
he turned back toward it and, as though afraid the some-

what loose glass would break in its worn frame, he carefully led the door back into its doorway.

Having reached the middle step, the man stopped, turned sideways and, somehow sliding back, found himself flat against the wall. There he froze, supporting the wall with his back. He suddenly looked so relieved that one might have thought he had been trying to reach that spot for a long time and had finally taken a position that suited his body.

Outside the door there was a lighted electric bulb. Its light shone through the glass panel on the man standing against the wall. From the street, through the glass square, one could see only the man's torso and head bathed in a greenish light.

The first thing that attracted attention was the man's cap pulled down to mid-ear, pinning down the lobes that folded upward. The headgear gave the man a pitiable and shameful air.

The cap was made of light summer material that had grown dark from being used in all seasons. It was covered with stains and had acquired a shapelessness similar to the conical bubbliness of a chef's hat.

The man was fat and apparently rather short. His whole weight was concentrated in his belly which he apparently supported with his hands clasped just under it.

His head rested on a neck drawn into his shoulders. Actually, he couldn't stretch his neck because his fat shoulders pressed against the back of it, causing his head to bend and dooming his eyes to look upward forever.

The man wore a quilted jacket into which his big torso could hardly fit. Indeed, he had to use several bits of elastic to keep the two halves of the jacket joined over his belly and under his chin.

The jacket had burst under the armpits. Cotton wool stuck out of the cracks, curling on both sides of his back, in a manner somewhat reminiscent of winglets.

The man seemed to be staring at one spot, somewhere downward, in a shadowy corner of the passage.

From time to time the man shivered all over, perhaps because of the dampness.

From time to time, he would lift a stubby arm and scratch his chin with the air of one who had stumbled on a pleasant idea in a stream of gloomy thoughts.

Now and then it looked as if he were dozing off. In any case he started to sink, his quilted back creeping down the paneled wall, sinking until his hands clasped around his belly fell apart. Then he woke up with a start and resumed his former position.

When the door opened and people came in, he rushed very eagerly to meet them and close the door behind them.

This man was a beggar.

The night advanced. The door opened less and less often. All unnecessary bulbs were turned off in the pharmacy. The beggar began to show signs of despondency. Apparently he expected that the pharmacy staff would soon discover his presence on those steps and that he would lose his shelter. Now he no longer dozed off. He kept turning his head toward the door at the top of the steps, raising himself on tiptoe and pricking up his ears. Suddenly he'd grab the doorhandle as though preparing to flee.

In the end they did kick him out all right and he found himself in the street.

It was raining; the street was deserted. The beggar walked faster and faster until he was running, his cotton wool winglets flapping.

He stopped at a crossing. Water dripped from his cap and ran in streamlets down his face.

Water babbled under the curb. He looked down: the water was swimming under the stone like a fish. To keep warm, he began to jump up and down.

Now, someone who wanted to have a laugh could imagine this man as an aging cupid because of his rotund form and his winglets. Besides, he had no socks and kept skipping around.

This is how, calmly, in the old realistic style, I'd have liked to begin my novel, *The Beggar*.

I don't know how others write novels.

Zola made a very detailed plan, determining with the greatest precision the date and the hour when he would set down the final period. And his estimate was never wrong. He knew in advance on what date of which month a given chapter would come to an end.

But I have never even attempted to draw up such a magic timetable.

In my files I have at least three hundred pages, each marked with the number one. These are the three-hundred-odd openings of my novel, *Envy*. And none of these pages became the final opening.

The mastery of writing technique is attained through daily, regular writing, like going to an office. Alas, we do not know how to work.

I had come to Odessa for a rest.

The summer house is on top of a cliff with a steep descent toward the sea. I sit on a bench a couple of steps from the precipice.

The sea is before my eyes. I look straight ahead without rising or glancing down. I see only the farthest plane of the panorama, its backdrop: sea and horizon.

But there are many planes in reality. The first is formed by crests of the slabs that have broken off the cliff. They slope forward somewhat, as if their gabled structure might disintegrate if merely brushed by a bird's wing. They are so dry and wind-blown; ordinary clay resembling granite in the desert landscape and the bright sun; castles in the air casting mighty shadows like craters of the moon.

Beyond them were ledges with vegetation powdered with dust that made it look like German silver.

What kind of flora is that? In the South, on the coast, I didn't find anything that could be described as grass.

Wiggles, dwarfs and freaks stick up out of the scorched earth among the hillocks.

It is true that I was making these observations at the

beginning of August and that I was roaming through the countryside as if through a town after a big fire.

And indeed, my foot suddenly gets entangled in a long stalk ordained to curl, a dry, rough stalk like a wire in its insulating covering. I'm scared to withdraw my foot, for I can't see the beginning of the stalk: it could be that any movement might dislodge an attached protruding rafter. In fact, to stop toying with imagery, the rafter is nothing but a gray, dusty tree trunk.

I am sitting on a bench.

Size is a relative thing.

On the very edge of the cliff, or even just beyond it, something umbrella-like is growing. It stands clearly outlined against the sky.

This tiny plant is all there is between my eye and the sky.

I look at it with ever-increasing concentration; suddenly a shift takes place in my brain: the focusing of imaginary binoculars.

And the focus is found. The plant stands before me like a culture under a microscope. It is gigantic.

My vision has acquired magnifying power. I become a Gulliver in the land of the Brobdingnag giants.

The impressive appearance of the puny, straw-like plant awes me: it is terrifying. It rises like a construction of some unknown, grandiose civilization. I see heavy spheres, pipes, joints, levers. The dim reflection of the sun on the rickety stem looks like the shine of metal.

Such is the phenomenon of vision.

It is not difficult to induce it. Any observer can do it. It is not a question of the peculiarities of the eye but of objective conditions: a combination of space, object and vantage point.

There is an Edgar Allan Poe story about a similar phenomenon. A man sitting by an open window saw a fantastic monster crawling over a distant hill.

He was seized by a mystical fear.

Cholera was raging in that region; the man thought he saw the incarnation of the disease: cholera itself.

A moment later the huge monster turned out to be only an ordinary insect; the observer had succumbed to an optical illusion, caused by the fact that the insect was making its way across a spider's web quite close to his eye and between it and the remote hills in the background.

We must see the world in a new way.

It is very important for a writer to engage in such magic photography. And this is no twist, no expressionism! On the contrary, it is the purest, healthiest realism.

I tire of looking at the sea. I make my way to the rear of the summer house.

I go through the garden gate. Expanse of steppe. At a distance a trolley line leading to Lustdorf.

On the steppe rises a water tower. (For a description of the tower, see the passage above, although that was another water tower amidst "outlandish vegetation" and with "outlandish windows." Here, there's no vegetation whatever: a tower of about two hundred feet sticks directly out of the naked earth.)

The ground belonged to someone named Vysotski. The nearest trolley stop is called Vysotski Tower to this day.

Vysotski once took it upon himself to supply water to the whole area. For this purpose, he built the tower. Someone sued him; afterward someone bought some part of it all: The details have been forgotten.

The tower has been in disuse for a long time now, but it preserves certain romantic characteristics: it dominates the landscape, looms black in the sunset, casts a long shadow, and is criss-crossed by the flights of birds.

There is a tunnel leading into the tower. It is a meeting place for buzzing flies attracted by excrement.

Once an aristocratic-looking old lady came, with two girls in cotton dresses. All three sat down on big stones near the garden gate. The old lady placed a book on her knee.

I read: Emile Zola. *Lourdes.*

The paws of reading glasses stuck out of the book.

The girls sat quietly, with dignity. Out of discretion, I walked away. Whispers wafted through the summer house.

The old lady was Vysotski's widow and the little girls her granddaughters.

Ten minutes later, I came back.

"This was ours," the old lady said, poking her finger into space.

"What was?" the left granddaughter asked.

"The park," the old lady said.

"Which park?" the right granddaughter wanted to know.

"This one here," the old woman replied.

There was no park there. There was just a yellow space. On the horizon, corn was swaying.

The girls kept a dignified silence. They saw what could be seen: the steppe.

The grandmother saw the park.

The park had been razed during the years of famine, its trees felled and turned into firewood by the people of the area. Not an oak, not a linden tree was left, nor even their roots. Then, for many years grain was sown where the park had been. Now, the harvest had been gathered.

August. Stubble. Here and there, some weeds.

The old woman sees the park. And, really . . . I suddenly remember.

When I was a high-school student, I came to visit the writer A. M. Fedorov at his summer house, the same one in which I'm staying now. And it is true that there were bunches of green clustered by the foot of the tower, white arbors were scattered amidst the greenery. I remembered: there was a park here, the famous Vysotski Park.

"That also belonged to us," the old woman announced.

"What?" her left granddaughter asked.

The girl sees little poles, barbed wire, vegetable patches.

"Pumpkins?" the right granddaughter asked.

"The house with the colonnade."

The old woman can see things that cannot be seen. This resembles paleontology. The old woman is a sort of paleontologist: she sees the past of the earth.

The girls gradually become dizzy.

"Was that also ours?" a girl asks, turning her head toward the trolley stop.

"The rosarium?" the grandmother says. "Yes, it was ours too."

Prediluvian roses are blooming before her eyes.

In the evening, the three of them sit on a bench near the edge of the cliff.

I walk over toward them. The silhouette of the old woman's head is like a heart.

The moon rises. The sea growls quietly. I am trying to hear what they are saying.

This time, the grandmother talks like a true paleontologist.

"The sea," she says, "was formed later. Once this used to be dry land."

"Was it ours too?" the granddaughters ask.

"Yes," I say, "it was. Everything was yours! Some scientists claim that the moon is a part of the earth that was once ripped away by some planet. In the place where it was torn away an ocean formed, the Pacific. Now, as you can see, the moon exists independently. But that doesn't mean a thing. It was once also yours!"

(1930)

SPEECH TO THE FIRST CONGRESS OF SOVIET WRITERS

There is good and bad in every man. I don't believe that a man can exist who would be unable to conceive what it is like to be vain, or cowardly, or selfish. Every man may suddenly feel in himself the appearance of some double. This phenomenon is particularly acute in an artist; one of the most amazing things about him is his capacity to experience other people's passions.

In every artist the seeds of an entire range of passions, bright and dark, are implanted; he knows how to make them grow and turn them into trees.

There are some supremely beloved plants in Tolstoy— Platon Karataev is one, Captain Tushin another. Nevertheless, in the mind of Tolstoy the artist, such terrifying scenes as Father Sergius succumbing to his lust for the short-legged little imbecile Maria also grow very readily and are visualized with unrestrained sensuality. It is impossible to describe a third person without becoming, if only for one minute, that third person.

All the vices and all the virtues live in the artist.

Often people ask him: "How could you know? Did you make it up yourself?"

Yes, the artist makes everything up himself, although obviously it is impossible to make up anything that doesn't exist in nature. But then, the relations of an artist with Nature are a bit special: she confides some of her secrets to him; she is more communicative with him than with others.

I can create a portrait of a coward from some quite flimsy childhood recollections, using my memory that has kept the hint, the trace, the outline of some perhaps barely initiated action, the reason for which was cowardice.

It should be possible to write a book entitled *The Transforming Machine* which would tell how an artist works, how certain things that impress him in the course of his life are transmuted into artistic creations in his mind. This is an unexplored process, a process that seems mysterious because it is still beyond our grasp.

The functioning of this "transforming machine" greatly affects the whole organism of the artist. The running engine inside him does not leave him unscathed, and constitutes the difficulty of being an artist.

An artist's relations with good and evil, with vice and virtue, are not at all simple. When you portray a villain, you become a villain yourself as you dredge from the bottom of your psyche everything evil and unclean. Thus, you become convinced that this evil does exist inside you, and thereby take upon your conscience a very painful psychological burden.

Goethe once said: "I wanted to reread *Macbeth*, but I couldn't take the risk. I was afraid that, given my condition at the time, it would kill me."

A fictional character *can* kill an artist.

Six years ago, I wrote the novel *Envy*.

The main character of that story was Nikolai Kavalerov. People told me that Kavalerov had many of my traits, that it was an autobiographical portrait; that, indeed, Kavalerov was me.

Yes, Kavalerov did look at the world through my eyes. Kavalerov's colors, light, images, comparisons, metaphors and thoughts about things were mine. And they were the freshest, the brightest colors I had seen. Many of them I had carried with me from boyhood and I pulled them out from the most sacred corner of that box of impressions that can never again be experienced.

As an artist, I expressed through Kavalerov the purest force within me, the force of first creation, the force created by the impact of first impressions.

But then, people declared that Kavalerov was a vulgar, worthless man. Knowing that Kavalerov embodied so much of myself, I took these accusations personally and was shocked.

I didn't agree, but I said nothing. I didn't believe that a man with an unspoiled curiosity and an ability to see the world in his own way could be vulgar and worthless. I said to myself: So all your ability, all that belongs to you, all that you yourself consider to be your strength, is just useless and vulgar? Is that really so? I wanted to believe that the Comrades who had criticized me—they were Communist literary critics—were right, and I believed them. I began to think that everything that had seemed precious to me was really nothing but beggarliness.

And this is how I conceived of the beggar; I imagined myself a beggar. I saw my life as very painful and bitter, the life of a man from whom everything had been taken away.

But then creative imagination came into play. Under its warming breath, the barren concept of social uselessness gradually turned into an idea and I decided to write a story about a beggar.

Think of it—I had been young once, I had known childhood and youth. Now I am living unwanted by anyone, vulgar and quite insignificant. So what can I do? I became a beggar, actually a real beggar. I stand on the steps of a pharmacy and beg; my nickname is the writer.

This is a story that moves me very much, for it is so delightful to be sorry for oneself.

Having hit bottom, I roam across the country, barefoot, in a torn quilted jacket. At night, I pass by construction sites, scaffoldings, lights; I walk barefoot.

Once, wrapped in the cleanliness and freshness of the morning, I pass by a wall. It happens sometimes that, in the middle of a field, not far from an inhabited area, one comes upon a half-collapsed wall. A meadow, a few trees, the piece of wall, the shadow of the wall on the meadow, even sharper and more angular than the wall itself. I approach it obliquely and see an archway in the wall, a narrow entrance with a rounded top as in a Renaissance picture. I come closer to it and see some steps leading to the archway. I look through it and see extraordinary plants. . . . Perhaps there are goats grazing? I step through the archway, look at myself and see that my youth has returned to me.

Youth has suddenly and for some unknown reason come back to me. I am wearing an undershirt. I look at my arms and see that the skin on them is young; I am sixteen. I need nothing: all my doubts, all my torments are gone. Young again, my whole life is ahead of me.

I wanted to write a story like this. I have thought about it. And I have come to the conclusion that my greatest wish is the right to preserve the colors of my youth, the freshness of my vision, to defend that vision from assertions that it is not needed, from accusations that it is vulgar and worthless.

It is not my fault that when I was young the world around me was horrible. But it would be absurd for me not to make use of the colors on the palette of my youth for that reason.

I never wrote the story about the beggar. At the time I could not understand why I couldn't write it, what was stopping me. Later I understood: it dawned on me that the trouble was not myself but my surroundings. My youth is still in me because I am an artist. And an artist can only write about things that are in him.

While I was thinking about the story of my beggar, our country was building factories. It was the time of the First Five-Year Plan, the very time when the socialist national economy was being created.

But this was not a subject for me. Certainly, I could have gone out on a construction site, lived in a factory among the workers and described them in an article or even in a novel. But that was not my theme, the theme in my blood, in my breath. I couldn't handle that subject matter as a true artist. I would have been forced to contrive, to lie. I wouldn't have had what is known as inspiration. It is difficult for me to conceive the type of a worker, a revolutionary hero. Because I cannot be him.

It is beyond my strength, beyond my understanding. And this is why I do not write about him.

I was frightened. I felt I was not needed, that there was nothing to which I could apply my peculiar artistic endowment. That is why the appalling picture of misery grew in me, the figure of the beggar tormented me.

During that time, the country was growing young. There are young people of seventeen today none of whose thoughts link them to the old world.

At the time when I was making up the story of the beggar, I peeked through the enchanted archway without understanding the main thing: that what I believed in was the youth of our country and that it was not my own youth I wanted to recapture. I wanted to recognize signs of the country's youth. That is, the new men.

Now I see them. And I have the boldness to consider that their young years are to some extent the return of *my* young years.

The most terrible thing is to humble oneself, to tell oneself: You're nothing compared to a worker, to a member of the Communist Youth Organization. How can one do that and go on writing?

Although I was born into the old world, I am proud enough to feel that there are many things in me—in my heart, in my life, in my dreams—that make me as good as the worker, as the Young Communist. And when a Young Communist or a worker advises me on how I should live and work, this is not a lecture in which one talks while the other listens in silence, but a true exchange, in the course of which we stand united and discuss the best alternatives.

There are many things from my youth, in my dreams, in my outlook, things that even today I could present in my writings as belonging to a man of the new world, to a worker, to a Young Communist. The world has become younger. A new crop of young people has sprung up. I have grown mature; my thoughts have become firmer, but the colors inside me have remained the same. Thus, the miracle of which I dreamt as I peeked through the archway has come about. Youth has come back to me.

This, of course, is a solemn, figurative way of putting it.

Actually, it is much simpler than that. The heroes who have built the factories and great construction works, who have collectivized the countryside, who have made things I cannot understand and which have made me a beggar; these people—glory to them!—have bypassed me with their amazing activity. They have created a world power, a socialist country, our motherland.

In this country the first new generation, the first Soviet man, is now emerging. Being an artist, I pounce upon him.

"Who are you? What colors do you see? Do you ever have dreams? What sort of things do you long for? What do you think of yourself? How do you love? How do you feel about the world? What do you accept and what do you reject? Which is stronger in you, reason or emotion? Can you cry? Do you know what tenderness is? Have you understood all those things that used to frighten me so, that I couldn't comprehend, that bewildered me? Tell me, what kind of a person are you, young man of the socialist society?"

I cannot write until I establish a common ground with him.

I would like to paint a portrait of this young man, endowing him with the best of what there was in my own youth.

I consider that the historic task of the writer is to produce books that will evoke in our young people a wish to emulate, a desire to be better. We must pick out the best there is in us and use it to produce a portrait of a man that may be offered as a model. A writer must be an educator, a teacher.

Personally, I have set myself the task of writing for the young. I shall write plays and stories in which young people will cope with moral problems. Somewhere inside me there lives the conviction that Communism is not only an economic system but a moral system as well, and that the first incarnations of this aspect of Communism will be our young men and women.

I'll try to put into my writings all that I sense of beauty, of grace, of nobility: my entire vision of the world. Things like a dandelion clock, a hand, a guardrail, a jump; the most complex psychological nuance; everything. I will try to prove that the new socialist way of looking at the world is also the most humane.

Such is the recapturing of youth. I did not become a beggar: the wealth that was mine is still here. It consists of the knowledge that the world is a beautiful place, with its grass, its dawns, its hues; of the realization that what made it bad was the power of money, the power of man over man. Under the rule of money, this world was whimsical and tricky. Now, for the first time in the history of civilization, it has become real and just.

[Stormy applause]

(August 22, 1934)

A LIST OF ASSETS*

CHARACTERS

LOLA GONCHAROVA, a Soviet actress
ORLOVSKY, manager of a theater company
GUILDENSTERN, played by an actor called Nick Ilin
KATIA SEMYONOVA, an actress in Lola's company
DUNIA DENISOVA, a professional beggar ⎫
PETER IVANOVICH ⎬ Lola's neighbors
BARONSKY ⎭
A YOUNG MAN WITH A BOUQUET
MADAME MACEDON, a landlady
LEDA TREGUBOVA, a dressmaker
FEDOTOV ⎫
LAKHTIN ⎬ members of a Soviet delegation abroad
DYAKONOV ⎭
TATAROV, publisher of a Russian émigré newspaper in Paris
HENRI SANTILLANT, a member of the French Communist Party
THREE MEN WITH GUNS
DMITRI KIZEVETTER, the unemployed son of a Russian émigré
MONSIEUR MARGERET, manager of a music hall
ULLALUM, a famous popular singer
A LAMPLIGHTER
A LITTLE MAN LOOKING LIKE CHARLIE CHAPLIN
TWO FRENCH POLICEMEN
A CROWD OF WORKERS

* © 1963 by Bantam Books

A SECRET AGENT
AN ADOLESCENT
A MIDDLE-AGED MAN WITH BODYGUARD
A WEAVER
HIS WIFE
POLICE CHIEF and detachment of POLICEMEN
Shakespearean ACTORS and MUSIC HALL PERFORMERS
A MESSENGER

SCENE 1. *Prologue.*

A theater after a performance of HAMLET, *which has been followed by a discussion that is now over. On stage are King Claudius, Queen Gertrude, Horatio, Laertes and Hamlet, who was played by* LOLA GONCHAROVA. *She wears riding boots and holds a rapier in her hand. In the foreground, a plain table covered with a red cloth.* ORLOVSKY, *the manager of the theater company, is presiding.*

ORLOVSKY (*ringing a bell*). The discussion is closed. Now Goncharova will answer the written questions. Comrade Goncharova. (*Hands her a pile of paper slips.*)

LOLA (*reading the first two questions*). "Are you going abroad? For how long?" Yes, for one month. "The play we have been shown, *Hamlet,* was obviously written for the intelligentsia. A working man can't understand a thing in it. It's absolutely nothing but foreign junk and corny stuff. Why bother to show it?" *Hamlet* is one of the best works of art of the past, in my opinion, at least. Probably it will never again be performed for Russian audiences so I decided to do it once more. (*Scans some of the notes.*) All right, let's go on reading. "You impersonate Prince Hamlet, that is, a man. But, looking at your legs, one can tell immediately that you are a woman." Well, judging by the great importance this note attaches to external forms, I'm sure its writer is not a member of our Party.

(ORLOVSKY *jingles his bell.*)

LOLA (*reading*). "You are a famous actress and make a good living. What else do you want? Why, on all your photographs, do you have such worried eyes?" Because it is very difficult to be a citizen of the new world. (ORLOVSKY *jingles his bell.*) What's the matter? Have I said something wrong?

ORLOVSKY (*addressing the audience*). Comrade Goncharova is expressing herself in the style of Hamlet's monologues. (*To* LOLA.) Please answer more plainly.

LOLA. You interrupt my every sentence with the jingling of your bell. Anyone would think my words were a flock of sheep. Why, am I bleating?

ORLOVSKY. Please continue answering the questions.

LOLA. "What will you do while you're abroad?" Well, I'll do things of professional interest. I'll go to theaters, get to know actors, see some famous movies I couldn't see here.

ORLOVSKY (*ringing*). Comrade Goncharova has an exaggerated opinion of foreign films. Our own films, such as *The Battleship Potemkin, The Turksib,* and *The Descendant of Genghis Khan,* have won full recognition in Europe.

LOLA. May I go on? (*Reads.*) "Why stage *Hamlet?* Aren't there any contemporary plays?" The contemporary plays are unimaginative, sketchy, false, heavy-handed and obvious. Doing them impairs one's acting ability. (*To* ORLOVSKY.) You needn't jingle your bell, Comrade Orlovsky; I know what you are about to say: it's only my private opinion.

ORLOVSKY. I wasn't ringing the bell. Why do you say that?

LOLA (*reading*). "How does one become an actor?" One has to be born with talent.

ORLOVSKY (*nervously*). How many more questions are there?

LOLA. Just a few. (*Reads a note, tears it up; reads another aloud.*) "In our era of reconstruction after the Civil War, when we are all involved in the breathtaking whirl of national development, the slobbering soul-searching of your Hamlet is unbearably sickening." Take hold of your bell,

Comrade Orlovsky, I am about to make a shocking statement. (*To the audience.*) Esteemed Comrades, I submit that in this breathtaking, swirling era, an artist must keep thinking slowly.

ORLOVSKY (*ringing*). Just a minute. Comrade Goncharova is giving her personal opinion. . . . As far as our theater is concerned, we do not fully share that opinion. This is what we might call an arguable point. Now, please continue. . . .

LOLA. The last note. (*Reads.*) "We request that you recite once more Hamlet's monologue about the recorder." Well, I don't know. . . .

ORLOVSKY. Do it.

LOLA. Where is Nick Ilin, our Guildenstern? I hope he hasn't removed his make-up.

GUILDENSTERN. Here I am.

LOLA. What do you say? Shall we do a repeat at the request of the audience?

GUILDENSTERN. All right.

(*They act.*)

LOLA-HAMLET. O! the recorders! Let me see one. To withdraw with you—why do you go about to recover the wind of me, as if you would drive me into a toil?

GUILDENSTERN. O! My lord, if my duty be too bold, my love is too unmannerly.

HAMLET. I do not well understand that. Will you play upon this pipe?

GUILDENSTERN. My lord, I cannot.

HAMLET. I pray you.

GUILDENSTERN. Believe me, I cannot.

HAMLET. I do beseech you.

GUILDENSTERN. I know no touch of it, my lord.

HAMLET. 'Tis as easy as lying. Govern these ventages with your fingers and thumb, give it breath with your mouth, and it will discourse most eloquent music. Look you, these are the stops.

GUILDENSTERN. But these cannot I command to any utterance of harmony, I have not the skill.

HAMLET. Why, look you now, how unworthy a thing you make of me! You would play upon me, you would seem to know my stops, you would pluck out the heart of my mystery, you would sound me from my lowest note to the top of my compass—and there is much music, excellent voice, in this little organ—yet cannot you make it speak. 'Sblood, do you think I am easier to be played on than a pipe? Call me what instrument you will, though you can fret me, you cannot play upon me.

(*Pause.*)

LOLA. Well, that's that. No one's applauding. That's all right with me. Close the discussion, then, Comrade Orlovsky. (*A note falls to her feet; she picks it up and reads it.*) "What was the question you tore up? Give us an honest answer." The question was: "Will you come back from abroad?" My honest answer is—yes.

CURTAIN

SCENE 2. *The Secret.*

LOLA GONCHAROVA'S *room. Evening. A send-off party. Lola's friend,* KATIA SEMYONOVA, *an actress in the same company and Lola's senior by ten years, has brought refreshments. Both are busy preparing for guests.*

LOLA. When I go tomorrow, I'll leave you the key, Katia. Please come in from time to time and remove the cobwebs from my Charlie Chaplin. (*There is a large portrait of Charlie Chaplin on the wall; to the portrait.*) Ah, Chaplin, Chaplin, the little man in frayed pants! I'll see *Circus* and *The Gold Rush.* The whole world raves about them, but years have gone by and we still haven't seen them.

KATIA. Slice the apples, we'll make some champagne cup.

LOLA. I'll get to Paris. . . . It'll be raining. . . . I know it'll be raining. . . . A sparkling evening, with slush on the ground, slush like the slush in Maupassant. Can you imagine it? Glistening sidewalks, umbrellas, raincoats. . . . Ah, Paris, Paris, all the famous books about it! And I'll

walk along its walls, under its windows, on my own, free
and happy. And then, in some small movie house, in some
out-of-the-way quarter of Paris, I'll watch Chaplin's movies
and cry. (*Pause.*) This is a journey into youth. What shall
I take along with me? That suitcase there, and this little one
too. Now listen: the desk . . . wait! (*Pulls out a drawer.*)
There's an exercise book here. . . . I told you about it.

KATIA. The diary?

LOLA. It must be better hidden. . . . Let's stow it in here,
for instance. You'll keep the key. Unless, do you think I
ought to take the diary abroad with me?

KATIA. What's the point?

LOLA. Why, I might sell it.

KATIA. What, as the "Diary of an Actress"?

LOLA. No, it's not the "Diary of an Actress," it's the
secret of the Russian intelligentsia. Would you like me to
show it to you?

KATIA. I don't think I'd be interested.

LOLA. That depends.

KATIA. And what's the secret? Gossip?

LOLA. The whole truth about the Soviet world.

KATIA. About the bread lines?

LOLA. Idiot, let me explain to you. . . .

KATIA. I've no time.

LOLA. Look: the exercise book is divided into two. Here
in the first half is a list of the crimes of the Revolution.

KATIA. I guess you'd better hide that thing.

LOLA. Don't worry. Or perhaps you imagine that there
are vulgar complaints about food shortages? I assure you
it's something quite different. I'm talking here about crimes
against the individual. There's a lot in our regime that I
cannot accept. Come here, closer. In the other half is a
list of the regime's assets. You may imagine that I don't
understand and appreciate the benefits of the Soviet regime.
Now, we'll put the two halves together. And that's me, my
worries, my nightmares. . . . Do you understand now?
Two halves of one conscience—confusing me and driving
me mad. I'll hide it in this suitcase, because I can't leave

it behind. Anything could happen. Someone might find it. That'd be terrible! They'd misinterpret it and decide that I'm a counter-revolutionary. (*Puts the exercise book into the small suitcase.*) Well, I suppose that's all. I have no other instructions, Katia.

KATIA. Now that I think of it, I'm beginning to wonder why you shouldn't really sell it abroad.

LOLA. What do you mean? Should I tear out half of it and sell just the list of crimes against the individual? You must realize that they wouldn't give me a kopek for a list of assets that the Soviet regime offers. Do you really expect me to show them only the grievances while keeping secret the things I so admire? Oh no, this exercise book cannot be torn apart! I am no counter-revolutionary, but a woman from the old world engaged in a debate with myself. But let's forget all that and make our champagne cup.

KATIA. Taking everything into consideration, I've come to the conclusion that you'll stay abroad.

LOLA. I'll be back very soon and I'll bring you a present.

KATIA. But what if someone over there falls in love with you and you marry him?

LOLA. Marry whom? I hate those vulgar, petty feelings! The Revolution has freed us of such sentiments; that is one of its benefits.

KATIA. Is there a can opener around here?

LOLA. Look in the drawer. No, not in that one, in the one over there. Ah, as you can see, I'm a hopeless housewife.

KATIA. There's nothing to prevent you from having a nice home.

LOLA. I don't own a thing, no books, no furniture . . .

KATIA. Well, why don't you buy them?

LOLA. I have no dresses. Ah, and this place! I have been living in this hole for five years. I'm a homeless tramp.

KATIA. It's just your nature. . . .

LOLA. Homelessness?

KATIA. You've only yourself to blame for it.

LOLA. There are those among us who carry only one list

in their hearts. If it is the list of crimes, if those people
hate the Soviet regime, they are happy people. The bold
ones among them either rise in revolt against it or escape
abroad. The others—the cowards, the adaptable people—lie
and write all sorts of gossipy anecdotes about the new
order, and them I loathe. Now, if one carries only the
other list, the list of the regime's assets, he is enthusiastically
engaged in the building of a new world, of which he feels
himself to be a member, a part. . . . But I, I happen to
carry two lists, credits and debits, in my heart: As a result
I can neither revolt nor flee, neither lie nor build. All I can
do is try to understand and keep my mouth shut. A home,
furniture, things. . . . What do I want with them? Do you
think I'm *living?* I keep flowing, flowing. . . . I cannot
accept the new world as my homeland and that's why I
cannot make myself a cozy home. We know how people
live in their homelands—they have things, words, concepts.
. . . (*Pause.*) Jasmine.

KATIA. What?

LOLA. A few days ago we gave a performance at a
horticultural commune. They took me to the gardens and
I saw bushes of jasmine in their greenhouses. I thought:
What strange jasmine. It was really quite ordinary, but it
suddenly occurred to me: jasmine found in an unfamiliar
dimension is no longer a thing, but an abstract idea. And
so, this new-world jasmine—whose is it? Mine? I don't
know. There's no private ownership. Yes, yes, that's the
primary cause. There are no longer flowering hedges that
belong to someone else, through which a beggar, dreaming
of riches, tries to steal a glimpse. . . . And there is a connection, you know, between the concept of jasmine and the
order under which it exists. One can't get the full sensation
of the jasmine's fragrance and color . . . the flower is
turned into a vague concept because a series of familiar
associations has been destroyed. . . . Many concepts get
lost, bounce off the eye and the ear, do not penetrate the
consciousness. Thus, for instance, concepts such as "fiancée," "guest," "friendship," "reward," "virginity," "glory."

. . . To achieve glory is to become higher than all others. That's why I know I'll keep watching Chaplin's films: I'll think of the fate of little men, of the sweetness of vengeance for insults suffered, of glory. . . .

KATIA. I'd have thought glory was the last thing you'd cry about.

LOLA. What kind of glory is it that doesn't permit me to swagger? I have no right even to feel better than others. And that's the regime's main crime against me.

(*A knock at the door.*)

LOLA. Who's that? Come in.

(*Enter* DUNIA DENISOVA, *a neighbor; she's middle-aged and wears an old, cheap dress.*)

LOLA. Ah, hello, Dunia. (*Aside to* KATIA.) I don't think you've met her before. My new neighbor, professional panhandler. They say she's unemployed. Just scum.

KATIA (*horrified and embarrassed*). Lola!

LOLA (*to* DUNIA). What do you want?

DUNIA. Some apples been stolen from me.

LOLA. What apples?

DUNIA. Half a dozen. I brought home half a dozen apples, left the room for one second, and they were gone, stolen.

LOLA. Who stole them?

DUNIA. How should I know?

KATIA. Is she implying that we stole her apples?

DUNIA. I'm not implying nothing. I can see there're apples here, that's all. (*Exits abruptly.*)

LOLA. Did you hear. Don't you think it's a crime? Well, I do and I'll add it to my list. (*Gets out her notebook; dictates to herself as she writes.*) "The Actress who played Hamlet for the New Man lived next door to a panhandler in a dirty hovel of a house."

(*Enter* DUNIA *and* PETER IVANOVICH, *an educated neighbor.*)

PETER IVANOVICH (*to* LOLA, *sternly*). Why do you steal apples? (*To* DUNIA.) Do you recognize your apples?

DUNIA. She's cut 'em all up in pieces.

PETER. You should be able to recognize the pieces.

LOLA. Yes, I have to admit it. We stole your apples.

PETER. So, it's plain enough.

DUNIA. Why did you cut 'em up? You had no right!

PETER. She needs whole apples. She intended to bake them.

LOLA. Well, that's really too bad. Now you'll just have to have stewed apples instead.

PETER. No one's asking you for advice.

KATIA. Now, look here, you! How dare you accuse us of stealing those apples!

DUNIA. My door was unlocked. If it'd been locked, you couldn't have stolen 'em.

PETER (*to* KATIA). Was the door unlocked?

KATIA (*flustered*). I don't know. . . .

DUNIA. Why waste time on all these questions? She couldn't have stolen my apples if the door was locked.

KATIA. Do you know who we are, after all? She is Lola Goncharova, the famous actress. She's going abroad.

PETER. Abroad things may be different but—

DUNIA. Just fancy: she's telling *me* to make stewed apples! I treat myself to apples once a year and she—

LOLA (*hysterically*). Get the hell out of here!

(*A knock at the door.* BARONSKY, *a neighbor from the next room, bursts in.*)

BARONSKY (*in a loud, shrill voice, gesticulating wildly*). I heard everything through the wall. Scandalous! A lady talking down to plebians!

KATIA (*defensively*). They're accusing us of stealing some apples.

BARONSKY. What a shocking tone to use! Really outrageous! (*To* LOLA, *advancing on her.*) What are you, an aristocrat at heart? Is that it?

LOLA (*calmly*). You've broken into my room without asking.

BARONSKY. Come on, don't try that on me! It won't work, you know. Better tell me who gave you permission to mock these people? Is it because they come from the masses,

while madam is an actress? Well, why don't you answer?
They are practically some sort of farm animals to you. So
you're an actress! Well, I for one don't give a damn: acting
is the lowest form of parasitism. I see you don't like what
I say? Of course you don't. But calm down and understand
that you're in no way—in absolutely no way—any better in
the eyes of the future than Dunia Denisova. Don't be in-
timidated by her, Dunia. She drinks water from the communal water supply just as you do. All right, madam, tell
me yourself: you drink water, don't you? And bread—do
you consume bread? And the stores cater for all citizens,
remember. Do you use electric light, too? Don't be afraid
of her, Dunia. The consumer's needs—d'you hear—the consumer's needs, is the formula that makes everyone equal!

KATIA. Why don't you answer him, Lola?

LOLA. Because I couldn't care less. This man is shuffling
about, jumping around, posturing, but I couldn't care less.
Through the mist of my journey, I can still see you,
Baronsky, but I can no longer make out your features or
hear your voice. . . .

BARONSKY. You can't hear? But we all heard you!

LOLA. What did you hear?

BARONSKY. That you intend to escape from the country.
(*Pause.*) You're scared now, aren't you?

LOLA (*emphatically*). I spit in your face!

BARONSKY. So you spit on us! Did you hear, Dunia?
Dunia, go shouting through the house that Actress Goncharova is planning to escape abroad.

(*The door opens. Enter* ORLOVSKY *followed by a* YOUNG
MAN *with a big bouquet of jasmine.*)

ORLOVSKY. Here she is.

YOUNG MAN. Good evening, Comrade Goncharova.

ORLOVSKY. This is from the horticultural commune for
you.

LOLA. From whom?

YOUNG MAN. From the horticultural workers with thanks
for the performance.

LOLA. Oh, that's so nice of you. . . . Thank you!

YOUNG MAN. I hope the smell of jasmine will remind you of us!

LOLA. I would like to write them a little note. Don't you think I should, Orlovsky? (*To the* YOUNG MAN.) Will you deliver it for me?

YOUNG MAN. Sure.

LOLA. But I'm in such a mess—can't even find a scrap of paper. (*Searches around.*)

YOUNG MAN (*picking up her notebook*). Here, tear a page out of this notebook.

LOLA. No, no. . . .

YOUNG MAN (*holding the notebook*). What is it? Your part in a play? I'm very curious to know how actors work. . . .

LOLA. Give it to me—it's a part.

ORLOVSKY (*professionally*). What part?

LOLA. A very hard part to play, Orlovsky. Well, just tell them thank you from me, that I'll be back soon and that I'm very proud to be an actress in the land of the Soviets.

CURTAIN

SCENE 3. Invitation to the Ball.

The living room of MADAME MACEDON's *boardinghouse. Enter* TREGUBOVA, *a forty-five-year-old woman who tries to look younger than her age. She sells dresses and is now carrying a large cardboard box.*

TREGUBOVA. Good day, Madame Macedon!

LANDLADY. Do you have the dress?

TREGUBOVA. I have a real miracle here today. . . . This is a dress such as—

LANDLADY. You're late—the American woman has left.

TREGUBOVA. But I was thinking of the Russian woman.

LANDLADY. Who, Madame Goncharova?

TREGUBOVA. That's right.

LANDLADY. You want to try and sell the dress to her?

TREGUBOVA. Is she young?

LANDLADY. Oh, yes.

TREGUBOVA. Pretty?

LANDLADY. Oh, yes.

TREGUBOVA. I saw her picture in a newspaper but that's not enough to give me an idea of a suitable dress for her. A press photograph has the same relation to the model as a glove to the living hand, don't you think? The complexion, the hair and the way the eyes darken or grow lighter . . .

LANDLADY. Do you realize that she's a well-known actress?

TREGUBOVA. A gentleman friend of mine showed me the papers. She seems to get big headlines: "Soviet Actress Goncharova Arrives in Paris." (*Pause.*) Is she coming to the ball?

LANDLADY. Who, Madame Goncharova? I really don't know.

TREGUBOVA. Surely, she must be.

LANDLADY. Everyone in town is talking about the ball.

TREGUBOVA. Yes, and the dressmakers are working without pause to have everything ready for Sunday, in time for the International Actors' Gala.

(*Enter* LOLA.)

LANDLADY. This is Madame Goncharova. Here's a dressmaker who would like to see you, Madame.

LOLA. Who?

TREGUBOVA. Good afternoon, Madame Goncharova.

LOLA. Good afternoon.

TREGUBOVA. I have the dresses—

LOLA. For me?

TREGUBOVA. If you're interested.

LANDLADY. This is Madame Tregubova. Many of my tenants have used her in the past.

TREGUBOVA. Here, look at these models I have created. (*Shows drawings.*)

LOLA. I see, yes—but I don't need any dresses just now.

TREGUBOVA. Why not have a look all the same?

LOLA. Are you Russian?

TREGUBOVA. Yes, I am. (*Pause.*) Why, you seem dismayed.

LOLA. The thing is that, in Paris, there are Russians with whom—

TREGUBOVA. I understand. You mean the émigrés. Oh no, I've been in Paris for twenty years. Madame Macedon can confirm that.

LANDLADY. I certainly can.

TREGUBOVA. Well, then, Madame, I have a superb ball gown—

LOLA. I really think you're going to a lot of trouble for nothing.

TREGUBOVA. Oh, think nothing of it! (*Opens her box.*)

LOLA. Oh, what a beauty!

TREGUBOVA. You see, with your hair—

LOLA. But this must be awfully expensive.

TREGUBOVA. In a world-famous *maison de couture,* this model would fetch at least ten thousand francs. You'd pay that at Poiret's or Lelong's or Armand's. . . . But there you'd have to pay for the label. They try to assure you that their model is inimitable, unique; and they're right, because they destroy the design. But there are ways of copying the original all the same. . . . We introduce some changes, of course . . .

LOLA. It looks like silver. . . .

TREGUBOVA. And so a gown that you would pay ten thousand for at Poiret's will cost you only four thousand here.

LOLA. Four thousand francs?

TREGUBOVA. That's all.

LOLA. Close that box.

TREGUBOVA. You don't like it then?

LOLA. It's not that. It's the price.

TREGUBOVA. It's not expensive if you think of the sensation you'd cause.

LOLA. I don't intend to cause a sensation anywhere.

TREGUBOVA. And what about the ball?

LOLA. What ball?

TREGUBOVA. The International Actors' Gala, of course.

(*Enter* FEDOTOV. LANDLADY *rushes to meet him and they hurriedly exchange a few words.*)

TREGUBOVA. Just think, it's no ordinary event. Paris is organizing a gala for the world's actors. . . .

LANDLADY. A gentleman to see you, Madame Goncharova.

LOLA (*to* TREGUBOVA). Will you excuse me?

TREGUBOVA. Please. (*She doesn't close her box.*)

LOLA (*to* TREGUBOVA). You can put it away. I won't take the gown.

TREGUBOVA. Just as you wish, Madame. (*Closes her box. Exits.*)

FEDOTOV. Comrade Goncharova? My name is Fedotov. How do you do?

LOLA. How do you do? Have you come from Moscow?

FEDOTOV. No, just the contrary—I'm leaving for Moscow. I'm on my way back from the U.S.A. I was just passing through Paris and thought I'd come over to pay my respects.

(*They shake hands.*)

LOLA. How kind of you. Do sit down. So, you've just come from America.

FEDOTOV. That's right.

LOLA. What did you do there?

FEDOTOV. I went there about the tractors, you know, with the Lakhtin delegation. There were three of us: Comrade Lakhtin, Dyakonov and myself. Well, now that we have made each other's acquaintance, if you're not too busy we could perhaps— You aren't in a hurry, are you?

LOLA. No, not at all. I'm very glad—

FEDOTOV. I'm a great admirer of your company, you know.

LOLA. Are you really?

FEDOTOV. Yes, really. And so you must realize how happy I am to meet a fellow countrywoman like you abroad.

LOLA. How did you find out I was here?

FEDOTOV. From the newspapers. Your arrival has caused a sensation in Paris. There's this Actors' Gala coming up, and the newspapers are announcing that the star of the evening will be the Soviet Actress Lola Goncharova.

LOLA. What nonsense! I haven't even been invited.

FEDOTOV. So much the better. By the way, do you know what sort of ball it is?

LOLA. It's the International Actors' Gala, isn't it?

FEDOTOV. And who do you think is organizing it?

LOLA. I suppose the local actors' association.

FEDOTOV. And who's pulling the strings?

LOLA. I have no idea who's pulling the strings.

FEDOTOV. Let me tell you. The ball is being organized by Lepelletier, the financier. You know, the older Lepelletier, the textile manufacturer. He has been hit by the crisis and has had to close his textile mills. But, since he must keep up appearances, he is giving this ball. You understand, it is his attempt to demonstrate that everything is just fine. The affair will be attended by all sorts of scum, by Russian émigré celebrities, by famous fascists. . . . But at the same time, another demonstration, much more consequential, is also afoot—the unemployed are getting ready to march on Paris.

LOLA. The unemployed?

FEDOTOV. The hunger march of the unemployed. And you talk about a ball!

LOLA. It wasn't me. You were the one to bring it up.

FEDOTOV. Ah, please excuse me. I got a bit carried away. Probably because I haven't addressed a political meeting for a long time now. But if you are invited, I advise you to refuse and to publish a notice to that effect in the Communist press. (*Pause.*) Yesterday I was at the Soviet Embassy. They're expecting you there.

LOLA. Yes. I must go over some time.

FEDOTOV. Why don't we go together?

LOLA. Good idea.

FEDOTOV. What about the day after tomorrow? Shall we meet at my place?

LOLA. Where is that?

FEDOTOV. Lakhtin, Dyakonov and I are staying in a boardinghouse in the rue des Lanternes. I'll write down the address. Let's meet at 7 p.m. the day after tomorrow, all right? (*Writes.*) Well, how have you been spending your time in Paris? Visiting museums, I suppose?

LOLA. Well, I mostly just wander about. . . .

FEDOTOV. Just wander about?

LOLA. Yes, but sometimes I stop and look, and I see my shadow. I look at it and I think: my shadow lies on the stones of Europe. (*Pause.*) I have lived in the new world and now I feel tears coming to my eyes when I find my shadow on the stones of the old world. I remember what my personal life was like in the world that you call "new." It was all in my thoughts. The Revolution has taken my past away from me but it has failed to show the future to me. And so thought became my present. To think. . . . I think that I did nothing but think. I could only reach through reason that which I couldn't reach through feelings. A human life is natural when reason and feelings are in harmony. I was deprived of that harmony and, for that reason, my life in the new world was unnatural. My reason fully comprehended the concept of Communism; my brain believed that the final triumph of the proletariat is in the natural pattern of things to come. But my emotions were against it, I was torn in half. So I fled here from that sundered life, for if I hadn't fled, I'd have gone out of my mind. In the new world I was like a fragment of the broken glass of the world in which I was born. Now I have returned. Here, the two halves have been fused: I live a natural life. I have recovered the present tense of verbs. I eat, I touch, I look, I walk. . . . A speck of dust from the old world settled on the paving stones of Europe. They are ancient, great stones, laid by the Romans. No one will be able to budge them.

FEDOTOV (*heatedly*). Those stones will soon be torn up and barricades built with them. You say your shadow lies on the stones of Europe? Did you see only your own shadow? I see other shadows. I see people turned into shadows, people crushed under the stones of Europe. . . .

LOLA. Maybe so, maybe so. I don't know. I've been resting from thoughts of the Revolution for three weeks now. . . .

FEDOTOV. Resting from thoughts of the Revolution? What do you think about instead? One can only think of the Revolution or the counter-revolution, because there's nothing else to think of these days.

LOLA. Everyone wants to think only of himself.

FEDOTOV. That sounds pretty selfish.

LOLA. It's human. I'm an actress and I must be human to the core.

FEDOTOV. There is no such thing as being human.

LOLA. Oh, how boring! What are you trying to say—that there is no such thing as just a human being, that everyone, willy-nilly, represents a class? What a bore! I've heard that before, thought of it, worked it out. It just isn't true. An actor becomes great only when he participates in a popular, universally understood and moving theme. . . .

FEDOTOV. That theme is socialism.

LOLA. That's not true.

FEDOTOV. What then?

LOLA. It's the theme of human destiny; it's the theme of Charlie Chaplin. An ugly freak longs to be beautiful; the pauper dreams of riches. The lazy idler hopes for an inheritance. A mother wants to be with her son.

FEDOTOV. You mean the theme of selfish interest then. It's a theme worthy of a *kulak*.

LOLA. *Kulak* if you wish.

FEDOTOV. I'm glad you understand that at least.

LOLA. I understand everything and that's what makes it so hard on me. Help me. I don't know what's come over me. I'm all alone in the whole wide world, and the Old and the New are fighting in my heart. You know, it's not against you I'm arguing, but against myself. I'm having this long, painful argument with myself, an argument that is withering my brains. Look at me—my hair's turning white. The day I graduated from high school the acacia was in bloom, petals fell on the pages of the books and into the hollow of my bent arm. . . . I visualized my future life—it looked beautiful. That was the year of the Revolution. . . . And since that day, I have knelt like a stone statue of a beggar woman, with my hands, coarse and rough as sand, outstretched in supplication.

(*A silence.*)

FEDOTOV. Why haven't you called at our embassy?

LOLA. I didn't want to see anyone.

FEDOTOV. You're officially supposed to report at the Soviet Embassy, you know.

LOLA. I don't know. . . . (*Pause.*) Listen!

FEDOTOV. What is it?

LOLA. Would you do something for me?

FEDOTOV. I'd be very happy if I can. What is it?

LOLA. Give me some money. (*Silence.*) Forgive me, I was just joking of course. I didn't mean it.

FEDOTOV. Comrade Goncharova, you're a mixed-up person.

LOLA. Have you just noticed it? Ah, you're quite a subtle observer! But, if you really must know, I was serious when I asked you for money; I need some because I don't want to go back to the Soviet Union.

FEDOTOV. It's terrible the things you say! Why don't you forget all that nonsense, Lola Goncharova? What's happening to you? You ought to be ashamed! So you're wavering? Splitting in two? Are you just going to stand and watch the hunger and unemployment around you? Even the blind are beginning to see, and they're gnashing their teeth. . . . What is there to philosophize about? There's a struggle for markets, for rubber, for oil. . . . New weapons are being invented, war is drawing near . . . and you come fuss about your private feelings. What are you complaining about? Do you feel you're being oppressed as an individual? Do you think that your intellectual grudges are in any way different from the grudges of the *kulak,* the rich peasant who screams that collectivization of the land has deprived him of his farm? You're exactly alike; no difference at all. What did you say? You don't want to go back home. You'd rather stay here? Is that it? Imagine this coming from a person like you, who has lived in the land of the Soviets, who, with the proletariat, has started building the new world, has started the great, incomparable glory of the proletarian revolution! And now you degrade yourself by considering staying here, defecting from the best society, from the most intelligent, the most progressive, the only thinking environment, from the hard-working people of the Soviet Union. You're dreaming, Lola Goncharova, you must be. You're delirious. I don't believe you! Yes, we're in Paris today. But let me tell you, Lola, the Paris that existed in your dream, the Paris you were longing to see, that Paris no longer exists—it is nothing but a mirage. Their culture is doomed. Do you imagine that this bourgeois Europe is as young as yourself? It is a collapsing temple and you're worshipping its ruined columns. But if you're sure you'd like to stay, at least be consistent: If you do intend to join the shopkeepers, the *kulaks* and the small capitalists, then you must join the police in firing on the unemployed masses of Europe. It is the same thing: a person who complains against the Soviet regime is bound to sympathize with the capitalist police who are shooting down the unemployed. No need for you to pretend and put up a philosophical smokescreen, because your philosophy is of the shopkeepers and the cops. You're on their side now. Then your position, whether here or at home, becomes crystal clear. Are you with us or with them?

LOLA. Kiss me on the forehead. Officially. On behalf of the Soviet Embassy.

FEDOTOV. So you see . . . very good then. (*Pauses.*) But you'd very much like to get to that ball, wouldn't you?

LOLA. Don't tell the Ambassador—I would very much.

FEDOTOV. You'd like to show yourself off?

LOLA. Yes.

FEDOTOV. All the greater challenge for you then, to make them angry: refuse if they invite you.

LOLA. You're a nice, cheerful person.

FEDOTOV. So are you.

LOLA. All right. Good-bye now.

(FEDOTOV *produces a revolver.*)

LOLA. What's this?

FEDOTOV. Just a habit left over from my fighting days—to have my gun always close at hand. (*Puts the revolver away and crosses toward the exit.*)

(*At this moment* TATAROV *appears outside the glass door.* FEDOTOV *stops and waits.*)

TATAROV. Unless I'm mistaken, you're Madame Goncharova?

LOLA. That's right.

TATAROV. How do you do? (*Offers to shake her hand.*)

FEDOTOV (*shouting from the door*). Comrade Goncharova, don't talk to him! (*Comes toward them.*) What do you want here, mister?

TATAROV. Excuse me, but I've come to see Goncharova, the actress who has defected from Moscow.

LOLA. I don't know you.

FEDOTOV. Don't say a word to him, Lola.

TATAROV. Is he your husband? Have you escaped together?

LOLA. I haven't escaped from anywhere.

FEDOTOV. Who are you?

TATAROV. Tatarov's the name.

FEDOTOV. The publisher of the émigré daily, *Russia?*

TATAROV. That's right. I'm here to do battle for the lady's soul: you're the angel; I'm the devil.

FEDOTOV. Get out at once.

TATAROV. My dear sir—

FEDOTOV. Are you trying to provoke her?

TATAROV. I didn't come here to talk to you.

FEDOTOV. Get out of here or— (*Puts his hand in his pocket.*)

TATAROV. Or you'll shoot me? You won't risk it. They don't like murderers too much around here. Here a human life is not an abstraction but something quite real. First of all, French cops with little black mustaches and wearing dark capes will appear. They'll grab you by the arm, take a moderate backswing, and bang you against a stone wall until your kidneys are loose enough. Then, when your kidneys are wandering and the blood is frothing from your mouth, they'll drive you off. . . .

FEDOTOV. My hands are itching. Once I used to be a brigade commander.

LOLA. Shall I tell you something, Fedotov? He interests me. A very lively fellow, this refugee. Let him have his say. Later, when I'm back in Moscow, I'll be able to tell everyone I've seen a real live Russian refugee. It's a shame that I'm a bit nearsighted. Won't you turn a bit, please; I'd like to look at you from the rear. Now walk up and down a bit. Now I recognize you—you're a cartoon! I've often seen you on the first page of *Izvestia*: a pen-drawn manikin. How dare you offer me your hand to shake, since you're nothing but a two-dimensional creature—you're a shadow, I'm a statue. Shaking hands with you would be a contradiction of physical laws. (*Pause.* TATAROV *remains motionless.*) Come, Fedotov, I'll see you off; as for him, he'll vanish like a shadow. (LOLA *and* FEDOTOV *exit.*)

TATAROV (*alone, to himself*). A shadow? Well, nothing wrong with being a shadow. But whose shadow? Yours perhaps?

(*Enter the* LANDLADY.)

LANDLADY. Mister Tatarov! (*He doesn't answer.*) What's happened, Mister Tatarov? (*No answer.*) Your friend, Madame Tregubova, was just here with some dresses. Have you come to pick her up? She left ten minutes ago. Have you quarreled or something?

(*Enter a* MESSENGER.)

MESSENGER. A letter for her. (*Hands her the letter and leaves.*)

LANDLADY (*reading the sender's name*). "International Association of Actors." Ah, Mister Tatarov, she's a Russian. I wish you'd seen her. She'd be very much to your taste, I'm sure. Madame Tregubova tells me you prefer blondes.

TATAROV. Let me have that envelope, please. I'll hand it to the Russian lady personally—an excellent opportunity to make her acquaintance.

LANDLADY. Poor Madame Tregubova—you're constantly unfaithful to her.

(*Enter* LOLA. *The* LANDLADY *sidles out.*)

TATAROV. Madame Goncharova. (LOLA *stops. Pause.*) That young man prevented me from carrying out the errand entrusted to me by the International Actors' Association. . . . (LOLA *stands off to the side of him and waits.*) I've come to present you with an invitation to their ball.

LOLA. Give it to me. (*Takes the envelope and tears it into shreds.*) And now get out.

(TATAROV *leaves.* LOLA *remains alone, then the* LANDLADY *returns.*)

LANDLADY. Well, did you like the dress? She's a first-class dressmaker, you can take my word for it. Moreover, she accepts payment on the installment plan.

(*A man bursts in through the glass door. Later in the play, he will be identified as* HENRI SANTILLANT, *a French Communist leader. Obviously he has been running. He rushes about the place like a man pursued.*)

LANDLADY. Help! Help! (*Becomes panicky.*)

(*Enter three men in civilian clothes, carrying guns in their hands; they grab the first man.*)

LOLA. What is going on? What is it?

ONE OF THE GUN-WIELDING MEN IN CIVILIAN CLOTHES. Get her out of here.

(*His two colleagues push* LOLA *out through the glass door, while the* LANDLADY *darts out and escapes upstairs. They close the glass door. Complete silence.* LOLA, *horrified, watches through the glass door as the three men seize the man who was trying to escape them, swing him and bang his back against the wall.* LOLA *pounds the glass door with her fists. The man receives a bad beating. He falls down but doesn't shout or moan. The entire sequence takes place in complete silence. Then they drag the victim toward the exit. The* LANDLADY *comes downstairs looking half dead with fright.*)

LANDLADY. What do you want, gentlemen? What is it?

(*Behind the glass door,* LOLA *is almost hysterical. She shouts but her voice is only heard very faintly.*)

LOLA. Let me in, let me in! How dare you! What have you done to that man?

FIRST ARMED MAN (*to the* LANDLADY). Who's she? Does she live here?

LANDLADY. She's a Russian actress.

THE VICTIM (*as he is dragged off, half conscious; in a hoarse voice*). A Russian? Long live Moscow!

CURTAIN

SCENE 4. *The Silver Gown.*

In TREGUBOVA'S *apartment. Evening.* TREGUBOVA *and* TATAROV *sit talking.*

TATAROV. I went to see her soon after you'd left. But it turned out that the Soviet Embassy had assigned a Secret Service man to guard her. Before I could say anything to her, he began threatening me. (TREGUBOVA *raises her hands in a gesture of hopelessness.*) Ah, the bandit! (*There's both indignation and envy in* TATAROV'S *exclamation.*)

TREGUBOVA. My God, you frighten me so. . . .

TATAROV. I left empty-handed. But had she been alone, I'd have found some way to make her talk.

TREGUBOVA. She's terribly careful. She said there are many Russians living in Paris who are to be avoided at all cost.

TATAROV. Meaning the refugees?

TREGUBOVA. Exactly.

TATAROV. That aloofness will last a week. We've seen plenty of saints out of the Soviet paradise who, after inhaling the smells of Paris for a while, renounced their faith forever.

TREGUBOVA. I got the impression that she's very proud.

TATAROV. She's a saint in the land of temptations. I wouldn't bet on her virtue, if I were you. We'll get her where we want her. What, you don't think we'll succeed? Why are you staring at me like that? Well, what is it? I don't understand that fixed look in your eyes. Turn that faded turquoise of yours away from me.

TREGUBOVA. I was thinking of something else.

TATAROV. What?

TREGUBOVA. Since you're capable of such implacable hatred, you must also be capable of burning love. (TATAROV *is silent.*) But you've never loved me. (TATAROV *is silent.*) All right, I can do without your love. Don't get angry, I won't talk about it any more.

TATAROV. To read what's going on in her soul, they've assigned a gun-packing angel to watch over her person. Assign me to her instead of that Soviet Secret Service fellow and all her secrets will be uncovered.

TREGUBOVA. She was still a girl when you fled from Russia, so how could you have known her?

TATAROV. I did know her though.

TREGUBOVA. Anything's possible. I know many things about your past. Tell me, could this actress be your daughter by any chance?

TATAROV. Could be.

TREGUBOVA (*with great feeling*). Is it really true?

TATAROV. Or perhaps she's my niece.

TREGUBOVA. Your niece?

TATAROV. Or perhaps she's not even my niece but the niece of some lawyer who looks very much like me.

TREGUBOVA. What lawyer, Nicky?

TATAROV. Or perhaps not a lawyer, but a bank manager. Or a member of some local government, or a professor. . . . What's the difference? She's of the same caste and tribe as we, the Russian émigré intellectuals. But I'm a poor refugee while she is the haughty visitor from my native country. I know she feels very miserable. Even if she's mute, like a reflection in a mirror, I'll still hear her voice; I'll make her scream in her despair.

TREGUBOVA. It may turn out though that your suspicions are quite unfounded.

TATAROV. Do you think she's sincerely with the Bolsheviks?

TREGUBOVA. I do. You've read me newspaper articles about her yourself and you should know how highly the Bolsheviks value her.

TATAROV. Nevertheless, I say she's lying to them and I'll prove it.

TREGUBOVA. She's very popular with Soviet audiences.

TATAROV. That only makes the case more interesting. Yes, she's quite popular over there. They gave her plenty of leeway. She produced *Hamlet* over there. Just think—producing *Hamlet* in a country where art has been reduced to the level of propaganda for breeding pigs or digging silage ditches. The Soviet regime has treated her as its pet. But despite that, I maintain that her desire all along has been to defect and stay here. The very fact that such a highly successful person escapes at the first opportunity will prove once again that life in Russia today is worse than slavery. The whole world is repeating it. But what does the world actually hear? It hears the complaints of woodcutters, the vague mooing of slaves who can neither think nor shout. But now I'll extract a protest from a highly gifted person that will intensify the horror the world feels at the very mention of Soviet Russia. The famous actress from the land of slavery will shout to the world: Do not believe! Do not believe my glory! It has been conferred upon me for my willingness not to think. . . . Don't believe that I was free—I was a slave despite everything.

TREGUBOVA. Why, but she doesn't look like a slave. She looks very much like a happy woman.

TATAROV. Happy? Proud? Incorruptible?

TREGUBOVA. That's my impression.

TATAROV. A saint? No sins, no vices?

TREGUBOVA. Yes, that's how she strikes me.

TATAROV. Well, I am convinced that she does have a sin on her conscience and if she hasn't, I'll invent one. (*Pause.*) They've invited her to the ball and that in itself is an important trump.

TREGUBOVA. She wouldn't buy the gown.

TATAROV. That was because the gown came first and the invitation to the ball only afterward. If it had been the other way around—

TREGUBOVA. She has no money.

TATAROV. That's our second trump. Give her the gown on credit. It's very easy to get entangled, to slip and fall, while wearing a gown weighed down by credit.

TREGUBOVA. You know very well that there is nothing I wouldn't do for you. But I'm afraid—

TATAROV. Afraid of what?

TREGUBOVA. You wrote of her: "The beauty from the land of beggars." Tell me, have you fallen in love with her?

(*Enter* DMITRI KIZEVETTER, *a lean, fair-haired man of twenty-five.*)

TREGUBOVA. What are you doing here, Dmitri?

KIZEVETTER. I'm looking for you, Nick.

TREGUBOVA. Nicky, I've asked you not to make appointments with this man in my house.

TATAROV. He lives with me because he hasn't a penny or any relatives, and because his father used to be a great friend of mine.

TREGUBOVA. See him at your own place.

TATAROV. But why can't I receive people I happen to like in your house?

TREGUBOVA. I'm afraid of him.

TATAROV. You've decided to break with me then?

TREGUBOVA. Ah, you're driving me mad. . . .

KIZEVETTER. Why does she say she's scared of me?

TREGUBOVA (*to* TATAROV). Can't you see he's insane?

TATAROV. What nonsense.

KIZEVETTER. How does my insanity manifest itself?

TREGUBOVA. I don't want you to come to my place.

KIZEVETTER. But why am I insane?

TREGUBOVA. Leave me. (*Starts to cry.*)

(*A silence.*)

TATAROV. Leda, my dear, stop it. Come here, give me your hand. (*Kisses her hand; raises her head and kisses her on the lips.*) I want you to be nice to Dmitri. You must remember he's unemployed. Five thousand of them have been laid off.

KIZEVETTER. What am I supposed to do, fire into windows perhaps, just because they've laid me off?

TATAROV. Fire at the Soviet ambassador.

TREGUBOVA. Why do you say such things in front of this madman?

TATAROV. Europe has gone blind. Give me a platform and I'll shout into the face of Europe to warn it: You're being infiltrated, I'll shout, their cheap bread, every grain of Soviet wheat is a bacillus of the Communist cancer. Each grain means one more man unemployed. Hear me, Europe, it'll eat you from within, the cancer of unemployment. Give me a platform! A platform like the Pope's. I'll put a crown on my head and don papal robes! Ah, it's me and not that flabby Italian who must raise Europe to fight against Communism.

KIZEVETTER. You'd look really cute in a crown. And the lady is looking at me in horror. She's surprised: Dmitri's kidding. Why, my dear lady, I'm blond and a graduate of the army officers' school. But, above all, I'm a good, kind man. I have no wish to kill anyone, I swear it. Why must I concern myself with such grave problems, why? (*Silence.*) Do you hear, Nick?

TATAROV. Well?

KIZEVETTER. I'm young, do you understand?

TATAROV. So?

KIZEVETTER. Have the young always been forced to face such difficult, intricate dilemmas?

TATAROV. He fled Russia with his father when he was twelve.

KIZEVETTER. What? Youth? Has it always been like this

for the young or was it different before? Chopin. . . .
Did the young Chopin have such a strange life?

TATAROV. The young Chopin lived on the island of Mallorca. He had TB.

KIZEVETTER. How wonderful. I agree. Let my own blood
gush from my throat. But why must I make blood gush
from another man's throat? Why?

TREGUBOVA. He's raving. Don't you understand, he's
raving?

KIZEVETTER. I, for instance, I've never seen a starry sky
through a telescope. Why is that? Why can't I look through
a telescope while I'm young?

TREGUBOVA. I can't bear to listen to him.

KIZEVETTER. I have no tie. But there are plenty of ties
around. I have no money. And who has money? Give
money to everyone. Are there too many people and not
enough cash to go around? Then, if the population increases, it must be destroyed. Wage wars. (*Silence.*) Or,
for instance, I've never been engaged to be married, but
I want to have a fiancée, I want to!

TATAROV. I'll never have a fiancée either.

KIZEVETTER. Why not?

TATAROV. Because the stuff that holds time together has
disintegrated.

KIZEVETTER. Who must I fire at because that stuff has
disintegrated?

TATAROV. At yourself.

TREGUBOVA. Out! Do you hear me, out! I can't stand it
any longer.

TATAROV. All right, all right, calm down. Go, Dmitri,
wait on the bench outside.

(*Exit* KIZEVETTER. *A silence.*)

TREGUBOVA. Are you leaving then? I thought you might
spend the night.

TATAROV. Listen carefully now: go tomorrow to her
boardinghouse and take along the best dresses you have.

TREGUBOVA. I've shown her one that she called "the silver
dress." (*Pulls her box into the middle of the room.*)

TATAROV. It's a magic box. You don't know how to think in symbols, Leda. Sequins, brocade, like shimmering heat waves; do you know what it is? It is something that people in Russia are forbidden to think of. It represents the longing to live for yourself, aspire to personal riches and happiness and glory. It is a human need and it is called light industry. It is a waltz coming through the window of another man's house. It is a ball which you long to attend. It is the tale of Cinderella.

TREGUBOVA. You kissed me so tenderly a few minutes ago and I'd like to pay you back. (*Kisses him.*)

TATAROV. You said she was a saint, sincere, incorruptible, loyal. . . . You saw in her brocade and silver lamé which do not actually exist. And the Bolsheviks, to whose advantage it is, see that attire of honesty and incorruptibility in her. But I see very plainly that the queen is naked. And only now will we be showing her to the world as she really is, when she puts on your gown.

TREGUBOVA. You kissed me so tenderly. . . . Now I want to give you back your kiss with interest. (*Kisses him.*)

(*A knock at the door.*)

TREGUBOVA. Who's there?

(*Opens the door; enter* LOLA GONCHAROVA.)

TREGUBOVA. Ah, it's you. . . . Please come in.

(TATAROV *crosses to front stage, sits down in an armchair and, turning his back on the women, puts on dark glasses.*)

LOLA. Do you recognize me?

TREGUBOVA. You're Madame Goncharova.

LOLA. I got your address from the landlady of my boardinghouse.

TREGUBOVA. Sit down, please.

LOLA. I must have a gown.

TREGUBOVA. I'm at your service, Madame.

LOLA. But the trouble is— (*Hesitates.*) My landlady says that you accept payment on the installment plan. . . .

TREGUBOVA. I do, Madame.

LOLA. I'd like to have that . . .

TREGUBOVA. The silver one?

LOLA. Yes.

TATAROV. Who's that, Leda? Who are you talking to?

TREGUBOVA. A lady has come for a gown.

TATAROV. I dozed off.

(LOLA GONCHAROVA *seems embarrassed by the presence of another person.*)

TATAROV. Please excuse me for keeping my back to you —you're sitting close to the lamp and the light hurts my eyes.

LOLA. Oh, it's perfectly all right.

(*A silence.*)

TREGUBOVA. Shall we try it on, Madame?

LOLA. Yes, let's.

TREGUBOVA. This way, please. (*Points to a cupboard which partitions off part of the room.*) This screens off my workshop.

(LOLA, *carrying her little suitcase, and* TREGUBOVA *go behind the cupboard where the former tries on the silver gown.*)

TREGUBOVA. Are you going to the ball, Madame?

LOLA. Yes, I thought I would.

TREGUBOVA. They don't have any balls in Russia now, do they?

LOLA. No, they don't.

TREGUBOVA. Now you'll see what it's like—a ball.

TATAROV. When a person outside hears a waltz coming from the windows of a strange house, somehow he starts to think of his own life.

(*A silence.*)

LOLA. What does your husband do?

TATAROV. I write fairy tales.

LOLA. When did you leave Russia?

TATAROV (*lying*). Before the 1914 war, when the world was still very vast and accessible. (*Pause.*) Do Soviet children read fairy tales?

LOLA. Depends on what fairy tales.

TATAROV. Things like "The Ugly Duckling," for instance.

LOLA. No.

TATAROV. Why not? It's a marvelous story. Do you remember it? They pecked him but he kept silent; they humiliated him, but he went on hoping. He had a secret: he knew he was better than the others. He bided his time. He knew one day he'd be vindicated. And then it turned out that the proud, lonely duckling was a swan. When a flock of swans flew by, he took off and joined them, his silver wings flashing in the air.

LOLA. A typical little piece of bourgeois propaganda.

TATAROV. How do you come to that conclusion?

LOLA. The petty bourgeois writer Andersen expresses the dream of the petty bourgeois. To turn into a swan means to become rich. It means to rise above others. That is precisely the dream of the petty bourgeois: to suffer hardship, to amass money, to be secretive, to maneuver and all that, in order to finally acquire wealth and power —that is, to become a capitalist. It is a dream of capitalist Europe.

TATAROV. In Europe, every ugly duckling can turn into a swan. But what happens to the ugly duckling in Russia nowadays?

LOLA. In the first place, they're trying to make sure there won't be any ugly ducklings. They're helped to become normal, not to turn into swans. On the contrary, they're made into gorgeous fat ducks. Then they're exhibited. But here begins another fairy tale of the capitalist world.

TATAROV. Which fairy tale?

LOLA. The fairy tale about Soviet exports.

(TATAROV *is silent.*)

TREGUBOVA. What sort of dresses are they wearing in Russia this year? Long or short?

LOLA. Something in between, I'd say.

TREGUBOVA. And what's the fashionable material?

LOLA. Where?

TREGUBOVA. In Russia, Madame.

LOLA. In Russia? Steel is very much in fashion.

(*Silence.*)

TREGUBOVA. And what sort of dresses do they wear in the evenings?

LOLA. I believe the same as are worn in the morning.

TREGUBOVA. What do people wear to the theater?

LOLA. Felt boots.

TREGUBOVA. You mean men wear tailcoats and felt boots?

LOLA. No, just felt boots.

TREGUBOVA. Why? Don't they go for tailcoats?

LOLA. No, that's not the reason. It's simply that they like the theater.

TATAROV. Is it true that they're systematically doing away with the intelligentsia in Russia?

LOLA. What do you mean by doing away with them?

TATAROV. Doing away with them physically.

LOLA. Are they shooting the intelligentsia?

TATAROV. Yes, are they?

LOLA. They're shooting those who prevent them from building the socialist state.

TATAROV. Of course, I don't follow politics too much, but I understand that the Bolsheviks are shooting the best people in Russia.

LOLA. But there isn't any such thing as "Russia" any more.

TATAROV. How can you say that there's no Russia?

LOLA. There is the Union of Soviet Socialist Republics.

TATAROV. That's Russia's new name.

LOLA. No, it's quite different. If tomorrow a revolution takes place, say, in Poland or Germany, then that country will become a part of the Soviet Union. So how is that Russia, if it is Germany or Poland? Therefore, Soviet territory is not merely a geographical concept.

TATAROV. What kind of a concept is it, then?

LOLA. A dialectical concept. Therefore, even people must be valued dialectically. And you must understand that, from the dialectical point of view, the best and the nicest person may be a villain and a criminal.

TATAROV. I see. Would you say, then, you consider that in some cases, shooting people may be justified?

LOLA. I do.

TATAROV. And you don't view it as a crime committed by the Soviet regime?

LOLA. In general, I know of no crimes committed by the Soviet regime. On the contrary, if you wish, I could read you a long list of its assets.

TATAROV. I'd be glad if you could mention one such asset.

LOLA. Since I've been here, many things have become clear to me. I'll return home with a list of crimes of the capitalist regime. Take the matter of children, since we were speaking of them earlier. Do you know that in Russia marital laws have been abolished? We have already become quite accustomed to it and no longer think of it. But in your capitalist world, you still have the concept of illegitimate children. Religion and the authorities penalize a child conceived in love but without the sanction of the church. That's why there are so many ugly ducklings. We don't have any ugly ducklings, we have nothing but cygnets and swans. (TATAROV *remains silent.* LOLA *speaks to* TREGUBOVA.) I love this gown. But now let's get to the main point: it costs—

TREGUBOVA. Four thousand francs.

LOLA. I'll pay you in a few days.

TATAROV. Are you expecting to receive money from Russia?

LOLA. That's right, and besides I think I'll give one performance at the "Globe."

TATAROV. At the "Globe"? What performance will it be?

LOLA. I'll play a scene from *Hamlet.*

TREGUBOVA. Would you be so kind as to sign this little note. . . .

LOLA. Of course, of course. . . .

TATAROV. What are you doing, Leda? Are you looking for a piece of paper? Your accounts are very poorly organized. Here's some. (*Takes a pad of notepaper from his pocket, tears off a sheet and gives it to* TREGUBOVA.) Write

—no, no, on the other side. (*He dictates;* TREGUBOVA *writes.*) "Received from dressmaker, Madame Tregubova, a gown valued at four thousand francs" . . . Insert the word "ball" . . . so it should read "a ball gown valued at four thousand francs. I promise to pay the above mentioned sum on" . . . When?

LOLA. In three days.

TATAROV. Write "Wednesday, the eighth." . . . Now sign.

LOLA (*signing and mumbling*). Lola Goncharova.

TREGUBOVA. Thank you very much.

LOLA. That's that. Good-bye.

TREGUBOVA. Good-bye, Madame.

TATAROV. Best wishes to our Russian compatriot.

(LOLA *leaves with the gown wrapped in a package, but forgets her suitcase.*)

TREGUBOVA (*to* TATAROV). So you see, my dear, you were wrong—she's a patriot of her new country. She even justifies their shootings.

TATAROV. And while justifying those murders, she adjusts the pleats of her gown.

TREGUBOVA. And her cheeks were afire when she was speaking of the illegitimate children.

TATAROV. When a citizen of the Soviet Union keeps denouncing the bourgeois, while at the same time longing to attend a bourgeois ball, I cannot believe too deeply in her sincerity.

TREGUBOVA. She looks divine in that gown.

TATAROV. Those are swan's feathers appearing on the duckling.

TREGUBOVA. And it flew away.

TATAROV. Leaving in my hand a little feather. Look at what is printed on the back of her IOU.

TREGUBOVA (*reading*). "*Russia,* the Daily Newspaper published by the Association of Russian Manufacturers."

TATAROV. Your incorruptible Soviet actress has signed her name on a piece of notepaper with the letterhead of the Russian émigré paper and she thereby acknowledges receiving a ball gown. That's quite cute, isn't it? In any case, it will be quite a sensation when it appears in tomorrow's issue of our paper: "A Saintly Woman Prepares to Attend a Ball."

TREGUBOVA. She forgot her little suitcase.

TATAROV. What did you say?

TREGUBOVA. She left her suitcase behind.

TATAROV. Ah? Let's have a look. (*Picks up the suitcase.*)

TREGUBOVA. Watch out; I'm sure she'll be back for it in a second.

(TATAROV *opens the suitcase, hurriedly searches through it, finds a notebook, scans it. A knock at the door. Pause. He hides the notebook inside his jacket and sits down again in his armchair.* TREGUBOVA *closes the suitcase.*)

TREGUBOVA. Come in!

(*Enter* LOLA.)

LOLA. Please excuse me, I—

TREGUBOVA. You left your suitcase behind?

LOLA. Yes.

TREGUBOVA. You didn't really have to take the trouble. I'd have sent it to you.

LOLA. Oh, I'd have hated to trouble you. Thanks.

(LOLA *opens the door, bumping into* KIZEVETTER. *For one second they stop and stare at each other. She's taken aback, he's frightened by the unexpected sight of this woman. Then she leaves. Silence.*)

TATAROV (*holding the notebook*). I've discovered her secret, Leda.

TREGUBOVA. Is that her diary?

TATAROV. That's her sin against the regime that I mentioned to you.

KIZEVETTER (*firmly*). I insist that you tell me who that woman is who just rushed out of here.

TATAROV. She's the beauty from the land of the poor.

KIZEVETTER. I *demand* that you tell me who she is.

TATAROV. She's your fiancée.

CURTAIN

SCENE 5. *The Recorder.*

Backstage of the music hall, the "Globe." Evening.
M. MARGERET *is talking to* LOLA, *who is dressed as Hamlet.*
On M. MARGERET's *desk there is a glass of milk and a loaf*
of French bread.

LOLA. I've put the costume on to give you a better impression. (M. MARGERET *remains silent.*) Perhaps you're too busy now?

MARGERET. Why do you say that?

LOLA. You're running such a big outfit after all.

MARGERET. Why do you say "big"?

LOLA. Well, a music hall . . . so many performers . . . it's not so easy, I'm sure.

MARGERET. Why "not so easy"?

LOLA. You have a very funny way of talking.

MARGERET. What's so funny about it?

LOLA. Whatever I say, you keep asking why—

MARGERET. It's because I'm busy.

LOLA. Well, that's just what I was afraid of in the first place.

MARGERET. Why were you "afraid" of it?

(*A silence.*)

LOLA. Perhaps you'd like me to go away?

MARGERET. Go away then.

(*A silence.*)

LOLA. Would you like to audition me?

MARGERET. I would.

LOLA. I could perform a scene from *Hamlet* for you.

MARGERET. Why from *Hamlet?*

LOLA. Well, I had something running along these lines in mind . . . on the posters, you know: "Famous Soviet Actress, Lola Goncharova, gives some excerpts from *Hamlet* . . ." (MARGERET *remains silent.*) Well, all right, I'll act for you now. . . . Well, I suppose the dialogue with Guildenstern would be best.

(*She acts, shifting from one spot to another, playing both parts.*)

"O, the recorders! Let me see one. To withdraw with you—why do you go about to recover the wind of me, as if you would drive me into a toil?"

Now it's Guildenstern speaking. I'm sure you know this scene so I won't bother to explain it to you.

"O! My lord, if my duty be too bold, my love is too unmannerly."

Now Hamlet says: "I do not well understand that. Will you play upon this pipe?"

"My lord, I cannot."

"I pray you."

"Believe me, I cannot."

"I do beseech you."

"I know no touch of it, my lord."

" 'Tis as easy as lying; govern these ventages with your fingers and thumb, give it breath with your mouth, and it will discourse most eloquent music."

MARGERET (*waves his hand*). No, no, no, that won't do.

LOLA (*shocked and indignant*). Why not?

MARGERET. It's not interesting. Recorder—yes. You play the recorder?

LOLA. Why play the recorder?

MARGERET. Now you're beginning to ask me "why." You'll just have to take my word for it: it won't do. What is it? An eccentric number with a recorder? We must give them a shock, don't you understand? "It will discourse . . ." that's not enough.

LOLA. You didn't listen. You didn't understand. . . . It's not that at all. . . .

MARGERET. If it isn't that at all, tell me what it is. Maybe something else will be of interest. An interesting number with a recorder might go like this: first you play the recorder, then—

LOLA. But I can't play.

MARGERET. You can't? But you yourself were saying that it's very easy.

LOLA. But it wasn't I who said that.

MARGERET. You even put it very elegantly—that it is just as easy as lying.

LOLA. You weren't listening. You're too busy to listen.

MARGERET. So you can see I'm busy and don't even have time to drink a glass of milk, and still you waste my time. Let's make it short. In order to make this act a success, it should go something like this: first you'd have to play the recorder, some minuet or something, just to put the audience into a melancholy mood. Then you could, for instance, swallow the recorder. . . . That would make the audience gasp. The mood would change to one of astonishment, then of alarm. At that point you'd turn your back to the audience and there would be a recorder sticking out of a part of your anatomy from which recorders don't usually stick out. That would be quite titillating in view of the fact that you are a woman. Now we have something. I've hit on a wonderful idea here! You'll start blowing into the recorder from what we might call your reverse end. But this time it won't be a minuet, but something more cheerful, something like "Oh, Joseph, Joseph, Can't You Make Your Mind Up." . . . Do you see what I mean? That'll bring the house down.

LOLA. You were complaining that I was taking up your time and now you're wasting it yourself on these jokes. . . .

(*A phone rings.*)

MARGERET. Hello? What? He's arrived? Impossible! I have a heart condition, remember? I couldn't stand it. So he's really arrived? Hurry! Quick, quick! (*Tosses the receiver to Lola, tears up and down the stage.*) He's arrived. Did you hear? He's arrived!

LOLA. Monsieur Margeret, I'd like you to listen seriously for one moment.

MARGERET (*coming back to his desk, looking as though he's caught sight of LOLA for the first time*). What? Ah, it's you. Yes, of course . . . please excuse me. Of course, we were having a conference. But I have a terrible habit: when my head is occupied with something, I listen to people without understanding a word . . . and sometimes I make quite unrelated remarks. For a whole week, my head has been occupied with the question: will he come or won't he? And now, he's arrived! He intends to dance at the International Actors' Gala. Now my head is free. What do you wish? You play the recorder?

LOLA. I am a tragedienne.

MARGERET. Why a tragedienne?

LOLA. There you go again with your questions.

MARGERET. You're right, you're right, thank you for stopping me. My head's full of thoughts again.

LOLA. You're a very funny man. What's your head full of now?

MARGERET. Wait a second. (*Touches his forehead with his finger.*) There's something bothering me in here.

LOLA. You were waiting for someone and he's arrived. What is it now?

MARGERET. Wait. . . . Yes, yes, yes, give me a chance to get it out of my head. All right, I've got rid of it. Why, it was you sitting in my brain. Isn't that funny? What do you want of me?

LOLA. Back home, in Russia, I was a well-known actress. . . . But do I really have to start the whole thing all over again?

MARGERET. Yes, yes, yes, I've got it! I understand perfectly now. Very good then! How did you put it? Why did you say "start all over again"? Right, right, right!

LOLA. You don't seem to have an inkling of who I am.

MARGERET. Very good. An excellent idea. At first no one has the slightest inkling. . . . They won't know you're a celebrity; they'll think it's just an ordinary number. . . . And no posters! I'll have all the posters destroyed. Here's what we'll do: this very night you'll make your first appearance. The celebrity will come out in the middle of the program instead of a routine number; she'll come unannounced, unadvertised. Hurray! That'll be more effective than any publicity.

LOLA. What, tonight? But it requires preparation. . . .

MARGERET. Who has to prepare? He?

LOLA. Ah, I misunderstood you, I thought you were talking about me. I've had just about enough of your way of thinking and talking. . . . (*She pauses.*) Ah . . . (*Pauses again.*) Is it really possible? Tell me, who is it who's arrived?

MARGERET. He. He's come to attend the ball. Yes, and he has agreed to give one performance for me! . . .

LOLA. I know, I know. . . .

MARGERET. If you know, don't say another word or you'll ruin my whole plan. Remember, the public has no inkling whatever. . . . Keep your mouth shut. (*Seizes her arm and squeezes it.*) Yes, yes, yes, it's him all right!

LOLA. He! Is it really possible? Is he about to walk into this room? Please, please allow me to stay. . . . I'll accept any conditions you choose to make.

MARGERET. My conditions? Ten American dollars a week.

LOLA. Ten dollars for what?

MARGERET. For your work, of course.

LOLA. What work?

MARGERET. For the recorder act, damn it! It's really rather difficult to talk to you.

LOLA. You ought to be ashamed—

MARGERET. Why should I be ashamed? Isn't ten dollars enough? Do you really want me to believe that it's all that difficult to bare one's behind and play some minuets?

LOLA. When he comes in, I'll tell him how you, a famous European impresario, are treating a foreign actress. I need money, a thing that could happen to anyone. I was humble where I might have been arrogant. He will understand; he is the very incarnation of culture, of human virtue, of civilization. He will be outraged by your behavior; he will defend me because he is better than any of you. He is the nicest man alive in your world.

MARGERET. Who is? Who is the nicest man alive in our world? How can you say such a thing! He is nothing but a vulgar, greedy, petty creature.

LOLA. That's impossible! I don't believe you.

MARGERET. Oh, sure, you're prepared to let him get away with anything. People have turned him into a god. The world's got a fixation on sex. To men, he is a man, to women he is a woman. Perhaps he's really a god after all. When I hear him sing, it makes me feel as if a woman, destined for me, is slowly undressing before my eyes. Then I watch the female faces in the audience. It's phenomenal! He sings, and all those eyelids droop like hen's lids, their eyes become glassy, dead. . . . It is ecstasy. Yet what does he really sing? Silly, idiotic songs. But there is some secret in his erogenous notes.

LOLA. Oh, I thought you were talking of someone else.

MARGERET. No one else can touch him. He is a god.

LOLA. I thought that Charlie Chaplin was coming here.

MARGERET. Why Chaplin?

(*Great agitation and noise.* ULLALUM *is approaching.*)

MARGERET. Here he comes. The great Ullalum!

(*Enter* ULLALUM *surrounded by music hall performers.* ULLALUM *looks at* LOLA. *They all notice he is looking at her.* LOLA *almost reels back.*)

ULLALUM. Who is this, Margeret?

MARGERET. I prepared her for you.

ULLALUM. Who are you? (LOLA *doesn't answer.*) I am Ullalum.

LOLA. Never heard—

ULLALUM. Who are you? An African savage? No, your hair is of gold and your complexion is an immaculate white. What are you? A Gaul? An ancient Gaul?

LOLA. I've never met you before. What makes you think you're entitled to talk to me in that tone?

ULLALUM. I am Ullalum.

LOLA. Never heard of you.

MARGERET. She's trying to intrigue you.

LOLA. Leave me alone.

ULLALUM. Wonderful! Last night, I dreamt of my childhood. A garden. Stairs with a wooden guardrail. . . . I was going downstairs, my hand sliding down the wooden guardrail that was slightly polished by the rays of the sun. You are the embodiment of a metaphor. Please take off your blouse, I beseech you! Your arms are round, like the guardrails.

LOLA. You're a very strange man.

ULLALUM. People have made a god of me. But I was a boy once, too. There were green hills there. You have come out of my boyhood in the city of Nimes. It was founded by the Romans. Come here!

LOLA. For some time now, life has seemed like a sort of dream to me.

MARGERET. Go to him. Good fortune is smiling on you.

ULLALUM. Come here!

LOLA. This whole thing is very funny!

ULLALUM. All right, I'll come to you then. (*Crosses to her.*) I'll kiss you.

LOLA. Oh, I remember now! I heard a song—one of your records—in Moscow, last winter, when I was longing to go to Europe.

ULLALUM. May I kiss you then?

LOLA. You may.

(ULLALUM *kisses* LOLA. *Pause. General, rapturous silence.*)

ULLALUM. Who are you? (*To* MARGERET.) Where did you find her, Margeret?

MARGERET. She plays the recorder with her rectum.

ULLALUM. Brrr . . . What if she then plays it with her mouth without washing it?

(*Laughter.*)

LOLA. But it isn't true. Tell him, Monsieur Margeret, that you made all that up yourself.

ULLALUM (*ignoring her*). Margeret, do you want me to go on stage right away?

MARGERET. Yes, I want you to strike them like a bolt of lightning.

LOLA. Monsieur Ullalum!

ULLALUM. What do you want?

LOLA. You have offended me.

ULLALUM. How's that?

LOLA. You don't know me. Perhaps you think it's true what he said . . . with the recorder. . . . But I came to this theater on business. . . . I thought it was a real theater, but it's turned out to be a torture chamber. That was so beautiful, what you said about your childhood.

ULLALUM. Memories of childhood are blown to pieces like a dandelion clock.

LOLA. You are a strange man.

ULLALUM. No woman can resist falling in love with me.

LOLA. I know. . . . Of course. . . . (*She pauses.* ULLALUM *is silent.*) I used to dream about Europe. I would hate to give you the wrong impression of me. Back in my country, they thought I was beautiful. . . . Even you looked at me—

ULLALUM. Come tomorrow.

LOLA. You don't understand what I'm trying to say. . . . I'm going crazy. . . .

(*Distant clapping. A number is finished. People rush up to* MARGERET.)

MARGERET. Just a moment, just a moment. . . . Ready, Ullalum?

ULLALUM. All right, let's go. (*Exits.*)

(LOLA *is left alone. From the audience come shouts, clapping, stamping. After a second of silence the storm breaks. Then silence again and the piano accompaniment to the song starts.* ULLALUM *begins to sing.* LOLA *leaves the music hall. Passages, corridors, steps . . . She goes downstairs. The singing fades. She stops and listens. Humiliated and lonely, she hears the sounds of a party going on behind strange windows. As she listens, she thinks of her life.*)

LOLA. I want to go home. . . . Where are you, my friends? The new world, the shabby crowds . . . my youth . . . I was about to sell my youth! I was dreaming of you, Paris. I was impatient to see your glory. But I knew—and I don't understand how I could have forgotten it—there is no greater glory than the glory of those who are rebuilding

the world. Every woman who is the mother of children
born into the new world and who stands in line outside a
food store shines with greater glory than all the stars of
Europe. What did I want? A ball gown? Why do I need
it? Wasn't I beautiful in my patchwork dress? I want to go
home. . . . How are the performances without me? Oh,
my country, I'm so thirsty now for the din of your debates;
worker, only now have I fully grasped your wisdom and
generosity, only now have I looked closely at your face,
turned toward the starry sky of science. Before, I used to
look warily at you out of the corner of my eye, a stupid
chicken distrusting the hand that feeds it. Forgive me, my
Soviet land. I am returning to you; I don't want to go to
their ball. . . . I wish I were back home, standing in line
and crying. . . .

(*Change of scene. A street. Leaves. The pavement is
glistening. A bench, a* LITTLE MAN *sits on it.* STREET LAMP-
LIGHTER *comes over to him.*)

LAMPLIGHTER. Hey, what are you doing here?

LITTLE MAN. I'm eating my supper.

LAMPLIGHTER. Eating dreams?

LITTLE MAN. No, I dined in my dream. I tried to leave
some onion soup for supper but unfortunately I woke up
too soon. . . .

LAMPLIGHTER. I see. I suppose you're unemployed?

LITTLE MAN. I must say you're quite perspicacious.

LAMPLIGHTER. I'd give you something for supper but—

LITTLE MAN. Please don't worry about me. Can't you
see I'm having my supper as it is?

LAMPLIGHTER. You're a cheerful fellow. What is it you're
eating then?

LITTLE MAN. A tree. Do you see that tree over there?
Well, I'm eating it. It would be very much like a chicken
drumstick if it weren't for the leaves.

LAMPLIGHTER. Ah, now I don't understand you! I'm sure
if I was forced to eat trees I'd eat them with the leaves.
What's wrong with a chicken drumstick with salad?

LITTLE MAN. You're right. But I've eaten my fill. All I

need now is dessert. I'll eat the fence. See, over there. Ah, it tastes very nice, a bit like a wafer. But hell, something's got into my food. Ah, it's a woman. (LOLA *crosses toward the bench.*) She is an actress from the music hall.

LAMPLIGHTER. You've spoiled his dessert, Madame.

LITTLE MAN. Margeret sacked me. Tell him that the unemployed will set fire to his theater.

LOLA. Why did he kick you out?

LITTLE MAN. Because I expressed my sympathy for the unemployed. Besides, he hates artists who belong to a union. I'm the recorder player in the orchestra, who are you?

LOLA. I'm a union member, too.

LAMPLIGHTER. Give him some money for supper or he may get a yen for pork and eat a cop.

LOLA. I know, I know, of course. . . . (*Gives* LITTLE MAN *money.*)

LITTLE MAN. Give me your address, I'll pay you back.

LOLA. I'm leaving the country tomorrow. (*Walks away.*)

LAMPLIGHTER. But watch out, don't wake up too soon.

LITTLE MAN. I was wrong—she's not from our theater.

LAMPLIGHTER. Better count out the money. See whether there's enough for a plate of soup.

LITTLE MAN. It's too dark.

LAMPLIGHTER. I'll light the street lamp.

(*Raises his pole. A street lamp lights up over their heads. In the light the* LITTLE MAN's *resemblance to Chaplin is quite striking: the bowler hat, the hair, the mustache, the battered shoes, the walking stick. The* LAMPLIGHTER *helps him count, peering into the* LITTLE MAN's *hand.*)

LAMPLIGHTER. Oho! There's enough for a whole ocean of soup.

LITTLE MAN. And me, who was dreaming of an onion no bigger than my pituitary gland.

LAMPLIGHTER. Now you can offer yourself an onion as large as this street lamp.

(*Puts the street lamp out.*)

CURTAIN

SCENE 6. *Logic.*

A café on rue des Lanternes. FEDOTOV *and* LAKHTIN *sit at a table.*

LAKHTIN (*looking at a newspaper*). In the White émigré newspaper *Russia,* Fedotov, there's a little piece that says that yesterday, in a certain boardinghouse, you, a Soviet citizen, pulled out a revolver and shot and killed Tatarov, the editor of the newspaper. Taking into consideration the fact that the article appears in this White émigré rag, I suppose you didn't really kill the above-mentioned Tatarnikov. . . .

FEDOTOV. Tatarov.

LAKHTIN. Never mind that. As I was saying, you didn't really kill that Tatarnikov. I go further and assume you didn't even wound him. I wouldn't be surprised, as a matter of fact, if you told me you hadn't even fired at him, hadn't the slightest intention of doing so.

FEDOTOV. It's nothing but lies.

LAKHTIN. But is it possible that you were brandishing your gun in that dump?

(*A* WAITER *comes over to their table.*)

WAITER. There's a young lady asking for you.

FEDOTOV. It's Goncharova. (*Gets up; leaves, returns with* LOLA; *offers her a chair.*)

LOLA. How do you do?

LAKHTIN. Very pleased to meet you. (*They shake hands.*) Please call me Sergei.

FEDOTOV. We'll go to the embassy soon. Comrade Dyakonov is there now and will call when they're ready for us.

LOLA. Very good.

LAKHTIN. You remember me. We were introduced once in Moscow after a show. In your own theater. I used to wear sideburns then.

FEDOTOV. Did you really have sideburns?

LAKHTIN. Long ones, like this. Looked like lamb chops glued on.

FEDOTOV. Why did you let them grow?

LAKHTIN. I have no idea. Just a whim, I guess.

FEDOTOV. Just for a laugh. (*To* LOLA.) What are you playing now?

LOLA. Hamlet.

LAKHTIN. You mean Ophelia.

LOLA. No, Hamlet himself.

FEDOTOV. A woman, playing a man's part.

LOLA. Well, yes.

FEDOTOV. But anyone could tell by your legs that you're a woman.

LOLA. These days a woman must think like a man. All sorts of accounts are being settled in a very masculine way.

LAKHTIN. May I pour you some tea?

LOLA. I hate to give you so much trouble, although you seem to be so easygoing.

LAKHTIN. I believe I have the gout.

FEDOTOV. Perhaps it's not the gout.

LAKHTIN. Perhaps it's simply homesickness.

FEDOTOV. Or a chronic head cold.

LAKHTIN. Yes, I think I had the flu and neglected it. But do have your tea and eat something. Is this the first time you've been to Paris?

LOLA. Yes.

LAKHTIN. Have you come for a long stay?

LOLA. I intend to leave very soon.

LAKHTIN. Where are you going? To Nice, maybe?

LOLA. No, I would like to go back home to Moscow.

LAKHTIN. When are you leaving?

LOLA. The sooner the better.

FEDOTOV. Come with us then. We'll make the trip together.

LOLA. That'd be wonderful.

LAKHTIN. Very good then.

LOLA. Now tell me, what was it like in America?

FEDOTOV. Well, it's all right in the sense that there's plenty of everything. But it seems sort of unorganized. They have no ration cards. . . . (*A pause.*) Tell me, Comrade Goncharova, do you intend to go to that ball?

LAKHTIN. Where?

FEDOTOV. To the International Actors' Gala.

LOLA. No, Fedotov, I don't intend to go to any ball.

LAKHTIN. Have you been invited?

LOLA. Yes, I have.

LAKHTIN. What cheek, to invite a Soviet actress to that ball for trained monkeys! I'm sure you turned down their invitation.

LOLA. Yes, I did.

LAKHTIN. I bet you did. Just think what your comrades in Moscow would have said if they'd heard you'd attended a ball given by Lepelletier, the man who forces his workers to starve!

(*Enter* DYAKONOV.)

FEDOTOV. May I introduce you? Dyakonov, this is Lola Goncharova. . . .

DYAKONOV. Who?

FEDOTOV. What's come over you?

DYAKONOV. Who did you say she was?

FEDOTOV. Come on, what's up with you?

DYAKONOV. You're Goncharova?

LOLA. Yes.

DYAKONOV. Why did you come here?

FEDOTOV. You must be drunk.

DYAKONOV. Have you seen today's papers, Comrade Lakhtin?

LAKHTIN. No, not yet. What's the matter?

DYAKONOV (*sitting down next to him*). I've come straight from the embassy. I told them we wanted to come to the reception with Actress Goncharova. Then they gave me these newspapers to show you: three French ones and the two refugee sheets, *Russia* and *Return to the Homeland*.

LAKHTIN. The places marked with a blue pencil?

DYAKONOV. Right.

LAKHTIN. I started to read *Russia*. . . . Ah, I see, they're writing about you. . . .

LOLA. About me? What do they have to say about me?

LAKHTIN. What a filthy scandal sheet: No sooner does a person come from Moscow—

DYAKONOV. Please, Comrade Lakhtin, read what it says.

LAKHTIN (*reading aloud*). "Actress Goncharova, who has escaped from the Soviet paradise, had a talk with a correspondent of the newspaper *Russia* and informed him that she had at her disposal important material that would reveal scandalous facts about cultural life in the Soviet Union—"

FEDOTOV. Please don't worry, Lola, those people are great experts in slander.

DYAKONOV. But this time they've come up with the truth.

LOLA. What are you talking about?

LAKHTIN. Don't let's talk so loud.

FEDOTOV. Don't make a scandal of it, Dyakonov.

DYAKONOV. And what about this? (*Hands a sheet of paper to Lakhtin.*)

LAKHTIN (*to* LOLA). Did you write this?

LOLA. Let me see. That's the IOU for my dress.

LAKHTIN. Where did you get the stationery with the letterhead of the émigré paper?

LOLA. I have no idea.

LAKHTIN. I must say it does look rather bad.

DYAKONOV. Now read what it says in *Return to the Homeland* and in the French papers.

LOLA. It's all nonsense.

LAKHTIN. Please, not so loud. They have it under the headline "Secrets of Soviet Intelligentsia Exchanged for Paris Gown." Did you sell your diary to the Russian refugees?

LOLA. What diary?

LAKHTIN (*reading*). "Every line of this document is smudged with tears. This is the confession of an unhappy woman, of a highly talented actress suffering under the yoke of Bolshevik slavery. This is the blinding truth about the way the dictatorship of the proletariat deals with what we consider the world's greatest treasure—the freedom of human thought. On the first page we found a list of crimes of the Soviet regime."

FEDOTOV. Is this true?

LOLA. Yes, but it isn't like that. I have a notebook. It is divided into two parts. . . . Hear me out, please! This is terrible. . . . Let me explain. That notebook contains two lists: one of the regime's debits, its crimes—the other of its assets, its benefits.

LAKHTIN. I don't understand a thing.

LOLA. I never sold it. It's some sort of a slander. I have no idea how it got into print. Come to my boardinghouse and I'll show you my notebook and then you'll understand. Shall I go and get it now?

DYAKONOV (*pulling* LOLA'*s notebook out of his briefcase*). Is this it?

LOLA. Yes. . . .

LAKHTIN. Where did you get it, Dyakonov?

DYAKONOV. This diary was sent to our embassy along with the IOU and an insolent letter from the émigré newspaperman Tatarov who contacted Madame Goncharova.

FEDOTOV. Was it the same Tatarov I met at your boardinghouse?

LAKHTIN. Let me see it. (*Reads.*) "List of Crimes."

LOLA. But look further, further, you'll find the "List of Assets" there.

LAKHTIN. No, there's no other list here at all.

LOLA. What? One half has been torn out? Who could have done it?

DYAKONOV. You tore it out yourself to get a better price for it.

LOLA. I did nothing of the sort.

LAKHTIN. Wait, Dyakonov. (*To* LOLA.) Tell us exactly what happened.

LOLA. I wanted to go to the ball. Yes, that's true. So I went to the dressmaker, took the gown and left her the IOU she demanded. I didn't realize I was writing and signing it on the stationery of the refugee newspaper that her husband—who I now realize was Tatarov—had given me.

DYAKONOV. The gown costs four thousand francs. Where did you hope to get such a sum?

LOLA. I thought I could earn it.

DYAKONOV. That's just it. You thought you could get that sum for your diary. And that is exactly what it says in the French newspaper.

LAKHTIN. Wait, Dyakonov, the newspaper may be lying. I don't trust them too much.

LOLA. I give you my word of honor, Comrades, I've never sold a thing to anyone.

LAKHTIN. I believe you. So you wanted very much to dance at the ball?

LOLA. But is that really such a crime?

LAKHTIN. But you knew very well that it is an open secret that the ball is organized by fascists.

LOLA. Yes, and that's why I hadn't made up my mind whether to go or not. I was hesitating.

LAKHTIN. I see. Nevertheless, you went ahead and bought yourself that gown. And it was the acquisition of it that led you to the refugees.

LOLA. I got trapped.

LAKHTIN. Yes, you got your little claw caught.

DYAKONOV. But that proves that she did have claws at least.

LAKHTIN. What I think happened is that they stole your diary and had it published without your knowledge. Now if it hadn't existed it couldn't have been stolen. Your crime is that you secretly hated us. And perhaps you hated us because we have no balls or magnificent gowns.

LOLA. I loved you, I swear.

DYAKONOV. I don't believe you.

LOLA. I'd like to prove it to you, but how?

DYAKONOV. Now, since this slander has been published, you must prove it not to us but to Paris and Moscow. Even if we believed you, the proletariat wouldn't.

LOLA. I understand. So what am I to do now?

FEDOTOV. We must go to the embassy immediately.

DYAKONOV. I'm not at all sure the Ambassador would receive her. The general rule that applies here I suppose is that once a Soviet citizen has passed into the camp of the émigrés he's outside Soviet law.

LAHHTIN. That's not your problem. Let them worry about that in Moscow.

LOLA. I'm an outlaw now?

DYAKONOV. Legally speaking, yes.

LOLA. I'm a traitor? If so, all intellectuals are traitors! The whole lot of them must be shot!

LAKHTIN. Why are you slandering the intellectuals now?

FEDOTOV. Calm down, Lola.

LAKHTIN. I'll call the embassy.

(LAKHTIN *and* DYAKONOV *cross toward exit.*)

DYAKONOV (*to* LAKHTIN *as they walk*). I'd have just put that woman up against a wall and shot her. (*Exits.*)

LOLA. Fedotov, what will happen now?

FEDOTOV. Take it easy, Lola.

LOLA. What if I walked on foot and hatless across the whole of Europe and arrived at Triumph Square at the hour of the general meeting and fell on my knees and—

FEDOTOV. No need for you to go on foot through the whole of Europe. Let's simply take the train: Paris–Berlin–Warsaw–Negoreloye. . . . Now stop philosophizing. As it is, your philosophizing has served the purposes of certain people very well. But never mind, the hell with them. You are no criminal. Dyakonov's just in a temper. Let's forget about it all until we get to Moscow and then we'll talk it over. Moscow has forgiven much more serious crimes, forgiven its open enemies.

LOLA. Will they try me? But I am my own judge and I've condemned myself, long ago. Is my life a real life, do you think? (*Stops.*) I feel faint, Fedotov. . . .

FEDOTOV. Wait. I'll get you some— (*Exits.*)

(LOLA *puts her hand into* FEDOTOV's *overcoat pocket, draws out his gun and slips away.* LAKHTIN *returns.*)

LAKHTIN. The Ambassador will receive us.

FEDOTOV. But where is Goncharova?

LAKHTIN. What can this mean? Where is she? What are you doing?

FEDOTOV. Nothing. It's just such an unpleasant business.

LAKHTIN. Do you trust her?

FEDOTOV. Yes. But I'm afraid she'll do something very stupid. Perhaps we spoke too sharply to her. I think she's on our side, don't you?

LAKHTIN. But where could she have vanished to? What shall we tell the Ambassador?

FEDOTOV. You go on ahead to the embassy while I look for her. She may have gone back to her boardinghouse.

LAKHTIN. If you find her, tell her it's nothing to worry about.

FEDOTOV. I'll tell her it's nothing to worry about.

LAKHTIN. Tell her it'll be all right and that we'll all go to Moscow together.

FEDOTOV. I'll tell her we'll all go together.

LAKHTIN. Tell her, as she herself would put it, that the proletariat is magnanimous.

FEDOTOV. I'll tell her that the proletariat is magnanimous.

CURTAIN

SCENE 7. *The Bouquet.*

At TATAROV's. *The silver gown lies in an open box.* TATAROV *and* LOLA *face each other.*

TATAROV. If you've only come to return the gown, you're at the wrong house. This is my apartment; Madame Tregubova has a place of her own. But, since you've taken the trouble to find out my address, I suppose you have a special reason for wanting to see me. Yet now that you've found me, you won't talk. I don't understand—are you offended with me by any chance? (LOLA *scowls at him but says nothing.*) And I imagined you'd be grateful to me as

long as you lived. (*A pause.*) The Soviet regime won't last
very long—it will be destroyed by the war that's going to
break out any day now. In Russia they'll form a government of intellectuals—scientists, technicians, and humanitarians. Obviously there will be repressions at first. The
Communists and those who co-operated with them over-
zealously will be prosecuted. Vengeance is bound to be
exacted, although I'm certain the new regime will show
great magnanimity. But, at first, military dictatorship is inevitable: the general who will occupy Moscow will act
sternly as a Russian patriot and as a soldier. That can't be
helped. The humanitarians will just have to look down at
their waistcoats for a while. . . .

And now imagine what would have happened if your
diary had remained in your hands? Suppose you returned
to Moscow and continued to pretend you were a Bolshevik,
until the Soviet regime was overthrown. One day at dawn,
you, among many others, would be brought to the com-
mandant's office. By then it would be a bit late for you to
try and prove your case by referring them to the allegations
in your diary. They would shoot you, as they'll shoot all
those women who work for the Cheka. Isn't that so?

Now, however, you are clean: Your diary has been published. It is being read by Milyukov, General Lukomsky,
Russian émigré financiers and, most important, by young
people impatient to storm Russia and avenge their fathers
and brothers who were shot to make the Reds pay for
forcing them to spend their youth in exile. They are reading
your confession now and thinking: She was a captive, they
made her suffer, forced her to serve a regime that she
loathed. She was secretly on our side!

So you see, I have helped you to justify yourself before
those who will be called upon to re-establish the order in
Russia. (*Pause.*) Why, it's quite obvious. Somewhere just
beneath the level of consciousness you have felt a constant
uneasiness, a responsibility for the blood the Bolsheviks
were spilling with your tacit approval. Now you have nothing to worry about. I have cured you of your fear, like a

doctor. (*He stops for a few seconds, waits, looks at* LOLA, *who still says nothing.*)

Now you can be at peace with yourself. Our motherland will forgive you, better still, she will reward you. You won't have to wait too long. You'll have your own house, your own automobile, a private yacht. In your silver gown you'll be the star of the ball. I'll be the publisher of a great national daily. I'll come to your theater loaded with roses wrapped in cellophane. Our eyes will meet and we'll firmly press each other's hands. . . .

LOLA. Stand against that wall, you scum!

(*She rises abruptly. The revolver is in her hand.* TATAROV *throws himself on her. There is a scuffle.* LOLA *drops the revolver.* KIZEVETTER, *who until this moment has been sleeping on a bed screened off by a curtain, appears. He picks up the gun.* LOLA, *in torn dress, lies on the sofa where* TATAROV *has thrown her. Silence.* KIZEVETTER *turns the gun in his hand.*)

TATAROV. Give me that gun! (KIZEVETTER *doesn't answer.*) I said, give me that gun!

KIZEVETTER. Don't come near me. (*To* LOLA.) Please don't be afraid. I'll be your dog. (LOLA *looks at him without answering.*) I don't know you. I've only seen you once before. Listen, we met in the doorway—do you remember?—and you've filtered through all my glands. . . .

TATAROV. You can act this scene without the gun.

KIZEVETTER. I'm penniless. But rather than let you sell yourself for money, I'll become a thief and a murderer.

LOLA (*jumping up, rushes toward the door, shouting*). Let me go! Let me go!

KIZEVETTER (*rushing after her, putting his arms around her knees*). Don't go, please don't go! The world is so frightening. . . . A black night is hanging over the world . . . but I need nothing. . . . Only, two creatures—a man and a woman—must press each other in their arms. . . .

TATAROV. Let go of her!

KIZEVETTER. Don't leave! (*Fires at* TATAROV, *misses him. Silence.*)

TATAROV. Ah, the epileptic!

KIZEVETTER (*putting his face on the table and weeping*). Ah-ah-ah . . .

(*Noise outside in the passage. Knocking at the door.*)

VOICE OUTSIDE. Let me in, you Russian!

TATAROV. The gun went off by accident.

(*Receding steps outside the door. Everything grows quiet.*)

TATAROV. They must've gone to call the police. (KIZEVETTER *is motionless. Silence. To* LOLA.) Where did you get that gun? (LOLA *ignores him.*) It has "To Alexander Fedotov, Brigade Commander" engraved on it. They gave it to you at the Soviet Embassy. What a careless way to do things: if they were sending you to kill me they should have given you an unmarked weapon.

LOLA. No one sent me. I decided to kill you myself.

TATAROV. That's more like it. But the French police will find it more advantageous to disbelieve you. On the basis of this evidence, they will accuse the Soviet Embassy of instructing its agents to perpetrate terroristic acts against Russian émigrés. (*Pause.*) That's a good pretext for acts of reprisal by us. Such as, say, an attempt on the life of the Soviet Ambassador.

LOLA. I see.

TATAROV. By trying to settle personal accounts with me, you may have caused the Soviet Ambassador's death. Do you understand? And it may go beyond that and unleash a war. The powder is dry as it is, and in Russia, they'll say you've ignited it. (LOLA *is silent.*) You've got yourself into a real mess this time. But never mind, I'll render you one more service. . . .

(*A knock on the door.* TATAROV *rushes to it.*)

TATAROV. Who's there?

VOICE OUTSIDE. Open in the name of the law.

TATAROV (*to* LOLA). Hide yourself.

(LOLA *hides behind the curtain.* TATAROV *opens the door. Enter two French* POLICEMEN *with little black mustaches and black capes.*)

FIRST POLICEMAN. What's going on here? Please explain.

TATAROV. The gun went off by accident.

FIRST POLICEMAN. Did it fire in the air?

TATAROV. Yes.

SECOND POLICEMAN. Into the ceiling?

TATAROV. Into the corner I believe. . . .

FIRST POLICEMAN. Who fired it?

TATAROV. He did.

FIRST POLICEMAN. Who are you?

KIZEVETTER. My name is Dmitri Kizevetter.

SECOND POLICEMAN. Why did you fire into the air? Is it your birthday or what? (*Silence.*)

FIRST POLICEMAN. What's your occupation?

TATAROV. He's unemployed.

FIRST POLICEMAN. I see. Where did you get the gun?

KIZEVETTER. I don't know.

SECOND POLICEMAN. Give him a sock in the mouth, Pierre!

FIRST POLICEMAN. Wait. Is this your gun?

KIZEVETTER. No.

FIRST POLICEMAN. It's a Russian weapon. Very interesting. The Russians are supplying the unemployed with arms.

LOLA (*coming from behind the curtain*). That's not true.

SECOND POLICEMAN. Ah, Madame! But let me tell you, Madame, beautiful women should stay out of politics.

KIZEVETTER. I fired the gun at him because of this woman.

FIRST POLICEMAN. Because of you?

(LOLA *doesn't answer.*)

KIZEVETTER. Yes, because of her.

FIRST POLICEMAN (*to* TATAROV). Is this true?

TATAROV. Yes, it is.

FIRST POLICEMAN (*to* KIZEVETTER). So you admit you attempted to kill him?

KIZEVETTER. I do.

FIRST POLICEMAN. You could get hard labor for attempting to kill someone, you know. (*Pause.*) Do you want to get hard labor?

(KIZEVETTER *doesn't answer.*)

SECOND POLICEMAN. Sock him in the jaw, Pierre.

FIRST POLICEMAN. Wait. If you'd like to avoid hard labor, you'd better forget your story about attempting to kill a man.

KIZEVETTER. All right.

FIRST POLICEMAN. So let's pretend that you just fired into the air.

KIZEVETTER. All right.

FIRST POLICEMAN. But you fired into the air from a Russian revolver. When an unemployed man fires a Russian gun into French air it goes without saying that his hand is guided by the Bolsheviks. In other words, the unemployed workers are trying to pull off a revolution with the assistance of a foreign power. Therefore, you're a traitor. And for that you can get the guillotine. Would you like to be beheaded by the guillotine?

KIZEVETTER. No.

FIRST POLICEMAN. So what shall we do now? (*Pause.*)

LOLA. This man has nothing to do with it. It's all my fault, do you hear!

FIRST POLICEMAN. Your fault? What did you do?

LOLA. I was the one who brought this revolver here.

FIRST POLICEMAN (*to* TATAROV). Who is she?

TATAROV. An actress.

FIRST POLICEMAN (*to* LOLA). Where did you get a Russian revolver?

LOLA. I stole it.

FIRST POLICEMAN. Where? (*Pause.* LOLA *is silent.*) Must have been in the Soviet Embassy. As you know, by virtue of international convention, the Soviet Embassy is guarded by French police. Stealing is not nice in general, but when it comes to stealing from a foreign power, it becomes outright discourteous. Now, since you have stolen something from a foreign embassy, I'll have to arrest you as a thief. For that, you could be jailed. Do you wish to go to jail for stealing from the Soviet Embassy? (*Pause.* LOLA *is silent.*)

TATAROV. She got a fright when that shot went off. She doesn't know what she's saying.

SECOND POLICEMAN. She your mistress?

TATAROV. Yes.

SECOND POLICEMAN. I like blondes too, you know. (*A silence.*)

FIRST POLICEMAN. Now, let's see what we have here. If we forget about the shot that was fired, we're left with an unemployed coward and a gun from the Soviet Embassy. On the other hand, we know that they are preparing a march of the unemployed. (*Pause.*) Now, since you like firing guns, go ahead, fire it off once more.

KIZEVETTER. At whom?

FIRST POLICEMAN. At several persons at the same time.

SECOND POLICEMAN. I think our police commissioner would approve of this.

FIRST POLICEMAN. We'd like you to fire into a crowd of the unemployed.

SECOND POLICEMAN. Yes, and you'll use this Bolshevik revolver.

FIRST POLICEMAN. They'll fire back and then our mounted police will be legally entitled to break them up and you'll avoid forced labor. Let's go then.

LOLA. You're a no-good crook, a criminal, a cheat!

FIRST POLICEMAN. Hide her behind the curtain, Gaston.

SECOND POLICEMAN. I don't want to touch her: I bet she scratches.

FIRST POLICEMAN. All right, all right, she'll calm down in the arms of her boy friend. Come on, on your way, young man! (KIZEVETTER *doesn't move.*) Well?

SECOND POLICEMAN. Give him one on the snout, Pierre! (KIZEVETTER *decides to go.*)

FIRST POLICEMAN. All right, you walk ahead and we'll follow you discreetly. (*They exit.*)

(*A few seconds' silence.*)

TATAROV. So you see: instead of having to walk through the icy rain to a drafty police station, you can stay cozily in a nice warm room. (LOLA *crosses to the door.*) Where do you think you're going?

LOLA. I'm going home.

TATAROV. Where? To your boardinghouse? But you haven't got any money.

LOLA. I'm going to Moscow.

TATAROV. How will you get there?

LOLA. I'll walk.

TATAROV. You must be crazy! I won't let you. There's a bad storm outside. Stay here. Don't be insane. I'll sleep on the sofa. (*A knock at the door.*) Sh-sh-sh! They've come for you. (*Seizes her and pushes her onto his bed that is screened off by the curtain. Opens the door.*)

(*Enter* TREGUBOVA. *Silence.*)

TREGUBOVA. I couldn't stay alone on such a night, Nicky. (TATAROV *doesn't answer.*) I brought a bottle of Lafite with me. Let's drink it together as we used to in the old days. I've also brought some asters to remind you of the gardens of our country. (TATAROV *looks away.*) Why do you look so worried, Nicky? Is something bothering you? (*Catches sight of the silver gown.*) Ah, I see, my heart didn't deceive me. She is here with you. (*Pause.*) She came to you in the ball gown. Her shoulders are so young. . . . (*Pulls the curtain aside.* LOLA, *immobile as though made of stone, is lying on the bed.*) So here you are, ugly duckling! Why don't you speak? Open your pretty eyes, I'll scratch them out! You dirty, nasty whore! You miserable slut! Take that! And that! (*Starts hitting* LOLA *in the face with the flowers she has in her hand.*)

CURTAIN

SCENE 8. *A Request for Glory.*

Night. A street. Workers.

A FRENCH SECRET AGENT. Comrades, I suggest we disperse.

FIRST VOICE. Coward!

AGENT. Quarrelsomeness doesn't mean courage. Rashness is a caricature of daring.

SECOND VOICE. You're a caricature yourself!

THIRD VOICE. Talk plain so we can understand you.

AGENT. It's impossible to talk plainly at night; at night people either whisper or shout.

AN ADOLESCENT. Go to hell, you lousy police spy!

AGENT. Why do you have to holler like that, kid? You're just a stupid kid!

ADOLESCENT. Long live Moscow!

AGENT. You stupid ass, do you ever read the newspapers?

ADOLESCENT. I don't know how to read.

AGENT. How dare you get mixed up in reorganizing the world when you're still illiterate? (*Mimics him.*) Moscow . . . Moscow . . . Ah, you dumb fish! Tell me, have you ever been there? (*The* ADOLESCENT *doesn't answer.*) If you haven't been there, just shut up. Now which of you has been there?

LOLA (*appearing among the crowd*). I have.

A CHEERFUL VOICE (*singing*).

In amidst the market place
Stands your basket full of lace
Blonde beauty
Blonde beauty
My beautiful blonde.

AGENT. Well, how wonderful. Then tell these ignorant fools about the Soviet paradise.

LOLA. Take off your hat when you talk to workers! (*Tears his hat from his head and throws it away. The crowd roars with approval, some laugh and clap.*)

AGENT. Ah, you damned slut, I'll wipe the streets with you, dragging you by the hair. . . .

(*The* ADOLESCENT *runs up to the* AGENT *from behind and kicks him in the backside. The* AGENT *stumbles and falls.*)

THE CHEERFUL VOICE (*singing*).

After market leave your lace
Come and see me at my place
Blonde beauty
Blonde beauty
My beautiful blonde.

(*A melee ensues. A* MIDDLE-AGED MAN *appears followed by a group of other men. They catch sight of the* AGENT *writhing on the ground and of* LOLA, *who is in a state of great agitation.*)

MIDDLE-AGED MAN. The revolution hasn't started yet, gentlemen!

LOLA. And that's why he's only lost his hat for the time being; when the revolution comes, his head will follow his hat.

MIDDLE-AGED MAN. Who's this fury?

AGENT. Some drunken whore.

(*A silence.*)

MIDDLE-AGED MAN. I came here to have a talk with you. Let's talk calmly.

LOLA. You should be calm yourself.

MIDDLE-AGED MAN. Listen, you little fool, if I were afraid of you, I wouldn't have come. Unless you imagine we're still living in the eighteenth century?

LOLA. Yes, I have visions of dukes and counts strung up on the street lamps.

MIDDLE-AGED MAN. I see that, politically speaking, you're quite immature. In our century, it isn't the kings and dukes who rule the world, it is the Machine invented by democracy and called Capital.

LOLA. What difference can that make? The street lamps are different too—many of them are electric now.

MIDDLE-AGED MAN. I am a lever of the machine you yourself have invented.

LOLA. You haven't introduced yourself yet.

MIDDLE-AGED MAN (*to the group of men following him*). You'd think she was an actress hired for a night to play the

part of one of those witches of the French Revolution.
Why are you getting so frantic? Do you take me for an
aristocrat? My dear girl, I am the son of a street-sweeper.
I was brought up in poverty. I worked as an apprentice
mechanic and later became a mechanic myself.

A MAN FROM HIS GROUP. The night is much too damp to
prolong this conversation.

MIDDLE-AGED MAN. I'm from the working class by birth
and can speak to you in your own language. What is it you
want?

A WEAVER. Bread!

LOLA. What? Just bread? No, no, no! Why are you
scared of him?

MIDDLE-AGED MAN. You're in my way. (*He raises his
stick to* LOLA's *chest, as though spearing her.*)

LOLA. You're hurting me.

MIDDLE-AGED MAN. Stop agitating people. You don't
look to me like a factory worker. I think you're employed
by the police!

(LOLA *seizes his cane and snatches it from his hand. The*
MIDDLE-AGED MAN *does not move. Men from his entourage
take the cane away from* LOLA.)

THE CHEERFUL VOICE (*singing*).

    First your shoes I will unlace
    Then your skirt strip off apace
    Blonde beauty
    Blonde beauty
    My beautiful blonde.

MIDDLE-AGED MAN. Things will get easier. All there is to
do is wait.

WEAVER. And starve while we're waiting?

MIDDLE-AGED MAN. What are you complaining about?
You get your daily plateful of soup, don't you?

WEAVER'S WIFE. And what about his children?

MIDDLE-AGED MAN. Why do you breed children in such
times? Tell your husband to control himself. Why should I
be responsible for his pleasures?

LOLA. Attack him!

(*She throws herself at the* MIDDLE-AGED MAN; *his body-guard pushes her off. She receives a blow on the head and falls unconscious. A sinister silence follows. Then a group of workers appears headed by the unknown man* LOLA *has seen beaten up in her boardinghouse. He is* HENRI SANTILLANT.)

THE CHEERFUL VOICE (*singing*).

Dare I but a kiss to place
On her back and not her face
Blonde beauty
Blonde beauty
My beautiful blonde.

MIDDLE-AGED MAN. That's Henri Santillant, a member of the Communist party, a former Deputy. (*To* SANTILLANT.) Hello, so they let you out of prison, I see? (SANTILLANT *does not answer.*) They respect you. You must warn them: they're blocking the street and it's nearly morning. You're preventing the city from awakening. The government will be justified in using mounted police to disperse the crowd.

SANTILLANT. We'll disperse ourselves if the government will listen to our grudges.

MIDDLE-AGED MAN. Go ahead, talk. I'll transmit your complaints.

SANTILLANT. It's a long list.

(LOLA *has regained consciousness and is listening.*)

MIDDLE-AGED MAN. Go on, dictate.

SANTILLANT. We demand—

A VOICE. Nurseries for our children, green playgrounds . . .

ANOTHER VOICE. Palaces of culture!

WEAVER. Spas to cure our sick!

VOICES. Guarantees to the workers!
Paid leave to pregnant women!
Abolition of child labor!
Communal kitchens for working housewives!

Self-determination of nations!
Six-hour working day!
Worker-run factories!
Confiscation of land from the landlords!
Science in the service of the proletariat!
All power to the workers!

LOLA. Bravo! Bravo! Do you hear? Read, read the list of the assets of the Soviet regime!

MIDDLE-AGED MAN. In order to make this list reality—

SANTILLANT. A social revolution is indispensable!

MIDDLE-AGED MAN. My former fellow deputy, you're a utopian! I think they let you out of jail a bit too early.

VOICES (shouting). Away with you! Long live the Soviets!

MIDDLE-AGED MAN. It's getting damper as the dawn approaches. Let's go, gentlemen. (Exits with his bodyguard.)

LOLA. I remember you. I remember everything. . . . The parks, the theaters, the art for the workers . . .

VOICES (shouting). Long live Moscow!

LOLA. I've seen a globe in the hands of a shepherd, I've seen Red Square. . . .

VOICES (shouting). Long live Moscow!

LOLA. I've seen the spark of knowledge gleaming in the eye of the proletariat; I've heard the slogan "Away with Wars!" I remember it all now.

SANTILLANT. How did you get here?

CHEERFUL VOICE (singing).
  Look who's come to close the case
  Blondie's man mad in my place
  Blonde beauty
  Blonde beauty
  My beautiful blonde.

(Enter POLICE CHIEF with a police detachment. Silence.)

POLICE CHIEF (to SANTILLANT). Who were you talking to? (SANTILLANT does not answer.) You must leave Paris by the following route . . .

LOLA (*catching sight of* KIZEVETTER *who's just appeared*). Careful. . . . Watch that man! The police have ordered him to fire on you. . . .

POLICE CHIEF. Arrest her!

(*A* POLICEMAN *steps toward her; takes out handcuffs.*)

POLICEMAN. Give me your hands!

POLICE CHIEF (*to* SANTILLANT). Your hands too. (SANTILLANT *doesn't move.*) Take him by force!

(*A* POLICEMAN *steps toward* SANTILLANT *and tries to slip handcuffs on his wrists.* SANTILLANT *hits him on the hand.* KIZEVETTER *fires at* SANTILLANT. LOLA *manages to shield him with her body. Panic. Anger.*)

VOICES (*shouting*). They've shot her! They've shot the Russian woman. Kill 'em!

LOLA. No, no, don't. . . . Don't rise to their provocation. . . . This man has settled a personal account with me. . . . Jealousy. . . . (*Collapses.*)

(POLICEMEN *run away. The revolver that was fired lies on the ground.* SANTILLANT *goes over to* LOLA *and picks her up.*)

LOLA. It was I . . . It was I who stole it . . . from a Comrade. . . .

CHEERFUL VOICE (*singing*).
     Bloody birthmarks now deface
     Blondie's neck so full of grace
     Blonde beauty
     Blonde beauty
     My beautiful blonde.

LOLA (*stretched out now at* SANTILLANT'*s feet*). I recognize you. . . . In my boardinghouse . . . the cops . . . and I was thinking about that gown. . . . Forgive me. . . . (*Falls silent.*)

VOICES. She's a thief!
He killed her out of jealousy!
He was her lover!
They were both working for the police!
She's a traitor!
A whore!

LOLA. Forgive me . . . I know . . . I can see: they're coming. . . . The Soviet armies are coming, carrying tattered Red banners, their feet battered by the long, stony marches. . . . The walls of Europe are crumbling. . . . Comrades, tell them I understood everything in the end and that I'm sorry. . . . (*She stands up.*) Paris! This, then, is your glory, Paris!

(*Falls. The* WEAVER'S WIFE *leans over her.*)

WEAVER'S WIFE. I can't hear. I can't make out a word.

(LOLA *pulls the woman's head closer to her mouth and whispers.*)

WEAVER'S WIFE. She wants me to cover her body with a Red flag.

SANTILLANT. The mounted police are coming. Raise your flags, Comrades! Let's march to meet them!

(*The unemployed exit in formation.* LOLA'*s body remains lying in the street uncovered. There are heard the strains of a march.*)

CURTAIN

(1931)

RUSSIAN LITERATURE
IN NORTON PAPERBACK

Anton Chekhov *Seven Short Novels* (translated by Barbara Makanowitzky)

Fyodor Dostoevsky *The Adolescent*
(translated by Andrew R. MacAndrew)
The Gambler
(translated by Andrew R. MacAndrew)

Nicolai V. Gogol *Dead Souls* (translated by George Reavey)
"The Overcoat" and Other Tales of Good and Evil
(translated by David Magarshack)

Robert C. Howes, Tr. *The Tale of the Campaign of Igor*

Alexandra Kollontai *A Great Love*
(translated by Cathy Porter)
Selected Writings (edited by Alix Holt)

Yuri Olesha *"Envy" and Other Works*
(translated by Andrew R. MacAndrew)

Alexandr Sergeyevitch Pushkin *The Complete Prose Tales*
(translated by Gillon R. Aitken)

F. D. Reeve, Tr. and Ed. *Nineteenth-Century Russian Plays*

Varlam Shalamov *Kolyma Tales* (translated by John Glad)

Aleksandr Solzhenitsyn *"We Never Makes Mistakes"*
(translated by Paul W. Blackstock)

Ivan Turgenev *"First Love" and Other Tales*
(translated by David Magarshack)

NORTON CRITICAL EDITIONS

Anton Chekhov *Anton Chekhov's Plays* (Eugene K. Bristow, ed.)

Anton Chekhov *Anton Chekhov's Short Stories* (Ralph E. Matlaw, ed.)

Fyodor Dostoevsky *The Brothers Karamazov* (Ralph E. Matlaw, ed.)
Crime and Punishment (the Coulson translation;
George Gibian, ed.)

Leo Tolstoy *Anna Karenina* (the Maude translation; George Gibian, ed.)
War and Peace (the Maude translation; George Gibian, ed.)

Ivan Turgenev *Fathers and Sons* (a substantially new translation;
Ralph E. Matlaw, ed.)